ASYLUM 54.0

THE BIONICS SAGA

nadège richards

ASYLUM 54.0
Copyright © 2017 Nadège Richards

All rights reserved. Except as permitted under the U.S. Copyright act of 1976, no part of this publication may be reproduced, distributed, or transmitted in any form or by any means, or stored in a database or retrieval system, without the prior written permission of the author.

First Edition: July 2017
Cover design by Regina Wamba at Mae I Design & Photography
Cover and book illustrations by Javier Chavarria at Mae I Design & Photography
Book design by Inkstain Design Studio
Edited by Carrie White-Parrish
Text set in Centaur.

The characters and events portrayed in this book are fictitious. Any similarity to real persons, living or dead, is coincidental and not intended by the author.

more books by
nadège richards

THE BLEEDING HEART SERIES

Burning Bridges

Deceiving Destiny

Fleeting Fires

Embracing Embers

THE BIONICS SAGA

Asylum 54.0

For everyone who's ever told me: "You can't."

I *did*.

When all the world *fades* to **BLACK...**

...who do you **BECOME?**

a letter from nadège

To the ones who have loved this story since 2013—

It's finally here. It's taken me four years (and some spare change), but I've begun Mathai's story in the best way I know how and I hope you grow to love her as much as I have. She was a difficult character to write. I often stopped writing for days to figure out how I could make her different from Echo Abbeny. Echo developed into such a strong character so quickly I wondered if I could ever separate her from Mathai in my head. Then, as I thought more and more during my days away from writing, I began to draw from a lot of my weaknesses and losses, my emotions and insecurities. Mathai, in every sense, is the version of me I hide behind tears during late hours of the night when the words stop making sense. She is my anxiety, she is my depression. She is my panic, my self-hate, and my loneliness. She is beautiful.

You may remember that Asylum 54.0 was first pitched as a dystopian novel when I introduced it in 2013, but I have switched everything up—the world, the characters, and the scenes. Forget everything you know when you enter this world I've built, because nothing is what it seems. I've given myself headache after headache, just to make this book something new and fresh.

The seven-book journey you are about to embark on with these characters will get scary and dark. It will be everything it was always supposed to be.

To the ones who are now joining my legion—

My words will often confuse you, madden and frustrate you, but if you are reading this, that means you've ultimately given them a chance. So in the end, I also hope they make you fall in love.

This story was something created from too many midnight snacks and my wild imagination. If you're all about it, Mathai's story awaits.

xoxo, Nadege K. Richards

ASYLUM 54.0

PROLOGUE

"SUN-SWEPT PLAINS"

They came at the break of dawn.

Mama held her breath at the kitchen table as the glass bowls shattered into fragmented pieces and the air vibrated with their call. I was first to sense the shift, the tear in the Ward. The unrest. Silverware and teacups shook, and my sister's helpless eyes fell on my bound hands as if I had caused it all.

I'd had this nightmare a thousand times, the one where they finally found me, and each time came with a thousand tortuous endings. It'd play out in slow motion. I'd never quite believe it until the very last second, because in that second it became much less than a nightmare. A chilled memory, perhaps.

It was always the same thing—the screams, the empty parklands, and the red skies and silenced voices. I knew every face, and yet the moonless nights couldn't account for much but shadows. We were captured and alone, and then we weren't. They were always watching.

In this second, it wasn't a nightmare.

This was my world, and it was colliding.

"Why?" my sister whispered. She took a tentative step back just as the windows imploded and threw the harsh wind at our faces. It tore a hole in the wall; the picture frames and paintings we had taken hours to fasten into the cement flew out like they didn't mean a thing. Like they never existed.

I dug my clipped nails into the wood of the kitchen table, grounding myself, and wailed for Mama, unable to form the words. I could see her through the dark screen of my hair, though I couldn't hear her. *Sound*. It was the only sense I had complete control over … and it was useless now.

I felt a tug on the back of my head, and I was dragged away from the table. As the walls of our piffling sanctuary caved, Mama hauled me through the blinking hallways, her fist wrapped in my hair. Les cried like always, though she had no reason—none of them did. *They weren't here for them.* She scurried after us and cradled what possessions she could in her arms. When the storm blew in and destroyed our bunker, it took with it a future we should never have sought for.

Mama stopped in the space she shared with Papa and an old desk piled high with maps. No bed, because they never slept. She released her tight grip on my hair and only then did I catch the glint in her doe-like brown eyes and the tired lines that surrounded them. I waited for her anger. Instead, she gave me her tears.

"Thai..." she said, patting the side of my face.

"M-Mama," I stuttered. I trembled and pushed my hands out in front of me. I'd kept them bound like she taught me, and not once did I run past the asylum Ward. I always listened and did everything right. Yet somehow, I knew this was my fault. I was terrified of the truth. "*P-Please. Make it stop.*"

"Stop your crying, girl." She rubbed harshly at her tears, then began to unwrap my numb hands. With a blink, they were free of their casing. I couldn't believe what she was doing. I sensed them ripping into the atmosphere—and she was doing the very thing they wanted.

"No!" My skin burned as if stretched too tight across my muscles. A slow ache began in my chest and festered until I forgot to breathe. Wind whipped my hair back and forth, and shattered my transparent soul in two. If I had to fight Mama again, I would do it. I'd torch this place to ash and brimstone. I'd take Les and run for the beaten Ward.

Gripping my shoulders, Mama shook me fiercely, ignoring Les' cries to stop. "Listen to me!" she screamed. She took my face, staring me in the eyes. I knew what would spill from her mouth next and I struggled in her hold. I dared to close my heart off to her. "*Thirty-six, forty-nine, sect. Sixty-four, eighty-one, sect,*" she whispered, she sang. "*Thirty-six, forty-nine...*"

An icy shiver slid down my back, calming me, her voice echoing through my skull like a melody. The repeating numbers took root and I blanked, I bottomed. Where there was once pain, there was now nothing. I reached out to touch her face, her lips. "I-I'm sorry, Mama..." My response was automatic, laced with uncertainty. I wasn't sure why, because I trusted her.

I felt feverish, like I had been angry about something. Every time I tried to recollect, I hit a black screen with the same blaring numbers that made me feel empty.

"I know," she crooned. "I know you are, but there isn't much time."

Papa suddenly broke into the room, breathing heavily. By the state of his jumpsuit, he'd gone out with the storm. He wiped his oil-stained hands on a map and began to throw things into a bag, thrusting it at Les. "Did you hide it?" he asked Mama. When she nodded, he finally looked at me. I wasn't good at reading people, and my encounters with others were limited to the three individuals standing around me, but Papa never made me feel like his own. I could recount his insults like the tallied letters along my spine, and all the remaining months he'd made it a point to ignore us. I could see it in his eyes when he looked at me. Papa hated what we were.

"Will they find it?" Mama asked.

"Not if they keep quiet," he said. "Why are you taking them?"

"You mean our *children*?" When she stood, I backed away and took Les' hand. She flinched when our skin met, but said nothing. Perhaps for my sake.

"They're targets, Rhea!" Papa opened the chest beneath the desk and rifled through the papers. "Always have been." He found what he was looking for, a string of keys, and pocketed them. "We push them out the door and never look back. I'm not losing you for these ... *things*."

"You wouldn't."

"Watch me." Papa took his bag and moved his way through Les and me, heading right out the door and into the storm that bled the sky to gray. Meanwhile, Mama could barely see through her swollen eyes and broken heart. She packed what she could and bundled the maps under the desk. After she clawed the shady memories from the walls—after one of the longest, most redefining moments I'd ever stood witness to—she looked at me.

"*Thirty-six, forty-nine, sect*," she cued.

"Mama, *don't!*" The words were pulled from my tongue and I sensed something cold peddling within my chest. The storm didn't matter. I watched her lips and hung from her next words, desperate to do anything she wanted. I swayed between the vacantness; my mind sunk deeper into the opalescent vacuum. When I released Les' hand, everything blurred in a haze of red. Below my feet rested my dirty bandages.

"You won't fear them. That's not who you are." Mama crossed the room and gripped my arms. Her nails dug into my skin, but I wouldn't feel the pain until this long became a memory. "That's not who you were created to be. *Fear*—it's not what we're here for. Promise me, girl."

I wanted to say no. I wanted to scream, and if I could—*if only I could*—I would have touched my unbound hands to the wall and disappeared to somewhere outside the Ward. Instead, I nodded, pretending to be unafraid and failing. "I won't fear them."

She leaned over and whispered the words into my ear. As she did, I grew colder. The walls toppled around us, yet Mama held my face like we had seven moons and a kiloyear left. I forgot my name first—I always did. Then I lost the ability to resist. Between her words, she released the series of numbers like a riddle forever unsolved. I was mercilessly ensnared.

"No, Mama," Les whimpered. She tugged at my overalls and tried to pull me away.

Mama stepped back, the remnants of her promise blazing in her eyes, and repeated, "*Thirty-six, forty-nine, sect. Sixty-four, eighty-one, sect.*" She said them until I understood, until I began to say them with her. "Let me hear you say it."

A hot tear spilled from my eye. "*Thirty-six, Forty-nine, sixty-four, eighty-one...*"

"*Sect.*" With a kiss to my forehead, she took my hand and led us out of the dark bunker. My footsteps were slow and unthinking, because her parting words had rendered some part of me blind.

I was dragged into the burning daylight and our city now flooded with fire, and all I knew was that I *feared* fear, despite what she told me. I feared death. I feared the inevitability of a conclusion, a voiceless void. I feared the things that called beyond the grave and the notion of knowing nothing. I feared an end. Like lightning before thunder, my life was evanescent. Besotted with the night. Nothing could make me forget this. Not even her.

Mama pulled sweaters from her bag and hastily tossed them to me, never taking her eyes off the dimming sky. She said, "Put these on. If they take one good look at you, they'll know."

"Know what?" Les cried. I helped her into her sweater before zipping up my own. I tucked her brown curls behind her ear and reclaimed her hand. In this way, she had her answer. Les and I made many promises while lying on the desert plains, during long hours of dreaming beyond the Ward and spitting seeds into the craters. This was one of them—her hand in mine, her faith in me, and my vow to save her life, even at the expense of my own.

"We're gonna be o-okay," I said. "Papa is waiting for us. We'll get on the fastest c-craft outta here. Got me?"

Les' frown lessened, though my words did nothing to assure her. She nodded anyway, squeezing my hand once, then twice. "Got you."

"Don't let—"

"I won't let go." She shifted her bag in her arms and her eyes went to the chaotic mess outside. The stars fell from the sky like enflamed rocks, and blood covered the dusty streets. Their aircrafts burned every building asunder and the west planetarium was torched to the ground. Just outside our window, where the red lands had once stretched free for miles, hundreds of cold, still bodies now lay. Dismantled and lifeless—that's how they wanted us, that's how they took us.

Mama spotted Papa across the swarming road. The burning skyscrapers cast him in complete darkness, yet I knew that green truck like I knew the color of my skin.

"Let's go," she said.

Taking my arm, she raced us through the running hordes. I recognized the faces as they flew by. Most of them were the abandoned children that had lived in empty bunkers, too afraid of life out in the open. One stood in the center of the road, screaming for someone with a white shirt raised high in the air. The wind flicked his frail body across the torrent. He caught sight of me as I rushed past and, with a blink, his brown eyes refocused to red.

He's like me, I thought with a grimace. My feet slowed as I watched him. Didn't he know they would see what he was? Desperation shone in his eyes ... and a sick feeling overwhelmed me. The white shirt held high meant he was surrendering. There were people who had disowned everything to find solace here, and he was merely giving in.

A large craft dropped from the sky, releasing its hooks, and illuminated his tear-stained face. In a blaze of shinning color, they tore into his skin and took him.

He didn't scream; he never called for his father again.

Gone.

It was the only word that described what we would become.

"Over here!" Mama cried. She and Les had run ahead while I remained frozen, confused. But as soon as I turned, pulling on my hood to hide my face, it was tugged back, a meaty hand clasped to my shoulder and spinning me around. My heart jumped at the idea that one of their crafts had found me. Would their hooks tear into me too? Would they take Les? The very idea made me wild, because they couldn't take her. Something urged me to fight for her, and like with everything I was told to do, I listened.

"L-Let go of me!"

But they tugged so hard I slipped out of my sweater. I allowed myself to look them in the face—the last thing you were *ever* supposed to do—and instead of the metallic suits and flashing green insignia of the Generators, I saw the man who lived in the bunker beside ours. The one Papa had caught smashing our windows and shooting off his revolver late at night. The madman they kept locked in a cellar, until now.

"I knew it was you," he seethed. Without warning, he fastened his hand around my throat and threw me against the side of a tower. The force was like an explosion of cannons in my head. "All they want is you. I should just give you to them! Maybe I'll get a little extra for the commissary or something, huh?"

"You'd g-get *nothing*," I spluttered, clawing at his filthy hands. "They will take everyone! Just l-look up." The truth stung; it did more damage than any storm ever could.

Cautiously, the man gazed up and his eyes widened at the sight of the darkening sky. If there was a moon hidden behind the clouds, you couldn't tell. Their crafts engulfed the azure and faded all to black. This was a harvesting, and they had come to reap what they had sown.

"Why couldn't you stay away?" With tears in his eyes, he pressed down on my throat, robbing me of my next breath. He watched me like I was something lesser, like everything wicked had been reincarnated and I was it. Instead of hating him or denying what he said, I felt ashamed. I felt sick with guilt. Like Papa, I hated what they made me.

"I-I'm so sorry," I whispered. I slid a hand down his arm and gripped his face. My mind tripped into overdrive—slowly, and then cataclysmically. It sensed his fear and fed from it. I had no time to think before it was done.

"You should have kept running."

My unbound palm radiated with heat, searing his flesh with angry sores. I watched the pain etch its way into the dark angles of his face. His hold on me weakened, just as my touch spread like a disease. When he screeched and ripped at his clothes, I fell to the ground. Below the dying sky, I lit him up like the **sun-swept plains**.

"You did this… You are … *darkness*," he continued to mumble between blistered lips. On my hands and knees, I crawled to get away. I didn't mean to hurt him. I didn't mean to hurt *any* of them, yet the people who ran madly around me might as well have been dead.

The man was right about everything, though. I was darkness. The sun had never shined the same since I'd been here, no matter how hard I'd crossed my fingers and played pretend.

"I-I didn't mean to…" Hot, sulfuric tears spilled from my eyes. He finally stopped moving, his face distorted with burns. I'd peeled away everything that made him recognizable.

With a single touch...

I sat motionless with my hands to the ground. If I touched my face, would I burn too? Could I ever touch anyone again?

An overhead shadow caught my attention and another craft descended from the sky. The Ward held up like a paper-thin fence; it never stood a chance. Their bloody hooks dug into the man in front of me, thrusting him into the sky. Conscious or not, they'd take anything with a still beating heart.

"Alessia Porter," came a booming voice, followed by flashing green lights. *Their insignia.* "Adriano Leif, Kaira Cruz, Isis Badden..." They rattled off names like they were broadcasting our time of death. In a way, I suppose they were. As they picked us out from the crowd and zeroed their lasers on our foreheads, I stumbled to my feet and broke into the mass, pushing my way to my sister. I wrapped my sweater around my hands, just to protect those that still survived.

I had to get to Les. If I regretted anything today, it would be promising everything would be okay and failing to make it so. She was the clarity I failed to see in everything, even in myself. The sanity I prayed for. They'd take that from her ... and it'd break her enough for the both of us.

As if she heard my thoughts, Les pulled away from Mamá and hurdled into the street in search for me. With everyone running in one direction, I moved against the grain, pushing and screaming, all with the green lights at my back. They knew who we were now. Their beams focused on us in the dark horde like spotlights. Mama cried as Papa pulled her into the truck, yet I knew he'd go without her if he really had to.

Bombs exploded around us, shredding into skin and bone, leaving nothing but suspended soot. I counted down the seconds, but I knew we were days too late.

From the other side of the crowd, Les reached her hand out for me. She'd just dug her nails into my palm when one of them grabbed her by the waist and flung her into the arms of another. *Generators*, Mama called them. They stood taller than average and their movements were quick and designed. Their metallic suits blocked all view of their faces, and their guns never left their side. Les' cries encased the storm and, ever so gently—like its strings were knitted together with twine—my heart quit beating.

Thirty-six, forty-nine, sect...

"Les!"

A Generator dove for me and I threw my sweater to block its view. It wouldn't harm me. They wouldn't kill me, because they needed me *alive*. When it jumped right, I feigned left, maneuvering through the crowd with shaking limbs. But they pulled Les further away, until I could no longer make out her wild hair and yellow sweater. I could hear my name on her lips, though, and I desperately chased after it.

"Alessia Porter, you have..."

No. I pumped my legs faster and broke free from the pandemonium, squinting through the abyss and watching as my sister was thrown to the ground and tagged, collared. Their pale, white hands crushed her to the dirt, her bags forgotten, and she cried out for Mama. She was only ten, and knew little of what was happening, although I was sure she sensed we were different from the others here at the asylum. You could only keep a secret from her for so long.

Her copper collar blinked green. She closed her eyes, releasing one last scream, and then her silence was like a sonic boom. Her lips moved with soundless music. They marked her like they did the rest, and when she reopened her eyes I knew I wasn't looking at Les anymore. I was looking at her shadow. She ceased fighting and her features softened. Slowly, they erased everything that made her my sister.

She'd become a blank slate, one of them.

"*No.*" The word felt numb on my tongue and I panicked so badly I began to twitch. I dry-heaved absolutely nothing. With my hands in the air, I spun and shouted for the Generators, and though our asylum was torn to shreds, I knew they saw me. I ran after their crafts as the wind beat my thin overalls against my sensitive skin. *This has to be it*, I told myself. I stopped running and raised my hands higher above my head, alone in the open plain. I was now the boy with the white shirt.

"Take me instead!" I screamed. The Generators on the ground quickly surrounded me and trained their guns on my head. "Release her and I-I'll go! Just don't hurt her."

"We've been waiting for you," one of them said.

"I know. I won't run again." I let the wind blow away my tears. As the lasers shone down from their crafts, I felt the ground shift beneath my feet. "I'll go with you if you release her. It's m-me you want, right?" I was bargaining with death. I knew nothing would come of me if I gave in, but if it could free Les from their collar, I'd sell my soul. Or at least the soul I assumed I had. My days were too bleak to know for sure.

The Generators gradually lowered their guns and hope dangled by a thread. Would they let me make the trade? A life for a life? I glanced at the unconscious Les, still lying in the dust, and internally begged her to get up. To run so far from here that she never dreamed of the Ward, or this asylum, again.

Les didn't move, though. She never got up, and hope's fragile thread snapped with the wind.

A soft click resounded from my left and I heard it as if it had come from beside me. A Generator in the back cocked his gun and raised it to my chest. It was the sound of my defeat, I realized. And I went from brokenhearted to enraged in a matter of seconds.

"You're not going to do it, are y-you?" I said. I lowered my arms and my hands curled into cold, tight fists. I could have strangled every one of them. "You're *never* going to stop."

When I took a step back, their guns buzzed. Nothing made sense, and then it did. The clouds lit up with their green insignia. "Alessia Porter, you have been activated."

"No!" My mind scattered to cling to something. None of the Generators would help. They stood around to watch my demise play out in slow motion; their faceless forms were like a wall around me. The sky shrieked those eight words over and over until I began to lose myself in slices. *Again.* My vision was a dark tunnel with no promising light at the end.

I opened my mouth to scream. Instead, I whimpered, "I'm sorry." The words burned with the knowledge that I would always belong to them in this way. With these few words, I'd become a heartless space.

"We know. We can help you. Wouldn't you like to come with us?"

"Yes." On the inside, I fought to break free. To defy them *just this once* and say no. I was moving without much control. A sorrowful hush quieted my mind, like a blanket to chase the cold.

My name . . . what is it?

When I glanced up, I saw Mama in the background standing beside the truck. Her jacket billowed from her rail-thin body and she cupped her hands to her mouth as she screamed. She was a broken kind of beautiful—a face so miserable it was impossible to look away. Her pain-streaked eyes shot right through me as she shouted louder, and after long seconds of tuning everything out, I heard her.

Run!

Run!

Run!

In a dizzying flash, my mind shrank and snapped, like someone's hold on my spine had been severed. A piercing screech resounded through the air. I put my hands to my temples and gripped my head to turn it off. It was too loud, too much, too fast. I grappled for a steady stream of thought and lost it in instants.

"Make it s-stop!"

"We can help you," they said.

"Come with us," they told me.

They spoke and my mind was awash with ice-cold water. The screeching ceased, the ground stopped shifting. I blinked, and then awoke.

Run!

With one last panicked glance at my sister, I dropped everything in the dust and ran for the open craters. My boots kicked back rocks at the promise of freedom and my heart had never driven me so fast before. Although I heard the click of their guns and my name in the sky, I refused to slow down, to stop the *smack-smack* as my feet kissed the red sand—or my tears that met the storm.

Sixty-four, eighty-one, sect...

Pain sliced into my back and a meteor of light blossomed behind my eyes. It beckoned like a perpetual crevasse, leading me into the unfamiliar. The Generators gave chase, and yet I didn't stop. I had to find a way to keep going. If I couldn't belong here, I'd die before I belonged to *them.*

The edge of the crater neared, along with the emptiness that lay below. I took one step, two, then jumped. The storm whipped through me as I opened my arms. I had been freed; I felt no fear.

I plummeted.

Then I flew.

ONE

"VACANT IMPRESSION"

BIONIC: ARI-0329

They said dying in water would be a peaceful mercy offered to few, yet it was the thing ripping me to pieces. My eyes blinked open as my lungs flooded with fire. One minute I was asleep, dead, and then I was wide-awake and drowning all over again.

Darkness crept in from all corners of my mind. The submerged pod surrounded me like four unbreakable pillars and the live wires stitched into my skin stung. I didn't remember where I was or how I'd gotten inside. I turned the last hours over in my mind, but got nothing. My fists shot out to pound against the glass, and in my reflection I saw a deep-set panic.

How am I still breathing? I wondered. Red lights flashed beyond the clear glass and the pod across from me was broken into, vacant. In fact, every pod in the dark room was empty—all but mine.

Something is wrong.

I beat harder, my movements slowed, and the force finally split the glass. I gave one more push and the barrier let way, spilling me from the pod with a gush of water. Cold air replaced the burn in my lungs and my hair clung to my damp skin. The hard ground felt like a thousand pinpricks below my fingers. Though it was nothing compared to the river of blood I lie naked in.

Choking down a scream, I scurried back, rising to trembling legs. Legs now dressed in red. *Did I do this? Were there people in those pods?*

The water on my skin dried to a sticky mucus. I took a step over broken glass and reached for a memory. I knew I should have been worried about a past I couldn't recall, but I was more frightened by the idea that there was nothing *to* remember. What if I forgot this revelation, this moment, right now? Was that normal? Wrapping my arms around my chest, I walked toward the flickering lights. A crushed mirror hung loosely on the far wall and my image gave me pause. Not only did my blue and green eyes appear hollow, but something heavy lurked within their depths. Like I carried two souls, instead of one. I took in my shaking form and pressed a hand to the mirror. Stuttered nothings escaped my lips as I thought, *Who am I?*

My descent down the long corridor was like a dance with the dark. I had no sense of left or right, up or down. My wet footprints stained the floor in red. Severed cables swung from ripped holes in the ceiling and the blinking lights mocked me. Windowless doors that led to more nothing sat on broken hinges; bloody tracks trailed the ramparts. Every hall appeared as if something evil had run away, destroying everything good and whole in its path.

My pace picked up as I rounded a stark corner. I didn't want to be here, yet I only knew of these empty walls and my broken pod. I didn't know where I was supposed to be, or where I had come from. Did I have a home? A family?

"H-Hello?" I called. My voice echoed in the recess and settled into the walls, where it vibrated. They shook and tore at the white panels, peeling back my sanity, until I realized it wasn't my voice at all. Something shook once more and I heard it for what it was. A bell, something like a buzzer. It lasted for one pulsing second before it ended, and when it did, the lights overhead began to explode, encasing me in a slow nightfall.

They were locking me in.

My hands followed the parapets as I chased the light down the hall. I didn't know what I was running to, but anything was better than going back. The beams blew out one by one, cloaking the room I fled. I couldn't turn around; I couldn't even *look*. Covered in blood and screaming jumbled words, I slapped the tiled walls and begged for them to hear me, to help me. I couldn't return to the pod. I couldn't keep dying over and over again, waking only to relive it. I couldn't remain comatose.

The lights won out and I met a red, locked door at the end of the corridor, right as I was swamped in blackness. "Can s-someone hear me?"

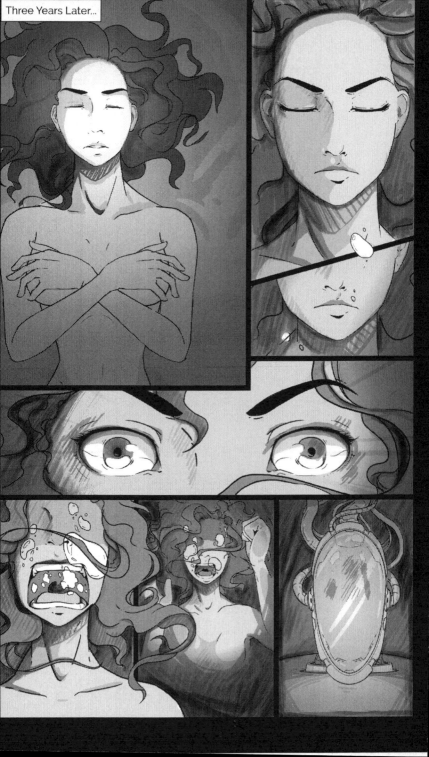

I wailed, banging on the steel door.

Nothing came. I sank to my knees and rocked myself to a quiet calm. The air wasn't cold, but a chill ran through me regardless. With the lights off, my mind began to play. I envisioned a pair of eyes and warm arms in the darkness. They didn't console me or answer my questions. They didn't bring me peace of mind or carry me away. But they were there. Something about not being completely alone silenced my cries.

When my eyelids grew too heavy to keep open, I allowed myself to drift. It was only a minute or two, and I knew because the blood on my skin had yet to dry. When I shifted on the floor, the lights blinked on like my movements had cued them. I wanted to be relieved. I wanted to call out and say, "I'm here!" Though they already knew where I was, and they came with their batons at the ready, guns in tow. They wore masks and suits—dressed in red, like me.

"I-I was quiet. I didn't mean to hurt anyone." Staring into their lights, I wondered, "Am I broken?"

I heard them say, "No, Ari. You've been reborn."

They reached for me, and then a sharp pinch at my neck stifled my thoughts.

"The subjects have escaped."

"And 0329?"

"She didn't go. Everyone else is gone."

"That's . . . impossible. Did you check the room?"

"Every pod was cleared."

"Where is she now?"

"Manis has her detained in the room. She's frightened and knows nothing. If you ask her something as simple as the date, she loses her mind. She's not making sense."

"She's changed."

". . . Why do you say that?"

"Watch her, study her. Her mannerisms are different. They did something to her and the key isn't working. We need everything she knows."

"What do we do? We've temporarily repaired her speech and detained her regenerative abilities, but she doesn't respond to—"

"Fix her. We need her."

"And if we can't?"

"She *will*."

The man with the scarred face slapped the folder down on the table and took a seat across from me. His scowl was growing tiresome, as were the cushioned, sterile walls that closed us in. I'd heard him call this the White Room, the room I'd awakened in. He spoke to someone through a device at his ear, though his words were in a language I didn't understand. Undoubtedly, he was talking to the rest of them, reporting on every question I answered wrong. I sat with my knees pulled to my chest while his long fingernails tapped out a rhythm on the glass. With the one door visibly locked shut and my hands cuffed to my chair, I decided right then that I didn't like this man.

"Let's try this again," he said. "What is your name?"

When he glanced at the camera receiver above my head, I stole a glance at the open files. "Ari. My name is Ari-0329."

"*Ari*—" There was no missing the contempt that dripped from his lips. "—Can you tell me what happened on your last crusade?"

"I told you. I don't know." I'd said it at least a dozen times, yet he continued to ask like I'd manifest the answer from sheer whim and feed it to him. I had opened my eyes to bright lights only hours ago. They said it was a miracle I was alive, that the others hadn't been so lucky. They said I was one of them and that they were there to help me. I believed them like they said I would, but the need to know for myself nudged at my psyche.

The man took another look through the folder, then sighed. "Three weeks ago you left with five other legionaries. You were supposed to go no further than the Ucilei coast, yet your craft was found miles from the next asylum. You had *two* days to report and you never came back." He leveled his gaze on my face, searching for my reaction. "Do you recall any of this?"

"Am I supposed to?"

"Why wouldn't you?" He sat back, crossing one leg over the other. "Something happened to you, Ari. Something that intercepted your code. Do you understand this?"

"My code?"

"Flawed or not, we found you," he continued, speaking right over me. "We can help you if you tell us what happened."

"I *can't*."

"Can't, or won't?" He spoke slowly. "We're you're family, Ari."

"Family?" This room didn't appear to be the epitome of a happy homestead. There was nothing welcoming about the veiled look in his eyes. "I don't have anyone else?"

The question shook him. His shoulders tensed and his small head cocked to the side, something like a bird listening for sound. Because I knew nothing else, I casually mimicked him. He dropped the folder and I knew I had done something wrong. "The legionaries you left with are gone, Ari. Why do you think there's anyone else?"

It's a nulled feeling, I wanted to say. I was missing someone or something, and I fought to decide which. I felt connected to another habitation, and although I trusted the men in the white jackets, I doubted how much of me they could fix.

"I don't know. I assumed..."

He arched a thin brow. "Assumed what?"

Exasperated, I tugged at my restraints and settled my feet on the mirrored floor. I was done with the interrogation, the pathless questions and his prying glare. Watching the second receiver across the room, I said, "If I remembered anything aside from my name right now, you'd know it. I woke up underwater, surrounded by blood. Write that down and turn in your file, because that's all I've got."

"No faces, names?"

"No, and I wish I was lying."

The man smiled. He *smiled*. "It'll come to you in time, and we won't hurt you. You mean too much to us."

"What does that—"

"It means we're done here." He picked up the papers, the ones splattered with data and my name stamped at the top, and stood. "Remember our proposition," he added. My hands itched to snatch the folder away. Did he know everything about me and refuse to tell me? Was this a test? He stopped at the door, which opened to a vacant hall and, with another smile to that scarred face, whispered, "Welcome back, Ari."

If those words were supposed to comfort me or make light of my situation, they damn well failed to do their job.

As he fled the room, the others that had watched from behind the walls came in and unbound me from the chair, releasing the beeping manacles around my legs. The scarred man took with him the heavy atmosphere I'd sensed since I awoke, and in its place left a numb awareness. I was aware of my own displacement, my conscious mind, and I wondered if that was the flaw in my code. The reason I didn't remember. Perhaps I wasn't supposed to doubt. Perhaps I did this to myself.

"It's time for your late-meal," one of the White Jackets said. He had pale yellow skin and blue veins that ran deep beneath its surface. No hair and a gaunt stature. He watched me emotionlessly, unblinkingly, with his back ramrod straight and his arm open to the hallway. When I took a step in his direction, he moved out of the way like he was doing his best not to breathe in the same rhythm with me.

I was released and shown out the room. The blank glass walkways outside were no better than the room. It was as if they were afraid to let any color in, and the partitions remained as cold as the men walking behind me. Color would be too loud, too mutinous, for a place like this. The large windows brought in beams of light, creating a mirage of shadows from the crafts in the sky, but that was it. No music, no sound. I was beginning to think I was the only one left when voices lifted from somewhere ahead, from another room. While the idea of confrontation made me wary, I yearned to see another face like mine.

I walked faster, stretching the sleeves of my shirt past my chilled fingertips. After they'd found me in the hall, I was allowed to shower in a small stall while two of them kept watch at the door. They gave me clothes that were too big and a stiff brush practically made of barbs. My footwear was nothing more than sole-worn boots. I took what I got and counted them as small luxuries, because they could have left me in the dark with nothing. They didn't, though, and that had to mean something.

I hadn't agreed to their proposal, yet one was made regardless. When the scarred man first relayed everything that happened three weeks ago, he promised I'd get my memories back. All I had to do was help them, and in return they'd help me. He didn't elaborate and I didn't ask him to. Getting my memories back was enough; knowing my name without thinking too hard was *enough*. I was desperate, and I'd endure every test they threw at me until I gained it all back.

We were legionaries. They said we were trained to protect the city from the dangers beyond the Ward, the things that waited within the sky. I didn't understand, or at least not at first. Then they hooked me to the loud machines and I recalled how effortlessly I had breathed beneath the water. I had considered my mismatched eyes in the mirror, thinking about how easily I had acquiesced to their commands. The scarred man had lied. We weren't truly like them, not in the ways that mattered. While they had time to mature and learn—to think without doubting their every thought—we only had creation and the bittersweet abyss that followed.

We were assassins, designed to kill. They'd sent me out to defend the Ward three weeks ago and I didn't return in one piece. Their whispered words couldn't hide that from me. I was broken, and they knew it.

The light in the hall shifted as we entered an outsized refectory, and I stopped to marvel at the framed glass that dropped from ceiling to floor. The wide view of the metropolis below captured my attention. The desert hills that climbed the sky and rivaled the tall towers was something I'd only found in my distorted mind. There were no clouds in the sky. In their place were three rings for a moon and an iridescent dome— the Ward that shielded everything. Hovercars flew in and out of view over arched speedways, some fading out to where the sand met water. Large screens dominated the top of every building; the sound of working machinery crescendoed as banners were strung from the highest rafters.

Majestic, this. It was stunning, as well as tragic. Whereas everything within this zone thrived, something deadly festered just outside. Paved roads turned to cracked dirt in a span of inches beyond the Ward. I squinted in search of another building, another field, and only found the stretching drylands.

"Your last-meal." The White Jacket pulled me by the arm and spun me away from the window. His touch was surprisingly warm. With the city now behind me, I took note of the people in the refectory, of their outfits that matched my own and the hundreds of voices that built to a cacophony. They jarred my senses. I pocketed every one and memorized their faces—freckles, smiles, hair color. Like I was standing right across from them, I heard each conversation and inhale-exhale of breath. Some spoke about the men that safeguarded the doors, while others sat in silence, pleased with their fare.

"You have twenty-five minutes." A White Jacket took me to a table and shoved a glass tray in front of me. It hadn't occurred to me what *last-meal* was until I took a better look at what was in the bowl.

"Mine?" I asked.

I could tell he didn't want to answer, though he nodded anyway.

Picking up my spoon, I watched, hypnotized, as the others dipped into their bowls and shoveled brown porridge into their mouths. *Food*, I understood. *They're feeding me.* Copying their movements, I cautiously brought a serving of porridge to my mouth and began to eat. The rich spices slid over my tongue and eased a waiting hunger. It didn't matter that most of the oats were uncooked, or that its consistency was near that of water. It could have been green and swimming in oil, I didn't care. I ate from the bowl until I was scraping it clean, until the ache in my stomach lessened. Truthfully, it felt like I hadn't eaten in weeks.

With my head down, I didn't realize someone had sat down across from me until she cleared her throat. She had long, yellow hair and a heart-shaped face. Her lips were pressed to a thin line as she observed me, hands fisted on the table. The girl was pretty, and her bright eyes made her even more so. However, when I glanced up mid-chew, her expression changed. Her anxious features flattened and she watched me expectantly, like she was egging me to say something specific.

"What?" I slurred, oats flying from my mouth.

I was sure there was a name for it, but a tiny light dimmed in the girl's eyes. She exhaled loudly and cringed at the mess I made, pursing her small mouth. "I'm Petra," she said. She unraveled the cloth around her silverware and handed it to me. "And this is a napkin. You got a little something..." She pointed to my hair, where oats stuck to my dark locks.

Despite myself, I smiled and took the napkin. "Thanks."

"Yeah, whatever." Petra still had a full bowl of porridge in front her, though by the way she glared at the thing, I had a feeling she hadn't sat to eat. She entertained the silence for a brief moment longer before she cracked.

"It's not much, but they give you five pairs of socks every month. Keep them, because the bedding is crap and those thin things are the next best thing. Hide your clothes, too. They wash and reuse them, but it's nice to have something that's yours, you know?"

I didn't know.

"And see those ones by the door?" Petra nodded toward the tall, faceless men in padded suites, the ones with the guns. "They bite. They don't talk unless they're giving us an order. Don't doubt what they'll do if you bite back, though. If you know what I mean."

"Why are you helping me?" I assumed that was what she was doing. She'd spat the information out like she was in a rush to get it all out, and looked about ready to run. "Do I know you?"

She shook her head, grimacing. "Not anymore, but I know you."

"You do?"

She paused. "I do."

I peered around the refectory, studying the faces I had just learned. No one appeared to notice I was there, or even acknowledged this side of the room.

Turning around, I said, "How?"

"How what?"

"How have I always been here," I said, "when I don't remember anyone, not even you?"

Averting her gaze, Petra swirled her cold porridge around in the bowl. "*Here* is Silo. Or at least this region is. You've lived here all your life, like the rest of us. And you could be sick. That happens often when they send us out during the storm."

"Storm?" I pressed my hands in my lap, leaning into the table. The Jackets grew antsy with our hushed voices, although they remained a few feet away from the table, giving me the remainder of my twenty-five minutes for the nothing it was worth. "What happens during a storm?"

Petra shook her head. I picked up on her emotions and cringed. *Disappointment.* She felt sorry for me. "They're electrical storms. They come and go when the Ward is its weakest, but that doesn't stop them from sending us out. If we don't go, we risk darkness. And darkness isn't good, for anyone." She said it like it was a delicacy, while absentmindedly mashing her porridge to a soup. "The storm debilitates our systems. Destroys us, if we're lucky. If not, we come back, heal, and go back out again."

"Oh, right." I observed her from across the table, warring with my thoughts. Storms were bad and I was sick. Possibly ruined, but only if I was lucky. Was I lucky?

Petra fed me my next questions, but I didn't want to ask them. I faked it instead. "If that's the case, I don't think the weather got much better..."

My eyes flashed from her to my bowl, and back. When she still didn't look my way, I scooped up my last mouthful of porridge and swallowed it stiffly.

"You know, I think, maybe, there's a storm inside my mind. It's calm now, silent. I can hear it sometimes, too. Just there—waiting, or something."

I pushed my tray aside and tucked my hands beneath my thighs on the bench. Petra was staring at me now. She didn't say anything, and in some way I knew she wouldn't. Her fingers played at her spoon. No rhythm, just a nervous *tick-tock*. When she turned her hand, I spotted a raised scar on her wrist. It wasn't red, and didn't look like a burn she got recently. It just looked painful. Instinctively, I reached out to touch her, to soothe her, and Petra flinched away just as quickly, folding her arms back.

Neither of us moved again, but there might as well have been ten yards and a chasm thrice as wide between us.

Collecting my thoughts, I asked, "You said the storm makes us sick. So is that why we stay within the Ward? To keep safe?"

"Safe." She stilled. "This isn't quarantine, if that's what you're thinking. We *are* quarantine. The Ward keeps us safe from the Seeming, but it's not impenetrable. It's why we fight—sun up, sun down."

"Fighting what?"

Petra had finally had enough of her porridge, and pushed it to the center of the table. "They didn't tell you?"

"Somewhere between chasing down a naked runaway and wringing me dry for information, I think they forgot."

The corner of her mouth tipped in a smirk. "You're witty. They won't like it."

"Should they?"

"I suppose not." Petra and her soft eyes could only silently regard me. A thousand miles more hung between her lips and her next words, and I sensed her hesitation like it was my own. When the White Jackets moved over to us, she casually stood, grabbing her tray to leave. "You'll figure something out, Ari. Because it's you."

I wondered about that. According to the scarred man, my psyche was on a loop. Every week I forgot the last one and I had to sit through constant questioning, the tests, just to salvage a piece of it. This was week three.

Although I didn't remember the other legionaries who had left with me, or the ones who were in the pods, I felt them there, just out of reach. Only I couldn't repair the disconnect. And it was destroying me faster than they could heal me.

When Petra stepped back, I grabbed her arm, right over the scar. "You didn't sit here to enjoy your last-meal with some invalid like me. You knew I didn't remember."

"I don't—"

"You can help me."

Her mouth opened with unsaid words and I felt sick to my stomach as she merely backed further away. Anger gripped me by the throat. Why would she give an inch, only to take it away?

Then the Jackets pulled me from the table and I reluctantly went. The refectory drowned in voices. My ire tasted better than the porridge and I feared the impassive looks I got from the legionaries in the room. They didn't recognize me; *I* didn't recognize me.

Petra vanished from sight and I was followed down the white halls again, this time further than before. Her words leeched at my mind, though, giving me some sliver of hope. Small, as it was. She knew me, or she knew something of me. She could help me find the missing fragments of my memory. In fact, she had given me more answers in twenty minutes than the scarred man had in hours.

I paced down a hall littered with steel doors, stopping in front of the fifth one—room 211. Without saying a word, the Jackets slid the locked bar open and nudged me forward. I was expecting a dungeon of sorts, a torture chamber where they'd skin me alive and force me to tell them everything I didn't remember. Instead, I peered inside and found two small beds crammed into corners and a frameless window that looked out at the Ward.

"You'll sleep here," one of the Jackets said. He reached into a bag on his shoulder and shoved folded cloth in my hands. I snickered humorlessly as I held them out.

"Socks." *Keep them, because the bedding is crap and those thin things are the next best thing.* "This is it, all I get?"

"For now."

A not-so-gentle shove toward the room thwarted my next question. When I stepped through the threshold, the door was slammed shut and locked behind me. From the outside. My footprints marked the tiles in the middle of the bedroom and I wondered how often I'd be let out. That is, if I was released from there at all.

A **vacant impression** swept through the air as I moved in. Then came the prickled awareness that skidded across my psyche. The room felt hollow, though other feet must have marked the spot in which I now stood.

Dropping the socks on the left bed, I retrieved the carrier of toiletries they'd given me and dug for the brush. The rough bristles jutted from a wooden handle, and on the back was a smooth carving of a flower. It was mine, I reasoned. The brush was the only thing that was truly mine.

Perhaps ... maybe.

I *hoped* so.

In the short five hours since I'd awoken in the pod, this was the only thing I felt some connection to. As little meaning as that held right now, it was still a healing balm.

Outside, the sky rolled to an amber-gold and I sat in front of the window, brushing my hair. I couldn't see the city from where I sat, yet I was content to stare into the oblivion, contemplating who would be sleeping on the second bed. Would they be a legionary, like me? Would they know my name or expect me to know theirs?

Beyond the questions, I began to feel impeccably small. I was a blink of insanity in a world I didn't understand. I had memories like everyone else, though mine were obscured so that I only knew who I had become today: the frightened thing that had lost it all to a storm three weeks ago. I wondered whether I'd ever be the same person again, whoever they said I used to be.

The arms and eyes I'd sensed in the dark hall returned, and I felt even more unfulfilled. They belonged to someone, much like my memories belonged somewhere, but visualizing a name or a face was hard. Though they reassured me. My past would find me eventually.

It was with that consolation that I found sleep, my fingers wound tightly around my brush.

TWO

"LETHAL ADDICTION"
BIONIC: ARI-0329

A *nightmare greeted me the next* morning. There were no voices, or names. Only an unsettling calm. Glimmers of light lay trapped within the shadows of my mind. The darkness stemmed, and then there was me—suspended above the waters of a crater, blood veins as black as the night.

Reality had a great way of escaping me, but never like this. My thoughts were never this vivid. The strangled feeling of drowning choked me awake and I was torn from the dream moments too soon. Coming to stifled a scream from my chest.

"I'm awake," I said, just to hear my voice. My skin was hot to the touch. Although light peeked through the window, the bedroom was otherwise dimly lit. I tangled my feet in the sheets and reminded myself that I was only dreaming, no longer in the pod. But I couldn't shake the weighty feeling behind my eyes. A part of me felt the dream like a memory.

And I'll take anything that comes.

"You were dreaming." The girl sitting on the bed across from me was hidden in a corner, yet I made out her short, cropped hair and high cheekbones. She leaned forward with her elbows braced on her knees, a silver chain wound around her thin fingers. "What I would do to know…"

"You don't dream?" I asked her. She must have come in some time during the night, perhaps after her last-meal. Or crusade. Did they send us out at night?

Giving me an odd look, the girl answered, "We never do."

"Right." I licked my dry lips, suddenly thirsty. "Of course not." I was learning that I often said the wrong thing. Probably something I'd done before, too—'old habits die hard' and all that rubbish.

If we didn't dream, though, what did I see? A projection? I attempted an awkward smile in the girl's favor, and when she simply looked away, I scowled and threw my legs over the side of the bed. "I'm not sure what it was. It could—"

"Your eyes." The girl, all stiff movements and plain features, shifted on her unmade bed. She hadn't slept. "You don't have to say anything," she said. "They say it all." Before I could ask what she meant, she went on, twirling her chain in a way that seemed rehearsed. "My name is Zayde, but they call me Zee."

"I'm Ari—just Ari." As I said my name, I thought of how funny this would be in any other scenario. Two detainees bonding over artificial names in a colorless room with no place to go, as if it would suffice. Knowing nothing would.

"Your eyes remind me of the skies just after third hour, when the moons crest above the Ward. First blue, then green," Zee said. She crossed her legs, and the movement put her in the light. I saw dark skin ... and a bandage wrapped around her forearm.

"Outside the Ward must look a world different, then. All I see is the sky, sometimes the city."

I suppose I expected her to confess the answers Petra had alluded to, though Zee appeared trapped in her own head. She spoke like she knew I was there, while not seeing me at all. As soon as she heard 'outside,' she jumped to her feet and tucked her chain into a pocket. She patted her pants several times before moving to the window.

"Oh, it is another world. This city is nothing without those fields. Pitch 'em in the dark all you want, but it ain't so bad."

"You're out there often?" I asked, cautiously broaching the subject.

"No." Zee shook her head. "They said I'm not as skilled as the others. I just help out in the sanatorium, fixin' up the others. Still, I wish..." There was a flash of longing in her features. It was so bizarre that I swore it was a shadow, nothing more. The look vanished in an instant. Zee scratched at her bandage, her words lost. Like she'd forced herself to forget them. "We have to go soon. It's almost sixth hour."

"Go where?"

She spun from the window and her hand went back to her pocket. I sensed she wanted to say more. I sensed her trepidation and it poured from her, wrapping around me in the way all emotions did. It was chaotic. Just as I rose to stop her frenzied pace to the door, a bell resounded outside the wall.

"What was that?"

Silence was Zee's only response. She straightened her shirt and smoothed down the side of her bandage, then touched her chain again. I recognized a habit when I saw one. I said stupid things; the scarred man had a knack for asking stupid questions. It was basically the same addiction.

Zee grabbed the golden handle on the door, which was, surprisingly, unlocked. Even though the bell meant nothing to me, and I was 99 percent sure that Zee had left the right side of her mind in the fields, I prepared to follow her to the sanatorium. Assuming that was where she was going. I didn't know the difference between sixth hour and the other five.

Zee's scabbed knuckles slid over the cool metal of the door and I was standing right behind her when she shakily turned around, gaze alarmed. She went from nonchalant to frightened—a flipped switch.

Backing away from me, she mumbled, "Your eyes."

"I know—"

"They remind me of the skies just after third hour, when the moons crest above the Ward. First blue, then..." Zee looked utterly lost. I tried to understand why she repeated herself, but quickly realized she didn't know either. When I reached for her arm, she pulled away, scratching her bandage. The wound was either healing or infected. She stared at me like she had never seen my eyes before.

"Zee?"

The second bell cut between us and Zee somehow pulled herself together long enough to open the door. The hall flooded with bodies as the other legionaries followed the shrieking sound through Silo. While I stood admiring the colorful faces, Zee fell into the aligned throng in a rush to escape me. She didn't say any more, like Petra.

Was it memory loss? I wondered.

I swayed with the crowd like a wave was pulling me out to sea. The boys walked on one side of the large hallway, their gaze focused on the path before them. Girls moved in the opposite direction and I stood in the very middle, confused about the rhythm and the pattern everyone but me obviously knew. They marched to a tuneless beat. Their eyes never strayed from *forward*, no one bothered to walk around me. More than once, I caught myself trying to move my lips the way they did. I tried to copy the expressions they made and swing my hands in similar motions. Though no matter how hard I tried to fall in line, I was caught in an endless flow of dysfunction.

Someone to my left helped me as I stumbled, then continued walking without a trace of emotion. This was how they lived, how they were synced. I wished this had been the one thing I didn't forget, because while I could pretend with the scarred man, I couldn't pretend in front of the hundreds of legionaries who knew something was wrong with me. I spun in the direction the girls were headed and concealed half of my face behind my hair, forcing myself to stare at my feet until they caught up with the beat. No need to copy the others; they were waves ahead of me.

The line trickled through the halls of Silo and rooms continued to spill with the rest of us. Perhaps we were going to first-meal and this was a standard morning procedure. I wasn't hungry, but I doubted my ability to find the sanatorium without Zee's help, and the last people I cared to see were the Jackets.

A loud grunt made me look up. In the opposite line, third from the back, was a tall boy who tripped and looked around the hall in awe, much like I had. He stopped walking every so often and sidestepped to evade the masses. I didn't know why he flinched every time he looked out the window, but he was easily the most interesting thing I'd seen since awakening. He wasn't like the others. Instead of looking vacantly ahead, he painted the white walls with his bewildered gaze and took in the actions of the others—carelessly and without shame. His mind was eager.

I studied the boy for long moments without breathing. He didn't know I was staring … and that somehow made it even better. People were their best beautiful when they were unaware. It was something in the face. Their features were relaxed, unimpressionable. They didn't inhibit the simple things or bury beneath a façade. They were the most exposed, right in that moment when they put wonder first.

When the boy stopped to observe the overhead lights, I killed all movement. The shift in the line must have startled him, because he looked my way the second I planted my feet. When he caught my gaze, it stuck. *He knew I was staring.*

I should have kept walking, but again, I said and did stupid things. Call it a forté.

The boy gradually reached up and pushed a strand of hair out of his face, tucking it behind his ear. Cocking my head, I mimicked him and settled my curls behind my shoulders. I didn't understand why I did it, or how he knew I would imitate him, until he smiled. Then I smiled. Our flash of teeth among the blurred crowd of bodies became an unspoken language. We were the same—in this way, in *some* way.

He was broken, too.

I lost him in the traffic and his face disappeared from view. There was little chance I'd see him again, but his smile had stained my dark mind with light.

I trekked through the staircase that coiled down the center of our floor. The bell died as we descended. We passed the refectory, and the further we went, the darker it became. The walls turned from white to blue. The female legionaries knew where to go without the bell, without a voice guiding them. If Jackets led in the front, they were impossible to see from where I stood.

Could I break away? I thought. No one would notice; there were too many of us.

When the lines instantly narrowed into a single file, I found myself jammed between tall bodies. My smallness didn't register until then. The others had a decent two inches on me and their pale, faultless skin was a stark comparison to my red undertones and freckles.

Perhaps I'm different and the others like me were hurt in the storm...

I spotted a set of large doors with LVL 9 written above the frame. We were on the very last floor, I gathered. There were no windows down here. Glass walls turned to concrete. If I broke free, I'd have nowhere to run but back to my room, and from what I'd seen of Silo so far, there weren't too many doors leading outside. It was here or *there*. I didn't know the people around me, but here I found familiarity in numbers.

A loud screech erupted from the front of the group. With mild interest, I moved forward and observed as the LVL 9 doors slid apart and revealed another room. Only this one was different from the refectory, and even from this hall. Everything was made of dark colors and square surfaces, floor mats, and dartboards. Four levels were stocked with tables, all lined with bits and scraps of machinery. Steel pillars supported the top floor, which was essentially a balcony. A large screen took up its central wall and it glowed with a single word: CAMP.

"Frontward!" barked a Jacket.

The bodies sprung to life around me and everyone rushed into the room, heading in the same direction. When the legionaries stripped, regardless of who was watching, I knew exactly where I was.

In quick, reflexive movements, they dressed in the black jumpsuits from the bins behind the doors and moved to their stations at the tables. Some headed for the floor mats and threw themselves into an entanglement of hand-to-hand combat forms. Several Jackets watched over their every step.

They're training us, I understood.

I shrugged out of my white uniform and slid into the jumpsuit, keeping my eyes on the ground. There wasn't anything interesting about the space between my feet, but hell if I would look a Jacket in the face while I changed. I tossed my used clothes in the opposite bin and climbed the stairs to the second floor.

Assuming we had full reign of our camp assignments, I settled in at a table in the back of the room. A girl with long red pigtails sat in one of the chairs. She didn't look up when I moved in beside her, or stop what she was doing with the machinery on the table. They looked like random scrap pieces at first, but when she clicked the last parts together in her hands, she held a gun.

"Huh."

The girl glanced at me then, if only momentarily. I watched her stand and then point her gun straight ahead at the red target on the wall. The other legionaries in the room did the same, and then all at once they fired away, sullying the boards with their bullets. While the resounding *boom* didn't stun me, the way they disassembled their guns and quickly mended them again did.

Only 9.53 seconds, I registered. That's how long it took for each of them.

My eyes zeroed in on the girl's hands and I mentally slowed down her movements, tracing every piece of the gun and their placement. After a few moments, my hands began to move too, and I plucked black pieces from the table and clicked them together. The metal vibrated beneath my fingertips. With every slide and twist, my heartbeat pulsed harder. In a little more than eight seconds, I had put the gun together perfectly.

Unless amassing machines was a part of our makeup, I had fed from an old skill. We were programed to know a lot of things, but this felt different. I transferred the heavy gun between my hands, the thing like a **lethal addiction**, and smiled. *I remembered.*

I missed the collective shots taken at the targets, but still rose after they had all gone on to start over. I held the gun steadily and closed one eye, taking aim. My vision focused and refocused until a gold, shimmering ring circled the center of the target. No one else could see it, though it was there like the board only sat a few inches away.

I turned off the safety and braced my finger on the trigger. The whole thing felt hot, like if I didn't hit bull's eye, it would detonate in front of me.

I held my breath. I counted to five, pausing at four. The gun slid a fraction in my sweaty palm, and then I pulled the trigger. Without changing my focus from the gun, I knew I'd hit the target dead on. It didn't sound like a *boom* to me this time. It was more like a subtle hush. It didn't echo around the room, but it did echo inside me.

"I hit it," I said, lowering the gun and admiring the hole in my board.

Even if my mind hadn't quite pieced together all of my past, my body could pick up where it had left off. Perhaps I hadn't forgotten everything, like how potent I felt with a gun in my hand.

I knelt to reach for my bullet shell. The others didn't bother to pick theirs up, yet I needed mine. I needed the tangibility. As I crouched below the table, my gaze shot up at a large carving of a letter.

P.

The letter had crooked wings, four arched lines sprouting from the back. It was quick work, something done in the heat of a moment. I searched the rest of the table frame for other letters and found nothing. Just the *P*. Curiosity beckoned and I placed a finger to the jagged carving. Maybe it wasn't a *P*? Had someone just scraped along the table too hard?

My finger slid against the "wings" and dizzying light flashed behind my eyes. I saw an image of myself in the light, setting fire to a wooden shack. When it went up in flames and crumbled to the ground, I turned and ran into the trees, my coat flowing in the harsh wind. I was sitting right here, though, and that put me out. I wasn't setting fire to a single thing and there were no trees in Silo.

I wrenched back from the table when someone cleared their throat, and bumped my head on the chair. I thought I was messing with the girl's concentration, or in the way of her next shot. But rather, two Jackets stood beside the man with the scarred face and a tall woman with a clipboard. She was the important one—short black hair slicked back on her head and a face too perfect to be pretty. Her pursed lips were tighter than our jumpsuits. She tapped her feet against the floor, waiting.

I shot up with a half-smile, rubbing the back of my head. "Hey, uh, *hi*," I said, and then mentally pushed myself out a window. They didn't smile back. If anything, their scowls deepened.

The scarred man sighed and pointed to the woman's chart as she checked something off. "We're still working with her. The progress is..." His eyes surveyed the gun in my hand. "...*Slow*."

I placed my hand on the table, trying to act casual, though my nonchalance was anything but bulletproof. While trying to get a peek at their chart, my hand slipped and I knocked gun parts from the table.

I closed my eyes and gritted my teeth as they clattered to the ground and pulled the attention of everyone in the room.

When the woman glanced at the scarred man for an explanation, he could only say, "Again, we're still working with her." They moved around the table and evaluated the other legionaries as they got back to work. I didn't breathe again until they were out of earshot, and even then I kept my breathing shallow.

I couldn't afford to mess up.

I spun to clean up my mess and Red Pigtails stared right at me. "I suppose you want to help?" I asked. She blinked once and then busied herself with her gun. "Yeah, fair, I wouldn't either."

I got down on all fours and grabbed the gun parts, then found my bullet shell. I held it up to the light and studied its gold design. It was still warm. I stared between it and the *P* beneath the table. Slipping the shell into a pocket in my jumpsuit, I wished I could take the carving as well. It could have meant nothing, or everything. Or I had sat at this table once before and the *P* with the wings was simply familiar.

When I rejoined the legionaries in the endless rounds of point-and-shoot, my mind was no longer on finishing in 9.53 seconds. It was on the pair of green and blue eyes hiding within the burning trees.

Me.

THREE

"FUEL TO THE FIRE"
BIONIC: ARI-0329

I *wrote out the three letters* of my name in the fogged mirror, then wiped it away. My reflection shimmered beneath my wet palm. I wanted to say I recognized myself, but truths were only lies swathed in gold. I could have woken up in another body, and if the Jackets had said it was me, I would have believed them.

My eyes were like two misplaced jewels that found the oddest chemistry within me. I passed my brush down the length of my hair and busied my mind. The legionaries moved in and out of the showers, getting ready, while I took far too long with my reflection, wondering why they called me Ari.

What did it mean?

It sure didn't feel like me.

But who was I?

The legionary at the sink beside me went about brushing her teeth and I mimicked her, spitting out the tasteless paste when she did. I was learning their routine now. It was a vortex of mechanical actions no one paid mind to, like they were simply the unseen outline of a masterpiece.

I could be mindless, invisible.

As the scarred man said, I was halfway there.

The bell rung outside the door and everyone filed out of the shower room, already dressed. I stood in my towel, minty froth at my mouth—one shoe on.

"*Dammit.*" I rushed into a stall and threw on my white uniform, then tucked the hairbrush into my bag. I made it down the hall while limping into my second shoe. I was only late by a few minutes, but the line had progressed around the corner. When I caught up, they were all seated in a classroom of sorts, their attention on someone who spoke from the front.

I was hesitant to walk in. Everyone would turn to stare at me in unison, because sure—*of course*. I had enough unease to go around for weeks.

I pushed through the door and my eyes went directly to the empty seat at the rear of the room. I noticed that everyone had styled their hair the same: tight bun, white ribbon, and not a stray hair in sight. As if I didn't look unprepared enough, they all held the same leather-bound book while I stood empty-handed.

"Come *on.*" With soaking wet hair and equally drenched shoes, I sped for the desk and plopped into the seat, shrinking into myself. The person at the front of the room had stopped talking the second I entered.

"Ari," he said. He looked like the scarred man, minus the scars. "You're late?" It was phrased as a question and I understood why. We were never late, we *couldn't* be late.

"I was brushing my teeth," I said. In my mind I took another plummet out the proverbial window. "I mean, I got back from camp late, so I had to rush."

Instead of entertaining my lie, the man went back to his speech about the new facility on LVL 9. When he mentioned our punctuality, he stared right at me.

Not only did they train us; they taught us, too. The man I presumed to be the instructor wrote a series of numbers into a glowing pad in his hands and they flashed in the air before the room, fading after a moment. Everyone quickly flipped to a page in their books and began to read the text aloud. I didn't understand what they were saying until I grasped that they were speaking another language altogether. Then my ears translated the twisted tongue and I heard them, word for word. They were reading from Chapter Twenty-five, the history of Caeshua—the world Silo settled in. They listed all the asylums governed by a presidium, and followed along with the map that spanned over two pages.

I listened. I listened and absorbed the information as if I were hearing it for the first time, even though the previous me had probably known the codex by heart.

When they flipped to another page and read an index of regulations, I peered over the shoulder of the girl in front of me. I wasn't discreet, I knew this, but the Jackets hadn't given me a codex to follow along. Just some socks and a petty *good-luck* shove.

Someone tapped my shoulder and a copy of the codex was slid onto my desk. It was from another girl nearby, but I knew the codex wasn't hers. I took it and, a few seats down my row, caught Petra eyeing me. She looked away instantly. She never stopped reading; she never lost her rhythm—and that confused me. Why was she helping me, and then pretending like she didn't know who I was? Like Zee. Were their memories flawed, like mine?

I slumped further into my chair and zoned out as I opened the codex to a random page and began to read silently to myself. It was in the same language they spoke—symbols, numbers, and unusual encryptions. My eyes scanned the page quickly, taking it in. I spat the numbers back out in my mind, and the symbols began to rearrange on the paper. When they stopped, clear and concise words lay on the pages.

It was a chart of colors, and the colors seemed more like titles. BLUE was the first. Its letters shimmered as I passed a finger over the page, and below them lay a long list of numbers: *0478, 6201, 7401...* They were legionary codes. As I skimmed, I recognized the colors as legions. Bold arrows in the margins indicated what station each legion member held, whether it be guarding the Ward from first hour to tenth hour or working in the artillery factories. Without the actual names, we were just numbers, faceless machines.

The GREEN, RED, and BLACK legions followed, their lists not as long, but I found my number on page four of legion BLUE: 0329. The old me had been a part of a legion. I had belonged somewhere before and, ideally, I could belong here again. Ideally, that was. When I slid my finger to the next column, searching for my station, the blank space filled me with dread. It was like I had almost been erased. If you removed my four numbers, I wouldn't be in the codex at all.

Further down the list was another legionary code, but it had been efficiently crossed out. So were two other codes in crew RED, one in BLACK, and four in GREEN. Apprehension pulled at my psyche immediately. With an eerie itch, I pushed through the pages of the legions, looking for an explanation. Had they switched legions? Was not having a station a *good* thing? I was aware of the noise I was making as I shuffled the pages around on my desk, but I couldn't hear it. My mind became a motor, reading words faster than I could process them and internalizing them for later. It was all statistics and creeds and *nothing* about the crossed codes, or why it was so off-putting. I felt like the faster I flipped pages, the madder I grew.

"How can they just stop being a legionary?" The words, bitten off in frustration, ricocheted around the room, hitting me last. Everyone stopped reading and the man in front watched me with a dull look, like he'd expected the outburst.

"0329," he said, and I groaned. "Is there a reason you haven't been reading along?"

Yeah, there are codes *crossed out in my codex.*

Like a sensor had blinked on my forehead, every legionary in the room swiveled to glare at me, waiting for my response. "Pardon—" I added **fuel to the fire.** "—I just lost track." My mistake was palpable. At this rate, I was sure there wasn't a thing I could do to redeem myself.

The instructor wrote something down on the pad at his podium, and then flicked his hand in the air, closing the holograms. When the loud buzzer sounded, signaling the end of an assignment, he didn't even bother to dismiss us. Everyone got up and left, and this time I made sure to leave last.

I watched them place their books on the glass racks below their desks, then casually slid mine up my shirt. I crossed my arms over my chest like the codex was my lifeline and paced quickly out of the room, my head down. I'd put the codex back, of course, but I'd spend the night dissecting it first. And I'd unearth those legionary codes.

Since everyone made a left down the corridor and headed toward the refectory, I veered right and marched the soundless building to my room. With everyone gone for second-meal, I'd have a chance to skip to the next chapter in the codex and hide it from Zee. I didn't know her, so I didn't trust her. The last thing I needed was her calling the Jackets. They'd raid the room until they found the book.

Or worse, they'd take my socks.

I smirked at my own joke, sobering the second I turned down the wrong hall. Room 211 was in the east wing and I was approaching rooms 400 to 630 in the west. With the leather of the codex pressed to my stomach, I spun and rushed down the other end of the hallway. From what I'd seen of it so far, Silo was huge, and I had yet to step a foot outside.

Nothing about these walls struck me as ominous—not like the dark ones from before—until I neared two doors that beamed a bright blue light. I reasoned it was another classroom and the holograms were emitting the lights I saw. As I grew closer, though, I saw that it wasn't holograms, but a machine.

I made sure I was alone before tiptoeing to the door and peering through the window. The machine wasn't like the one I had been hooked to, all screens and monitors that tracked the pacing of my heart. This one was something like a chair. A legionary sat upright with his arm outstretched as he spoke. By his furrowed forehead and pained expression, I knew something serious was bothering him.

They tried to talk him down, asking him simple questions like where he was and his name. But he couldn't give an answer. He was covered in sweat and bleeding from open sores on his neck. He was afraid, for sure, but the Jackets moved around him like he wasn't two minutes away from slipping into a stupor. One held a needle filled with a purple serum to his arm and said nothing as he injected it into his bloodstream. When the legionary struggled to stay still, they just strapped him down.

I almost didn't want to blink. My breath fogged up the glass, but I couldn't move my eyes from them. Not even when my heart beat through my chest.

The Jacket disposed of the syringe and turned to the keypad on the side of the machine in which the legionary sat. As he screamed and thrashed his head from side to side, I wondered if this was normal. If this would happen to me, too. Would this help him? The more I thought about it, the less I doubted it. It was the one thing I couldn't bring myself to second-guess: my trust in the Jackets.

Of course it was meant to help him...

The legionary was lowered into the machine and the lights beamed brighter. The chair hummed to life, and with a pulse, an invisible energy wrapped around him, pouring through his mind. His back arched and his knuckles reddened. His face turned a hideous shade of blue, like he couldn't pull in enough oxygen.

Despite his screams, they didn't stop. The energy beat on until the legionary gave in, finally lying still. The intensity I'd seen in his eyes just moments earlier was gone. He blinked several times before he glanced around, then sat up while the machine powered off. This time, when they asked for his name, he told them. He answered every question, succinctly and by script. My teeth set into my bottom lip as I battled to make sense of it. Whether this was helping him or not, it didn't feel right.

They wrapped his injection site with bandage and he immediately began to itch, as if he was digging to get to something under his skin. It was the same itch Zee had. Same location, same bandage.

"I need my memories back," I whispered. I pulled away from the door, determined to put distance between the machine and me. The room wasn't in some secret, hidden corner of Silo. It was in plain sight, discoverable by anyone. Which meant it *was* normal. I just didn't remember.

The codex in my hands suddenly weighed a ton. I was the only one in the corridor, and yet I felt like I was being watched. I retraced my steps and rounded corners into familiar hallways. Rather than watch ahead of me, I stared at the ground and focused on the glass tiles that viewed the city below.

I headed east through Silo. A few girls trickled into the hall from the refectory, but they didn't glance my way. I slowed down and allowed them to pass, then escaped down the last hall to my room.

I counted the footsteps to my door like a maniac. My mind was elsewhere. Honestly, I felt like I was hiding an explosive beneath my shirt. When I turned, my shoulder collided with someone else and sent the codex crashing to the floor, pages flying through the air. It might as well have detonated in front of me and soiled the halls in blood.

Panicking, I kneeled and hurriedly pieced the book back together. "Look, I'm going to return it. I was just reading—"

But it was Petra. She bent to help pick up the pages, though her movements were slow. With her hair tucked neatly into a bun, it was hard to tell her apart from the others.

I was certain we weren't supposed to feel such strong emotions, but shame was scribbled all over my face.

"I don't remember, so..." I swallowed the sentence and it went down like a knot of thorns. Petra handed me the last pages wordlessly. "You gave me this codex. I know you did. I didn't see you, but I *know* it. And just now, in that room with the boy..." I was running out of air between my words. "I'm not crazy too, am I?"

She gave me her sympathy for all of one second. I was captured between wanting to run and begging her to explain. The latter was what I had done yesterday, and she'd shot me down. Tucking the codex beneath my arm, I said, "*Speak* to me. Didn't you tell—"

Petra's eyes widened. Her gaze slinked down the hall, and when she saw no one, she slapped a hand over my mouth and pushed me out of the way. With my back pressed against a wide window, I watched her. The tick above her right eye, the red to her cheeks, the grimace that tugged at her lips. This was the thing that made her different from the rest. Emotion.

"The walls appear thick, but they're as hollow as the nights are black," Petra said, slowly removing her hand. "All voices carry."

"Then whisper. As long as they're actual words, I don't care for the tone they come in."

"You can never be fixed."

I gave myself a minute to digest her words, and then shrugged. "That's not true."

"Isn't it?"

"It's *not*." I moved until I stood shy of her chest. "They said with training I could—"

"It won't help." Without preamble, Petra spun me around and

gathered my hair in her hands, rendering me silent. It took me a moment to realize what she was doing. She swept my hair back and began to wrap it into a bun using pins from her ponytail. My curls hadn't fully dried and they were brittle to the touch, but by the time Petra slid in the last pin and tucked away a stray strand, I realized the neatness bothered me something fierce.

"I don't want to look like the others." I reached back to pull out the pins and Petra slapped my hands away.

"You can't. You can *never* look like them. Like us." She must have heard the vigor in her own voice, because suddenly she cleared her throat and stepped away.

I glanced at my reflection in the mirror. The city blurred below when my eyes came into focus. I couldn't write my name on the glass this time, but I didn't need to. In less than twenty-four hours, I had pieced together the shell of *her*—the girl I used to be. Just the shell, but she was tangible. I felt her there in my subconscious, keeping company with the eyes and hands that waited in the darkness. She stood on the other side of the glass, my reflection. With one tap into the right memory, the mirror would crumble to my feet. Then I would become her, wholly and at last.

Clutching the codex, I spun on Petra. Her face was impassive, until I spoke. "I may not know who I am yet, but when I remember..." She arched a brow, daring me to finish. Because that was it. What would I do once I remembered? "I'm *going* to remember." Silence. "And I'm keeping the book."

I walked away before my own words could haunt me. I wondered if I'd gone too far, and then squashed it. She'd never refer to me in the same sentence with "never" again.

"Good. It's yours anyway," Petra called out. From the corner of my eye, I caught her grin and that green light in her eyes. I'd had no name for it when I watched it diminish before, but it was obvious now as it rekindled in her irises. *Optimism.* That's what I would call it.

The buzzer went off on cue, a loud *tick-tock* that signaled another part of our day. As Petra disappeared into the refectory and legionaries, both male and female, joined us in the glass halls, I found myself pushing through the crowd in the opposite direction. The current headed toward me and I moved faster to meet it. I held the codex in front of me; I didn't hide it.

I was a hurricane of *emotion.*

FOUR

"ONE OF THE SIX"

"**There have been reports of** activity beyond the Ward. Forward action?"

"Have the Reapers pick up faces. ID them, tag them, and bring them in."

"What if it's not a legionary?"

"A legionary is no longer a legionary after days outside the Ward. Kill anything that moves."

"It's not that simple. It circles the Seeming before disappearing altogether, then returns days later. The Generators always find nothing. It's like it wants us to see it, but only when it's ready."

"Chase it off."

"It could be **one of the six**."

"Well—"

FIVE

"DEAD RINGER"
BIONIC: ARI-0329

"I have questions first."

The scarred man—who I'd learned was called Manis—wasn't surprised by this. His faceless men strapped me into the chair, and then they took their place behind him. They watched me with vivid interest. I wondered if they could sense the lies that burned on my tongue.

"Questions?"

"I told you all I knew—honesty. You asked for it, I gave it." I shrugged. "I want the same."

We were back in the White Room. Two cameras were drilled into the two-way mirrors on either side of me, but I was damned if I would look into them. I knew they were watching, studying me.

Manis cocked his head, and I fought not to do it too. "I gave you honesty."

"Did you?"

I had been dragged out of bed before dawn and had two seconds to hide the codex before they discovered it. Zee was fast asleep. She'd crept in during the night again, her bandage gone. She hadn't been able to see me in the darkness, but I saw her. I saw her momentary relapse as she forgot where she placed her chain over and over again, even though it lay in her hands. Because I valued her space, I hadn't said anything. Not until I was forced into this room, and thoughts of the glowing chair brought the words to my lips.

"I want my questions answered by you," I said, adding, "Alone." Manis knew exactly what I meant. He regarded me for a short moment, his jaw tense. He pressed a button on the underside of the table and the red glow of the cameras flickered out. I still didn't trust the mirrors, but it would do.

"Tell them to leave." I nodded at the Generators.

"They stay. It's protocol."

"They stay or I talk. *Pick one.*"

I didn't blink. I stared into his bottomless eyes until he finally gestured for his Generators to leave. When it was just us, when I was sure I could no longer hear the hum of the cameras, I glanced down at my open files on the table.

"What do you remember, Ari?" he asked.

"I remember yesterday."

"That's a good start."

He has no idea.

Instead of hiding the folder from me, Manis spun it around and flipped through the pages. He pointed to a blurry headshot. It must have been taken several years ago, because my hair was several inches shorter and my face didn't hold the same lines as it did now. I glanced from the picture to the scrawling of notes that essentially made me real. How odd, to see your entire existence in a three-paged folder.

"I remember bits, like my name. But is that really justified when you had to teach me what it was?"

"Of course it is."

I grimaced. "You promised me honesty. A vein in your neck twitches when you lie."

He did that thing he did before, the thing that made my blood crawl. smiled and didn't say a word.

"I remember most when I touch things, certain things I've touched before. Like a gun." My fingers danced on the metal of my chair. "I remember how good it felt to hold one in my hand, like it belonged there. I assume pulling the trigger must have come easy to a killer like me."

"You're not a killer."

"*Legionary*; same thing."

"No," Manis said. "*Killer* implies that you destroy your own kind. A legionary is a fighter. They protect."

"And what do I protect?"

"The Ward." I'd made the mistake of giving away his tell. Manis reigned in his features and I could no longer differentiate his lie from his truth. "The Ward is your home."

"Why would my home need protecting?" I gauged. I watched his lips pulling the words from his throat. I wanted him to say it, the things Petra held from me. The things I had found etched into the back of my codex, written in light ink so as not to stand out. I knew already, but I needed to hear it.

Manis pulled his chair into the table and said, "The Leviathans."

The things that await in the sky.

I hadn't slept last night. Combing through the torn pages of the codex consumed me like a mad disease, and I read from page 1 to 276 before the sun greeted me through the window. The pages were bookmarked. Black marker ink led trails throughout Chapter Twenty, and I recalled the greediness with which I followed them. I understood why Petra didn't say the words in the refectory. During some late hour of the night, the cold cement wall at my back and my hairbrush by my side, it finally made sense.

All voices carry... They're as hollow as the nights are black...

We were built to protect the Ward and to fight against the black-eyed beasts the Jackets codenamed Leviathans. They had no true origin, and no one lived to see them until they tore from the clouds, inhabiting bodies and rendering them undead. The book called it styxing, but I preferred *leeching*. Because that's what they did best—destroy and control the mind, all while feeding from a tattered soul.

They covered Caeshua like a thick, miasmic fog. They took and took until they were the only ones left among the red fields, searching hungrily for new flesh and always finding that one helpless straggler. Most people fled, and now we were what remained of a world below a green sky.

The Ward needed protecting because the Leviathans looked just like us, and it was probably the worst threat yet.

The Jackets built Silo, along with the other asylums, to guard the few thousands of survivors. Before that? Perhaps nothing like Silo had ever existed in Caeshua and some degree of concord was actually visible. Now, the idea of those black eyes tearing into my soul beat at the back of my head.

Manis said no more, as if he was waiting for the right reaction from me. I wasn't supposed to react, of course, which was why he stared so intently. Emotions—they burned deep in my veins.

"Why would I protect a home I don't remember?" I asked.

"Because you belong here."

"Do I?" The buzzing of my manacles replaced the hum of the camera, but it was unnerving all the same. They tied me down for a reason, I knew they did, but I didn't believe for a second that Manis was afraid of me. If anything, he was taking precautions to assert his role. His role, the one that placed him several echelons above me. Me, who, for all intents and purposes, was supposed to be the stronger one.

My home was a lab, cold lights, and a vat of synthetic embryotic fluid. It was countless tests, training, and never thinking on my own. I was generated and hatched into this world, bleeding and angry, and taught how to use a gun before I could form my first sentence. The goal was to kill for the Jackets, to become one of them.

I was failing.

This wasn't the problem, though, and I knew all of this barely ten minutes into my reintegration testing after waking up in the pod. The problem wasn't that I knew, either. The girl I used to be before the storm sat in those classes and learned every page of the codex until she could recite it on command. She belonged here. She was the fighter.

The problem was that this information about who I was, and what I was meant for, now bothered me. Like it was *wrong*, even though I was told it was right. Every cell in my body wanted to override and purge it out, despite that I couldn't. I snapped back every time. I trusted them, yet I still wanted my memories back.

"It's going to take time—" Manis began.

"Do you think I find comfort in time?" I didn't move. "These walls get stranger every day. You promised me my memories and I *want* them. If I once fought to protect the Ward, I want to do that again. I want whatever comes after this oblivion."

"Ignorance is bliss..."

"Until it kills you." I didn't realize I was stretching over the table until the manacles on my wrists screeched with my movement. It was therapeutic, though, knowing that they couldn't completely detain me.

Perhaps that was what Manis wanted—for the idea of being controlled to frighten me into compliance.

With a deep sigh, he pointed to the bottom of a page in my folder. "We need you to remember what happened out there, Ari. It's the only way we can help you."

"I said I don't remember."

"Try harder."

"*I am.*" But I was a blank slate before two days ago. Progress wasn't progress unless I was actually going somewhere, and I felt stuck. "There have to be methods other than tying me down, surely. Or fooling me into thinking we're alone."

"We *are* alone."

I scoffed. "Yeah, right, and I can leave this room any time I want."

Manis was learning my habits and colloquialisms as fast as I was learning his, if not faster. He stood without the folder and began to pace from one wall to the next. "You said you had questions. Let's start there," he said. My eyes darted to the mirror for a fraction of a second, and he saw. Rather than trying to reassure me again, he stood in front of the small speaker below the camera. "They can see you, but they can't hear you."

"How can I be certain?"

"You trust me."

I did, for whatever unknown reason. I trusted Manis ... and I trusted the Jackets.

My fingers began a slow strum against my chair. "Just two, actually," I said. "I have two questions." When Manis only nodded, I continued. "I saw something yesterday. I don't know if I was supposed to, or if I was allowed to go down that hall at all. At first I thought it was normal, but truly, it was as normal as our situation is right now." Manis didn't laugh, not even a twitch. "They put him in a chair. Not like the one I'm in, because his was larger. It glowed, and he seemed afraid of something..."

"They were healing him," Manis answered, as easily as one would count to three. "Some legionaries experience different traumas when they're out defending the Ward. That chair's electromagnetic currents are meant to repair. It's a conciliatory recess." He seemed proud of his answer. "Next question."

My pointer finger paused over the metal of my chair and I watched it, the slight tremor in my hand. I had been right to some degree, then. They were going to put me in the glowing chair. At least, if I ever left the Ward.

Would my veins be pumped with the same serum? Would I lose myself in fits of panic like Zee, only to return to a reality I didn't recognize?

I opened my mouth to voice this, then decided to keep it bottled until I could figure it out on my own. Because I wasn't going into that chair.

Taking on Manis' change of subject, I peered down at my folder, catching sight of my code: 0329. The file was primarily about me, but Manis had asked about the legionaries who left with me on March 19, and they weren't listed anywhere in the folder.

"Who were the others you mentioned, the ones I'm supposed to remember?" I asked.

Manis stopped pacing and cut me a look made of obsidian. "I can't tell you that."

"Why not?" I asked. "They were in my legion, weren't they? Just give me their names. Maybe I'll remember something."

"You remember or we tell you nothing at all."

My mind revolted. "I just want their names. I can't fabricate an image of who they were if I don't have something as tangible as a *name*, Manis. I want to know what happened on that day just as badly as you all do. Lately, it seems I want it more."

"Then remember."

"I can't!" I shouted, frightening myself. Though I didn't shut it down. Words spilled from my mouth and I began to feel like that sick thing cowering in the dark hall. "I-I can't remember, I don't know who I am, who I was. I'm trying to fix myself, but it's hard to put something back together again when you don't have all the missing pieces!" My hands were hot in the manacles. Tiny prickles danced down my spine, igniting something cold in my blood. Something long repressed.

Manis didn't look half as frightened as I felt. Instead, he looked surprised, his pale smile itching at the corners. I understood too late that he saw the emotion he was looking for earlier. The entire time I gauged him for information, he was testing me.

And I had failed.

Again.

I sat back, jaw clenched. The Jackets were going to inject me with as much material as they could without giving me too much, then yank the lost memories from my mind before I could ever truly have them. It was taking too long and they were growing impatient with me. I couldn't even pretend to make progress anymore.

"When do I get to go outside?" I said.

"You can leave when we're done. First-meal should—"

"No. *Outside*."

I allowed myself to feel expectation for the first time since I awoke drowning in a pod, but like everything I'd learned since then, it was good for nothing.

Manis spoke quickly, refusing to look at me. "You're not ready and we don't know how hyperactive you are beyond these walls. You could eclipse or…"

A single breath escaped me. "I can't just *stay* here. My life revolves around these white walls, and then camp. I can show you how I shoot, if that's what you want. I never miss, Manis. I hit it every time. I can show you," I pled. "Anything to escape this, please." With my hands bound, I couldn't wipe the angry tears that warmed my cheeks. I didn't blink. I only stared at Manis' lips in some pitiful effort to get him to say *yes*.

He tapped on the mirrored glass, and the door leading out into the hall unlocked. The two Jackets that had waited outside returned, and then the cameras flickered back on.

"We're done for today," Manis said. To me, his movements toward the table seemed pressed into slow motion. I watched him reach for my folder—all the information I was still missing. Manis' smile was becoming eerily familiar.

He shuffled the papers together and something about the careless action poisoned my mind. I hated it, how easily he could pack me up and stuff me back into an envelope. All at his beck and call.

My shaking hands heated the beeping manacles to boiling point. The bounds shook, then snapped. The Jackets didn't know I was free until I was halfway out my chair. When I gripped Manis' wrist, I didn't have time to process how I did it. I wanted the papers, and no amount of trust in them could deter me.

"You promised you would help," I said, cautious and vibrating with energy.

Manis glanced down at my hold on him with wide eyes, and I swore I could read his mind. He was trying to figure out how I broke free from the steel cuffs, because somewhere in the back of my muddled mind, so was I.

The tick in his neck was back.

I chanced it and tried to snatch the folder away, only to be pulled back by the two Jackets. My fingertips were a breath and a hair away, and then Manis stepped back.

"Take her. She'll eat her meals in her room until she can remember something."

"Manis!" The fiery energy inside me swelled as he neared the door. I didn't have a name for the emotion yet, but it was a dark weight. Something so apart from who I recognized myself to be. It was someone else, it was *her*. And she was angry.

I slid back from the glass table, pushing it out of the way with little effort, and dodged the Jackets. As Manis stepped towards the door, I picked up my chair and threw it with all my strength. I wanted to hit him. I wanted him to hurt, but I must have hesitated.

Because I missed.

And I never missed.

Manis ducked low just in time and the heavy glass chair crashed into one of the mirrors behind him, splintering the glass but never breaking it completely. We stared at the cracks—him in awe, me in disbelief. My **dead ringer** was there. Wild hair, dark eyes, and those hands… They vibrated.

Manis ignored my trembling state and tapped the mirror harder, hurrying the Jackets. The first thing they did was arrest my arms behind my back, pushing my head down.

I missed, I seethed.

Manis followed as they hauled me out and walked me back to my room. Keeping my chin up was my last bid in defiance, yet it was futile. Everything I did from then on would be, especially when they were the healing balm to my past and I was nothing.

If I made it to next week with the same memories, I'd remember this moment in a haze of deformed shapes and holed thoughts. The night I learned what I was and the morning I realized I'd never officially become it, not again. Not in the same way.

They pushed, I pushed back. The Jackets held a firm grip on my arms, their colorless fingers digging into my skin, but I was numb. So numb, and to everything but the rapid beating of Manis' stone-cold heart.

"You promised," I said, dragging my feet to stay in line with him. "I need help."

"That's without question." The Jackets slowed as Manis swung to face me. The broad window behind him, one filled with a picturesque sky and city lights, was a great contrast to the darkness I found in his gaze. "Do you trust me, Ari?" he asked.

It was the question I always had an automatic response to. *Yes, I do.* Only, I hesitated again and the question confounded me. It was full of numbers and racing equations, figures and erratic symbols. My mind couldn't route the five simple words. I heard them play over and over again, yet Manis had only said them once.

"I-I do," I stuttered. I glanced down the hall. My thoughts screamed in my head. "But I-I don't think I want to." I smiled with the confession. There it was. Something I designed, a response derived wholly from *me*, and it had only taken a complete meltdown to do it.

"Then I suppose it's better that you have no choice in the matter," Manis said, cutting into my smile.

Futile. Everything may have been futile, but that didn't mean I wouldn't try.

Manis gloated in his response and I beat him to his terrible joke. I brought my head back and knocked him in the face, then kneed him in the gut. "I *want* a choice," I said. As Manis keeled and fought to keep the vomit in his throat, I pulled a hand free and elbowed a Jacket in the chest. He took it with a loud grunt, much harder than the second Jacket, who yielded with a punch to the face.

What am I doing? I thought, breaking away. I was stronger than my tiny body afforded me, but I wouldn't stand a chance against a Generator's gun. I wasn't invincible. Not yet.

The Jackets had pulled me from my room this morning before I got to my shoes, but I didn't let that slow me down. I took off down the hall, my arms pumping and socked feet beating the glass floors. I ran more in the promise of the outdoors than anything else. Behind me, I heard the Jackets release the siren.

"Don't let her get far!" Manis yelled, nursing his bruised nose.

I didn't know where I was going, but I knew I needed to get away from the scarred man. I rounded new corners, turning back every so often to make sure I stayed a step ahead of Manis. First-meal must have been over, because legionaries, both male and female, crowded every inch of the halls. Anxiety crawled up my back, a twitch or two in my psyche to remind me that I was also running from myself. I forced it down with everything else. Saved it for a time adrenaline wasn't beating me blind.

I stopped in a large, forked foyer to breathe. I didn't have the codex, my brush, or my shoes. My hair was a mess of tangled knots and my sweaty shirt clung to my back. I calculated the distance of the nearest Generator, how long it would take for them to rope me down and throw me back in my room, but it wasn't enough time.

5.25.

I could hear their guns, their manacles. The Generators stormed down one hall and the Jackets bounded down the other. The flashing blue lights above me were like wild triggers, sparks skittering across my synapses.

Manis is lying to you, I rehearsed. *He's not telling you something.*

4.29.

I glanced around the foyer again and found a door with a red lever. Whether it led to the White Room or LVL 9, I didn't care. I closed it behind me and beat the handle for good measure. When I was done, it looked like someone had put it through a grinder and my wrist throbbed with shot veins.

"Ari!" Manis slammed against the door just as I finished twisting the handle over the lock, making it difficult to open. "You're not ready!"

4.22.

I hadn't entered a room at all. It was a gallery flooded with legionaries, the other half of Silo that hid behind a door. The colorless walls and frameless windows were the same. I had walked through a door into nothing but the usual. Only, a few stragglers stopped to stare at me. In a small crowd of six, they still managed to look identical.

"How do I get out?" I asked, fists at my side. I breathed deeply, focusing on their faces. If they didn't tell me the way out, I'd find it myself. With four minutes left.

No one moved or shouted for the Generators. I felt my mind reach out for theirs, stretching across the feet between us and taking hold. All I had to do was think about it. I had to want it bad enough. I found their racing thoughts and quickly reprogramed them, faster than a speeding bullet. It was instinct, taking control, even though I had no intention to. They were legionaries, better off than I was, and yet their minds snapped like a twig in the wind.

Incensed, I ran up to one of them—a boy with a young face and hair that matched the walls—and gripped his shoulders. I shook him and my desperation drove into his mind. "*Please*, you have to help me. How do I get out?"

I watched his irises refocus. He was cold to the touch, they all were. They always were. When his forehead furrowed and he took a step back, I watched him pluck a light in the void of his mind. Or perhaps it was a light I placed there. He raised a shaking hand and pointed down the opposite hall. The other legionaries copied him, a shaking finger angled south.

My hold on them abated. I knew because a tightness in my chest quit and I didn't feel tethered to them anymore. A second ago, we felt like one whole entity. I stepped around them and ignored how nauseous this made me feel.

Did I. . .? Could I. . .?

The south hall was as bright as the rest of Silo. The only difference was the large elevator that slid open with a frantic push of a button. The legionaries continued walking. The sirens doused the blank walls in red, but nothing mattered to them except getting to their next assignment.

1.87.

When the crystal-clear doors of the elevator flew open, I threw myself in, hitting the very last button on the panel. Glass walls closed me in, and I saw everything. I saw everyone. The Generators pushed legionaries aside with their readied guns, and then there was Manis. Poor Manis. He ran down the hall with a bloody nose and an equally red face to boot. I prepared to fight them if I had to, if they made me. I watched them through the sticky strands of my hair. The tube of the elevator sunk and still I counted.

0.

If Silo was this building, I had no idea what they called the city surrounding it. Hands pressed against the glass, I beheld the jagged skyscrapers and busy highways that hung suspended below the Ward like rainclouds. The people walking through the streets were tiny blots of light and darkness, fading in and out as they entered shops and markets. It was foolish, but right then I wanted to be that inconsequential, a pebble in a field of boulders. The further down I escaped toward the city, the more I wanted it.

The sirens stopped on LVL 1. I could still hear them coming for me, but somehow being closer to the ground made this easier. When the doors slid apart, I was immediately encompassed in dry heat. I took one step, two, then fell. My socked feet hit the edge of the tube and I ate dirt the second my body collapsed. The pain that exploded in my right ankle didn't stop me, though. My eyes lifted skyward and I crawled to my feet, mud beneath my fingernails. I had to do it. If not for me, then for her.

The dead ringer in the mirror.

I caught sight of the tallest building 25.3 feet west and sprinted for it. The crowds were thinner in the city, but the rhythm confused me no less. Everyone had somewhere to go, and I was unsure whether I passed by legionaries ... or something else altogether. I ran, sometimes backwards, and took in the world I must have seen with innocent eyes once. Now all I saw were the faceless Generators approaching in forms, and my freedom lying facedown in a gutter.

I pushed someone in a cloak out of the way and whispered a half-hearted apology. The tall building was halfway down a broad alley with no doors or windows. It was early morning, though I was cast in the dark.

"Do it," I whispered. Pulling the sleeves of my shirt over my fingers, I clung to the steel bars on the side of the building and began to climb. I dug my feet into the holes and grooves, using sheer upper-body strength to scale the tall structure. My feet bled through the socks and I thought of Petra. My nails chipped and peeled back, and I thought of Zee. My legs trembled and I thought of the boy in the hall, the boy in the glowing chair. Again and again, the pain reminded me that I could never be them.

"She's over here!" came a voice. In a matter of moments, the alley flooded with the clicking sound of their guns and a team of Jackets led by Manis. They watched me climb the building, their frustration palpable.

"Ari!" Manis shouted. "You're not ready!"

My grip faltered. "I'll come down if you answer one last question."

Manis was restless.

"What were their names?"

"Ari—"

"*Their names.*"

I gave him five seconds to follow through and he blew it in two. He sent his Generators back to get the hovercrafts and the Jackets called in reinforcements from Silo. Manis would have climbed up after me if he could, snatching me back and shackling me to a leash. But I wasn't coming down without knowing their names, and he knew it.

I continued the climb. Sharp ledges made me stop to readjust my sleeves over my fingers, but it was all fleeting, especially when I was this close. I watched the light stream down from the vivid sky and chased after it—a beggar to gold. Looking down wasn't an option. I questioned several times whether I was sane, though sanity couldn't explain why I was running away from the people who'd created me.

I was *in*sane, perfectly and willingly.

I was criminal and chaotic.

Everything they designed me to hate.

I—Ari.

0329.

My right hand hit the flat top of the roof and I hefted myself over the edge, then rolled onto my back. When I thought I couldn't get up, when I thought I had to take a break, a feather-light brush against my psyche got me moving again.

I shed my socks, and my bloody feet trailed along the surface. I didn't stop until I was at the other side, staring off into the expansive hills. It was the closest thing to serenity—the sky and me.

The Ward was a thick screen that cradled the city. It was placed this high so that it couldn't be compromised, but here on the top floor of the tallest building, hidden behind a column, I could reach out and grasp the Ward in a bruised, angry fist. My hand slid through it effortlessly. If I wanted to, I could bend it to my will. The realization brought a wicked, deeply satisfied grin to my lips.

It was odd. The eyes and arms that found me in the darkness weren't hiding in the dark anymore. They were paired with a mouth, shallow breathing, and all right in the light of day. This time they spoke to me, uttering a single letter: "H."

When Manis found me hours later, it was with both feet dipped into the emerald sky.

SIX

"BLUE MOON"

BIONIC: ARI-0329

"Update on Subject 0329."

"She's resisted treatment for four days. The Generators deliver her meals to the door as instructed, but she refuses to eat. She only drinks the water."

"Does she speak?"

"Yes. Manis reported a slight break in her psyche when she tried to escape."

"Break?"

"The stuttering is back, mildly."

"Does she remember anything?"

"When they ask, she doesn't talk. She won't look at Manis anymore."

"But she is remembering?"

"We... We're not really—"

"She is. She's relapsed seventeen times since the incident and she comes back as something different every time."

"I don't understand."

"0329 is intelligent, smarter than anything we could ever recreate. She can't be duplicated. It's a game she plays."

"Game?"

"If we believe she's impossible to fix, we'll dispose of her. And that's what she wants, whether she knows it or not. She wants us to believe we no longer need her."

"What do you want us to do?"

"Nothing."

"But what if—"

"Do nothing. We'll play her game."

I made it to the next week. I entered it in much of the same way I re-entered Silo—confused, cold, and confined. My only source of comfort was my bed, and I wasn't deserving of good sleep. They took everything else, so I spent every waking hour counting, calculating.

2,481 strangled breaths.

1,901 paced steps.

12 minutes before they returned.

Ten days.

Ten days had gone by since I awoke in the pod. I'd etched lines into the bottom side of the bedpost so they couldn't tell I was keeping track.

Words hadn't left my lips in forty-two hours, and my thoughts raced faster than the flighty milliseconds between my heartbeats. I blinked 29,135 times a day—181 times to chase the tears away. They wouldn't see me cry.

Manis only showed his face four times, but in those four times I wanted to waste two minutes and eight paced steps to smother him unconscious.

I was livid, but passive. When the Generators slid my food through the door, I left the meals to rot in the corner. Anything they gave me would be laced with sedatives. I learned well after the third day, when the Jackets restrained me and forced the food down my throat just to keep me alive. My screams were nothing new to Silo; just new sounds in the chorus of agony. I'd felt fine for a while; then the sky turned upside down and the walls disappeared around me. When I awoke, Zee's bed was gone.

They were going to put me in the glowing chair. Manis alluded to as much when I refused to talk to him for the fifteenth time. He grew angrier; his face would get so red the scar across his face practically bled anew. Manis was an itch, an *unrelenting* itch. He couldn't be ignored, and I couldn't move two inches in his direction before being contained, but that didn't stop me from studying him, his weaknesses. He knew I was smarter than him. He watched the way *I* watched him, understanding that even though he sometimes said nothing, I could wrench the words from his small mind in the time it took me to blink twice.

And he wasn't in full control, not of anything. He was as much a coward as he was an itch. He took orders from someone else, then reported back when the day was done. He promised he wasn't going to hurt me, but he would have buried me alive the second I broke from the pod. In his eyes he carried a deep hatred, and he wasn't hiding it anymore.

The door squeaked open and footsteps clamored into the room. Zee sat the tray down in front of me without looking up, like she'd done periodically all day, and stepped back. It was some sort of soup with a side dish of crackers. She set the cup of milk down last.

"I..." My voice was rough from disuse. I cleared my throat and tried again, finding Zee in the half-lit room. "I wanted water."

"They only gave me this."

"Zee, please." Digging my broken nails into the floors had centered me for three days and now it did nothing. "Water is the only thing I-I can see through. It's the only way I know they aren't poisoning me."

"I can't." Zee shook her head hard. She'd refused to look at me since they carried me in from the building's rooftop, and I knew they'd told her to. Now she fought herself, slowly peeking my way. Something clicked in her mind. I felt it. "Your eyes remind me of the skies..."

"Zee—"

Like she'd realized what she did, Zee slapped her hand over her mouth and briskly left the room, leaving me with the cold soup. Bits of noodles and vegetables swam around in circles in the bowl. The broth was a red-orange and the crackers looked like the hardiest thing I'd seen in days. I picked one up, and then threw it back down. If I blacked out, I wouldn't be able to live with myself, not even behind these four walls.

"First blue, then green," I whispered. Instead of for feeding the beast in my stomach, I climbed to my feet and padded over to the wall beside my bed. Both hands pressed to the cement, I felt around for the right spot with my eyes screwed shut.

Eleven paces to the right.

Twenty-six finger-taps south.

One step forward.

When I opened my eyes, there was the slanted hole in the wall—the one I'd hurriedly closed off before the Jackets returned this morning. I pulled back the slab of cement and set it on my bed. I hadn't dug the space out with my hands, and Manis never sent my food with utensils. The space had already been there, and the moment I realized they weren't letting me out, I'd hid my book all the way in the back.

I fished it out and blew the lingering dust away. I'd been too afraid to take it out until now. Crazed ideas of the Generators raiding the room in search of it made me anxious, like it'd somehow vanish in the hole. On nights when I couldn't risk it, I'd lie with my ear pressed against the wall as I counted the distance between it and the window. Seventeen shaking, tiptoed steps—the distance it would take to free it, even if I couldn't free myself.

But this night, I held it.

I lay with my back to the floor, the book opened to page thirty-four, where I left off. This was my bedtime story, and it was the best, and only, one I'd ever heard. I read of the day the yellow moon became a **blue moon**. There were many more cities like Silo, and the Jackets weren't the only beings that survived. I re-read this page the most, tracing the words with memory.

I read aloud, softly at first, through chapped lips and with tired eyes. I didn't stop until my arms grew too heavy to hold up the book.

Five pages more.

One bookmarked edge.

Never enough air to breathe.

I didn't sleep on the bed.

SEVEN

"BONE WHITES"
BIONIC: ARI-0329

The *unlatching of the bar* outside my door awoke me. I didn't like sleeping, not if I could fight it. I'd lost count of the hours and wasn't sure who had come for me. It could have been anyone, but the color of the sky told me it was Manis.

I quickly hid the codex in the hole in the wall, then crawled over to my spot in front of the window. The door swung open, though no footsteps sounded for a while. I half-thought they were letting me out, but when I turned my wary eyes to the door, there stood Manis. Only observing me.

It was mid-afternoon, and he was right on time.

"You're going to wither away," he said. He waved for a Generator to enter the room, and it set a tray of food before me. A sandwich this time, and water. I gave the clear glass a long look before I picked it up and chugged it down. My dry throat was instantly soothed.

"But that doesn't seem to be your plan, does it?" Manis continued.

I watched him above the rim of the glass.

"Does she speak?"

I tipped the glass over, stretching out my tongue for the last drop. When I was sure it was empty, I set it back down on the tray and pushed it all away.

"*She* has a name."

"Ah, so she does!" Manis chuckled, and the sound was grating. He stepped into the room and purposely stopped in front of the window, blocking my view of the outside. "And what is her name?"

"Ari, 0329."

Manis wore long, dark pants and a collared shirt. His lab jacket touched the floor and his eyes looked tired today. My resistance was breaking him down as much as it was me. He crouched to my level and picked up the cold sandwich. "I've seen what days without food does to a person. You won't survive on half a glass of water, and your few breaks to the lavatory will become no more." He brought the bread to my lips. "Eat."

"No." The sandwich was filled with meat and some sort of sauce. I wanted to grab it and eat my fill, just to lull the pain in my gut, but not at the risk of blacking out.

I had to stay in control.

Manis' eye twitched, and he shoved the sandwich at my mouth again. If his gaze were a furnace of tall fires, I would be a carcass sitting in flames.

"*Eat.*"

I opened my mouth and feigned taking a bite, then pushed the sandwich away, repeating, "*No.*"

Manis didn't know what to do at first. If he shoved the sandwich in my face again, he knew I would only deny him. I watched in mild fascination as his reaction blew through his features. The bow of his eyebrows, the lack of blinking, and the subtle way his pale ears turned red. It was my friend, emotion, and I would have considered it beautiful had it not been on his face.

"Your days will rot away faster than you do." He dropped the now squashed sandwich, then took ten steps to the door. I counted. Only he didn't leave and slam the latch like he usually did when he visited. He sent his Generator down the hall, and a moment later it came back with a group of Jackets. Bald heads, white coats. They looked so much alike it made no sense. "Make sure she's well fed," Manis told them. "She's missed five days worth of meals."

His words instantly put me on my feet. My knees were a little unsure, but I was up and backing into the furthest corner in moments. They were going to force me again.

"Manis!" I screamed, gripping the wall. The Jackets swarmed the room and tugged at my legs, my hair. They swatted away my useless attempts to keep them away. Their cold hands dragged me to the bed and strapped me to the posts with the same manacles. "Manis, please!"

One Jacket pulled at my mouth to connect the hooks while the other readied the tube. Fear knocked on every damned door of my mind.

I was going to meet the darkness.

I couldn't keep count there.

I would lose track of the hours, the minutes...

My hands gripped the sheets below me and I shouted, "I'll eat! Manis, *I'll eat it.*" It was the saddest thing—my voice. I would meet the same darkness with the sandwich, but perhaps I wouldn't meet it confined to my bed. I'd have a chance to run. Somehow, that was better.

Manis shut the door, but I heard him say, "I'm sure you will."

I did this to myself. My eyes went from the door to the ceiling. There was nothing there, though I pretended there was. A sky, a few mountains. Perhaps a few birds and people who smiled, like last time. Tons of color. Sometimes I even had a family who waited for me. A mother ... or a sister.

The hooks forced my mouth open, and then the Jackets fed the tube down my throat. I shut my eyes against the pain and imagined I was far, far away. Among the desert hills, maybe. A scene where the sky looked just like me.

Sleep came easily.

I dreamt of sallow silhouettes and broken cries.

Fiery nights and muted tones.

My mind clung to the images like *his* hands did, and deep inside the shaking home, burrowed beneath the burned blankets, they held me. I couldn't guess why we were hiding, or from whom we were running, but suns fell outside the window and it explained everything I needed to know. A grey, gaseous fog enveloped the small space. When people shouted to leave, we remained.

Sheltered ... yet, *not*.

I felt the tears on my fingertips and the need to be closer—so much closer. I felt the *pitter-pat* of our slowing hearts as I was rocked to a lullaby, then embraced by a body that smelled of the sea. *Famine* was what I called it. I clawed at skin and breathed in between the caresses that scorched my soul, starving for solidarity. Anything but the darkness that would surely leave me without. I figured that if we never moved from where we were, where we were never supposed to be, I could scour through the sands of time like the morning skies chased the stars. I could be invincible, I could be different.

When the clouds rolled overhead, the room gave out. Fog seeped in through the locked doors and shut windows, separating our lips and dividing our intertwined hands. I watched the people disintegrate. I watched with bleeding eyes as, all together, everything stopped and I was left with a benumbed sense of *hollowness*. In that nothing, I caught: "We are the **bone whites**, the soundless, the unsung. The harbingers of deceit."

A chant, a battle cry.

I came to with a jolt, staring into wide eyes that weren't my own. I pushed the vomit-soaked sheets away and rubbed my sore throat. I must have been screaming in my sleep, soon after the Jackets untied me and left. "Petra? What are you doing in here?"

She stood beside my bed, her face hardly discernable in the dark. I hadn't slept long, I estimated. A few hours at most, but they were still hours I couldn't get back.

"You were dreaming. I was watching you remember, in the dream," Petra told me. "How do you..." When I didn't agree, she sat down beside me and pressed the back of her hand to my forehead. "You haven't eaten properly in days. We need to go."

"Go?" She pulled me up and toward the door ... and I didn't argue. If Petra was getting me out of Silo, I'd follow her barefoot and blind until I was miles away from the Ward. Unless she was working under Manis, that was. Then I'd endure another week of sparse water and four blank walls if I had to.

I turned back to get my book, but she stopped me. "Leave it. You're coming back."

"Are you kidding me?"

"I don't *kid*," she said.

"Then where are we going?"

The door opened a fraction and a sliver of light spilled into the room. A girl poked her head in and Petra nodded for her to come closer. She was average height and had the face of every legionary in Silo. She was a little weird, though, like Petra. She looked right at me and grinned.

There was nothing empty behind her eyes.

"The Generators aren't watching, but there are heat sensors in the walls. They know if *and* when you leave. They stop every ten minutes for rotation," said Petra.

"Ten minutes—"

"Starts now." Petra took my hand as the girl climbed into my bed. I watched her take the same position I'd slept in, moving slightly to show that the body in the bed was breathing.

"Tell her to lie on the floor."

Petra volleyed me with sad eyes, but nodded for the girl to get on the floor. When she took my favorite spot in front of the window, I allowed Petra to hurry me down the hall.

Her footsteps were quick and quiet, trained. We entered the shower room after dodging the hallway cameras and headed for the exit out the back that led to the central stairs. I had only been locked away for a handful of days, but walking these halls again felt like I was encroaching on new territory. Every breath I took felt too good to be true.

I stopped Petra in front of the sinks. She was sweating and her hair was unraveling from its bun.

"We need to *go*," she urged, trying to take my hand. The silence around us was eerie, yet welcomed.

"Tell me where we're going first. If this is Manis' new joke, I'm turning back. I'll tie myself to that bed before I let him get one on me again."

"There's no joke, Ari."

"Don't lie." I watched her outstretched hand like a timid animal. "You said the walls hear everything."

She nodded once. "Then let me *show* you."

Show, not tell.

Petra's palm was warm when I slid my hand into hers. I remembered the way she'd sat across from me in the refectory and handed me a napkin, her tone friendly even then. I trusted that she wanted to help me, but didn't trust that she would succeed. I was dancing on a thin sheet of ice—my mind—and it was destined to swallow me. So I had to trust *her*, the girl I used to be, and allow her to be my compass out of here.

With greater determination, Petra and I set off through the halls of Silo, hiding within every shadow we found. Generators patrolled the rooms, but that didn't stop us. Two quickened heartbeats in the black rivaled that of any siren. I looked around anxiously, but Petra never wavered. She had practiced this once before and had every step mapped.

We took the central stairs that led to camp, though we detoured another floor lower—to LVL 2. The doors opened to crooked wall panels and blinking lights. The holes in the ceiling were tiny abysses. It was nothing like upper Silo, or camp. The air felt different, and a niggling sensation told me that Petra was taking me back to the pod.

I tugged on her hand, forcing her back. Something didn't feel right, and my vision was growing hazy. The scratch marks on the walls were still fresh. My screams were still embedded somewhere deep in the floors.

And the blood.

It manifested before me and I choked on it, retching as it bubbled up my throat and burned me from the inside. Petra saw the panic climb into my eyes and immediately began to shake me. She didn't stop until her grip on my hands was painful.

"Ari!" she whisper-shouted, searching my eyes. "I'm taking you back."

"*No.*"

"What you're feeling right now is called fear."

"*Fear...*"

"They warned me not to show you too soon, but we can't wait. You're not fixing yourself."

She released my hands and the bloodstains evaporated, a figment of my poor imagination. "I don't want to," I said.

"Too bad." She continued to haul me through the entry. She liked to do this, I realized. When I closed my eyes, she forced them open with a slap to my arm. She didn't want me to miss a thing.

I entered the room with the broken pods, and the familiar shattered glass pinched into the heels of my feet. Everything was exactly as it was on the day I broke free. The mirror where I saw my eyes, the lights, and the same smell of dread that first awakened me. It was like I never left; they didn't bother to repair anything. They shut it behind a door and forgot it existed, much like they'd done to me.

Pressing my hands to the inside of my pod, I flashed back to the moment I was reborn. I recalled trying to form words as I crawled naked to the red door, and how speechless I was when there was so much to say.

If I had known things would be a slow burn from then on, I would have let the water take me. I would have relived my death until it became my whole world.

"It's in here." Petra stopped in front of a door at the rear of the room. She pressed her palm to a panel and it lit up, scanning her handprint even though pieces of the monitor lay on the ground.

"It's a vault," I said.

She asked, "Do you remember it?"

"I'll always remember the darkness," I told her. "I was birthed in it."

We entered the room and Petra shut the door softly. The panel beeped, locking us inside. She hit a switch above my head and I finally saw her in proper light.

Her bun was nonexistent, gone; thick strands of hair framed her sweaty face, doing little to conceal the exhaustion beneath her eyes. Her white sweatshirt was rolled up at the sleeves. She held a ring of keys, but dropped them on the floor when she made her way over to a lab table, like her mind had forgotten she held something.

There was an odd tension in her shoulders, too. I cocked my head, her hyperactive movements superseding what knowledge I already had of her. Whatever she had to show me was driving her insane. Her pallor mimicked the walls around us.

"Sit." Petra pointed to the only chair in the center of the room, right in front of a large screen with a crack down its side. She shifted from the table to a small refrigerator below an old chest. "It isn't much, I know, but

I hope it's better than water."

I sat in the chair and took in my surroundings. The vault wasn't empty, but it wasn't necessarily full, either. There was the table, the fridge, the screen, and a scattering of books and papers. It wasn't anything important, just a means to exist. Despite the chill in the air, it felt *lived in*.

"Petra, do you—"

Petra sat a plate in front of me: carrots and lettuce. Without waiting for me to react, she turned and made her way to the screen. "It's all I have, so eat it."

"Why do you hide here?" I asked, ignoring the food and my growling stomach.

"I don't hide," Petra said. She pressed a button on the screen and it lit up, fading in and out. "No one can hide in Silo."

"Then tell me what this is. How do you have access to this place?" The chill was seeping into my clothes. The pressure in my chest would kill me in moments if she didn't answer my questions and release me from this jail.

"How much do you remember about the day you woke up?" she asked, still tinkering with the screen.

"Not much. I just remember the feeling of drowning, dying."

Petra slid a small disc into the screen and the light stopped blinking. It flashed a solid blue color and cast a shadowy hue against the walls. She stood back, marveling at her work. "You were dying, Ari. Still, you are."

"But—"

She spun on me, tight-lipped. "I was there. I found you, curled up in a corner with your back against the floor like you were trying to somehow become *a part* of it. I found you. It was me, I was there."

I was struck by her honesty. It wasn't her words, but the fierce tone with which she spoke them. Petra had been the one to find me in the darkness, sedate me, and then deliver me to Manis? But she was the same one who gave me the socks and braided my hair; the one who gave me my codex of answers.

I shot out from my seat, knocking the plate over. "You don't get to do this! You don't get to play with my memories. It's not fair, and you *knew*."

She arched a brow. "Which is why you need to shut up and watch this."

"I'm not watching anything. I'm leaving Silo."

"And where will you go?" The question was asked in earnest, but because I didn't have a good answer, it only served to agitate me. "What you're about to see won't be easy, but I'm not asking you to trust me. I'm asking you to trust *yourself*," Petra said.

She hurried back to the screen before I could bring myself to walk out. When she clicked a button, a new, polychromatic realm exploded before my eyes, jolting me back a step. The screen played images in motion, one frame after the next. There was little sound, yet I could hear the voices perfectly.

"How?"

"It's called an audiovisual, Ari," she answered simply. "A video."

An audiovisual. I watched it, concentrating on the way the Jackets whispered around a table. They held folders and boards, writing things down as holographic data flew across their glass charts. At the center of the room was Manis, though he looked several years younger. His skin had color, a sun-kissed tan that spelled too many evenings below the Ward. He had hair, and the scar across his face wasn't there. This somehow made him less scary.

"What are they doing?"

Petra shushed me and tried to get me to sit, but I didn't budge.

"Code," Manis said, pointing to one of the opposing Jackets as he paced. The scenery around them was blurred out at the edge of the screen, as were the faces of the other Jackets. I hadn't seen much of Silo yet, but I saw enough to know they weren't in this building at the time this video was recorded. Their walls held maps and photos, charts and more flashing data. Silo was the very absence of those things.

"How old is this video?" I asked Petra. I wasn't expecting her to answer right away, but she did.

"About eleven years," she said.

Eleven years.

Manis' voice continued to boom through the screen. "There are 40,130 subjects and each were injected with case Y-506. Give me the strongest one."

"2,943 failed to complete the change," came an answer.

"420 completed the change, but failed to live through the second week," came another.

They bounced numbers around the room and the data on the table was checked and crossed as they progressed.

It took me a few moments to understand why Petra was showing me this. After all, an outdated video of Manis was the last thing I wanted to see, especially when my food was on the floor. Then I chanced a second and cut my eyes to Petra's face. I observed the way she was shifting uncomfortably from foot to foot. Occasionally she'd peek over, when she thought I was unaware, just to record my reactions to what was being said.

Petra was showing me how it happened. How I was created.

"Ari—0329," came the final answer from the video.

"What makes this one the strongest?" Manis asked.

"She's not. She's just the only one who survived this testing."

Every part of my body was attuned to the scene. I took a step closer to the screen, my shadow fading in the blue light.

"She?" Manis said. "Explain."

The Jacket who spoke my code cleared his throat and set down his chart. With a small voice, he answered, "She consumed the Y-506 virus."

EIGHT

"SCREAMS AND SHADOWS"
BIONIC: ARI-0329

A *veil of static swallowed the* scene, just before it changed. This time Manis was shown entering an underground vault similar to this one, and he appeared several years older. The vault contained a thick layer of glass that offered panels and buttons and separated Manis from the other side, where the single pod stood.

"What's happening?" Manis asked. He was talking to a Jacket on the other side through a speaker.

"It appears something is wrong with the subject, sir."

Manis nodded for him to finish. "Out with it."

The video zoomed in closer and I was able to see what was floating in the pod. Though I was sure it could only be a legionary, I wasn't prepared to see my face. I looked younger than I did in my data folder, much younger than I could ever have imagined myself being. I was a tiny thing connected to wires and sensors, breathing underwater. My home a glass barrier. How was it possible to look so fragile?

"Subject 0329 is scheduled to activate at the same exact time as the others. Not a second later," the Jacket nearest the pod said. He paced around the room, frantic.

"So what's the pro—"

"She's already awake." The machines around the room ticked. "That's the problem, sir."

Manis released the button for the speaker and took a stride back from the glass. He did nothing but stand there for about a minute. Fifty-two seconds—I counted. When he seemed to come to a decision, he shed his white coat and stepped through a small room leading down to the pod. It had two doors, like an in-between passageway. The door shut airtight and a chemical haze emitted from holes in the ceiling, sterilizing him from head to toe. When he finally exited, he was less confident than he had been when he first entered the scene.

"Ari—0329's mind was programmed with all the same logistics, calibrated just the same, but to better suit what we'd need her for..." The Jacket stopped pacing and his face glowed with a realization. "*Her mind.*"

"She doesn't have one. Not a mind nor a conscience," said Manis, forcing his skinny fingers into protective gloves. "Put her back to sleep."

"It's not that simple. You see—" He motioned toward the pod

emphatically. "—Her mind may be rejecting any and all programming in the same way she rejected the virus. So it's lapsing her back to something else."

"Back to what?"

"*Anything*. Her own rules, her own complex and dynamics. Her own being! She could create a new world if she wanted to."

With a shove, Manis moved the Jacket away from the pod and stood in front of the younger version of me. I couldn't have been any older than seven years old, I understood.

This is how they raised me.

Manis raised a finger to the glass of my pod, tapping twice. He hid his trepidation well from the Jacket, but never from me. "She doesn't get to decide who she is. We do that. And anyway, she has nothing to lapse back to. She's a blank disc, and so she will remain until Presidium says otherwise."

"Manis—"

"Wipe her."

"How much?"

"*Everything*."

Grudgingly, the Jacket left to take his place behind the panel of buttons and controls. The two-way passage shut Manis inside, alone with me. As he grew closer to the pod, I neared the video screen. I came face-to-face with myself, like proximity was the thing that could transport me into the scene. My scrutiny roved over my smooth skin and the tiny wisps of hair that floated around my face. I was innocent, and even though I was created to kill, I was always meant to be me. It was the one thing

Manis could never control—who I chose to be.

"Everything bleeds, everything dies, and everything can be controlled," Manis whispered, tapping on the pod again with a crooked fingernail. "Remember that the next time you try to be anything other than what you were designed to be."

He waited with his hand to the glass. I thought maybe he expected the Jacket to return with a report. There were no windows in the room, so there was no telling what time it was or how much time had passed.

Manis tapped again, and this time I responded in the pod by slowly opening my eyes. I didn't open them in panic, either. It was nothing like when I'd awoken several days ago. Rather, my blue eye and my green eye settled on Manis as I breathed calmly threw my nose, like I could hear him speak through the glass.

All was silent for a beat and a pulse. Even the machines in the room quieted to watch the scene unfold. I moved as close to the screen as I could and was completely cast in its blue light.

Manis tapped the glass again with a scowl that stretched his face, and the eleven-year-old version of me smiled. Smiled like her world wasn't so dismal and the man before the glass wasn't about to eradicate her, again.

I doubted I was much of a storyteller, but I would have put that smile in my book. On page 104, right next to the image of the Ward. I would have written it on my heart. I would have proofread it a thousand times under a thousand moons until a thousand tears thoroughly rationalized what it meant to me. Each time for when I'd met the darkness, and then succumbed. The smile read "you can't break me'"—bold and in italics.

Manis stepped away just as static took the screen and ended the scene. I looked at Petra. She hadn't moved or done anything other than watch with me. She leaned against the wall with her arms crossed over her middle, appearing far more relaxed.

"There's more, just watch," she said.

I was reluctant to turn back, but found myself dragged into the middle of another scene as the images quickly unraveled.

I had aged once more, looking somewhere between thirteen and fifteen. Nothing was dated and the scenery was all the same foreignness; static made the video hard to see faces. This scene was recent, though, and that made it the most important.

I was strapped onto a table in the same vault as the last. Only my pod had been replaced by more operating machines—and I was connected to every one of them. Several Jackets stood by my side as they asked me questions and readied something at a nearby table. I wasn't answering them, at least not coherently. A shake of my head followed everything they said to me.

I was wearing a white nightgown and bandages adorned my hands. My feet were covered in mud. Although my mouth moved, no sounds actually passed my lips. My eyes were like lasers, cutting into every direction. When a Jacket picked up a syringe and brought it to the back of my neck, I heard my cries for the first time.

"No, get up!" Smacking a hand to the screen, I yelled as if they could hear me.

My hair was pulled to the side then and I saw a series of numbers along the top of my spine: **0329**. It didn't look painted, or drawn. It was my tag ... and it was permanent. I absentmindedly slid my hand to my neck to feel for it. Was it still there?

The fluids were injected into my spine and my mumbling quieted. One Jacket cooed for me to take deep breaths while another shifted in front of me. I saw what was in the chair across from me then—another legionary. She wore a similar uniform to what I now wore. In black, block letters, the pocket of her shirt said 'DESNI—5590.'

The Jackets released me from the table, but my bandages remained. They positioned me in a chair opposite of Desni and proceeded to strap my hands down. I scanned the screen for the shadows that seemed to dance in Desni's aura. Her blank stare didn't surprise me; neither did her impassive features. She was hollow as they sat the whimpering girl—me—in front of her.

"Ari—0329," Manis said over a loud speaker. I couldn't see him, so his voice vibrated from the walls in the vault.

I didn't answer him. I couldn't, not while hiccupping through tears. The Jackets finished strapping me down, and even went so far as to chain me to the floor. Fifteen-year-old me glanced down at her hands and began to weep harder.

"No more hiding, no more running away," he continued.

The mud on my feet.

"N-no..." I said, and this time it came from the video. I shook my head from side to side, and pulled on my restraints. If I didn't look so young, I would have assumed this had happened just days ago. It was more of the same, the torment. It didn't change; it didn't stop.

"You need to complete the change," Manis said. "Finish it, or she'll do it for you."

"I-I'm *s-sorry!*" I faced Desni in my chair and called to her with slurred words. Why was I talking like that, like I couldn't put two sentences together without choking? Desni proffered silence and I had no choice but to take it, with my dirty toenails digging into the chains as I tried to push away.

"Begin."

"Desni, s-stop!" I called across the room. I watched, face to screen, as panic opened my eyes wide and compelled my body into shock. Energy skidded over my skin when Desni set her eyes on me. She focused so hard that a vein began to pulse in her forehead. She was relentless, unrestrained, and controlled while I only cried to get her out of my head.

Desni tethered her mind to mine. I couldn't see it, but I could *feel* it, as if I were remembering the exact moment it happened. She wasn't telling me what to do or how to feel. Desni perched at the window of my mind, where I fed from the light, and wrecked it all.

She broke me easily. I was holding something in and she sought to scrape it out.

"Look at her!" Manis commanded.

The small thing that was once me shook her head again. I was losing the battle, and Desni only grew stronger the more I resisted.

"You h-have to stop!" I tried again. I bit into my lip and blood gushed into my mouth. A wicked current blew through the room, and I knew it was Desni. Wind picked up her hair and her body pulsed in the splintering chair, like she was finally coming to life. Desni was a storm, and I was standing in the eye of her.

Around the room, machines sparked and valves shattered against the walls. When she stood with an unwavering gaze, her power knocked into me like a blow to the face. It sped across the room in visible, lightning rays.

"*Look at her!*" Manis pounded on the overhead glass and, slowly, the fight left me. It fled my system and I quit crying. Desni was encroaching too far into my head. She left so much pain, pitting me into a hole of nothing, like her. I didn't want to hurt her, I knew, but whatever I was holding back ... I didn't know how to control it. I didn't even know what it was.

"Petra... Wha—"

"*Watch.*"

I locked eyes with myself in the video and the change was instant. The wind changed directions, stealing Desni's next breath. I had zeroed in on her mind with skilled force, I remembered. I was supposed to find something—*anything*—but I was only wandering in a wasteland. It made it too easy, it made me reckless.

How was I doing this? I wanted to ask Petra, but my mind was no longer in the present. I was lost in the video, in the past.

"Desni!" Her name was a plea. I needed her to back down. She was strong only because they told her to be, but I looked like I had played this game far too many times, giving in at every go. Desni didn't stand a flick of a chance.

I did what I had done to the legionaries during my flight through Silo. I reached into Desni's mind and turned everything off. I pressed so much power into her that her limbs grew slack and her skin drained of color. Most of the Jackets fled the second the overhead lights crashed to the ground and upturned the table. A small fire started by the in-between exit, chasing up the walls.

The colors of my eyes deepened to an inky black. A sneer curled my lips, and I let loose. I was controlling Desni with my mind, braving the beast inside. Her eyes began to bleed and her skin chipped away in scales. She grasped her head and screeched. She was going blind, and by now she had lost all hearing. The room continued to fall around us, though the me in the video cocked her head instinctively and pushed Desni farther. I was turning into the perfect assassin, spurred by desperation. *This* was my training.

I was completing the change.

"Petra, turn it off." I searched for her and Petra came up behind me, forcing me forward. Wordlessly, her hands fastened on my shoulders, making me finish the video.

I finally stood from the chair, and with every step I took toward

Desni, panels ripped from the walls and slapped against the glass shield protecting Manis against the hell I raised. Tiles lifted below my feet, levitating in mid-air. I was a vision of **screams of shadows** in my sullied nightgown. My bandages slipped down my arms and I, at last, saw the evil in my touch.

"*Jaaa!*" I bellowed. My fingers curled and a rush of energy flew from me, attacking Desni and hurling her back into the fiery wall. Her neck gave out an audible *crunch*, and then she dropped to the ground with blood-ringed eyes that took in everything, while seeing nothing.

I thought I would have stopped, but I didn't even go near her. The Jackets who remained in the room tried to soothe me in the same way they did before. They approached with faces that said they could be trusted and raised guns that said otherwise. I knew the guns well. The clicks, the lasers; the speed at which they traveled through the air and shocked my body cold.

Before they could pull the trigger, I evaporated around the room in a thick, red cloud. So red I could hardly tell the difference between it and Desni's blood. I deftly dodged each bullet. I was a constant blur of in-and-out motion, stopping only to catch my breath and materialize by the passageway. They did their best to track my shadow, but only released aimless bullets into the walls. Spinning in my nightgown, I ran for the passageway.

"Get her under control!" Manis called from somewhere above. I found him still standing behind the scratched glass frame, with his steel eyes fixed on me.

His Jackets were burning in the flames one by one; there was no one to control me.

It happened so seamlessly I had to look back at Petra for confirmation. When she nodded I knew that what I had witnessed myself doing with my mind, and now with my body, wasn't an apparition in the video. It was me, and I had ... *abilities?* Did Manis do this?

I fled the room before the burning Jackets could pull me back and locked myself in the passageway. My trembling hands slid the panels closed. When nothing happened and the other door refused to budge, I set my eyes on the glass and focused hard. There was a thundered explosion as it caved around me and shattered to diamond rain. The tiny particles ripped into my skin, but it was as if my body didn't respond to pain anymore.

I bent, picking up a large fragment, and held it at my side. With slow, untiring strides, I entered the control center of the vault. I moved with a pledge. If Manis had run, he couldn't have gotten far.

The video was scratchy and froze in places, but the one thing that was always crystal clear was my face. My eyes were hooded and my breathing hadn't been stable since they'd sat me in the chair. Blood crusted at the corners of my mouth. Fire clung to the hem of my nightgown. I listened closely for movement, then tiptoed through the vacated vault.

I passed the empty desks and lab tables. Everything vibrated as I moved, waking at my call. The Jackets were gone, but they couldn't have left. I could hear their racing heartbeats through the screen. They came from the floors, and I stepped on them, my bare feet sliding over their sad song.

I heard their labored breaths as they waited for me, too. Twenty Generators—ten to my right, three to the left, and seven guarding *Manis*. I honed in on his heartbeat as I ascended the stairs. When I entered the final room with the window overlooking Desni's ashen body, none of us were surprised.

"Ja," I said brokenly from the doorway. What did it mean? Was it what I called him?

Manis stood confidently behind the Generators with his hands in his pants pockets. Somewhere under the false bravado was a scared, little boy. "Congratulations," he said. "You passed the final test."

A Generator trained his light on my face.

"You've overshadowed the others and denied all strands of the virus. Your body regenerates before you can ever feel any pain." Manis laughed manically. "Even when we buried you, you somehow crawled your way out. You are ... growing, changing, *toxic*. You'd kill anything in your path, wouldn't you? You are death itself. You are our greatest creation."

"*No.* Ja!" My lips quivered and my hold on the shard of glass slipped. I examined the Generators like they mocked me, even though they had no faces. I was confused. All I knew was *Ja* and that I wanted Manis to stop hurting me, at whatever cost.

Manis was taunting a raging fire. He thought his words would detain me, bottle me up and out me. He didn't know they stoked the flames higher.

"Who are you now?" he asked, arching a dark brow. "What's her name?"

I didn't answer him, probably because I didn't know how. I didn't know how to speak or formulate sentences longer than several words.

"Who will you become next?" Manis' eyes went to the glass in my hands. They paused there, and then narrowed on my face. "Take her back. She passed, but she isn't ready."

"No..."

"And keep her away from the others."

The Generators opened fire and I dematerialized around the room, blazing in and out in that same storm of red. I deviated their needled bullets to the ceiling and resurfaced behind their backs, choking them unconscious with my arm pressed tight to their necks. I never let any of them touch me. I was a blur as I clawed at their eyes and pushed them through walls. I was too fast; the camera—a security measure pinned to the ceiling of the room—shuddered to keep up with me. The entire time I kept my sight on Manis and the smug look of satisfaction on his face.

I wanted to turn that face inside out, I thought. *I wanted to kill him.*

By then a quarter of the Generators lay numb on the floor and two others were pressed to the window, held up by invisible bonds I fashioned with my mind. They spasmed as they tried to breathe, and something about the way their robotic forms twitched brought a smile to my face. I watched them, then I watched Manis watch them, knowing he had underestimated how well I would pass his senseless test.

The remaining Jackets crowded around him. They wanted to flee, I saw it in their eyes. Something made them stay, though. Was it loyalty? Or were they so afraid of me that they risked their lives to take me down?

With the ease of a simple thought, I jerked their heads around and their bodies pooled at my feet—gasping, grasping, gaping. Manis was next and he sensed my intent, but I bided my time, my stare sliding from the dead Jackets to him with an intensity that forced him backwards. He contested it, like I knew he would. So I stepped over the Jackets and pushed more energy through him. The closer I drew, the stronger I became. Manis' skinny face was distraught and his legs shook. He was a fly caught within my web, and this time there was no one around to free him of my clutches.

"Please *stop*," I said, pulling my curls back with one hand to unveil my face. "No more."

"Yes, *more*," Manis retorted. He reached for something at his side and I inclined my head, commanding his hand against the wall behind him. His shoulder rolled and popped, and his hurt couldn't be mistaken. "0329!"

"Name. I have *name*."

Manis snorted. "You don't have anything! You destroy everything you touch."

I cocked my head in another direction and Manis' right knee gave out, twisting his leg in a strange angle. His screams skated over my psyche and fed the darkness.

"Name!" Gripping the shard of glass, which now dripped with my blood, I stopped in front of him and took in his terror up close. It parroted my own. Despite how strong I was—how strong I knew I was and how little I knew how to control it—I was more afraid of Manis than he could ever be of me. Because he made me; he unleashed me. In the end, he would always be the baser evil.

Getting close enough to smell the blood on him, I whispered, "Sleep now." I didn't wait a second before lifting the glass over my head and swinging it down. I couldn't have possibly missed his chest, but I never got to find out. The lights suddenly flickered down in the vault and I was snatched away from Manis. The only thing the glass managed to touch was his face, cutting into skin and muscle.

His scar. *I did that.*

The screen went black soon after. I only heard voices and footsteps for the longest time. Petra breathed heavily behind me, reliving the moment as well. Her face was as pale as her hair. Several minutes later I was able discern things in the blackness, and the video scratched back and forth through beams of penlights. It sounded like more Generators. Or Jackets? The lights returned and they ran, exiting the vault and breaking into a room with five pods. There were people in them, sleeping. Petra opened her mouth to explain, then was interrupted by a *bang* that ricocheted through the screen.

There were four Generators and a bleeding Manis on the screen, kicking down numerous doors. It was a long hall with eight doors and they found me hiding in the fifth. The door didn't have a sign like the others, and it was left ajar.

They raged into the room and their lights hit my face as I curled up in a corner. That's how they found me, like I wanted to be seen. The instant resemblance to how they'd found me mere weeks ago was not lost on me. The Generators shifted aside once they saw I was no longer a threat, allowing Manis to step forward. He sighed with a palm pressed to his wound.

"We can help you, Kyra. Would you like to come with us?"

Kyra—not Ari. I didn't understand.

I nodded my head, rocking back and forth. The light shifted around the room as the video jumped between the security cameras, and I got a better look at the corner I had crawled into. I held something. Or rather, *someone.* I pressed my palm flat to the screen and squinted. My lips were pressed to the person's forehead as I cried and whispered incoherent nothings. My pupils were dilated, my nightgown soaked.

My cries had different frequencies. Before, in the vault, they were somber and quiet, yet powerful enough to conjure wind in a room with little air. A stormless sky. But now, as I held the person in my hands, my heart bled and I painted the walls with all the colors of my pain. The thing I held in my arms was covered in blood and its name was Desni. She was dead and I had killed her. I glanced up into the lights from where I sat in the corner and saw all their faces. My knees buckled as the stories aligned in my mind.

Her, them, *they*—they were me. Desni and Kyra had the same eyes and the same hair. Only one was dead and the other was well on her way to being so. They were carbon copies, exactly the same. Kyra, fifteen-year-old me, had been forced to kill herself.

The Generators swooped in and I wailed harder as they carted me away from Desni's body. They struggled, tripping on things as they went. I could barely digest one reality before another hit me in the chest.

They tripped over me. *Me.* The room Kyra had hid in was jam-packed with dead bodies that looked just like me, even down to their white uniforms. Their shirts read different names, different languages, though it was always the same face. There were at least fifty in the corner they found me in. Kyra had dragged them all here, into this room of ghosts. It was her prison, where she went to both mourn and condemn herself.

"*Jaaa!*" Kyra shouted, red-faced. They took her, kicking and screaming, and locked the room away. With the turn of a key, my cries no longer held a frequency at all.

They just stopped.

NINE

"MATHAI PORTER"
BIONIC: ARI-0329

"**Ari.**"

Petra shut off the screen after the video ended, but I remained standing in front of it, shock-still.

"Ari, do you—"

"Is that even my name?" I asked.

Petra calculated her response perfectly, leaving no remainders. "No, not really. It used to be, but you're not Ari anymore."

"What happened to her?"

"The same thing that happened to the others. You killed them. Before Ari you were Kyra, and before Kyra you were Desni."

"How?" When I turned my eyes to Petra, they pierced her to a spot.

I didn't blame her, but why would she wait to tell me this?

"There's a virus called Y-506. It creates the leviathans, destroys any legionary. It ... *is* them, and it was extracted to make you." She paused. "Only you."

"I don't understand." I ignored my food on the floor and took my seat. No matter what I did, though, the ground still felt absent beneath my feet.

Petra said, "Manis was obsessed with those things that fell from the sky. He tested them, dissected them. He spent years and years studying them until he was able to find what made them so strong and indestructible. It was the virus." Crossing her ankles, she continued to explain. "He needed a plan. Humans were too weak and lacked the numbers the leviathans came in. So by duplicating the DNA of those who died, they—"

"*Designed* us. In a lab, like we're expendable," I finished, hating the words. It didn't help that Petra appeared guilty.

"They had no choice. The leviathans were feeding on them."

"You're actually defending him?"

"Absolutely not," she said. "But if it wasn't for Manis' twisted mind, you wouldn't exist. None of us would, because we'd all be dead."

"Yeah, well..." I glanced down at my hands, the hands that had moved objects without touching them. "Perhaps it would be better if I was."

Exhaling loudly, Petra came to me and sat at my feet. She didn't slap me or try to get my attention. Rather, she just waited. Then she said,

"The virus didn't kill you like the several other legionaries they tested. Instead, it became a part of you, enhancing the abilities you already had. All legionaries have abilities, but not like yours. Not unless they're outside the Ward. You were *stronger* than any other. You killed more leviathans, too. It really didn't make sense."

"And the ones I killed, who looked just like me?"

"Versions of you—mock copies. When they created you, they couldn't exactly control you."

"And that means what?" I asked.

"You have a mind of your own. You were right, you are broken. But in the best way. You feel things and you have a conscience. You have a choice." Petra considered something, then began again. "You dealt with your memory loss by conceiving someone new every time you came back. They'd wipe who you were, hoping to program you like the rest of them, but they couldn't. Even though you became these different people, a true part of yourself always bound them."

"So I duplicated myself?"

"No, Manis did that. He siphoned parts of the girls you became and plugged them into clones, then made you kill them as part of your ability training. It was all a game to him, a way to keep you from switching up again," Petra said unapologetically. "You fell for it every time. You were killing yourself repeatedly, so how could you not want to be someone else?"

How could I not? My hands were unmoving in my lap, but they might as well have been dipped in fire and bursting with energy. What she was telling me… These things I did with my mind…

"Is there a way to reverse it? So that I'm normal again?"

"What is normal?" Petra asked in jest. "As far as I know, there's no way to reverse it. *You're* the virus now."

I nodded, understanding and accepting my lot. My mind flipped through emotions like I'd flipped through the pages of my codex. I couldn't decide on any individual one, so in the end I chose them all, casting my mind into free fall.

"Who am I now? If I'm not Ari, who did I choose to be this time?"

For once, Petra didn't hesitate to give me the answer I wanted, needed. "You're Mathai, the girl you became first. The true you. They showed you an old file and gave you the wrong name because you may have seen or heard things you weren't supposed to, as Ari. They reached for those things without resetting you. Again, it was the plan. They'd get the information and you'd still be their sanctioned legionary."

"*Muh-tie*, Muh-*tie*," I whispered, feeling out my new name. "I'm Mathai."

Petra smiled. "Yes."

"Then who are you?"

Without a word, Petra licked her finger and brought it to the back of her neck. She swiped, then showed me the black ink. It was the code from the top of her spine, but it wasn't permanent. Unconsciously, I reached for my own at my back.

"I'm not like you and I'm not like them," was all she gave me. She wasn't a legionary, programmed to kill. She hadn't spent her life in a pod and she hadn't been forced to destroy her clones. It was childish and stupid, but I envied her. I wanted to be originless like Petra.

"How many duplicates were there?"

"I can't say for sure. There might have been a few ... hundred or so. It really—"

Unceremoniously, I jumped from my seat and left the vault, passing my shattered pod with one glance. Petra knew where I was going without asking. She knew I had to see it for myself.

I trailed down the same hall from the video and counted the doors. The lights blinked as I stopped in front of the fifth door.

"No, wait," Petra called. She was too late, though, and I had already pushed through the door by the time she reached me.

I didn't know what to expect. I knew this was the same room they took Kyra from, and if they had done as they did with my pod, it would have looked exactly the same. Only that was the problem. It did and it didn't.

I stood in the doorway and scanned the white walls and the sterile floor. There were no bodies, just an unsettling chill. I felt like I had when I entered my bedroom for the first time. Like someone stood beside me. There was no one in here except me, of course, but I didn't feel so alone.

I walked inside and my hand went to the wall. As my fingertips memorized every bump and groove, I remembered being Kyra and Desni. I remembered escaping every fourth day, purely by habit, and the way rocks shredded my bare feet while I felt nothing but the wind on my face. Bits of my memory fell into place. I recalled it all, and through a gust of blue and green, I saw this room covered in blood.

Only it wasn't visible. I spun around and counted the white panels that started at the floor and touched the ceiling. They were off; they felt wrong. White—the absence of color, feeling, emotion. They hid the colors Silo lacked, and the panels suddenly became the focal point of my rage.

I took to one side and dug my nails in deep. With trembling hands and a new resolve, I began to rip the squares from the wall. I didn't slow down to count or watch where I threw them aside. I pulled and pulled, angry tears ready to fall, until I stood in a room of stained cement walls.

They had tried to wash the blood away, wash *me* away, and failed. The panels couldn't hide the colors and handprints, because they told a story. I envisioned Kyra in this room. She would hastily write messages to herself in blood. She'd returned to this room to remember, like I now did.

"You're not Desni or Kyra, or Ari," Petra said from the door. She said it slowly, afraid I would fall apart. "You're not four numbers. You're **Mathai Porter.**"

I sank to my knees and pressed my hands to a dark stain. Whenever I touched the wall, I thought of the last scene in the video. I wondered what their names had been. "And what *is* Mathai?"

"Whatever she wants to be," Petra answered.

Was it that easy? Could I collect all the parts of me and become Mathai? Most importantly, could I stop myself from repeating the cycle?

I sat with my back against the wall, my hands palm-up. Staring at them, I said, "She doesn't want to be a legionary, Petra."

She nodded around the room. "I think they all knew that, Mathai." Sifting through the torn panels, Petra found a good spot to sit beside me. She was quiet, allowing me to lose myself in my head as I calculated, thought too much, and sobbed once before turning it all off. She took up as little space as possible, and I appreciated it. There was closure in her silence.

I wasn't Mathai in this moment, I realized. I wasn't a legionary and I wasn't a person. I was an hour, a minute, a second. I was the timestamp of my liberation—right there, right then.

"Petra?"

"What is it?"

I smiled sheepishly. "She's pretty hungry, too." We laughed, the sound melodic and sour.

When my hands began to bleed from ripping the panels and I couldn't stand to sit on the sterile floor any longer, Petra led me out and back to the vault. She fixed me another plate of food and watched me eat with gusto. She grinned and handed me a napkin when I made a mess, too. This was no time for bonding, and I didn't fully understand her, but I was thankful for her help. Petra was my friend. She was the healing balm I searched for.

She treated the cuts on my hands and slipped extra carrots in my pocket. After I drank my fill of water from an old faucet, she took me back up the central staircase and through the halls we'd left from. Sunlight steadily peeked through the windows. They marked the glass floors with green hues. Petra said we had spent hours in the vault, but it didn't feel that way. It felt like years went by as I relived my past.

Suddenly, I missed the moons outside my window.

We maneuvered through the halls with the same stealth as before, entering and exiting the shower room into the east wing of Silo. The Generators that patrolled this level never saw us, and we only moved from the shadows when the cameras swiveled their focus to the opposite direction.

While we strode down the corridor to room 211, I said, "What happened on my last crusade?"

"That's for you to remember," Petra said. We came to my room and she quickly unlatched the bar, checking to make sure the hall was clear first. The girl who had come with her was still lying on the floor, and I wondered if she had really fallen asleep.

"But what if I never do?"

Petra pushed me into the room and the other girl stood up without saying anything to me. I faced the window as they began to close the door. I only turned back to get my answer.

"You always do," said Petra.

"We wait in the Seeming," said the girl, who shut and locked the door.

I was alone in my bedroom again, and it was disconcerting. Because the last time I had been here my biggest worry was being force-fed by the Jackets. Now it was that and so much more.

That night, instead of further abusing my back by lying on the floor,

I slept on the bed. The sheets were thin, the pillow was scratchy, and the socks I had shoved beneath the mattress weren't doing much to defuse the springs, but it was warm. It wasn't my pod or the vault.

I replayed all of Petra's words until I formulated a plan to escape Silo. It wouldn't be easy ... but I was prepared to fight for blood if I had to. I would bide my time and get out of this room. I was going to gain Manis' trust again, and to do that I had to be Ari just a little bit longer.

That night, I was deserving of good sleep.

TEN

"DEAFENING HEARTBEATS"
BIONIC: ~~ARI~~ MATHAI-0329

The days in my room passed quickly. Zee came in and out with her trays, and although I obeyed Manis by eating the food, I was numb to everything else. Numb to Zee's miserable side-glances and numb to the Generators that tugged me around like a puppet as they dressed me in new clothes every morning before sunrise. I let them believe I had given up.

On the first day after Petra showed me the video, Manis had come to speak to me again. He was angry about the sandwich, yes, but was surprised when I answered all of his questions. He asked me what my name was, and I told him I was Ari. He asked what my duty was as a legionary, and I told him exactly what the codex told me: *shoot, detain, kill.*

I thought he would give up once I continued to respond with succinct answers, but Manis was nothing if not persistent.

I had spent hours that morning preparing for the question, so when he asked me what had happened on my last crusade, I looked him in the face and lied like I believed it.

I told him my legion and I had moved north beyond the Ward to barricade the asylums from the leviathans. I told him one of us had been bitten and was changing fast—five hours until they, too, would have had black eyes and an even blacker soul. He asked for more and I delivered, saying we had carried the fallen legionary to an alcove. We remained there until sun-up since our radiocoms had been destroyed with our craft. It was in the alcove, near the coast, that the electrical storm found us, killing everyone but me. I told him it took my three days to find my way back to Silo. I told him all these things born of my imagination ... and meant none of it.

On the second day, they gave me water. They didn't drug any of the food, though I reasoned the glass of lukewarm water was a sign of trust. Some sort of trade between Manis and me. I gave him the information he wanted, albeit the wrong information, and he gave me the water. Zee brought a glass of it with all three meals that day and I swigged it down in place of eating the food. No, it didn't satisfy my hunger and, no, it didn't taste the best. I drank it because I wasn't so sure I'd get any the next day, and the water meant I was one step closer to getting out of Silo.

They let me out of my room on the third day. After I swore I wouldn't run, I was ushered to the refectory, where I ate first-meal alone. The legionaries didn't pay me any mind, and I liked it that way. I got to observe them; I mastered their movements and attitudes to better my charade of the perfect legionary. And when the Jackets shifted their attention, I slid my fork into my boot.

I finished eating in minutes and was allowed to see the city. I caught things I'd missed while trying to run away, like the homes that smelled of bread and the small children. The buildings and signs were colorless and the people here weren't legionaries. They were anthropoids, flesh and blood through and through. They weren't designed in a lab and appeared very much like the Jackets, only less vile. The speeding highways above our heads trafficked iridescent, hovering cars. The glass roads were lit up with lights. When someone spoke, in a different language or not, everyone understood. My view was limited to shades of white, gray, and black.

The Generators crowded around me from every side as I walked. We drew many wandering eyes, though no one tried to speak to me. A child once stared for a moment too long over its mother's shoulder. I made an attempt to smile, but I must have looked like some unkempt beast, because the child immediately began to cry.

If only Manis reacted the same way, I'd thought wryly.

I strolled through the city without growing tired. Silo was large and wide and I was obsessed with seeing every part of it. The Ward dimmed at a certain spot in the middle of the city. Five legionaries wearing matching uniforms partitioned the tall exit gates that led outside. They held hands, with their heads tipped skyward and their eyes closed. They concentrated on something hidden, and I didn't see it until I stopped to feign interest in a holographic street sign. Energy emitted from them, like a force field. It enveloped them, and then legionaries pushed it upwards toward the highest building I had climbed. Squinting, it didn't take much to come to a conclusion. Those five legionaries were the powerhouses behind the Ward. Without them, we were open to the leviathans.

When I tried to approach them from across the street, a Generator butted me with his baton and propelled me forward. A whizzing car drowned the string of curses I released on them, but I didn't bother to hide my sneer. I took their aggressiveness with a grain of salt. I couldn't mistake this paring of independence for open chains. I couldn't fight back, because I knew Manis was always watching.

Training came on the fourth day. I floated between constructing guns, exercising, and hand-to-hand combat, digesting the instructions I was given. I was proficient, firm. My blows landed and stuck, and I managed to get my opponent down in three minutes every time.

When I had a second to spare, I tracked the movements of two Jackets who bounced between training rooms. They hadn't worn lab jackets, which made them easy to pluck out from the groups. Each Jacket held a set of keys to unlock the doors. One room appeared empty, but they entered it anyway, exiting several moments later with folders. What they didn't do was lock the door, and I hid my smile behind my gun. To remain inconspicuous, I trained until my body grew sore, then trained even harder.

Camp concluded with a run on the treadmill, and I took to the machine between two girls. They'd been running for a while and their mileage climbed quickly, by the hundreds. It was a competition, whether they knew it or not. Jackets stood behind every machine and recorded numbers. They compared notes to see who ran the fastest, while Manis stood at the back of the room. Although there were at least fifteen other legionaries around, his viperous gaze was fixed on me.

I jumped on the treadmill and began with a steady pace. The Jacket in front of me stared as my numbers increased. If there was a goal or a limit, I didn't know it. I focused on my breathing and keeping my feet planted. But then the Jacket tapped on the treadmill, signaling that I was falling behind.

"Faster," he said.

It wasn't like I was going too slow and tripping over myself. I always ran at this pace.

Manis was far behind me, but I swore I heard him snicker. His scarred face goaded me in the mirror, like my ability to run fast was laughable, at best. While the goal was to remain compliant until I found my opening to get away, I couldn't resist this time. I took his doubt and ate it, driven by the need to prove him wrong.

I held on to the handles of the treadmill and pumped my legs faster. My thighs grew stiff with the exertion. If I let go, I would have sputtered off the machine and collided through the glass wall.

My mind, and my memories, crystallized on one, sweet thing: He won't win.

Sweat dripped down into my eyes. It burned, but they didn't know it. The ponytail broke free sometime after I hit three hundred miles. Four hundred miles flew by … and I quit counting after six hundred. My **deafening heartbeats** became a testament of how badly I wanted to see the disappointment in Manis' eyes. In the final moments before my treadmill powered off, flashing a four-digit number that was two times greater than everyone else's, I realized I could never be Ari again. Ari was a prisoner—a slave to Silo. She was weak in every way Mathai was strong.

I slowed, and then hopped off the treadmill, grabbing a towel from a rack in the corner of the room to wipe my face. When everyone left for the shower rooms, the Generators parading them out, I backed into the laboratory the Jackets retrieved folders from. Forget not knowing what they needed the folders for—I'd take them regardless.

Once in the room, I headed straight for the cabinet behind the old equipment. It had four shelves and each one was overstuffed with files. I ran my fingers through the order, stopping at section A. There were hundreds of names, but none of them were mine. I looked for Kyra and Desni, then resorted to opening ones I grabbed at random. For some reason my file wasn't there. Did they keep it in a separate cabinet?

I thought better then and flipped through section M. Even though it didn't make orderly sense, I went right to the last file and tugged it out. I spread it out on the table beside the cabinet and, undeniably, it was mine.

My face headlined the top of the first page. It was a recent picture; more recent than the picture I'd been shown from Ari's file. My code was the same, and all the reports were on the right pages. My escapes, the date I left with my legion, and every person I became after Mathai. It was all there. The file was exactly the same as Ari's, only the name was changed and Y-506 was stamped across every sheet.

I was killing time and knew I wouldn't remain unnoticed for long, so I placed the file back where I'd found it and closed the cabinet. I tested the bottom drawer marked with an "O" to see if there was anything more—anything I was missing—and discovered it was locked, which confused me since the files were easy to get to. What were they hiding in the drawer?

I pulled my hardest, with no luck. Checking to make sure no one was at the door, I searched around the room for the keys. My palms were sweaty and my breathing hastened. There were no keys by the files or at any of the desks, and I began to wonder if the Jackets just carried the keys with them. The drawer could have been empty, but I needed to know for sure.

I was turning to go when a box on the side of the cabinet caught my eye. It was small, hardly anything at all. Though when I opened it, three keys fell out and spilled onto the floor. They were each engraved with a letter, and the one with the "O" had to be the perfect match.

Instead of opening the drawer right away, I put the other two keys back and made sure things were as the Jackets had left it.

I grabbed my towel to leave ... but stepped back into a tall frame. My reaction was instant. I jerked forward and spun to face the Jacket, who watched me with a look of mild speculation. How long had he been there? Did he see?

"0329," he said.

There was no way I could have hated four numbers any more.

"I was looking for fresh towels. Found one," I lied. His eyes went to my hand and I remembered the key in my palm. My pants didn't have pockets, but there was a rack to my left. I made a show of hanging up the towel while my attention never left him. With a flick, I sent the key tunneling into the long sleeve of my shirt. The action was quick enough that the key made no sound.

"This is a restricted area," the Jacket said.

It couldn't be that restricted if the door was open, I thought snidely. He reached over to pull me out and I skirted around him, avoiding his touch. The key was at my elbow. One hand in the wrong place would put me back in containment, and I wouldn't give Manis that satisfaction again.

The Jacket stayed behind to study the room, probably to find something out of place. If he ever did, it was in the time it took me to slip back into my room and hide the key in the wall. I placed it next to my codex and the fork I'd stolen.

The rest of that day was spent in deep thought, tracing things into the glass of my window. *P*—the letter with wings. *H*—the letter whispered to me when I pushed my hand through the Ward. *O*—the letter that allowed me to see who I really was. The three letters that followed me around Silo like a shadow I couldn't lose.

It took a lot of searching, but I found Petra on the fifth afternoon. I was on my way to the lavatory as she walked out. Although I hadn't seen her since she showed me the video, we left each other notes beneath the second sink. The messages were short and often rushed. I'd write that I wasn't remembering anything new, and how despite that, I was determined to leave Silo. Seek shelter somewhere until I figured out what to do next. Petra didn't say the words, but I hoped she would come with me. I didn't belong here, and neither did she.

She silently passed me in the hall. Her stare was on the path before her, though at the last moment, on cue, Petra glanced my way. Only her eyes moved and it was for a split second so that the Generators trailing behind me couldn't see. The single look said something grave, important.

I sped up and hurried through the door of the lavatory. It was the only place I was allowed to go alone. I was given ten minutes each day, and the Generators stood right outside, yet it was always enough time for me to find Petra's note and scrawl a reply.

I ducked to make sure the toilet stalls were empty, then went straight for the sinks. We hid our notes on the smooth underside of the countertop. There were spaces between it and the actual basin, perfect to squeeze a crumpled paper into. I snatched it out, along with the pen she'd left, and unfolded it. She'd scratched out my previous words, and written on very bottom. In tiny, jagged letters, she'd spelled out:

They are coming.

They? It gave me pause. Petra and I had discussed my departure from Silo, through and through. We hadn't missed a single detail. But this ... *they?* It wasn't what we talked about; it was completely unscripted.

I tapped my foot against the tiles in a nervous jig to clear my mind. I wondered if I had missed something in her notes, but then it was just like Petra to throw me left when I wanted to go right. *They* could have meant the Jackets or the Generators. Manis had tabs on every singular minute of my life so it couldn't have been him. It was *they*, plural.

I huffed and put pen to paper. In a little under five minutes, the Generators would barge into the lavatory and force me out. They wouldn't care if I was in the stall, and they surely wouldn't care if I was caught up writing a message to Petra. So biting down on my lip in tense concentration, I wrote down, *I'm ready*.

It was gone in a crumbled fist and then tucked back under the sink. Petra would read it and then find a way to burn it. Better to squash the evidence before it wiggled free anyway.

When the Generators came for me, I was waiting. I didn't fight their rough hold on my arms, either. I treaded the hallways made of glass for perhaps the last time, smiling through the loose strands of my hair.

Euphoric hope was my lifeblood and I was high on promise. I wasn't coming down until my feet hit the ground outside the Ward.

Today was the sixth day. I woke before sunrise and crawled beneath my bed. I listened to the pendulum swing behind my ribcage as I scratched away at the wood. I let it comfort me, humming along. There was nothing to do today but wait and, taking full advantage of being left on my own, I spent hours beside the bedpost. Tomorrow Manis would inevitably take me to the White Room for questioning and I'd tell the same lies.

I scratched until my thumb turned red and I had to switch hands. I tallied the fifteenth day, then added something just below it. In large letters—so that it could never be mistaken for anything other than what it was.

MY NAME IS MATHAI PORTER.

ELEVEN

"UNCHECKED EMOTIONS"
BIONIC: MATHAI-0329

"It's 6243."

"How do you know?"

"Its face was detected by a Reaper, west of Asylum 10. Different clothes ... but I'm sure. Its code read the same. We don't believe—"

"It's not lost."

"No. It's searching for something."

"And the others?"

"Still unfound."

"So what's it doing in Asylum 10?"

"That *I'm* not sure of."

I had become great friends with the darkness. I knew it well, and recently found myself consoled by it. It never changed, and I knew what to expect. I was only wary of the shadows that blinked back; but even they were unmovable. Or at least that's what I first believed.

It was nighttime and I was locked in my room. The city was asleep, so there was little to no light shining through the window. Shapes and faces danced in the shadows. I reasoned it was all in my head, but they seemed blacker tonight. Untrusting, I sat up with my knees to my chest. I had been trying to rest for hours, though to no avail. I passed the time by humming. I would wait out the sun and be wide awake when Manis came for me.

Suddenly a silhouette to my right froze for an instant, then swayed again. It grew a face, a body, and hooded eyes. In its depths I saw that there was a girl, and she *was* the shadow. She rocked and it moved with her.

"Mathai." She walked right through the wall, like there was a door, or a portal, on the other side. The shadows slithered away soon thereafter, while I sat agape as she approached me.

It only took me a moment to identify her as the girl who'd come with Petra. It seemed she had abilities too—abilities that allowed her to move through walls. Did that mean Petra did as well?

"How did you do that?" I asked, scanning for more shadows. They were gone.

"That's not important right now."

"Then why are you here?"

She offered her hands and I realized she held a bag. When I didn't rise from my bed to get it, she removed its contents and offered them again. "Petra said you would need these. For tomorrow."

"*Tomorrow.*" I went to her and took what she gave me. It was an outfit, paired with a green jacket and a cuff bracelet. Wrapped inside the shirt were my files, bandages, and a pair of gloves. The clothing looked worn in the worst way, but also warm and just my size. I pressed the jacket to my nose, and even though the girl stood right there and it was plenty awkward, I sniffed it.

"You wore it the day of your last crusade. We would have found you something else, but it was all you had here. I'm sure—"

"It's perfect," I said, breathing in the scent of myself, and something akin to sandalwood. "Where did you find it?"

She showed me her palm and the key I'd stolen during camp. "In the cabinet."

"But how—"

"That's not important right now," she said again.

"And I can't think of five words I hate more."

The girl grinned. "Petra was right. Your attitude never left."

"And it never will."

Instead of feeding into my lashing sarcasm, the girl took the things from me and spread them out on the floor. I knelt by her, staring at the jacket and the holes that dimpled its fabric. She rearranged everything, as if to present it to me, then handed me the bandages.

This was a goodbye gift from Petra, the last piece of my past. She must have known I'd go back for the cabinet. And as sure as she'd walked through the wall, this girl had taken the key and finished the job for me.

Now it made sense why they locked my clothes away. A name on a piece of paper was one thing, but physical proof of my previous existences was everything. It solidified every reason I had for leaving Silo. If it weren't for Petra, I might have been repeating this loop as Ari—or someone else—already.

"Here, like this." The girl grabbed the bandages and began wrapping them around my left wrist. "Your hands are your most lethal weapons, Mathai. You can create and destroy, all with one touch."

"But my abilities haven't returned yet," I told her. I took note of how she tugged and tucked to keep the bandages in place.

"*Yet.* They will; they always do."

"When?"

"When you need them most."

I searched her face as she concentrated on my hands. Her hair was a deep brown, almost black, and pin-straight. Strands slipped in front of her eyes, though they never broke her trance. I questioned what kept her here. Was it me? Was it Petra?

The girl said, "When they do return, it will hurt like nothing has before. The bandages keep you controlled to some degree. Wrap your hands every night, like this."

"I don't know. Being force-fed kind of defeats all competition."

"It's worse."

She moved to my right hand and I narrowed my senses on her. "What happens if I don't wrap them?"

"You don't know many things right now, but this is..." She slowed her movements to glare at me. "You'd rather not know everything, believe me."

"I want to know your name."

"That's not important right now."

I frowned, then nodded. "Then what *is* important?"

She finished wrapping my hands and proceeded to push them into my gloves. "Tomorrow you will leave," she said, "and you won't come back."

Strange, the way she phrased her words. "Why would I want to come back?"

"You're bound to this place. You'll want to come back, every time. It's all you know, but swear you won't return." She pulled at a finger of the glove, making sure it fit over my knuckles.

"I won't—"

"*Swear it.*"

I didn't respond immediately. I tried to read her first, to get a sense of where her head was. The look she flashed me was both stoic and filled with empathy. Although I couldn't comb her mind the way I had with the legionaries, to miss the candor she sat there with would have made me a damned fool.

"Okay, I swear," I finally said. "But you and Petra are leaving with me, right?"

She adjusted the other glove, and then pulled away dismissively. I saw her decision before she made it. Switching around my things on the floor kept her busy until she was ready to answer my question. And even then, it wasn't much of an answer.

"Do you sing, Mathai?"

"I barely know the sound of my voice," I said.

"Good." She folded my clothes, placing my files under them. "Keep a song in your heart. You'll need it."

"What does that mean?" She didn't look at me, so I moved into her line of vision until she had no choice.

"It means the walls hear everything." Not in here, though. I'd made sure of it after hours of searching every corner of the room. Petra said there were only heat sensors; no cameras. No speakers. Just my bed and me. I opened my mouth to say this but the girl pressed a finger to her lips, shushing me. "My ten minutes are up." She handed me my stuff and stood.

"They'll find out if you stay," I called, rushing before she disappeared through the wall. The girl had her back to me, but halted with a hand pressed against the white cement. "Manis will know you and Petra helped me, so don't stay."

She wanted to consider it, I could see that, but her mind was set. Her decision had been final from the moment she materialized in the shadows. Maybe Petra's had been too, since before I became Ari.

"Keep a song," were her last words before she left with the shadows.

They didn't dance this time. They didn't linger and they didn't blink. They were just gone, taking the nameless girl with them. Darkness was a constant.

I dawdled in the room, pacing from window to door. That's all there was to do. Several ten-minute intervals passed as I waited for the sky to signal sixth hour with its green and blue hues. I kept count since there was no clock, and it settled the noise in my head.

It took me far too long to pick up the things she brought me, but when I did there was enough sunlight in the room to see what I was doing.

I stripped. I peeled off my white uniform until I stood in my undergarments. I was a madwoman, clawing at my clothing with **unchecked emotions** like fear crippled my spine. I reveled in the agony because I knew sweet release was soon to follow.

I wanted to trash the uniform. Instead I kept it, chucking it aside to the bed. Putting on the tank top the girl gave me was difficult at first. There were too many holes and I didn't understand how a shirt with no sleeves worked. I successfully pulled it over my head after three tries. It was faded—grey now, not black—and there was a stain by the hem. Though it fit.

The pants followed, and getting into them was easier. They were tight in a few places and loose in others. They had just enough stretch to affirm I had worn them before. I buttoned them at the top, and then moved on to my gloves.

The girl had wrapped all my fingers carefully. While I pulled the bandages away, I recalled her movements. She had covered my skin from wrist to middle finger. It was a technique, and I taught it to myself in the blooming trapezoids of light that washed from the window. I wrapped and unwrapped until my joints were too stiff for another round.

You'd rather not know everything, believe me.

The girl's voice followed me around the room, like she was still there in the walls. Once I was done with my hands, I took my bag out from beneath the mattress—the bag the Generators had given me with the socks. There were no more socks, but there was my brush. I shoved my gloves and bandages inside, along with everything else she'd brought, and tied it up. All that was left was my uniform, and I reluctantly put it on to hide my new clothes.

It will hurt like nothing has before.

There were some odd hours left before Manis would come to retrieve me, and I used them all to stare at the ceiling. Not really thinking about anything, yet still concentrating on everything. Wishing the girl would come back and tell me her name.

Just her name, that was all I needed.

My mind was a sequence of revolving events, and it only hushed when I hummed.

So I hummed the tune that came at will. It wasn't sad, it wasn't happy. It was like the darkness—constant. It came from Ari, and I imagined she lay beside me, the moon in her eyes as she led me in song.

TWELVE

"DIRTY REVENGE"
BIONIC: MATHAI-0329

"*What's in the bag?*" *the* Generator asked. It stopped me in the doorway and my hand stilled on my bag of clothes.

I was half-asleep, but awake enough to answer. "Socks. I'll drop them off at camp." The Generator's roving sensors took in my messy curls and the circles that rimmed my eyes, and then turned away. It had no reason to believe I was lying. Though if it had looked long enough, it would have seen my tank top peeking out from under my collar.

It was sixth hour, exactly. Two Generators flanked my sides as we hiked the halls. The traffic of legionaries was expected, but they were conscious of me, like a splotch on a canvas. They swerved in and out around me. Not once was I elbowed or trampled. It was something about being ushered by the Generators. The legionaries treated me like the plague I was and not just a broken, wayward thing.

I walked in front, assuming we were going to the White Room. Manis would be waiting for me with a rich smile and an eager pulse. He'd be sitting in the opposite seat with my file open on the table and would ask the same questions. Not because he didn't know the answers, but because he'd want to make sure I hadn't changed the story. I'd ask if they could hear me on the other side of the wall, and he'd lie. They could hear me. He'd ask about my last crusade, and *I'd* lie. My legion was dead.

I stepped down the passageway leading to the White Room, but the Generators tugged me in another direction. They did it with firm coercion, too, seizing my arms and yanking. I didn't have a chance to brake my heels on the tiles.

"We're not going to the room?" I asked, masking the tremor in my tone. I'd purposely missed first-meal and camp wasn't yet for several hours, so they weren't leading me downstairs. Where else would they be taking me?

"No," one of them answered. I couldn't tell which; my gaze was set on the walkway before me.

Their footfalls accelerated. Within a few short moments we were on the other side of the building, bypassing windows and screens and laboratories. They carried me across the glass sky bridge between the divisions of Silo before I could take in the city. A light shined from behind a door at the end of the corridor ... and the ground dropped beneath me.

"M-Manis is waiting for me in the White Room." I burrowed my nails into their hard armor and forced my head back like it could slow them down. I didn't want to know what the light meant. But it grew closer and closer, until I met it with a frustrated roar. Then they swung the door open and shoved me in, not caring whether my feet reclaimed the ground.

"He'll see you here," a Generator said. I crawled to my knees and turned back to scowl. I imagined them hanging from the walls, like in the video. They wouldn't be able to haul me around then.

Shifting to my feet, I took note of my placement in the huge room. There was a glass partition, and then a space beyond it. It looked like the White Room. Only there were no chairs for me to throw. It was just a box with nothing in it. This must have been what the other side of the two-way glass looked like.

"You've made progress, Ari."

I spun and came face-to-face with Manis. After seeing the younger, scar-free version of him, he seemed more like a skeleton. A silhouette.

He approached me with his hands clasped behind his back. "You must be wondering what we're doing here."

I nodded, refusing to give him my words. The right words had power.

"You're going on a crusade," he said.

I put space between us. If he got too close, he'd see I wore two layers of clothing and notice that my bag was too heavy to hold just socks.

"I know I said you weren't ready, but you've proven that you are." Manis watched the room, then me, smiling. "Crusades are very dangerous tasks, Ari. Many legionaries don't return. Like your legion." He paused; I began to sweat. "If they do, it often takes them years to mend. Crusades are thorough, they're dangerous." He cocked his head. If he did any more of that, the frail thing would roll right off his shoulders. "They say the mind can conjure terrifying things when left alone with time, but nothing instills more fear than the reality of those creatures. I know, because I've seen them."

He was trying to scare me. Between my strange nightmares and the descriptions in my codex, I knew exactly what the leviathans could do, what they looked like. He didn't have to tell me.

Manis shook his head like he forgot something. "But of course I'm only helping you. Not every escape is sweet."

Escape.

I watched him knowingly. Even though he didn't say the words, Manis seemed to sense that I was up to something. My eyes lowered to his hands, clasped behind his back, and my grip fastened on my bag. I remembered the door behind me and wagered how hard I would have to hit it to knock it down.

I finally spoke. "When do I leave?"

"Today."

Today?

"I haven't completed my training. I can't go."

"Of course you can," he said. "Your new legion will be there to guide you."

New legion?

Manis stepped aside and I saw something I missed when I fell into the room. It was the glowing chair—hooked to machines and ready. I had only seen it through the window of a door, though now that I'd been forced into a room with it, I knew it was no chair at all. It was a noose fashioned with false assurances, and it panted for the drop of my weight.

"You can't–" I stepped back and right into a Jacket's arms. I grounded my anger as he moved me further into the room and strapped me to the seat. On the surface, I was stiff and resisted very little. Manis had to believe I wanted this; meanwhile, he had no idea of the danger brewing inside me.

"This is normal procedure, of course," he said, following the Jacket to a table, where they mixed vials of liquids and arranged equipment. His movements were fluid, excited. I studied them, though I only took notice of his face. Because his face—the scar, his deep-set eyes, and a mouth to match—was the complete opposite. Manis was anxious. Either to get this over with or to see my reaction. Regardless of which, he was determined. And stars burned to the ground because of determined men like him.

He filled a syringe with the same purple liquid he'd given to the panicked boy, then flicked the side to free the bubbles as he raised it to an overhead light. "You said I have no family," I said. Anything to distract him. "But you're it, aren't you? You created me."

"Family?" He tapped the syringe again, then slid his hands into lab gloves. "You were an accident turned liability. There is nothing about you, me, it, or them—" He motioned toward the other Jackets in the room. "—That resembles a family."

"But you created me."

"What good is a creation if it cannot be perfected?"

Perfected. Manis' useless attempts to make me like the other legionaries were catching up to him. I wasn't perfect before the crusade, and I still wasn't. I was a virus in his carefully constructed technologic masterpiece—and I wasn't going away.

"This is how you do it, isn't?" I fisted my hands and ignored the beeping of the machine I sat in. Impatience stole through me. When Manis turned around, I noticed that at least one-fourth of his determination had chipped away. "This is how you erase me."

His jaw clenched like he hadn't expected my words, though he must have known. If he had the patience to revive me from the pod every three weeks and pretend to help me, he *had* to know.

"On her back," Manis said to a Jacket. The chair reclined until I was lying flat, a bright light piercing straight into my eyes. Manis moved into view and his facial features blurred. "Hold her down."

"*Wait.* I can tell you more about the crusade." Despite my plea, the Jackets yanked my head back and tugged it beneath a metal brace. I strained to see the needle Manis held poised at my arm.

"You're out of time."

I seethed. "I need *more* time, Manis."

More time for Petra.

He leaned in close. So close, I could smell the acidity of his breath. "Funny—you say that each time, right before your eyes go blank." He brought the needle to the exposed juncture where my bicep met my forearm and I kicked up, wiggling my arm to throw him off. "Who will you be next, Ari?" he cooed.

I screamed and spat. His words were too similar to the video. A Jacket scurried to pick up the trays I'd knocked over and contain the bars locking my feet. His pathetic figure faded in and out of the light like a shadow come to reap the dead. When the needle pinched my skin, when Manis began the transfer, venom to vein, I dug a little deeper into my share of depravation.

"She won't know anything—the next girl," I told him. "She'll be just like me."

The needle and the serum stopped and Manis arched a brow. He didn't empty the syringe, but I already felt the affects of whatever it was. Sweat beaded at my temples and slid down to my neck, and my mouth was dry. Numb. The injection site burned. No matter how fuzzy my mind became, though, my eyes never left his hands.

Manis didn't leave time for error. He whistled for a Jacket to restrain my other arm and my knees. Pressing down on the needle in warning, he said, "Then I've got the wrong one."

Wrong one.

Wrong girl.

Wrong version of me.

From the very corner of my eye, I saw Manis shove the needle in completely, eliciting a strangled cry from my lips. It burned like liquid fire—like someone was lighting me up inside, one blood vein at a time.

I had two options, and option one was defeat—to lay still and hope the pain knocked me unconscious before Manis did. Then I pictured Petra searching Silo for me with my ticket to the red fields, and option one was instantly omitted.

So I grappled for option two, with my eyes on Manis' syringe and my nails scraping across the cold steel of the machine. I slowed his movements with my mind and tracked them, then reversed them. I did it repeatedly in a span of seconds, until my vision distorted into one monochromatic streak. When I screamed again, it was cathartic, separating from me in aftershocks that juddered everything in the room. A shock to the heart gave way to a dark power.

The syringe flew from my arm and crashed into the wall behind Manis, though no one in the room had moved. He cast wide eyes on the other Jackets. "She needs another dose. That wasn't enough to contain her," he said, confused. "Hurry, another dose!"

The Jackets flew around the room to prepare another dosage of the narcotic while Manis monitored them. I watched them with sick interest, noting that they had released my hands. And while my right arm had gone stiff from the serum, my left was mobile enough to push against the straps.

I didn't know where the power came from. It had no source inside me, and that was perhaps the most unsettling thing of all. It might have been my callous thoughts, or just the need to see Manis crawling around in his own blood. Whatever it was, it didn't matter.

I leered around the room and sipped from the energy like it foamed at my mouth.

One moment I was lying down, the next I was ripping free from the machine. I pushed aside their useless braces and removed the gauze around my injection site. When Manis turned around again, it was to watch me dismantle his plans entirely.

"Hold her!" A Jacket charged for me and my mind flipped. Grabbing a tray from the table at my side, I struck him across the head and sent him, the needles, and remnants of the serum soaring across the room. The machines were silenced; the only humming came from inside my head.

Needles skittered over the floors like rain. But I knew they wouldn't stop. Seeing me hit a 120-pound man three feet into the air only spurred them on, as it should. Manis immediately opened the doors for the Generators, and the room exploded in chaos.

With a flick of my wrists, I levitated the snapped needles off the ground and focused them above the Jackets' heads. I nodded once and they hissed through the air, striking through wide, frightened eyes and pumping their veins with their own poison. As their screams bounced around the room, a smirk twitched at my lips.

My *abilities*.

They were back.

I moved my feet for the first time since breaking from the chair, spinning on a Jacket as he dove for my midsection. I looped my arm around his neck, tugged, and then swiveled in time to plant my boot in another Jacket's jugular. His gurgled yap was pathetic. He collapsed onto two *other* Jackets, who lost track of their syringes among the disarray. The one in my arm, blue-faced now and fighting for oxygen, tapped his sides repeatedly in submission. Instead of releasing him, I pulled him closer.

Generators fenced me into a tight circle the second I glanced up. Some wielded guns, and others held giant nets. Were they trying to capture me like a wild animal? String me up and tag me? The guns clicked and I jumped into action, kicking over a nearby table so hard it skidded and bowled into them.

The connection of the metal table and their suits became visible, a red, electric force bursting into the air. It surrounded the collision like sound suddenly had color. First there was silence, then the thundering *clash*. The sharp corners of the table dismembered three, leaving two.

"Lock down the doors!" someone shouted. "Code Y!" From the corner of my eye, I caught Manis—*that seedy bastard*—backing into the control panels that monitored the room. With shaky hands, he tapped in a password and turned a key. I anticipated what happened next. When the lights in the room began to blink on and off, I counted. Once, twice, then again. The rhythm was blinding, and with Manis' serum rushing through my system, I found it hard to stand upright.

But I had to. Unlike the time when I'd run away to Silo's tallest building, I couldn't let Manis win. He wouldn't get away—*I* would. It was my turn.

I dug my nails into the limp Jacket in my arms and round-housed the next Generator who rolled my way with a net. I ducked, then struck its knee with a knuckled punch. Though the force threatened to shatter every bone in my hand, I didn't feel a thing. I hit again and this time pulled away parts of its suit, my movements laced with determination. The Generator's right knee buckled and it collapsed on its left. Transferring my grip to the Jacket's throat, I fed the power into my leg and kicked the Generator right in the chest. The pieces of its suit shattered as the blue force knocked it back.

I was rushing across the room before I gave myself time to think, running my fists through every pale face I saw. My unconscious Jacket hung on. If I couldn't hold his neck, I tethered him to me by wrapping his lab coat around my arm. I tossed him through the air like he weighed nothing, catching him in the next instant as I swung around to face another Generator.

My pores expelled **dirty revenge**. If I stopped moving for a second, I knew I'd be trembling. I knew the moment would catch up to me and I'd black out—from the pain or from the power. Though that never slowed me down. Amidst the madness, I wondered if anything could...

I ducked through the nets that stretched for me as my eyes adjusted to the sputter of the lights. The blows I wasn't fast enough to thwart were a shock to my system. I felt the serum leaking into my mind, yet my body still moved, wrought with unbridled adrenaline.

When a Generator wouldn't stay down long enough for me to rip into its suit and unplug the blue source that fueled it, I traveled to that cryptic part inside me and used my abilities to control it. One Generator imploded with a tic of my lips, while several others barely made it two feet within my perimeter before they ascended, dancing in the air with the lab machinery like loose particles.

I felt the darkness take me, but I wasn't afraid.

And what did that make me, if not the perfect assassin?

"0329!"

The sound of my code halted me, midway between stifling a Jacket with my uniform sleeve and ignoring the growing pain in my back. Manis stood by the two-way glass, gun in hand. The barrel was pointed directly at my chest, but his gaze was all over the place. I watched him with hooded eyes, listening for his labored breaths. They echoed in this room of motionless bodies.

"Release him, or I'll shoot," Manis said.

It took me a second to trace his meaning, and then I shifted my gaze to my frail hostage, who slowly woke to consciousness. I moved, carrying him with me. The room seemed smaller now that it was only Manis and I who stood. I was sweaty and drugged. And his lab coat was still whiter than the stained walls.

"You won't kill me."

"And I have no intention to." Manis tapped the trigger. "If one dose won't do it, fifteen to the heart will."

I failed to conceal the scowl on my face. I could propel the gun out of his hands with one thought, but it was too easy. And since my weeks in Silo had been anything *but* easy, I planned to pay Manis back in full.

I inhaled, then dove for a station to my right. Gunshots rang across the lab, whizzing past my ear. Manis didn't aim. Instead, he gripped the gun like he'd never held one before and emptied the magazine of needles into my shadow. When he wiped through one, he clipped in another. My heartbeat tripled as I slid across the floor and sat the Jacket in a wheeled chair.

The dark corners of the room were my allies. Before Manis could find me again, I pushed the Jacket to the other side of the room and grabbed the first sharp thing I could find lying on the floor. It was a scalpel, but it would double as a weapon. I placed it between my teeth, then counted how many times Manis pulled the trigger. The gun couldn't hold more than eleven rounds, and the sixth one had just blown past me. I rolled up my sleeve and detached the rubber tourniquet from above the injection site, my lips moving as I counted. Round seven smashed through the two-way glass, and Manis laughed maniacally as he called for me and tiptoed around the room. I was only four paces to his right, but he didn't know it. I crouched low, rolling down my sleeve and taking the scalpel in hand.

"There's nowhere for you to run, Ari," Manis said, like we were playing some sick game of hide and seek. "It's just you and me now."

No, just me, I thought.

I stood and sprinted across the room, right at him. Manis spotted me immediately and shot off his eighth round, but I dodged it with a quick tumble and was up again before he could follow my movements. My breath came erratically, and sometimes it didn't come at all. My body hurt and my eyelids felt heavy. I was tired and shutting down. Given a few more moments, Manis wouldn't have to sedate me. I'd crumble at his feet.

Shut down later, not now.

I sped toward him just as his finger pulled the trigger again. I grabbed his arm in that 2.1-second window and cranked it out until his bones snapped several times, the agony visible on his face. The scalpel was now at his throat. The *boom* of the needle leaving the barrel sounded right by my ear.

"N-No more games," I slurred, Manis' figure blurring in my vision between the sweaty wisps of my hair. "No more lies. Tell me who y-you created me for."

The pale-faced idiot laughed. The blinking of the lights made him appear more sinister than he could have been with a broken arm and a blade at his neck. "What makes you think I made you for someone?"

"Because as demented as you are, you're not selfish." And I knew that as fact. Manis' obsession with perfecting me wasn't a personal agenda. It came from his resolve to satisfy someone else.

Despite his cracked bones, he tried to move his wrist and reposition the gun. His eyes flashed and I grunted, taking the scalpel and digging it into his shoulder. Blood poured from the wound, spilling over my fingers. The shock of pain brought him to his knees with his hands raised above his head.

He was insane if he thought he'd win this one. Taking the gun from his crippled hand, I stepped closer and admired his scar.

"I can help you, Ari," he said. He lied. He was reaching for anything now that I held the gun to his face. "Would you like to come with me?"

"Y-Your keys don't work on me anymore. You can't control me, and I don't trust you."

"I can—"

Infuriated, I fired a needle over his head. Once to threaten him, like he'd done me. Then I made quick work and shot the last round into his chest before he drew his next breath. "You were wrong. You had the right one."

His blue veins turned black as the serum entered his bloodstream. I had no idea if it would kill him, or if it would just wipe his memories like it was supposed to do to me. Only when his eyes rolled back in his head did I release my hold on the gun and the Generators that hung in midair. I turned away from Manis as their metallic suits dropped around me one by one.

It was time to go.

I shuffled over to the Jacket I'd left in the station chair. He was awake, but watching me like I was going to hit him next. I didn't carry him around just to kill him, though. Grabbing his lab coat, I pulled him over to the control panel and dropped him in front of it.

"Open the d-door," I said.

Without hesitation, he typed in Manis' passcode. The door to the room slid open, and I found my bag by the electromagnetic chair and then ambled out the exit.

The lone Jacket said and did nothing to stop me as I left those white walls behind, unsure of what would greet me in the halls of Silo—but ready for it anyway.

THIRTEEN

"HARDER THEY FALL"
BIONIC: MATHAI-0329

There *was no one to* escort me out. Not a Jacket, not a Generator. No manacles waited to secure me. And Silo's sirens were strangely silent—a noiseless madness. I launched down the hall, looking for the closest exist. If I managed to get outside to the city before anyone else knew I'd fled, I could be too far beneath the sun to be dragged back. I could find Petra.

Then destroy the Ward.

I was cutting through memorable hallways when I caught the sound of tromping footfalls. It gave me pause, and I stopped to listen before I attacked. *Three heartbeats.*

By the deep breathing and measured strides, I knew they were legionaries.

But why were they running?

They barreled toward me with glazed eyes, and I hardly had a moment to step aside before one of them collided with me, knocking my already-shaken body off-kilter. I grabbed her by the collar while the other two ran off.

"What's happening?" I asked, searching her eyes. They were dark and endless. They knew too much.

"Go," she said, tugging away. "Go, *now*."

"Go where?"

"The Seeming." Her eyes widened like she expected me to know what that meant, though I'd only heard of such a thing from the girl who walked through walls. Then she gasped. "*You*. You're one of us!"

One of them?

Without another word, she took my hand and pulled me after the others. And now I realized that there were no lights on this side of Silo. There were no sounds—and I missed the hum of the cameras in the walls, oddly.

When we crossed the sky bridge, colors blossomed from a doorway, twisting from left to right like they were moving to keep up with us. Colors had no place in Silo, and neither did I.

She guided me further, and then the refectory came into view. I had no business trusting her, but her *go* was my *go* too, regardless of what she was running from.

Ahead, the two other legionaries stopped before a Generator that had ruptured from the refectory. Its suit was smashed and it took longer than usual to detect us with its lasers. It backed us into the forked hall, towering above us by two feet.

"Ari—0329, Sabine—3118," it calibrated, its automated voice cutting in and out. Fear made me clutch my bag like its three pounds could do actual damage. There was never only one Generator. They would swarm like insects, then signal to their units with a whistle and a warning.

I was about ready to take the girl's hand and bolt back to the sky bridge when the refectory doors crashed open and the Generator lurched forward. The glow in its eyes drained out ... right before it shut down and dropped. The four of us stared in question, and our answer stood right behind it. A man with baggy, torn clothes and a gun the size of my head held the Generator's fake heart—a powerful green stone. He'd ripped it out. I didn't breathe as he crushed it in a fist and pelted it to the floor.

*The bigger they come, the **harder they fall**.*

"Let's go," he said. "The others will follow." At that moment, a group of legionaries darted our way from the sky bridge. They were equally sweaty, equally frightened.

"What's going on?" one asked, fighting to catch his breath.

"My training partner just tried to *strangle* me!" cried another. "She wasn't herself."

They all looked to the man and, admittedly, so did I. Manis wouldn't remain unconscious for long, but I couldn't be anywhere near Silo when he woke. If this man was going to get me out—whoever he was—he needed to get me out *now*. I pushed to the front of the group and surveyed the refectory behind him.

The tables were gone. The kitchen was empty and no one was lining up for porridge. The refectory was absolutely empty and a gaping hole destroyed the glass and the view I had admired so much. The rioting city quaked below our feet. And the colors I saw were really people dressed like the man. They blazed through the room, subduing Jackets and tearing through Generators that appeared to crawl from the walls. They were unnatural, out of place and far too bright.

A woman stood by the holed wall with a handle as she called over. I recognized her as the blonde who had stood with Manis while I trained in the gun range. At the time she seemed like another one of Manis' cohorts. Someone who made sure our training fell in line with their schedules. Now, though, I understood she was just like Petra. Originless. Disguised.

How much did I miss while confined to my room?

The once-mute sirens crackled to a buzz then, and began to blare the names of every legionary who had escaped. The lights flashed, and I wondered if Silo was this chaotic every time I cycled through identities.

"You either come with us or you stay behind," said the man. "That's life or death. Choose now."

He didn't have to explain. The legionaries pushed through to the woman and, one by one, took the handle to zip-line seven floors down, then disappeared into the city with a *whoosh*. The confusion unraveled before me and I was the last to move. I didn't understand any of it; I felt like I had appeared in a dream and at any moment I'd awake to find these people in color gone. The man—large muscles and a head full of hair—snapped me from the stupor with a hand to my shoulder.

"Mathai?" he asked.

I didn't say anything, but the lost look on my face must have given him his answer.

"We've got the one!" he shouted to the woman.

Generators appeared from the halls, and his people shot blazing bullets through the air, bringing the walls down around us. They communicated with gestures and grunts, like animals. If they didn't have hands and feet, I would have assumed them as such. The man shoved me toward the woman, who gave me the zip-line handle.

"Put your bag on your back. There's nothing much to this," she said. "Yank the handle once to slow, twice to stop. It'll lower you down. Hang on and don't let go until you hit the street."

"The street?"

She pointed down to where the legionaries were zipping down the lines that rushed toward the gates of the Ward. "Someone will direct you out once you're there."

"Why should I trust you guys?"

"Why should you trust anyone?" She pushed and I fell, dropping into the sky as the wind beat against my face. My heart plummeted to my feet. One pulse, two pulse, *three*. With my hands clenched tight to the handle, I glided across the line that connected me to a building below. The ground neared too quickly to do anything but hold my breath and hope I landed in one piece.

Over my shoulder I could see the entirety of Silo. Its walls caved out and the pretty glass that held it together collapsed in a dizzying pattern. Hundreds of those roguish people stood beside it, just outside. They pelted hooks into its frames with thick cords and pulled, beginning Silo's descent. Its structure crumbled into the streets as people dove from windows.

The words on the paper came back to me then: *They're coming.*

I refocused on the zip-line in front of me and yanked the handle to slow. I must have yanked too hard or not hard enough, though, because I dipped low, but didn't stop. I yanked again. The legionaries in the street waved for me to jump, but I was still too high. The line didn't lower. With my luck I'd break every bone in body, then dry out in the burning sun until Manis took me back.

Back to what? Silo's gone.

I yanked the handle again as I zoomed past the street and headed toward the glass skyway of speeding cars. I had to let go soon. Either that or I'd fly right into the connecting building.

I braced myself against the air current. My feet dangled several feet above a car, closer now, and I began to count. The distance of my fall and how far I had to throw myself in order to land on the sidelines. I could make it back to the other legionaries in seven minutes if I survived the drop. A drop at twenty feet would kill me if the traffic didn't, and there was no stopping anyone from hitting me.

I counted to ten, swung my legs, then released the handle. The glass skyway met me with a grunt as I rolled right into the second lane, my nails digging for leverage to stop the constant spin. Pain exploded in my frontal lobe. Horns honked in front of me, cars zoomed back and forth. Instinct kicked me in the gut and I doubled over in time to avoid being hit. I didn't stop spinning until I neared the edge of the skyway, where my head lolled over the side, hundreds of feet above the city.

An inch more, I chastised myself, feeling lightheaded. *An inch more and you'd be dead.*

"Mathai!"

I flipped over and landed on my feet, sighting the only car speeding toward me. It was white, like all the others, but Petra was driving and waving her hand out the slanted window. She zigzagged through the traffic with ease, ignoring the signals and the flow of the skyway.

She braked hard, then threw the door open. "Hurry! Get in."

Righting my bag on my shoulder, I dove into the passenger seat and buckled in. When I couldn't figure out how to close the door, Petra huffed and leaned over, hitting a black button above my head to shut it. Before I could utter a word, she sped off toward the ramp leading into the city.

"How did you find me?" I asked, then was immediately caught off-guard by what she was wearing. She wasn't in the same white uniform and boots. She was dressed like the man, like the blonde. All layers, all color.

"You're with them?"

"They're Outliers," she answered, eyeing the side mirror to make sure no one was following. "Yes, I'm with them."

"I don't understand."

"You will." With both hands on the steering wheel, she revved the car to the front of traffic and I held on to my seat. She spared me a glance only after we drove down the departing ramp and veered into the city. "You look terrible," she said.

I smirked, tossing my curls over my shoulder. "Does this sweat make me look fat?"

Petra groaned. "You were supposed to follow the others through the city. I only saw you fall into the skyway by chance."

"Good. Then you can get me out of here."

"No."

"What?" She swerved again and I slammed against the door. "You said you'd help me get out!"

"Yeah, *help*. I can't hold your hand and lead you out the gate."

"Then what can you do?"

Petra nodded to the city streets. "I'm taking you to the others. You have one shot at getting out of here, so make it count. Get out for good, Mathai."

"Where do I go?" The thought of wandering aimlessly and alone in those red fields frightened me. What if I ran into leviathans and had no means to defend myself?

"You'll figure it out. You always do." She side-eyed me again. "Just don't come back." She jerked around another corner, yelling for people to get out of her way. In thirty seconds flat, she stopped across the street from where legionaries were dropping from a disintegrating Silo.

"Wait, how do I contact you?"

"You don't." She reached over and hit the button. When the clear door slid up, she shoved me out. I landed none too gracefully in a puddle of dirty water. "Focus on saving yourself. Then find your legion. I'll be waiting."

Huh, wait—my legion? Petra and I never talked about my legion, much less about them being *alive*. "But—"

"If you're anyone other than Mathai the next time we meet, I'll throw you over the skyway myself."

She drove off, leaving nothing in her wake but my confusion. I gave myself a moment to chew my thoughts, then searched the city.

Get out for good, Mathai.

The tide of legionaries was leading down every dark lane and I followed, minding the drones in the sky that scanned for our faces. There were hundreds of us, though I looked comparatively different. Picking me out of any crowd would be easy—a white cloud in a dim sky.

I recognized this street from my journey through the city during confinement, when I had mapped the details of each building. I remembered the gate to the Ward, and the two legionaries who held it up. But everything was different now. Those in front of me trekked down the avenue, and I made a noted that the two legionaries were gone. The gate sat wide open, incomplete. The large sphere around the city flickered out like a candle, and then there was only the expansive outlands bathed in red dust.

"The Seeming!" a boy yipped beside me, joining a ruckus of glee.

City-goers gawked as we fled the city. I hurried over the threshold and my feet hit the dirt-packed turf for the first time. No glass, no white walls. Delirium passed through the lot of us like a disease. The city loomed behind us, a vast nothing ahead, but here we weren't mindless. Here we weren't legionaries; here we couldn't be controlled. I dared to smile, my first real one in so long. The boy, smiling with me, watched me as he ripped his shirt from his back and extended his arms. Running to meet the wind, he sprouted large, silver wings from between his shoulder blades and soared into the sky.

Wings.

I remembered what Petra told me then, about most legionaries only being able to access their abilities outside the Ward. As I ran, I counted each legionary, sifting through their emotions. Some ran faster than my mind could track, while others simply vanished, their bodies fading from corporeal to incorporeal within seconds. A girl to my right levitated, then shot up toward the sun with ground-moving energy.

This victory could have been false and flighty, but *damn*, did it feel like everything.

Crafts muddled the bright sky and I sped up. They were empyrean beasts as they dropped their hooks, fishing for bodies. Sweat flattened my hair to my face and my bag hung around my arms rather than over my shoulders. I dodged the crafts that dipped low, telling myself that if they took me back to the city I really would take that jump out the window. Manis wouldn't be able to revive me then—Kyra, Ari, or any other.

I pinned my shaky gaze to the trees and dark buildings in the distance. Around me, legionaries dropped with needles in their necks and I jumped over their still forms. Power, tempting and fierce, surged up my spine and I released it, feeling my body shred into a million little particles before I appeared again, whole and in a cloud of red. Though it wasn't like in the video. I didn't reappear miles away from my previous position. I glitched in and out, fading only to materialize a few feet away and still running, like I was passing between two portals.

The serum.

Whatever Manis had fed into my veins was taking hold. The dosage was right, but he'd underestimated the time it'd take to affect me. What control I thought I had over my body was leaving me in waves.

The sky offered no solace, but there was a crater only feet away. Although hundreds of us still ran, the crafts were working with limitless power. We couldn't run forever in an open field. So I bit into my bottom lip to counter the pain in my legs and sprinted for the crater, hoping no one would follow. It was a selfish thought, but I couldn't risk being seen.

I moved with the red cloud as it pushed me closer. Skidding, I evaporated for the last time and dropped into the crater. It was an empty, flat hole in the ground and I tumbled until I hit the bottom, pressing against the side of the dirt wall.

When I stopped rolling, when the pain ceased in my head, I laughed. I laughed as the crafts flew right over me and I laughed until the sound burbled in my ears. I imagined this was what accomplishment felt like, finding the Seeming. Finding myself. *Freeing* myself.

I laughed until I passed out.

FOURTEEN

"GOOD DREAMS"
BIONIC: MATHAI-0329

She touched my face.

We sat at the edge of the crater, biting into green fruit and laughing at senseless jokes until our cheeks hurt. She was young and I was so much bigger than her, but her toothy grin made up for it. Her hair was sandy, her voice soft. When she looked at me, and when she put her head on my shoulder, we promised to take care of each other. *Because we were the only ones left*, she said to me.

There were birds in the sky, and clouds. She pointed them out and traced them with a finger. My view of her was faint, but I felt her. She was warm. Her hazel eyes held an intense beauty, like a smothered rainbow. Still bright, still pure. Just somehow darker.

I missed her, though she sat next to me. My heart ached, though I didn't think it had reason to.

She finished her fruit, spitting the seeds into the deep crater, and then turned to face me. There were tears in her eyes and she didn't bother to wipe them away. She let them fall in the space between us as she clutched my hands.

The clouds moved too fast to be real, I realized a moment too late—white puffs that cast shadows across her face. When she spoke, her words were gentle. I wanted to use her name, but I didn't know it yet. She wouldn't tell me.

Why are we here? I wondered. *Who is she?*

She dropped my hands like my thoughts were razor-sharp and her tears turned to blood. They slid down her cheeks in dark smudges, staining her pretty face. While the ground shifted and moved, we remained still. The birds dropped around her, and then we were suddenly immured in a bunker. She spoke again when I was too traumatized to do anything but stare.

"Thai." The wind picked up and she stumbled. "Mathai! Get up. Get *up!*"

Get up? I was standing, wasn't I? I glanced down at my feet, but was distracted by my hands. They sparked with a blue energy, volatile threads slipping between each finger. That was why she'd let me go. Not because she heard my thoughts, but because she was afraid I'd burn her.

She lost her footing again as a hidden force lifted and dragged her through the roof of the bunker and into the sky. Not before she touched my face, though. Her nails dug deep as she wept and called my name. It echoed through the aphotic cloudlands.

Mathai.

Mathai!

Get up!

I was pulled from the dream like someone ripped me out and jerked upright, vomiting into the dirt with my heartbeat rushing in my ears. A headache beat away at my skull. I would have done just about anything for a sip of water and a few crackers. Or new boots—preferably ones with unworn soles. The heat of the Seeming was cruel, the land too rocky. My tongue slid over my cracked lips and I grimaced.

I need to get out of here.

The first thing I saw when I looked up was a gigantic sign. Tall and intimidating, it stood out in front of an abandoned skyscraper. I rearranged its odd letters in my mind, like I'd done at Silo, until I could read it clearly. *Asylum 10, Caeshua,* it said, and I huffed, getting to my feet.

I'd walked without stopping for a day straight. When the crafts flew back to their ports and most of the legionaries were dead or gone, I'd crawled from the crater and started in the direction of the trees. I'd wandered for hours without a compass or thought of where I'd go next. Petra left me with no way to contact her; she only said to find my legion, and my mind burned to think of all the possibilities that inferred.

My hunger had finally won out and I'd fallen asleep, not knowing I was close to anything other than the red fields. Now I saw that I was just outside Asylum 10, and it was vacant. Nothing like what I'd read about in my codex. The road I stood on was cracked and dimpled with weeds. It led down a shadowed street that curved to the left. A metal fence clanged in the wind in a nearby alley.

I assumed there would be people walking around, like in Silo. My nights of confinement were spent daydreaming about the different asylums in Caeshua, and I'd imagined they'd look completely different from the White Room and the refectory, as every asylum was tailored to fit an altered existence.

Asylum 10 was the "City of the Valiant," according to pages 24 and 61 in my codex. The legionaries in A10 ranked highest in agility, lowest in survival rate. When populations waned throughout Caeshua, they were exported like practicalities and sent to defend another Ward. They were the guardians of this city, as well as Asylum 4—18,963 feet from where I stood. Or so my codex had said.

Though all the asylums were connected, each synced individually to Silo. A10 provided a workforce, but as the closest asylum to Silo, it was practically a second capital. Skill, knowledge, technology—it supposedly had it all.

Truly, Asylum 10 *was* different. It wasn't valiant at all. It was dirtier, grittier, than what I'd believed it to be. The streets reeked of misery, even though no one was here. It just wasn't what I expected.

The air was wet. Dewy, almost. I combed a hand through my hair, flinching as my fingers caught in a tangle of curls, and squinted into the dying sun. I had a few hours before it got dark, so I needed to find food and shelter soon. And in that order. My stomach rumbled in agreement as I started toward the city.

I mined through my bag until my fingers wrapped around the leather-bound book. Flipping directly to the chapter on Asylum 10, I began to read. I knew the words like water knew the color blue, but perhaps I'd missed something. Did the people live in a specific location? Where were the legionaries? Were they hidden, or did leviathans ... *kill them off?*

The thought broke shivers down my back. Leviathans were swift, thirsty. It would only take ten of them to dismantle an entire metropolis without warning, and then they would move right on to the next asylum. Or *stay*, waiting for their next victim to wander in, oblivious and foolish. And I wasn't dumb. That victim could easily have been me.

I scanned the dark corners of the street with stalled breath, and then resumed reading. My boots scuffled along the broken pavements and the sound followed me through the asylum. I'd have to find an empty home, or search until I found someone. Silo hadn't prepared me to survive out here alone, but I was created with enough cognitive thinking to know I had to get high or keep low. Staying on-ground was the equivalent of standing in the middle of the road, shouting Manis' name into the sky, and hoping he wouldn't eventually find me.

My pants hem caught on a scrap of metal, and when I tugged, the toothed edge tore a hole up to my knee. Aggravated, I removed the uniform, revealing the clothes I'd hid beneath it. I would have ditched the uniform long ago, had I been thinking. I wiped the grime from my face with the shirt, and then rolled all the white fabric into a ball. When I brought it to the mouth of my bag, I realized it wouldn't fit. Shoving and folding didn't work, and I couldn't leave it in plain sight. Swapping it out with my bandages wasn't an option, either.

I eyed an enormous waste bin across the street, tucked between two buildings. It wasn't gasoline and a match, but considering my circumstances, it was the next best thing. I walked over with the clothing in tow and threw it over the side. Once it was out of my hands, I grinned, feeling like I'd finally gotten rid of Silo and Manis for good. Without the uniform, I could be anyone I wanted. I'd disappear into Caeshua.

With a second thought, I dove through the dumpster in search of food. It was disgusting and desperate, but I reasoned that nothing could be more than a day or two old. Ripe, but not rotten?

I found two copper coins and a key, then found the broken lock to match the key several seconds later. My body hung halfway out the dumpster now, and some sort of wrapper was knotted in my hair. I fished it out and sniffed it. It smelled stale, like it'd been something good one day, but that day was gone. I tossed it and pocketed the coins. When I eventually touched the bottom of the dumpster, the hunt was over. No food meant no people.

I jumped down from the dumpster and observed the sky. It was much darker now; I gave myself twenty minutes before nightfall. The chapter on A10 was short and sparse, but an uneasy sensation in my gut told me the darkness wasn't quiet here. Or welcoming. If I had to choose between shelter and food, shelter would win by miles.

I faced the dumpster and noticed a small window near the ground. It was a part of the building, its glass smashed in, and was the only one in what was possibly an underground bunker. The same windows were used for light in Silo, or as vents, but this one was pointless while broken. I reasoned someone either needed to get in or get out, fast. The skewered alignment of the dumpster and mashed mud in front of the window led me to believe it was the latter. They'd rushed, rolling the trash over toward the window in the hope of concealing their hideaway. It was a bang-up job; I would have missed the window had I not been diving for food.

Calculations ran amuck in my mind. I stepped around the broken glass, peered through the hole, and knew immediately that I had to go inside. Maybe someone was still there. Maybe they could help me. With minimal light from the sun, I saw only a desk in the center of the room. Zero movement. If there wasn't anything useful to me and I couldn't stay, I told myself I'd just look around. Wait out the moon and hope the night was a short one. Then I'd be back on my feet to search the city.

I fastened my bag on my back and kicked in the remaining glass in the window frame. When it was completely open, I got down on my hands and knees and crawled through, head first. Muck clung to my skin, dirtying my clothes, and tiny insects tickled my skin. If I had the room to cough, I would have, as dust and cobwebs clouded my entry. But when

I could see fully through the curtain of my hair, I knew I'd been right. Someone had been here, and this wasn't any ordinary bunker. I stared long and hard at the desk for a moment. It was an ... *office*?

I dropped down on the shaky countertop below the window and breathed heavily in the silence. After a beat, I stepped off the counter and padded into the cellar. Apart from the desk in the center of the room, there was a small cooking stove and a few pots. They were empty and the oven grills were cold. Whoever lived here must have discovered this place unoccupied, too. With only the desk and a destroyed kitchen, I wondered how they survived.

I searched through the tattered cabinets, tiptoeing to feel around the top shelf. My fingers brushed something solid and I climbed up to grab it. It was a small, silver can with a hook to pull. When I shook it, liquid sloshed against the sides. *Food*, my mind registered. *This was where they hid their food.* I peeled the lid off and sniffed the rim of the can. It smelled sour, with a trace of something sweet. Yellow, seedless chunks floated around in the thick liquid. I considered putting it back in case the person returned, especially since I didn't know what it was, but my stomach roared loudly, urging me to take a sip.

I knocked the contents of the can back and swallowed the pieces without chewing. Its heavy citrus flavor hit my tongue and I coughed several times before continuing. And even though the morsels of food were slimy and left a bad taste in my mouth, I searched the cabinet again, doing a quick dance when I counted ten more cans.

As I finished my second serving, I measured the room. The distance between its four walls and all its hues and shades. The ground was made of dirt—not red, like the rich sand that filled the craters—but dirt so black I wondered if I'd left my shadow outside. My footprints disappeared in its blackness. Then the light of the dying sun filtered through the window and highlighted the room's quiet nooks. Like Petra's vault, this bunker felt *lived in*. Blank walls, chilly air, and all. Almost like someone had stepped out and left a part of themselves behind.

I popped a yellow drupe in my already stuffed mouth and circled the kitchen. Curiosity led me to the desk, where I surveyed its scratched surface and the drawers cluttered with crumpled paper. This wasn't an office. I imagined an office had more to it, like one of those audiovisual screens. Maybe a computer or two, or a machine. But this desk was old like everything else here, and looked as if it was used simply as a place to sit down, not for hours of hard work. Because there weren't any graphs or diagrams, maps or analyses. Nothing my mind recognized or could dissect.

I sifted through the papers and found them marked with ink lines. Most lines were wide, uneven, and angry, bleeding off the page and onto the desk, but the narrow, subtle ones, the lines that barely made an appearance on the paper at all, grabbed my attention. It was as if they were there by mistake, like the mad artist who sat in this chair with murky thoughts and racing fingers, broke down from a high and allowing the ink to lead them, rather than the other way around. Like there was clarity in those last few moments as their pen glided over the parchment, like they had sovereignty over their mind once more. These lines, I realized, were wilder.

I placed my cans down on the chair and searched deeper into the stack of papers. The first few layers were nothing more than these scribbled lines, though at the bottom I found one that was different. It was a drawing of an eye. It had no color, but the black rings of the iris and strokes of the eyelashes were exact and unrushed, making it look real. Copied from an actual person. I held it up toward the window and touched the edge of the paper where the artist must have run out of room and sharply drawn an X across the eye. The other papers were practice, and while they'd finally drawn what they wanted, their canvas had been too small.

The drawing reminded me of the eyes and arms that often comforted me. They had little connection to a tangible person, but I was strangely obsessed. I wanted to know whom they belonged to, and then I didn't. Knowing solidified that I had forgotten someone, and that was a pain that occupied no space or time. It was a vacancy...

Forgetting someone.

I slapped the drawing back down and resumed eating from the cans. If I ever thought of returning to Silo, I had to remember that feeling of seeing, being, and knowing nothing.

The bunker was too dark now with the sun gone, but I felt my way around, a free hand pressed to the rough cement. I landed in front of a three-foot door with a jammed handle. Turning the knob swiftly to the right loosened it enough for me to slam against the frame with my shoulder. After a push or two, the wood splintered and the door broke open. I tripped into some kind of foyer, catching myself at the bottom of a flight of stairs. My good-for-nothing boots weighed a ton and my bag fell. I paused there, breathing deeply with my hand braced on the wall, and downed more of the sour fruit like a drunkard would a bucket of ale. Everything from Manis' serum to pure exhaustion was eating me alive. I wanted to stop and rest and I didn't care where, as long as **good dreams** were as frequent as my nightmares.

I stood, dragging my bag behind me as I climbed the stone steps. The room I found had a side table and a tiny bed pressed against the far wall. The sheets were thin and worn, a feather between my fingers. I could grip the width of the entire mattress without struggle. The bunker wasn't cold, but I feared that would change with the hour. When I searched the dusty floors for extra blankets, I found nothing but snapped pens.

"D-Don't think about it," I whispered, frowning at the break in my voice.

I left the cans on the side table, then lazily emptied my bag on the bed. Immediately, I separated my bandages from everything else. When morning came and I had proper light to see, I'd wrap my hands like I was taught to. But for now I resumed digging through the rest of my things, until my fingers passed over something sharp.

A fork, I thought, feeling over its prongs.

I smiled.

The girl—Umbra, I'd call her, for the shadows she moved with—had put the fork I'd stolen from the refectory in the bag. At the time I'd meant to use it on a Generator to cheat my way free, but I hadn't found a moment while bound and practically glued to their sides. Its use was limited now, so I cracked open another can of fruit and dug in with the fork instead of sticky fingers.

While I ate and counted the hours until the sky would be taken with the blue-green of a sunrise, my mind drifted to the girl from my dream. There had been no sound, only rolling images, but I heard her say my name. And as we laughed and drew pictures in the crater, I heard her say something else. It was silenced when the clouds took her away. Now it frolicked in the darkness.

Sister.

FIFTEEN

"AKIN TO LONGING"

BIONIC: MATHAI-0329

"*My name is Mathai Porter.* I am the cause, I am the walking virus..."

I released the button on the radiocom and listened as it played back my words. My voice sounded strained—though I could hear myself, and that was what mattered.

The radiocom was something like an armband. It had two buttons on the back—one to reset and one to record or send audio. But it was more technical than a piece of jewelry. It was made up of curved, smooth metal that lit up when I touched its screen and grew warm when I clasped it around my wrist, like it was adjusting to my body temperature. It estimated when I was hungry or tired, or when I'd wandered too far into A10 to pick up a solar signal. It told me the time and date, and placed me on its holographic map with a red dot. It became a part of me. And because I'd been stuck in this asylum for fifteen hours already, with no luck of finding anyone, the radiocom also picked up on my bitter emotions.

When I'd found it in my bag, I thought it had been some sort of calling device. It took me several moments to configure it, and I'd hoped the previous version of me—Kyra—had left a note about what to do next. But she hadn't, and the bright, virtual screen blaring "NO LEGION" mocked me until I began pressing random buttons. That was when I discovered how easy it would be to record myself, memorize myself. Words on paper were great, but I needed to hear it. So every hour, on the hour, the radiocom repeated my name, my code, and the message I'd programmed. It was meant to do so much more, but it served me best this way. *This way,* I'd never forget who or what I was again.

After it repeated my message for the seventh time, I powered the radiocom off and glanced down at the alley below. I was sitting on the rooftop of the bunker I'd broken into, my feet dangling off the edge. Fifteen hours had afforded me enough time to trek through A10 that morning, and it was probably more time than I needed. There was a house two streets down that must have lodged a family of five or more. They hadn't been there, but everything in their home remained untouched, like they'd evaporated into thin air. I'd targeted their bedrooms and taken any clothes that fit me, then bagged the canned food I'd found in the cupboards. I'd taken matches, books, and bed sheets—anything that would help me survive for some time on my own.

None of their bathroom showers worked, but half-filled water bottles had done just fine for removing the grime from my skin.

After that, I'd hopped from home to home until the plastic bags I was carrying grew too heavy. By the time I started back to the nest I'd built in the bunker, my radiocom was beeping with my reminder to eat.

It was almost third hour now. There were twenty-four hours in one day, I'd calculated. After the twelfth, time renewed and began at one again; the sun set a little after sixth hour. I grabbed my codex from the ledge beside me and opened to the page with Caeshua's map, and then held it up to the light with bandaged hands. It wasn't much to go on, but I'd marked points on the map to indicate where my legion could be. I'd search all four asylums since I didn't have a lead, and hopefully I'd find them alive.

When I dropped the codex, Silo's Ward was glimmering in the distance. It danced on the horizon above A10's tallest buildings, and I held up two fingers, shutting an eye as I imagined pinching the city into nothing. *If only it was that easy,* I thought. I had plans to put the city behind me. Good plans, *true* plans. With nothing here for me in A10, I'd continue the hunt for my legion in A4. Travel by foot, ration my food, and rest only when I absolutely needed to. I measured that in two days' time, I'd make it. And A4 was far enough from Silo that no one would know who I was.

"*Third hour! Third hour!*" My radiocom buzzed to life, its digital clock displaying the time. And the hovercrafts promptly dispersed from Silo's ports and freckled the sky. They worked on rotation, scanning Caeshua's desert hills every third hour. I'd discovered this earlier that morning, while rummaging for weapons in an empty bunker ten blocks north. The crafts had flown overhead, vibrating the objects around me and creating a hum in the air. At first I thought it was a seism, a quake in the terrain, but then I'd watched from a window as they activated their green sensors. The Silo insignia branded all five crafts.

I wanted to believe they were searching for every legionary who'd gone rogue, but I was smarter than that. Manis wanted *me*.

I stood from the ledge with perfect balance, then crossed the rooftop to the trapdoor and, before the crafts flew close enough to notice me, plunged down the hole to land in the room with a squat. The hinged door swung shut just as their green lights scanned the bunker. I held my breath, mentally counting as each craft passed by. When the last one hovered for several seconds longer than the others, I paused. How long would staying underground work? If I ran, would they shoot with the intent to kill?

The hovercraft was gone in the next instant and I rose to make my way to the bed, where I'd dumped everything I'd collected that morning. Other than the clothes, it wasn't much. And I would have to leave most of it behind in order to pack light. Because if it was going to slow me down, it had to stay.

I began with the food, opening my empty bag and shoving two small cans into the bottom. They weighed the least, but it'd be enough to get me to A4. Or at least halfway there.

I picked up another can to add for good measure, but in my haste I dropped it, and it slipped and rolled beneath the bed. When I ducked down to reach for it, I was caught off-guard by all the broken pens I found. I'd seen them last night, but it had been dark and I had been too tired to process much else beyond the pain in my body. And there hadn't been nearly this many pens last night, either. There were at least twenty, cracked clean in half. I waded a hand through the mess to grab the can and my fingertips met paper on the wall. Wide-eyed, I kneeled down further, with my face to the ground, and finally connected the pens to the artist. The bed covered most of the papers, but I knew ... they'd found their canvas.

With hurried movements, I slid the bed across the room until it was flush with the side table. Then I faced the wall with all its paper, growing cold at the sight before me.

It was the eye. Only, it wasn't on just one piece of paper—it was on several. Hundreds. The papers were placed together to create a collage of lines and shapes. To create a single image. And that foreign feeling of familiarity returned again, especially when I sat on the ground in front of the wall, my hands pressed to the drawing. I pulled free the page with the eye's iris. Devoid of color, I couldn't even begin to guess where the artist's inspiration came from. But I sensed that it was a place **akin to longing**. Like I longed to be more than an assassin, a project. *Silo's hound.*

A squawking noise from beyond the door jolted me from the reverie.

I rushed to fold the paper up and tuck it into a back pocket. I packed some clothes, a few bottles of water and my codex, and blank notebooks I'd found and tied it up. Without a backwards glance, I ditched the room and tiptoed to the broken window.

The sound could have been the wind, but I worried it wasn't. In my fifteen hours spent here, I'd been trapped in an endless silence. No people, no life—just me, alone with my thoughts. And now noise. Perhaps other legionaries had found their way to A10 too?

I peeked out the window, craning my neck to see down the alley. The waste dumpster shielded my view of most of it, but I saw a pair of dirty, bare feet. The squawk came again, followed by low groaning. It seemed like they were ... hurt? They had to be in pain. They didn't move, and the groaning grew louder and more grating until I was urged to help them.

I climbed out, making as little noise as possible. Scaring them away would be inevitable if I approached too swiftly. They'd run, and probably right into the hooks of the crafts. Nimble footsteps moved me through the alley; my breathing slowed. Without shifting my eyes from the figure crouching in the corner, I programmed my radiocom with another three-hour timer.

"Hey, are you hurt?" I called, stepping around the alleyway trash.

It was a small child, her head down as she groaned. Her back was to me, but I could see that the thin strands of hair desperately needed to be washed. Her hands snuck out to the side and the dullness of her skin made me wary. She was so pale. She was gangly, boney. The groaning continued like she didn't hear me.

"Are you lost?" I was right behind her, now, and I reached a hand out to tap her shoulder. Before I could make contact, though, she sniffed the air and swung around to look at me. The movement was so fast, her body blurred. And her head sat on her shoulders crookedly, like she'd taken a fall, broken her neck, and simply walked away. That's when I saw her pitch-black eyes and the blood that spilled over her cracked lips. She growled at me, a hiss coming from deep within her chest.

Leviathan, my mind processed, leaving room for fear.

Horrified, I jumped back and tripped over my feet. Near-dizzying adrenaline constricted my throat as the girl crawled toward me with twisted, jerky limbs. There was a dead bird behind her, I realized too late. That was why she was groaning. She was *feeding*, and I'd stupidly interrupted her.

I ran through everything my codex told me about these creatures—how they looked like us, had once *been* us. They were parasites; one bite from them and they'd possess your mind like a disease. That was, if they didn't devour you first.

My time was limited. I numbly inched backwards with my hands behind me. The child's black eyes rolled over in their sockets and she bellowed into the air. *Are they blind?* I wondered. I couldn't imagine they saw much through their inky irises. She sniffed the air again, as if something called her to me, and readied her body to jump. Acting quickly, I grabbed a shard of broken glass from the window and gripped it tight. When the beastly thing launched at me, I struck, lodging the glass in her eye as she released a bloodcurdling roar in my face.

Sorry, little girl.

Black goo dripped from her mouth and slid down my neck. She smelled horrid, like a week-old corpse. She wiggled around on the glass as I pushed it deeper. I didn't stop until I was sure it met her brain, and then I tugged it down, crying out when the glass cut into my bandage. Though it slashed right through her cheek, the shard didn't kill her. Instead, she screeched and scuttled away, digging for the glass in her eye with her small hands.

I knew opportunity when I saw it. I scrambled to my feet and immediately started running in the opposite direction. The girl continued to shriek, but other noises joined, surrounding me like a cocoon. My stomach bottomed with the idea that there were *more* of her, and it propelled me through the streets of A10, panic following suit. How did I miss them? Had they been hiding? Did they *smell* me?

I watched the open sky as I ran, remembering that I only had three hours before the hovercrafts returned. I couldn't spend too long running, weaponless and so exposed. So I made a beeline for the large, U-shaped tower at the end of the street, the one with the risers and blinking lights. It wouldn't take much to break through a door. Even if it only provided shade and a few moments to gather myself, it was easier than running back to the bunker.

Screeching resounded from behind me, and when I dared a glimpse over my shoulder, I counted four additional leviathans running alongside the child. Their movements blurred and their black mouths opened and closed like they could already taste the flesh on my bones. I wanted to vomit. The bodies they animated were dead, and if a glass shard to the eye couldn't vanquish one, what could?

Cars created a checkered pattern in the street, making it hard for me to run a straight path. They appeared deserted—doors wide open and seats filled to the brim with garbage. I zigzagged between the sidewalk and the street, pumping my arms, and dove for a car that blocked my route to the other side of the road. Though the soles of my feet burned, I hopped up on its roof and slid down the splintered windshield.

I was concentrating so hard on the leviathans behind me that I completely missed the one in front of me. It jumped out from beneath the car and a rawboned hand wrapped around my ankle. They were leeches, these things.

Even if I was the last thing alive in this city, I'd bleed myself out before I became one of them.

I yanked and the leviathan moved with me, crawling around in soiled pants, its right arm completely gnawed off. I braked, pivoted, and kicked my other leg out like a whip. The heel of my boot caught its jaw and an audible *pop* sounded as guck flew from its mouth. It freed me and collapsed to the ground. And because I would be damned if it got back up, I punted its head several times before taking off toward the tower.

It should have been a clear shot—779 steps. My eyes zeroed in on the building while everything else became hazy. I pretended it was the target from the gun range, and a gold ring appeared around the tower's structure. It gleamed and refocused as I moved, then disappeared just as suddenly when a swarm of leviathans rounded the corner and barreled toward me.

They were gathering, calling to one another. Their wails flooded my mind, and I stalled right there in the middle of the street, beady-eyed leviathans at both ends.

Think, Mathai...

I shook out my bleeding hand and broke into a run down another alley, winding through three more of them just to stay away from the main road. I moved like a serpent, curving through tight crevices, and circled around to the tower in hopes of losing them in the process. I thought that they would scatter, while the alleyway trash would mask my scent and confuse them. It was a long shot, but one I was willing to take.

Steadying my breathing, I continued to distance myself from the havoc. I merged with the shadows and ran like fire nipped at my heels. I was about two blocks away from the tower when loud thoughts inside my head slackened my pace. They weren't my thoughts, I knew, because they were too loud to be mine. They bobbed in and out of my mind like poor radio reception, and they were deep. I gripped my head to make them stop, though they continued as if I'd tapped into someone's mind by mistake.

Don't ... Back ... Lights ... City ... The thoughts came, as frantic as my own.

They disorientated me. For a brief, insanity-induced second I thought it was a leviathan, *speaking* to me. However, I doubted those soul-eaters thought about much but their next meal. Which meant it *had* to be someone else.

I sped across the street and entered the last alleyway, which would spit me out in front of the tower. My bag felt like it weighed a solid ton on my shoulders, so I reached back to unstrap it.

I'd only broken my focus for a fraction of a second, half a beat ... but it was enough for me to be blindsided by a dark, hooded figure.

SIXTEEN

"ATRAMENTOUS POWER"

BIONIC: MATHAI-0329

My psyche skidded into terror.

A muscled arm wrapped around my throat and I was hauled over to the brick wall in the alley. I tried to wrench away, but the leviathan was too strong.

Strong. Were they usually this strong?

With no room to breathe, I dropped my hands and met the wall with my feet out. As the leviathan shoved, I put one foot in front of the other and scaled the wall, then focused all my strength into flipping myself over. Blood rushed to my head, disorientating me, but as soon as I was back on my feet again, I lashed out with my fists.

My hair spun around me like a black cloak while I jabbed at my attacker with knuckled punches in quick succession. Though I never missed or failed to land a blow, it countered my every strike. *Is it mutated?* I questioned, whirling on my heels and aiming for its throat. It didn't move fitfully like the other leviathans, or mumble and groan. It grunted as it mimicked my every move and threw strikes of its own, each one fluid and precise. It smelled like sandalwood and rain and nothing like rotting flesh. Only when it caught my arm in mid-attack did it occur to me that it wasn't trying to eat me. Rather, it was trying to *hurt* me. Like I was trying to hurt it. And the hands that blocked my blows weren't bony or filthy. They were calloused and *warm*.

I froze with the realization, and so did it. When I ducked to peer under its hood, it turned away.

"Who are you?" I asked.

It actually responded. "*What* are you?"

Its deep voice shook me. Leviathans couldn't speak, could they? *No.* The fact that it wasn't trying to tear my flesh from my bones meant it wasn't a leviathan. Because it was a *he*. It was a boy, and he was probably running away like me.

I reached up to tug his hood and he moved quickly, dropping my arm and gripping my face like a vice. His strength startled me still. Then the lines of his face shifted into view—his full lips, sharp jawline, and piercing, hazel-green eyes. He was all color, shrouded in darkness. Russet waves of hair spilled over an eye. He leaned forward with a sneer and inhaled through his nose. I flinched like he was prepping to strike me again, but he didn't.

He did nothing more than inhale deeply, his hand unmoving.

Is he... Is he sniffing *my mouth?*

He brought his nose closer to my lips and I gasped.

Hell, he *was* sniffing my mouth.

Taking control, I knocked my forearm across his, breaking his hold, and then slammed into his chest with the heel of my hands. He shot backwards and his body whooshed through the alley, hitting the wall and cracking its bricks. Though his head took the brunt of the collision, he stood back up without faltering. He *shook it off*, like he hadn't put a dent in a fortified building.

A strange spell of energy descended over me, eating up my fear. Mutated leviathan or not, he was in my way of getting to the tower. If he wouldn't talk, then neither would I. And he wasn't interesting enough to risk getting stranded out here with a fleet of *actual* monsters—nothing was.

He walked to the mouth of the alley and watched me. I couldn't see his eyes, but I felt his gaze on me like a beacon of heat. His deep, ragged breaths stretched across the space between us. Did he think I was a leviathan? The idea was senseless, because his skin was as warm as my own. I knew he felt it. Or had he been sent by Manis to confuse me? It was a definite possibility. The crafts could have dropped him down, right into my path, to deter me. Manis could have been smiling from behind a monitor right then... Or maybe he was dead with the rest of Silo.

I took a step and the boy advanced. He'd been anticipating my next move for a while, so when he dove straight, I parried right, climbing a closed dumpster and leaping for the ladder that led to a window higher up. I clutched it and used the wall for leverage, then waited for him, analyzing his intent. When he charged over, I lifted and swung my feet out together, clocking him in the gut with a stressed roar. It didn't throw him as far as I needed to, but it agitated him. It was enough to set him off. He grumbled his frustration, like he hadn't expected such a fight.

I continued the climb, the seconds waning. My bandages began to unravel, but I didn't stop to right them. Now my bleeding hand left a red trail along the ladder. And my heavy breath came faster, my chest tight. I had one hand on the ladder and one on the window ledge when I felt a yank on my right leg. The guy wrapped his arms around me like I weighed nothing and pulled until my fingers started to slip, even though I held on so tight my knuckles turned white.

He's tall, I thought in annoyance. I wiggled and kicked to get him off and the bastard laughed, like I was trying to tickle him with my effort. I looked down at his dark hood, then back up at the window. *I'll knock him out first*, I told myself, wincing as my hands stiffened on the ladder. *The tower will have to wait.*

I dropped and landed haphazardly on his shoulders, my thighs wrapping around his head, balanced above him. Rough hands held my legs while I seized his hood, trying to tug it down. But he fought me for it, shrugging his shoulders so that I slipped around to his front, my body pressed too close for comfort. This guy was determined as hell.

We shared a look as he held me. "I'm not a leviathan," I said.

It fell on deaf ears. He rolled and I rolled with him, hitting the ground back first. My breath escaped from my lungs, and I had a little less than five seconds before he stormed me, crawling over my body with his face still veiled.

"I know," he finally answered, and it left his lips like it pained him to admit it. His hands descended and I dodged him once again, rocking away on the dirty ground and wrapping my legs around his torso. I maneuvered, flipping him over on his stomach and planting a knee on the back of his neck. I was strong. I'd spent hours training in camp without ever really getting tired. The other legionaries were never a good match for me, and I was often left to train on my own, working through fighting tactics with rubber mannequins so I didn't harm anyone. But this guy was different. He *matched* me. His strength rivaled my own, and I didn't like it. It made me feel unwrapped, incompetent.

"Where's Manis?" I slurred breathily, bringing my face to his. "He sent you, didn't he?"

Confusion marred the features of a face I could now actually see, then he smiled. In the next beat he threw me over his shoulder, never releasing his hold on my hand. He pitched me like a doll and then reeled me back, constricting an arm around my throat. Within the headlock, I could do little more than bite his thigh until he howled and turned me to face him.

I was growing weary of the back-and forth, his aloofness. Before he gained leverage on me, I fished my hands between us and pinched, digging my fingers into his sides. He snarled but didn't budge.

Now we became a knot of quick jabs and furtive strikes. I tried to grasp his throat and he aimed to do the same to me. His agility was a nuisance—one I couldn't track. I couldn't read his movements as easily as I could with the legionaries in camp, but he read mine. And my body ran hot.

I struck him once and he slogged me twice. We should have stopped and I should have run, because when I side-stepped to push him away, something cold zapped between us. Something *wrong*. His eyes lit up like fire blazed behind them. Our skin met and we were separated by a blast of **atramentous power**. It blinded me, and I didn't regain my sight until my body slapped the brick wall.

Pain fissured across my psyche. My radiocom buzzed with a two-hour warning, and I fought hard to keep my eyes open. But I could hear them, the leviathans. I'd been too distracted with the boy, and the leviathans had circled the block and were now closing in on us. I could fight off one, or two, but a horde?

I wiped the sweat from my face and righted my hair, and then stood upright. The boy did the same, and when we faced each other, only a few feet apart, I realized his body was aflame. Blue fire surrounded him, but he wasn't burning. He was perfectly fine. I knew he didn't understand what was happening, though. He glanced down at his hands and spun the sparks between his fingers. He then glared at me, green-hazel eyes covering me with bewilderment. And now that his hood was down, I saw the exact moment uncertainty set in.

Because I, too, was covered in blue flames. It didn't hurt and I couldn't feel it, yet I staggered back anyway, amazed at how easily I'd drawn from my abilities. But so had he. Just like he'd mimicked my every move, his fires imitated my fires too. The both of us a blaze of blue, wild energy. When I moved and my flames swished left, so did his, nipping at me with tiny flickers.

I spoke, steeling my mind against whatever wicked abilities he'd unleash next. "Did Manis send you?"

"I don't know who that is," he said nonchalantly, dropping his hands. He closed his eyes and concentrated. When he opened them again, his flames died out, cutting mine off as well. Like I was attuned to him. "But I followed the voice inside my head and it led me to you."

"It's called a conscience."

"Not that one." He smirked, flashing a row of straight teeth. "And why would it lead me to you? We're not supposed to have a conscience."

He knew I was different? He knew *he* was different? That changed everything, because Manis wouldn't send a broken legionary after me. Or would he? "So you're not like—"

"The five million other legionaries pumped through the veins of Caeshua? *No.* They couldn't exactly … control me." He shoved a hand in his pants pocket and raked the other down his face. Though I was no longer a threat to him, his stance remained timid. When he wasn't trying to throw me off his back, he seemed like someone else altogether.

"Then you're like me. From Silo?"

"I don't remember where I came from," he said.

I took a step away and squinted. I didn't remember much either, but I knew where I came from. That was something. "You don't remember? As in ... you forgot?" I gauged.

He sized me up once, eyes searching mine, then said, "I think so. I try to leave here, but I can't."

"Can't?"

He nodded. "I keep coming back."

It was a hard assumption, but he could have been a lost member of my legion, or from Silo. Maybe he'd forgotten for the same reasons I did. Maybe he was someone from my past.

He walked a slow circle around me. He was curious; he couldn't figure out what I was. I'd seen very little of the male legionaries in Silo, but I was sure none of them appeared the way he did. His face was too expressive, though his thoughts remained caged within the fortress of his mind. How strange it was, to feel someone in your head but be unable to comprehend *them*.

"Do you recognize me?"

"No," he said without hesitating. "I heard your thoughts from a block away and thought you were a Reaper. You wouldn't be the first one around here."

"You mean a Generator."

He stopped pacing. "Generators operate at Silo, where they guard and aid legionaries. Reapers are the ones who collect our dead bodies when the leviathans are done chewing on our remains."

"They're flying the crafts," I gathered. The Reapers were the ones who searched A10 every three hours, not the Generators. "Who are they looking for?"

"You, I imagine. Something tells me you're no average legionary if you can hear my thoughts so well."

It was the third time he'd mentioned it, and it confused me more and more. "I could say the same thing about you. Your thoughts cut right through my mind." I arched a brow, daring him to deny it.

Then he smiled. He was always smiling. "I think we can help each other."

I opened my mouth to question him, but he swiftly drew a gun from a holster at his back. He went from relaxed to tense in no time at all.

My body revved to move out of the way, but he snatched my shoulder and turned me into him so that my back met his chest. The trigger clicked and a bullet shot a writhing leviathan in the throat. It screeched like he'd set it on fire. With filthy hands, it ripped at its face until a black, wraith-like vapor escaped its mouth. And then its body dropped—only feet from where I was standing.

"See, now you owe me," he said, his breath on my neck.

I shrugged him off as the thundering footfalls of more leviathans approached. He holstered his gun and took my arm. He was like Petra, constantly pulling me to go somewhere. I walked alongside him like we hadn't just spent the last twenty minutes attacking each other. My feet moved, but I wasn't paying much attention to where he was leading. My eyes were glued to the quickly disintegrating body behind us.

"That bullet—"

"—Was made of amber. Only thing that kills them," he answered. "That and dismemberment."

"Normal bullets don't do it?"

We reached the other end of the alley, where the road seemed clear and the tower hovered a few feet away. He paused to load his gun. The yellow-orange bullets were small and smooth, and I wondered where he found them, because I'd spent hours searching for anything as little as a knife, and all sixteen bunkers had turned up empty.

"Silver bullets slow them down. It'll save you a minute or two if you're in a tight situation, but nothing more."

Dammit.

"How fast can you run?" he asked.

I smirked. "Is that a trick question?"

"Good point." My radiocom chirped incessantly, alerting me to the oncoming leviathans, and he handed me a gun. The black metal felt heavy in my hands. "Shoot their heads. If you can't, shoot anywhere close. The amber is like poison. It's most effective if it doesn't have to travel far." He tapped his temple and I understood. In order to put a leviathan completely down, I had to keep the gun up. A glass shard to the eye wouldn't do it.

I watched him as he readied his second gun. Most of his hair spilled to one side, drawing attention to the way he sneered while concentrating, his eyebrows drawn down and gaze searching. I was addicted to emotion and physical nuances, and he had so many. I couldn't trust him, yet something in me told me I had to. That he was my only way out of A10, and that he wouldn't have given me a loaded gun if he didn't, in some way, trust me too.

"We'll run toward the city and get in if we're quick."

I nodded, moving in the direction of the tower. But his hand grabbed my waist, stopping me. With amusement in his eyes, he pointed in the other direction, to where the leviathans had circled the block. Their screeching called from a nearby street. "The city is that way."

"What? But we're in the city."

"This isn't A10," he said with conviction. I was ready to call out his lie when he continued. "The leviathans ravaged most of the city years ago. When the Ward went up, people fled beneath it, leaving this," he motioned to the disgusting alley, "to the leviathans. The real city is further inland."

I was taken aback by what he said—and by the thought that I had wasted so much energy here. My legion could have been in the *real* A10 all this time. "Take me there, now," I said.

He looked at me like I was foreign. "You got a name?"

"It's Mathai."

"Muh-thai," he pronounced. "I'm Jon."

"Take me to the city, *Jon*."

He laughed, and my breath was instantly caught. Why was he so interesting to look at?

Don't trust him! a voice in my mind screamed. I snuffed it out and gripped the gun.

"We're going to get along just fine," he said.

He spun and broke into a jog toward the city he claimed was the true A10. As I followed him, eyes tracking the pack of leviathans, I wondered if he knew the code on the back of his neck was gone.

SEVENTEEN

"WANTED"
BIONIC: MATHAI-0329

I*t took us exactly forty* minutes. Twenty minutes to escape the leviathans and hop a barricade that led to A10, Jon's hand in mine as we moved quickly to get over; five minutes to recalibrate my radiocom, and another ten to slip past the Ward in disguise as legionaries returning from a crusade.

We progressed in line behind the hundred others, and I admired the colorful, burning sky and the clouds that floated like bundles of cotton in the air. The pathways glowed below my feet and people zoomed by in sleek vehicles with talking screens. I jumped to stay out of their way, surprised by their speed. And although it was near nightfall, I saw the homes beyond the silver bridges and the lights that flickered on inside them.

Jon snatched me out of line moments before a Generator spotted us, and we walked the remaining five minutes to the corner of a street, swaying namelessly through traffic. We took a main avenue south. Since he didn't specify where we were going, I assumed he was taking me to another hideout. Somewhere to lie low for a while and rest up. Perhaps wash. We were covered in foul leviathan blood, which clung to my skin like a gel. Jon's jacket was splattered with it, turning it from a dark grey to black.

He stopped abruptly and I slammed into his back, my tired legs working to keep me upright. That was when I realized we were standing across the road from a small parlor with a flashy, neon sign that read OPEN.

"Why are we here?" I asked, hiding my face behind my hair as a passerby stared too long. I didn't want to take any chances.

"Food," Jon said. "Come on."

We waited for a car to fly pass, and then crossed the street. When we entered the store, a bell chimed on the door and a woman behind the counter turned to watch us. There was nothing more here than a few shelves of food, all pre-packaged and arranged by row. And though I hadn't thought about my hunger in a while, I wasn't one to deny a proper meal.

"You have money?"

"No," Jon answered, his new favorite word. "So be quick about it."

He made for the third aisle while I remained in place. I glanced from the woman at the counter to the other people shopping around, perusing the store without noticing we'd come in.

We have to steal, I told myself with a frown. *Or I'll starve after my cans run dry.*

I disappeared down an aisle marked with a two. The stands carried little bags in various shapes and colors. When I picked one up and shook it by my ear, Jon hissed from the next aisle down, giving me a stupid look. But how else was I supposed to know what it was? I didn't understand how things worked outside of Silo. I had to relearn most of everything. And even though many things seemed simple, they baffled me. Like these bags—were they edible? Or was I supposed to wait for something to happen?

Indecisive, I put the bag down and picked up another, giving it a gentle shake. After moving through the entire aisle like this, I settled on a yellow one. The image of the food on the front of it looked good enough. It had to be better than nothing, right? Before I changed my mind again, I grabbed more, settling for six bags after Jon practically began jumping up and down and screaming for me to stop making so much noise. I smiled at him and waved, and he rolled his eyes.

A man followed me to the next aisle. He eyed a wrapped cake for a long minute, like he'd never seen something so good before. When he thought I looked away, he shoved it in his pocket and discreetly moved on. No one seemed to see him but me. It made me feel guilty, though, and guilt was an emotion I'd never had to process. I juggled the bags in my hands, counting them even though I knew the exact number, and swore I'd find a way to replace them.

While I strolled with hesitation, taking whatever caught my eye, Jon was on a mission for something. He skipped several lanes and I lost him near the back, where they kept food behind freezer doors. These aisles were colder and narrower. I shivered, and the lights above blinked in time with my footsteps. The woman behind the counter continued to watch me as I swung open the fourth freezer door. Really, I couldn't blame her. I was covered in blood and I'd tucked my gun into the back of my pants. If I wasn't the ugliest thing she'd ever seen, I was definitely in the top ten.

A gust of air from behind the freezer door hit me in the face. When it cleared, I was certain the purple vials, lined up in neat columns, weren't food. I leaned closer and tried to read their labels, but it all looked like gibberish to me. Another language, perhaps? Every freezer along the wall had them, each one containing a different color liquid. The man who'd stolen the cake returned, reaching in and taking one out. Without reading what it was, he pocketed it and walked away.

Maybe it was some kind of drink?

I shifted my food bags to one hand and stretched an arm into the freezer, my mind set on grabbing the green one in the third row from the very back. But just as my fingertips touched the cap of the vial, Jon caught my wrist.

"You like touching me, don't you?" I grumbled.

"That's not for you." He ignored my dig. "It's Evermore—a narcotic."

"In a public store?"

He shrugged, and I noted he held very little—a square, palm-sized case and a bottle of water. "I've seen worse."

I shut the freezer and headed back the way I came, gradually slipping the food bags under my shirt. They formed an uneven, abnormal bump. There was no way this wasn't obvious. "I don't think this looks—"

"*...In lieu of the missing legionaries. They are dangerous and reports from Presidium say they are armed...*" A holographic screen tethered to the ceiling was broadcasting a video of legionaries escaping Silo. Though there had been hundreds of us, they zoomed right in on my face, displaying everything from my false name to my height and age. "*They escaped seventy-two hours ago, with intent to harm all non-bionic bystanders. If you see these faces...*"

"We have to go," I called, but my voice was too quiet.

They showed my face for a second longer, and then ran through a list of other rogue legionaries. The last one, to my surprise, was Jon. They placed our faces side-by-side, slapping '**Wanted**' across the blurred shots. Like they *knew* we were together.

I forced myself not to panic, but dread ate away at me regardless. Anyone who saw the footage would be able to identify me. A new outfit wouldn't change that.

"Jon—"

"Keep walking." He casually slid in beside me, staying close as he steered me toward the exit. I didn't say anything, but I knew he saw his face up there too. I knew he saw that *I* saw. If he didn't escape Silo with the rest of us, why was he wanted? How long had he been missing? Did he really not remember? Because he was tense again, like when he'd pulled the trigger on a leviathan. Jon had two modes, and I understood neither.

We bypassed lane five, then stopped dead in our tracks. Five men with poorly concealed weapons were approaching from a door at the rear of the shop, and the one in the middle was the one who'd followed me around each aisle. Their attention was dead set on us.

Jon and I shared a quick look, thinking the same thing as the large men advanced. I dropped my bags and we swiveled in one smooth motion, at the same time, switching sides and drawing our guns from our backs. All thoughts of food flew from my mind as I targeted one man's shoulder, then another's leg. I pulled the trigger without thinking. Jon's gun clicked nonstop, and the second the men stopped to take cover behind racks, we tore back up the lane. Not even a moment later, bullets were ringing past our heads and shooting through the walls.

"You're wanted!" I spat, pulling Jon left while keeping low.

"Long story," was all he had to say. The woman at the counter was on the phone, talking fast. I had a bad feeling she was reporting us.

We ducked behind a row of fruit and I stopped to catch my breath. After Jon did a swift scan of where the men were shooting from, he pointed left. "Cover me."

Wait.

He jumped into the confusion, shooting twice before ducking into the next aisle. One of the men went down with a gurgling cry and I took the opportunity to fire at his bearded friend. He was smarter, though, and instead of shooting directly at me, he shot the light above my head, causing sparks to fly around the aisle and throw off my aim. By the time I was able to look over again, he had moved to another lane, much closer.

And he didn't stop. He shot round after round with a gun two times bigger than mine until I began to think the stands of fruit shielding me wouldn't hold up.

They must have seen the video, I thought. They must have seen us walk in and known who we were the whole time. They weren't Silo's men, that was for sure, and I'd never come across anyone like them before. So they weren't Outliers. They were too unstable, rushed to get the job done. One wore a suit and another wore rags for clothes. They weren't in sync at all. If anything, they were lackeys here to reap some reward for returning rogue legionaries.

"Mathai!" Jon called. He waved for me to cross over, even though bullets were still pinging through the air at random. He saw this and thought better, jumping into the middle of the lane and pelting a large tray of pies at the shooter. It was a distraction; the tray volleyed through the shop like a disk and Jon shot straight through the silver metal, killing the man with a bullet to the head.

Deep breathing yanked my focus from Jon and I turned to meet a man with his arms thrown out. By the time I thought to react, he'd already wrapped his hands around my neck and pressed down on my trachea. He was wearing a dark mask with cutouts for his eyes and mouth, and he was grinning eerily, like he'd just made his first kill and was sweeping in for the second.

My body went haywire, my gun falling to the ground and slipping beneath the racks. With about eight seconds of air left, I put my hands to work, clawing at his face and digging my thumbs into his eye sockets. He howled in pain and loosened his grip a fraction, and I peeled back his control, cutting into his psyche. All minds had a framework of walls that, when distracted by other means, crumbled under pressure.

His snapped like a rubber band.

With my mind latched to his, I compelled him to release me. Then I bent his fingers away from my throat, breaking three digits in the process. I deftly elbowed his chest and put him in a chokehold—all while keeping Jon in my peripheral. My movements were instinctual, recalled from my past. I only hesitated when the masked man began to struggle.

"Hungry?" I picked up an apple from the stand and shoved it between his teeth, cutting his scream short. I tightened my arms around his neck and pressed in until his eyes rolled back and his body slumped. When I was sure he was unconscious, I dove for my gun and shot one of the guys headed for Jon. The bullet clipped his shoulder without slowing him, so at the last minute I focused hard and used my abilities to throw his body through a freezer door. Jon shot a round into the last guy and added to the bodies around us.

I smirked. "Now you owe me."

I thought I was damned hilarious, but Jon was still serious. He sighed and examined the shop for any more of bizarre men. He found no one, and even the woman from the front counter was gone. She'd probably run when she had the chance. Putting his gun back in its holster, he motioned toward the door. "We need to go."

"Go where?"

"Anywhere we're not wanted," he said, his jaw clenched.

We escaped out the back door like the thieves and killers we were. But before I walked away and into the night with Jon, I spun around and shot a bullet into the screen still booming our names. The photographs of our faces fizzled to a static, and then to black.

They knew we were together.

They knew where we were.

EIGHTEEN

"POISON"
BIONIC: MATHAI-0329

The moons hung low for us that night.

Jon and I left the food shop behind and walked through A10 with our heads down the entire time. I followed him silently, trepidation in my every step. It felt like we walked forever. He offered to hold my bag several times, but I refused. The drawing of the eye still burned in my back pocket and my bag offered an inexplicable comfort, like I had control over my life even though it was rapidly unraveling in front of me.

Jon finally grew tired of walking and led me down a side street, where several people lay around but minded their own business.

"What is this?" I asked, eyeing the weeping old woman across the way.

"Our bed for the night," Jon said. He slid down the rough concrete wall and sat. I hated that he knew this city better than me. I hated that I had to trust him, and I had so many questions.

But I didn't ask them all at once. I sat next to him and allowed myself to rest for the first time since earlier that morning. The silence grew thick as I rehashed every moment in the shop, as I knew he was doing too. The way we'd been so close to being discovered.

Because we were wanted.

Suddenly, Jon spoke. "I took these for you." I looked over and he held out a yellow bag; the same one I'd tried taking from the shop. Why would he do that for me?

Despite myself, I was thankful. I reached out to take it and his gaze shifted to my arm. I didn't notice until right then, but my bandages had unknotted and were covered in blood—leviathan and mine. Moving fast, Jon began to unwrap my bound hand. I was stunned. No one had ever touched me without ill intent, save for Petra. I slapped a hand over his, and we glared at each other, waiting for the other to speak.

"You're hurt," he told me.

"I-I can't take them off," I said. I tried to pull away, but his grip was firm.

"You can put the bandages back on; relax. I'll just clean them first."

I couldn't find the words, and an infection was literally the last thing I wanted, so I nodded, giving him my arm. I took in his hazel-green eyes, wondering how long I had to stare into them before I understood him, like his eyes were the key to the enigma of his mind. His tan fingers slid against mine as he carefully exposed the cut I'd gotten from stabbing the leviathan with glass, his skin smooth. Not flawless, but the glide of his touch sent chills down my spine, shock through my psyche. It emptied my head. The constant flow of numbers and words that droned in my mind were quieted when he touched me. And all over again, I became unusually enamored with him.

He slid his fingers over the cut and I winced. "Is it bad?"

"Could be worse," he said.

I pulled my bag off my shoulders and handed it to him. I only had the things I'd stolen from the leviathan-riddled outlands and my codex, but he'd have to make do. I studied him as he sifted through the bag, eventually taking out a bottle of water and offering me my jacket, saying, "The nights get cold."

I accepted it wordlessly. Did he sleep outside a lot? Was he homeless?

He doused my bandages with the water from my bottle until the red stains turned pink and wrung them out, concentrating, but I sensed he wanted to say more. I caught him looking at me in the same way I assumed I was looking at him—with wonder, speculation, concern.

Pouring the rest of the water over my wound, I asked, "Why are you wanted?"

"I think..." he began. A dimple appeared over his left eyebrow as he thought about it. "I think I was an important asset to Silo once." He worked his fingers into my skin, removing the dried blood. The fact that he was doing all of this with his bare hands wasn't lost on me. And I realized that I didn't want him to stop touching me. "Maybe I ran away.

Maybe I was afraid."

"You don't remember that either?" When he shook his head slightly, I understood him. At least in this. "I lost my memory, too. I don't remember what my favorite color is, but I can't imagine what it must feel like to not know where you come from."

"But you don't know who you are," he said frankly. He had a point.

"Does anybody?"

"I suppose not, but when you're number one on Silo's most wanted list, it's kind of important, you know?"

Another point for Jon.

Nothing else really mattered if you didn't know who you were, and I'd never know until I unlocked the memories of my past. So far all I had was my codex and meaningless dreams.

"I think I have a sister," I said before I could stop myself.

Jon moved away to wring the bandages one more time and I sighed at the loss of contact. "How?"

"I don't know. It was a dream. I... I remember some stuff from my past."

"Past?" He looked me in the eyes and I so badly wanted to know what he was thinking.

"I'm a lot stranger than I appear to be. Mysterious, too."

He grinned. "So I'm learning. What does your sister look like?"

"I'm not sure. I've only seen her in my dreams. She could look like anything ... if she's real."

"So you have a sister *and* you dream?" He folded up my now-clean bandages while laughing to himself. I laughed too, and for no reason at all. Nothing was funny. If anything, it was sad. But his laughter was infectious, sweet. Better than any narcotic. "You are strange."

He placed the bandages in my lap, his face close, and I sobered up right away. I wanted to deny it, but couldn't. Jon was doing something to me and I didn't know how to stop it. I looked away first to inspect my wound. Only, there was no longer a wound. I touched my arm and met smooth, unmarked skin, like I'd hallucinated the whole thing.

"You heal fast," he said. "I'm guessing you didn't know?"

I shook my head, feeling incompetent. I'd never bled to know. "You said you heard me in your head. How?"

"I heard your thoughts. You were scared, anxious." His hands slid over my skin, higher up my arm. The wound was gone and my bandages were clean. He had no reason to touch me, but I had a feeling he didn't know how to stop either. "You were thinking about the tower. I felt the barriers around your mind, but they didn't stop me. They let me in."

Why would they do that? I wondered.

"A friend helped me escape from Silo. She didn't give me much information, but she said it was important that I find my legion." I scratched my brow with my free hand, then added, "We left for a crusade a while ago, never came back. I might have been someone else at the time..." I was mumbling and making little sense. Jon only watched me silently. "I-I think you might be one of them."

"Someone from your legion?"

I nodded.

He thought about the possibility. It was bizarre, but I wanted to believe it was true. That my legion wasn't already dead.

His fingertips passed over my knuckles and a jolt of energy jumped through my system. I brushed it off until it happened again, though this time with intense pain. Jon grunted like he felt it as well. I tried to pull away, but when I glanced at our hands together, I was shocked to see a web of black veins crawling up my arm, draining the color of my skin to grey.

The pain felt like a nail to the heart as someone beat it in with a hammer. Jolt after jolt choked me up until Jon finally let go, breathing in lungfuls of air. Once we were no longer touching, the pain receded. The color in my hands returned and the black veins vanished beneath my skin.

"What was—"

"I don't know," I said, turning my hands over. Did I do that? His touch had been addicting, until it wasn't.

I snatched up my clean bandages and, even though they were still damp, began wrapping up my arm.

"Mathai—"

"I don't know how to control my abilities, okay? I didn't even know I had them until a few days ago." And I didn't want them if it meant I hurt everyone I touched. Was this why Umbra, Petra's friend, had told me to keep my hands bound?

I wrapped faster, my focus on the other people in the street who were crowding around a fire barrel with scraps of food. I watched them without thinking, moving the fabric back and forth. When my hands began to shake, Jon touched me anyway, knotting the bandages for me.

And he wasn't afraid.

"I don't know how to control my abilities either," he said to me. "I could have been poisoning you."

"Wrong." He packed everything back into my bag, and then leaned against the wall. He was staring into the distant fire when I whispered, "Between the two of us, I'm the **poison**."

He didn't know the true meaning behind my words, but I did.

I knew where I came from; I knew who they created me to be.

And I *was* afraid.

"I'll help you find your legion," Jon said. "And you'll help me find my past."

I wanted to insist that the two might have been interconnected, but I was too tired. After minutes spiraled into hours and our silence became a comfort, I began to fall asleep. Fewer people remained in the street and Jon spoke, probably more to himself. But I felt him turn to me as my head drifted sleepily to his shoulder.

I dreamed of two birds in the sky. They circled above the street, their wings an iridescent silver. They spoke into my mind in the same way Jon had. They were watching us, I felt them. They were here and they were coming for us.

NINETEEN

"THIS GIRL"
BIONIC: JONATHUS-6243

She was the tiniest thing. Mathai, she called herself. She frightened me ... and then intrigued me in the cruelest way possible. My eyes darted around the street, observing everyone and everything like I always did, assuring that no one came too close. But when I looked at her face—her full, heart-shaped lips as they parted while she slept—I didn't feel the need to look anywhere else. Time was ceaseless. My mind went blank.

For the first time, my mind went blank.

I didn't want to move; I barely wanted to breathe around her, for fear I'd do or say something wrong to scare her off. And I wanted her to stay so badly. The reason for it gnawed at the corners of my mind, but nothing conjured any memory.

Though she reminded me of myself, when I'd awoken in my pod. She wielded her strength and perseverance like a gilded sword, and regardless of her shift to a world unknown to her, she was brave. And she was beautiful.

I feared she was too beautiful for Caeshua—for what we were about to face. Because everything ugly and dark lay ahead, and I knew, beyond any doubt, that she'd charge, flames blazing, into the chaos. I wouldn't be able to stop her or slow her down. I'd have to stand beside her, protect her. But if that was all I could do, I'd do it.

I'd do it.

My gaze shifted to her feather-like eyelashes as they fluttered against her cheeks. She was dreaming. I shouldn't have done it, but my palm itched, and disregarding the feeling was no longer a choice. I brought my hand up to her face and felt her lips. She was lightness and I was the terror in the night, starving for even a sliver of her glory. My touch would mar her beauty—dirty it, destroy it, break it. But I didn't care.

I was selfish as I watched her sleep, reveling in her nearness. She didn't have to know, but I lost myself in the sight of her. I wanted to know the inner workings of her mind. My hand slid to her neck and I felt her racing pulse against my fingertips. If she woke now, would she move away in disgust? Or would she crave my touch like she had before?

I tucked a curl behind her ear and the black veins appeared. They moved with my hand, draining her face of color. Her heart slowed and she pulled in a shuttering breath. I was a bastard, because I didn't let go until I absolutely had to.

Two minutes.

That's all I had.

I returned my hand to my side and clenched it, staring into the night that bludgeoned my hope.

And I knew, beyond any doubt, that I was going to kill **this girl**.

TWENTY

"OUTLIERS"
BIONIC: MATHAI-0329

Jon woke me before daybreak with a nudge to my side. A light sleeper, I shot up and rubbed my eyes until everything stopped spinning. "What time is it?" I groaned.

He was already standing, his arms crossed as he looked down at me. The sun peeked from behind the clouds and voices sounded from the main avenue.

"A little after sixth hour," he said. I peeked at my radiocom and it read the same. "But there's someone I need to take you to."

"Can they help me find my legion?" I stood, grabbing my bag, and righted my frizzed hair. Though one side refused to stay down.

"Maybe," Jon said, averting his gaze. "Do you know what they look like?"

Yeah, you. "No, but I imagine they're lost and forgetful too."

"Then we'll start there."

I tailed him through the street until we merged with the hustling crowds of A10. There were too many people, far more than I was used to. We stood shoulder-to-shoulder with strangers, only moving a few inches at a time. Red and green traffic lights told us when to stop and go. The large crowds made sense if hundreds of people had fled beneath the protection of the Ward, but didn't they worry about overpopulation? How did anyone make it anywhere on time?

Jon curved right and I followed the top of his head through the throng. He stopped before a platform as a shimmering glass bridge slid out and stretched across the chasm between buildings. While I was distracted, a group of little girls pushed me like they couldn't get me out of the way fast enough. They stepped onto the platform and it began transporting them across the sky, until they exited on the other side of the city. Silo had skybridges … but never like this. They never moved.

"Do you marvel at everything?" Jon asked, and I sensed the humor in his tone.

"Only everything." Biting my lip in concentration, I stepped to the edge of the platform and then leaped, landing on the glass beyond with a *yip*. My footprints left colorful spots on the bridge, and because I absolutely couldn't get enough of it, I tapped my feet around in several circles.

"You're like a child," Jon said, stepping up behind me. The bridge began to move and I slid around the glass walkway, awed by the sixty-foot drop and the cars that flew back and forth through the sky.

"If being a child means I get to see everything like this," I looked back at him, trying to read his mind and getting nothing, "then yeah, I'm a child."

We exited the bridge to the less-crowded side of the city and moved toward the broad streets, where very few people roamed, and the homes looked more like tall apartments with round windows and slanted doors. A neighborhood, I understood. And based on the silence, everyone was still asleep. We walked to the fifth building with black gates and climbed through the yard. The grasses were tall but neat, and the pebbled pathway to the stairs had been entirely uprooted from the soil. I had to jump around scraps of machinery hiked the stairs to the second door. It had a letter *N* on it, a mailbox stuffed to the brim with unopened letters.

"Who lives here?" I whispered as Jon knocked on the door.

"A friend," he said. When no one answered, he knocked again. "Hopefully."

On his third try, the door was yanked back an inch and someone peeked out, hesitant. "Jonathus, is that you?" a voice creaked.

Jonathus?

He nodded and the person behind the door gasped and quickly shut the door to unlock it. When it opened again, an older woman with a freckled face jumped into his arms, hugging him close. She instantly began to cry. "You're alive? You haven't used your abilities in public, have you?" she asked, pulling away to touch his face, making sure all the parts were still there.

Jon smiled and I watched their interaction closely. Was this his mother? He said it was his friend, but how had they met?

"I said I'd be right back," he told her, looking slightly embarrassed.

"Yes, but the riots at Silo had me worried. There were all those—"

He pulled away and the woman finally saw me. Her features turned from delighted to frightened, and I stood there nervously, not knowing what to do.

"This is—"

"Ari," the woman finished for Jon. "I recognize your eyes from the most wanted ad."

I cringed. "My real name is Mathai."

"Yes. Mathai Porter," she said.

Jon glanced between us like he sensed the unspoken words. All his confusion was directed at me, however, because I hadn't told him a thing about who I was at Silo. And it was a horribly long story.

"Come in, then," said the woman. "Sit, sit." She rushed us into her home and I was immediately hit with a warm, pleasant smell. She was cooking something in the little kitchen to the right of the sitting room. Her walls were covered in maps and photographs, leaving no room for anything else, and potted plants occupied nearly every surface. Though it was small and lit only by scented candles, her home was comfortable.

We gathered around a wooden table after she locked the door, and I sat my bag on the floor. "How do you know my name?" I asked.

Jon answered for her. "This is Niana, a technician who used to work for Presidium at Silo. She's taken care of me all my life."

In other words, she used to be a Jacket. A *female* Jacket. "You're his mother?"

"Something like that," Niana said. She clasped her hands in front of her on the table—nervous too, but also curious. She had slanted, animated eyes that crinkled at the corners and brown hair streaked with strands of grey. "I began caring for Jonathus when he was a small boy. I saw what Presidium had planned for him and I couldn't bear to be a part of it. The life of a legionary is ... *no good*. So after I spent years researching and identifying ways to destroy the virus, I was thrown out of Silo. And I snuck Jon out with me; I had to. Now I help him remember."

The virus. Me. I shifted uncomfortably in my seat and moved my attention to the room, wanting to look away from them. Jon *was* from Silo, then. Niana stole him—to protect him, I presumed—but not before they took away his memories like they'd done to me. "So you know who I am?"

"Mathai or Ari?" Niana asked. "Because if you're referring to Mathai, we've met before. You were about five years old or so. A head full of hair, bright eyes, and a penchant for hiding things in your pockets." She grinned, then immediately sobered. "But you were often troubled, never obedient."

"Do you know why I don't remember anything? They told me I went out on a crusade—"

"And you were the only one to survive," Niana finished, nodding. "All lies."

I held my breath, rubbing the underside of the table. Why had I believed anything Manis told me? "So I didn't leave for a crusade?"

Instead of answering right away, Niana stood, pressing down her ankle-length skirt, and moseyed to the kitchen. There, she put a tea bag in a cup and poured hot water from a kettle over it. While she did this I looked at Jon, trying to understand why he'd brought me to this woman. Was she supposed to help me remember? Or were we just passing through? I had a list of places I had to search in each asylum—and I didn't have time to kill.

"What are we doing here?" I whispered.

"I suppose you have the patience of a child as well," he retorted, rolling up his sleeves to reveal biceps of corded muscles. Nothing huge, like you'd see on someone trained to lift weights, but toned, like he spent hours a day engrossed in hard labor. He joined Niana in the kitchen and helped her strain the tea, leaving me alone with my thoughts. I teetered on the edge of my seat, caught between wanting to blurt a million questions and run for the door. In the end, I waited for them and tried my best to chill my frazzled nerves.

"Do you know your story, child?" Niana asked, appearing from the kitchen with a tray. She set it down at the middle of the table and slid a flower-painted mug to me. The tea smelled sweet, like the fruit cans in my bag.

"Of how we were created?" I sipped from my mug, eyeing the mint leaves that floated around the bottom. Then, though the tea was hot, I swigged it down and held the mug out for more. "I don't know much beyond what they told me. We were trained to kill leviathans, right?"

"Right. But you..." She stopped pouring the tea into my cup and placed her hand over mine. Her knowing eyes pierced right through me, and I knew she was going to say it. She was going to tell Jon. "You're different."

"How different?" Jon asked, standing now with his back pressed against the wall, a leg propped up.

"*Different*, different," Niana said. She set down the teapot and sighed. "I was there for the testing of the Y-506 virus, when Mathai, the last legionary to undergo the procedure, tested positive. It didn't kill her; she killed *it*. Took it in and made it a part of her."

Jon looked at me cautiously then, like the innocent girl he'd imagined me to be had vanished ... and a monster took her place. "The virus? As in the virus animating those black-eyed—"

"Yeah," I said, flinching. "That virus."

"You are to feel no shame in my home," Niana said. She sat in the chair next to me and busied her hands with the tablecloth. I understood her motherly appeal—her calm voice and caring touch. I much preferred her to Generators and a submerged pod. "The erasure of memories is standard protocol for legionaries. It removes all recollection of what you might have seen when you were out defending the Ward. That way thoughts don't haunt you, or distract you from executing your next crusade."

"That's some Ward." Jon scoffed. "Now they want us dead."

"No, not dead. Thirteen years ago, when I was there, they began using the chair for other means. Especially for you, Mathai. Maybe even for Jon."

"What does that mean?" I leaned closer to Niana. My right leg jittered under the table in unease at what she might say, but I had to know what information she had. "What did they do?"

"It happened after I left with Jon. They said you went with your legion on a crusade, but it was all lies. Terrible lies. You left to return to the others, to report back. You were secretly undermining Presidium and it was all *choice*." She swallowed and I fed off her anxiety. "Mathai, legionaries aren't programmed with choice."

I'd discovered that not even two days after waking in Silo. I was supposed to be a mindless machine, and I wasn't. Neither was Jon.

"What *others*?" he asked.

"The others are—" Niana's face lit up and she stood and retreated down a curtained hallway that must have led to the bedrooms.

When she was well out of earshot, Jon asked, "Why didn't you tell me?"

"What, that I'm Silo's lapdog and most skilled killer? Gee, that conversation would have gone over well."

"Things aren't adding up."

"Welcome to the last four weeks of my life," I mumbled.

Niana returned before Jon could respond. She pushed aside the curtains and walked toward us, holding a large book in her hands. It had to have over a thousand pages. She dropped it on the table, rattling the teacups, and opened to a marked page.

"I never saw them, but I heard things. They were wild outsiders that dedicated their lives to returning the leviathans to the sky. They were against creating legionaries."

"I went to see them?"

"I believe so." Niana skimmed through the page in search of something. She stopped on the ninth paragraph and pulled a pair of glasses from her shirt pocket. Sliding them onto her face, she said, "I wrote it right here. They believed that by separating the virus from Silo, they stood a better chance of defeating the leviathans left to roam Caeshua. No virus, no monsters."

"So they wanted to destroy me?" I asked, dumbfounded.

Niana looked at me. "No, not destroy. *Use*."

"She worked for them?" Jon asked.

This was too surreal, and I was more of a weapon than I had first thought. Was I really that expendable?

"Taking you against your will would have been too easy. Why not use Silo's own weapon against them?" Niana said. "Toughen the blow with your betrayal and it's a grand plan."

"But why would I work with them?"

"I can't be the one to say, child. It's possible Presidium believed you were working with them and gaining information they didn't have. When they couldn't pry it from you after you returned to Silo, they began stripping back the layers of the girls you became. One of them had to know."

Manis, I thought to myself. *What have you done?*

"But this isn't for certain, right? Maybe these people don't exist?" Jon started looking at the book with her, but I was suddenly too cold to care. And there weren't enough candles in the room to help.

"No, they're real. They called themselves ... something. Something with a K, or maybe a T? No, an *O!*" Niana removed her glasses and rubbed the bridge of her nose. "Overbearers, or the Officials ..."

"**Outliers.**"

"Yes, that's it!" Niana shouted. "How did you know?"

My right leg stopped thumping beneath the table ... only for my left one to pick up where the other stopped. To say I was anxious was an understatement. I was petrified. "They're the ones who helped me escape. Some were undercover, and I knew one of them. Her name was Petra. She's the one who told me to find my legion."

"*They* freed the legionaries?"

"Some," I corrected. I gripped my head to control my spinning thoughts. I couldn't decipher who the bad guy was in all of this, and it made me want to scream. "Most legionaries at Silo were the same—no emotion, always did what they were told—but there was a group of us who weren't. We were different. The Outliers knew because we fled the second we were given the choice. So they freed us."

"Why?" Jon asked.

"If I knew, maybe I wouldn't be here. But I am ... and I don't remember."

Jon shared a solemn look with Niana, then said, "There's something that may be able to help." He flipped toward the end of the book and I stood to peer over Niana's shoulder, trying to read the text.

"Did you write all of this?"

"Sure did," she said, and I glared at Jon. The book was long and thorough, with smudged notes in every margin. It must have taken decades of research to record all of it. Jon shook his head as if to say, *She's an old, crazy woman. Let it go.*

"This!" Niana suddenly pointed to a scraggly drawing, and I looked around the page in confusion. It had diagrams and colored arrows, and text written in different languages. The book was so old the edges of the page tore away as she held.

"This is going to help me remember? A circle?"

Jon choked down a laugh.

"No, child. It's a stone." Niana moved around me, carrying the book, and settled into a chair in the sitting room. Jon and I followed and sat on the floor in front of her draped furniture. She showed me her doodle again, emphatically waving her arms around as she explained. "A healing stone, born from fire. It can only be found near the Ucilei coast, but its healing properties are wild and beautiful. Take a look." She pointed to the paragraph below the stone and I read exactly what she told me. It seemed the stone was unusual, and a piece of what made the Ucilei coast sacred grounds. When acquired and mixed with other medicinal remedies, it was *otherworldly*, mending bones and curing the sick.

I read further, committing every word to memory. "Does Presidium know about these stones?"

"Yes, but they're considered an old practice."

"Niana believes they could help restore my memories," Jon said. "She's searched the markets, but no one's had a stone in years. Maybe decades, and gems of any kind are a rarity around A10. It's likely Presidium hid them."

"But we can try?" I looked up from the book hopefully, leaving a finger near the spine so that I didn't lose the page. "We'll just go to the Ucilei coast and get one."

"Mat—"

"Don't you want to know who you are?" I begged.

I had him there, and he glanced down at the book in my hands, weighing his options. Then he inhaled deeply, eyes going to Niana.

"You need to know, Jonathus," she agreed. Placing a hand over his, she smiled. And it was likely a smile reserved just for him. It said so much that I couldn't translate, but Jon knew. He nodded his head once and pulled away.

"Why don't you take a warm shower and I'll wash those clothes for you, Mathai?" Niana suggested, wrinkling her nose at my bloodstained outfit.

"I suppose a shower is necessary." Unwillingly, I tore my gaze from Jon and allowed her to lead me down the hallway to the bathroom. Jon stayed behind, seemingly lost in thought.

"He'll be okay," Niana told me with a pat to my shoulder. "He has you now."

TWENTY-ONE

"METHOD TO MY MADNESS"
BIONIC: MATHAI-0329

t the end of the hall, we came to two wooden doors. The one to the left led to the bathroom. Niana scooted me in and sat me down on the closed toilet seat. I pulled my bag to my chest as she moved about.

"Do you think I'm enough?" I asked her. Her hand slowed by the sink and I realized how oddly I'd phrased my words. "I mean, do you think I'm enough to help him?"

"Only time can tell." She withdrew things from the cabinet above the basin. "And you two have a lot of growing to do." Without explaining what she meant, she handed me a toothbrush and some toothpaste, and then set a bar of soap out by the tub. She finally motioned to my hair, which was no doubt as big as a nest. "When was the last time you brushed this?"

I shrugged. "Weeks ago?"

Niana *tsked* and went back to the cabinet, coming back with a comb with wide teeth. She called me over and when I moved in front of the mirror, she wet her hands beneath the running faucet and ran it through my hair, softening the curls.

"You must comb your hair every night, Mathai, or else you'll get knots."

I nodded numbly, and as she fixed my hair, I watched her in the mirror, trying to recall whether I'd had a mother to do these things for me; to teach me how to take care of myself.

Niana set the comb down now that my hair was soaking wet and left it hanging in loose, untangled curls. "There, isn't that pretty?" She moved my hair to the front of my shoulders so that it framed my face. I'd never considered myself pretty. Or *anything*, really. What made someone pretty or ugly? Was it my hair, my eyes? I couldn't imagine something so inconsequential was equivalent someone's self-worth.

"How far is the Ucilei coast?" I asked.

"A two-day trip by hovercraft," she said. "But I'm afraid you and Jon will have to make it by train and foot, since we don't have a craft. It may be a few hours longer."

I couple extra hours meant nothing to me if I could finally get my memories back.

"The territory hasn't been touched in years, but you'll find it." Her confidence in me, after only just meeting me, was disconcerting. Though

I supposed she assumed I was the same person I had been as a child. She left the comb on the sink, and then showed me how to work the shower.

"Leave your clothes by the door and I'll bring you new ones to wear in the meantime," she said. "Take as much time as you need."

She left the bathroom, closing the door behind her, and I counted to five before I set my bag down and began removing my dirty clothes. I switched the shower to the hottest setting and allowed it to run until fog clouded the air. I had every intention of taking my time. It was potentially my last shower for what could be days—a luxury I wasn't taking for granted.

When I unbuttoned the top of my pants, though, I remembered that I didn't have a towel. "Niana, I—"

I opened the door and Jon was there with a fluffy, purple towel in his hands. It was like we couldn't be apart for more than five minutes. He looked startled, like he'd been working up the courage to knock and hadn't expected me to open the door so quickly.

Hiding my body behind the door, I reached for the towel. "Thanks."

Our hands touched as I took it from him. It was only a brush of fingers, and there weren't any sparks or a fiery energy that called me to him ... but there was curiosity.

"I'll be across the hall if you need anything," he said, and I shut the door after he turned away. I tried to free my mind as I removed the rest of my clothes and the bandages on my hands, and hopped in the shower. I did a piss-poor job, though, because my thoughts shifted immediately to everything I'd learned. If I closed my eyes for too long, I envisioned leviathans scratching through the skin of my back while everyone in Silo laughed. They'd find humor in my tears, then piece me back together as whoever came after Mathai.

Standing completely beneath the water, I scrubbed my skin until dirt and blood ran down the drain. Then I rubbed some more, obsessed with being clean. I told myself that if I didn't have to see the blood on me, the thoughts wouldn't be so bad. But it was all lies. I washed my arms raw to the ticking of the numbers in my head, to the voices that never hushed and the calculations that refused to leave me alone. My scalp burned and the water grew too hot, but I couldn't stop. That was the worse part—not until it was gone.

In the silent breaks from my insanity, I wanted nothing more than to touch Jon's hand again.

I shut the water off quickly and pressed my forehead against the shower wall's tile. After sixteen deep breaths, I summoned the strength to step out and wrap the warm towel around my body.

There wasn't much in the bathroom save the shower, toilet, and sink. I stood in front of the mirror and wiped the condensation away until my reflection was clear. My blue and green eyes seemed more familiar now, but the color of my skin was washed out from days of unrest. Gingerly, I collected all my hair in a fist and pulled it back into a hair tie I'd found in the cabinet. I did my best to recall how Petra had spun my curls into a bun, but it didn't come together the same way, and the hairs at my nape started curling. I turned to the side to better see what I was doing in the mirror ... and the movement revealed the gaudy code on the back of my neck—0329.

Reaching to slide my finger over the permanent numbers, I thought of how bare Jon's neck was. I'd only seen a glimpse of it during our fight, but I was positive. He didn't have a code on him, and I now knew that it was because Niana had taken him away from Silo before they could mark him. To everyone outside this home, he appeared to be an ordinary boy. The irony of it all.

I cracked open the door and took the new clothes Niana had left for me in the threshold. The stripped bottoms were a little big, but the undergarments were just right. I assumed the shirt was one of Jon's because the hem dropped nearly to my knees. So I rolled it up, tucking it into my pants to keep it in place. When I finished my hair, I moved on to brushing my teeth, then bundled up my dirty clothes and walked out the bathroom.

A dancing light guided me down the dark hall. It took me to a small room and I saw Jon before seeing the bed and the dresser—and the loose sheets of paper scattered around his bedroom floor. He stood beside the bed, gazing down at something he'd laid out while he worried his bottom lip. I had so many questions for him; senseless questions, too. Like what was his favorite color, or his favorite book? Did he enjoy being alone in silence, or did he prefer the cacophony of crowds?

I tiptoed to the door and watched him open the small case he'd taken from the food shop. I'd thought it was a snack of some sort, but I could see now that it was actually a box of black, wooden pencils.

That's what he wanted to get?

He pulled a pencil out and twirled it lazily around his fingers. Next, he closed his eyes and focused, working the muscles of his jaw. I decided not to go in or bother him, because I liked watching him instead. And I did so for several minutes—until the moment seemed too private and my legs grew tired of standing. He was neither tense nor calm. He was a murky in between, and I liked it. Though I suspected that it was the perfect façade. He had to be as conflicted as I was, if not more.

"So you've lived here all your life?" I asked Niana, who was fussing around in the kitchen. She'd put me in the sitting room after rushing off to wash my clothes. While she told me stories of her past, I scribbled in the blank pages of my codex, replicating her vision of the healing stone so that I had it with me when I left.

"Yes, child," she said. "This was my parents' home, too. These walls hold many memories."

"Would you ever leave?"

She walked slowly from the kitchen with a steaming plate in her hands and I rushed to meet her halfway. Thankfully, it wasn't porridge. I slid the center table closer and set the meal of vegetables, stew, and bread down. As she spoke, I crossed my legs on the floor and dug in with a spoon.

"No, never. Home is home, and there isn't anywhere else for me to be. Or anywhere else I'd *want* to be."

"I want to be home too," I told her around a mouthful of bread.

"Finding your home isn't always about the house, Mathai. Sometimes it's about the people."

Jon walked in right then, freshly showered. In exchange for his hooded sweater, he'd donned a simple black t-shirt and grey pants. The wavy ends of his hair were darker when wet, and he pushed his hands through them, slicking the hair back and away from his eyes.

"I'll bring you food," Niana said, urging him to sit on the other side of my table. Though he looked reluctant to eat, he accepted a plate. He loved her, I could tell, and wanted to appease her.

I continued eating, scooping what looked like white, mashed food into my mouth. The flavor was new to me—buttery, yet not sweet—and I pushed everything else on my plate aside for it, eating with so much gusto that I was sure it got in my hair. I felt Jon's eyes on me, but glanced up only to grab another spoon from the table. It was *nonsense*, how amazing the food tasted.

Using both spoons, I funneled the vegetables into my mouth, working to consume everything faster and wondering why everyone didn't eat this way. Two spoons were definitely more useful than one, and Niana's cooking was better than any meal I'd had at Silo.

Then, from the corner of my eye, I caught Jon holding back a laugh. He did that a lot—laughing. "What? There's a **method to my** madness," I said, holding up my two spoons and licking the stew from around my mouth.

He smiled big and pointed to a napkin. "It's a good look."

"It's my *best* look."

When Niana returned to the sitting room, she held a tray of her own. She joined us at the table and we ate in silence until the scraping of plates became monotonous.

"How did you find her?" Niana finally asked Jon.

He stopped mid-chew to look at me, no doubt thinking the same thing I was. We couldn't exactly tell her that we'd about ripped each other's heads off in blind rage.

"We sort of ... um, ran into each other, actually," I explained.

Jon said, "I found her in the outlands, running from a pack of leviathans. She claims she didn't know, but she was projecting her thoughts clear across the city. That's what led me to her."

"She *what?*" Niana jumped and spilled her tea. Without bothering to clean it up, she said, "You heard her thoughts?"

"And I heard his. Is that normal?"

"It's normal... I just didn't think it'd be you two. Only members of a legion are synced that way."

"So then Jon's from my legion," I said too excitedly. "Even though you took him?"

"Legions are assigned at creation. I had no control over that."

Creation, not *birth*.

"Then where's the rest of the legion?" Jon asked.

"We'll find them. If they weren't taken from Silo like you were, then they were on that craft headed out with me. Which means they have to be somewhere in Caeshua." I wasn't done eating, but I moved my plate to pick up my codex. If Petra was a liar and she'd freed me for selfish reasons, the other members of my legion may not have been alive. But I had to get to them; I had to piece everything together, starting with them.

"There's a way. All six members of a legion are bound by more than codes. It's biology, it's science. You're drawn together by an uncontrollable force," Niana said.

Uncontrollable force. It explained why my fears ceased to exist when I was around Jon. Why my thoughts always circled back to him. He *had* to be in my legion. Maybe it was more than happenstance that brought us together in the alley.

"So we wander around until we feel a connection with someone?" I asked her.

She frowned. "It's not that simple, child. You'll know when you know."

Feeling restless, I flipped to the map in my codex and propped it up on the table. I pointed to Asylum 4, and then to the western region where the Ucilei coast was located. "Before I found Jon, I was going to visit A4 and search there. I'm still not sure where to look, but I figured it was a place to start."

"We'll pass through on our way to the coast. It's on our way, anyhow," Jon said, eyes tracing the details of the map. "Where did you get this?"

"Silo," I said curtly.

"They gave it to you?"

"I took it. They use it as some sort of rulebook to educate legionaries, but I think this one was mine. You know ... *before* I lost my memories. It has all these notes jotted down in the back, almost like notes to my future self. Petra gave it to me."

"Why did you trust that girl?" Niana piped in, arching a grey brow. She began to clean up the mess of food and plates on the table, and Jon reached over to help her.

As I thought of what to say, I considered the video Petra had played in the vault. "Because she showed me my potential," I told them. "The Jackets at Silo wanted me to feel ordinary and like all the others, but Petra showed me that I was never meant to be anything like them. I suppose I trusted her because she believed in me."

"That's home," Niana said. Her frown deepened like she didn't fully understand. And maybe I was a fool and falling for the same trap I had before the crusade, but I didn't regret leaving my room with Petra that night.

"The stone will help me remember why I chose to work with the Outliers," I said.

Jon stacked the plates on the tray and stood with it, headed for the kitchen. "And where you were going in the craft."

"The Underground," Niana responded, nodding her head. She looked tired. We must have been there for over two hours, and it was now early morning. But she didn't let it faze her. She reached into her book and unceremoniously ripped out a page. Tucking it into my codex, she told me, "The Outliers reside in a territory called the Underground. I don't know where it is, but I'm an old woman, child, and people say many things in my company that they probably shouldn't." She laughed a hearty laugh. "It's there you'll likely find the answer."

And hopefully Petra, I thought.

Jon mumbled something to himself as he entered the kitchen and dumped the dishes into the sink. Niana stared at me without saying a word and I played with the frayed ends of my hand bandages, pretending not to notice. After a pregnant pause, she touched my cheek with a gentle hand.

"They used to say your eyes came from your human counterpart. Yours blue, hers green. So beautiful."

And somewhere along the line, I assumed my genetics had grown too muddled to keep up, leaving me with hybrid phenotypes as a result of the DNA they stole to create me.

"You two should rest before you leave. It's a long trip."

"You're not coming?"

"I can't," she said. "It's not good for you to stay in one place for too long, and you'll need quick feet to make it to the coast. I'm afraid I'm much too slow, but I'll be here when you return." She stood and searched around the sitting room until she dug up a blanket from beneath one of the couches. She gave it to me and then pushed the center table to the corner of the room, where it sat with all her trinkets and plants. "It's not much, but—"

"—It'll do." I thanked her and she retreated to her bedroom to rest. While Jon washed the dishes, I made a small bed on the floor with the blanket and stared up at the ceiling, expecting sleep that never came. Filtered light poured in from the window curtains and a low hum sounded from the refrigerator. I waited and waited and waited for some feeling of fear to take me. I was, after all, so close to discovering the full and complete truth. But instead of fear, I felt madly determined. So much so that I worried there was too much adrenaline in my system to rest.

It was only a matter of hours now.

TWENTY-TWO

"OPEN NIGHTS"
BIONIC: MATHAI-0329

"*You remembered the bullets, Jon?*" Niana was dressed in her nightgown and slippers as she stood by the back door. It was late morning and we'd spent our last hours in A10 packing the essentials for our trip to the coast. She insisted on helping us, offering extra food, sweaters, and socks, burying them at the bottom of our bags so that there was no way we'd leave without them. She'd taken time to rest, but she was up and around like she never slept.

"Both amber and silver," Jon assured her, pushing the last of his things in his pockets. He had a separate bag for the guns and gadgets he'd kept locked up in his room.

"Five pairs of shirts?"

"Yes, ma'am." He waved one around over his head.

"Shoes?"

"I'm wearing them."

"Map?"

"Mathai has it."

I grinned at Niana's stressed expression and motioned to the codex in the bag on my back. She seemed content with this, dropping the extra food she was about to hand me and moving away as we exited the back door. Jon suggested it after Niana became paranoid of someone watching from outside. And with our Most Wanted ad occupying every screen in Caeshua, the possibilities were endless.

"Sleep by day, travel by night," Niana said. We spun and faced her in the threshold. "They won't know it's you. And Mathai, you keep those eyes of yours down."

I nodded, pulling the straps of my sleeveless shirt closer to my body. Niana said her goodbyes with a kiss to our foreheads and I followed Jon down the metal steps to the apartment garden. It certainly hadn't been cared for in years and a large tree arched towards the roof of the building. I kicked aside tangled weeds and stopped in front of the broken gate obstructing our path to the street.

"So you were right," Jon said. He tossed his bags over the fence and began climbing over. "I guess I am in your legion."

"What made you doubt me?"

"Something about a five-foot tall girl jumping on my back," he joked.

After he hopped down on the other side of the fence, he held out his arms to help me over. But I disregarded the assistance and threw my bag into his open hands instead. Placing my booted feet carefully, I pulled myself up and over.

"Five-foot-*one*, to be exact. And you were kind of asking for it."

"How?"

I jumped down on the street and took my bag from him. Righting the two braids Niana had plaited in my hair, I said, "You sniffed my mouth. That had to have broken some rule of conduct, right?"

"I was making sure you weren't a leviathan."

"Their breaths smell?"

"Like death," he said. "When someone's been infected, it typically takes five hours for them to turn savage. Rotting teeth is the first sign."

That made more sense. Leviathans killed their hosts from the inside-out, reviving dead bodies as a source of life. I imagined much more smelled than just their breath.

Jon and I walked at an even pace down the street, side-by-side. Though it was later in the day, the road remained somewhat empty and we only had to avoid the occasional car. Down the avenue was the skybridge we'd take back to the other side of the city, where we'd catch a train to A4.

"Can I ask you something?" I said.

Jon shrugged. "If I say no, you'll still ask anyway. So yes."

"Why were you in the outlands?"

"I was stuck; I told you that," he said, watching me from the corner of his eye.

"But don't you remember why you were there, what you were there for? How long were you there?"

His pinched brow made me think he'd forgotten that too, but then he said, "I was there to find something, but I'd bore you with silence if I took the time to figure out what it was."

"Maybe you were looking for me," I said, kicking a rock in passing.

"Maybe. But that still doesn't fill in the blanks. Something happened before I found you in the alley."

"Then do you really think the stone will work?"

Jon paused to turn to me, his hands lost in his pockets. But I sensed he had them there to confine them, rather than to keep them warm. With him standing so close, I could smell him, and he smelled like sandalwood and rain—a strange combination but it was wholly him. "Do you usually ask so many questions?"

"It's part of my charm," I told him. "And I can't quit the sarcasm. It's a two-for-one kind of deal."

"Then it's only fair I ask questions of my own, right?"

I narrowed my eyes on him. "What are you getting at?"

"Simple: question for question."

It killed me to admit it, but I liked Jon. He kept my mind entertained, always, and I supposed I was beginning to understand him because our predicaments were so interwoven. We were complete strangers, and then we weren't. I'd felt him in my head since the alley, and for the first time I wanted to know someone else's story besides my own. I wanted to know this boy.

"Deal," I said, crossing my hands. We made it to the end of the street and turned right. "First question."

"Why are you so predictable?" he asked, fighting back a smile.

I scoffed. "I'm not."

"Yeah?"

"*Hell* yeah."

"Afraid of the unknown?"

I shook my head. "Afraid? No."

"On a mission to defeat the bad guy who wronged you and save the day?"

"Sans mission," I said, "and the only thing I want to save is myself."

"Clumsy, except in all forms of combat?"

"My left hook is pretty lousy, actually."

He stopped the downpour of questions to look me up and down. "How lousy are we talking?"

Before he could stop me, I swung out and punched his shoulder hard, smiling when he howled and feigned injury. He even went so far as to buckle his knees like my hit rendered him weak. "I ... owe you ... an apology." He laughed so hard I could barely understand what he was saying. "That was the lousiest punch I've ever seen in my life. That was pitiful."

I rolled my eyes at him. "Save it."

"Did you fight your way out of Silo with that—"

I punched him again, this time swinging fast with my other hand. The blow made him trip over his feet. "My right hook is pretty good, though."

"*Predictable*," he whined. He popped a smirk, then winced, rolling his shoulder back to lessen the pain.

I did my best to hold back a smile and lost it. In the middle of the street, Jon and I laughed until we were red in the face and threatened to wake the neighbors. Then when the moment passed, we fell in step together, bouncing questions back and forth to pass the time. And I soon discovered that I liked the sound of his voice.

I asked him what his favorite time of day was as we crossed the skybridge into the chaos of A10 and he told me he enjoyed **open nights** the most. He liked to see the stars, he said, and pretended they were more than tiny suns billions of miles away. While I'd never seen stars myself, I understood the need to seek purpose in something greater. So when we moved through the city, guided by the shadows of the road, I told him my preferred time of day was dawn. A coruscant sunrise and the smell of the fresh-turned earth was all I needed. *Petrichor*, Jon called it, and it instantly became my favorite word.

We neared the backend of the Ward in A10, where five legionaries emitted beams of light to uphold the gate. They only opened it for outgoing legionaries and the trains that came and went. The circular platform they stood on towered above the entire city. And Generators orbited around them, guarding them, like I assumed was necessary in light of what happened to the wardens at Silo.

Furtively, I merged into the lines and became another anonymous face, sticking close to Jon with my gun at my back. Now that everyone was awake and about, the crowds were a lot less organized. I rocked impatiently from foot to foot until we crossed the plaza, with all its colors and lights, and we were able to board the long bullet train. Its clear doors slid out with a ring and we stepped in, finding many people sitting or lounging. When Jon nodded his head to vacant seats toward the back, I walked ahead of him, keeping my eyes down like Niana had said to. We didn't have tickets. Not only did we not have money for them, but running the chance of anyone seeing our faces wasn't in our schedule. We had two days to make it to the coast, two days to make it back.

I climbed into the window seat and Jon took the one next to the aisle. Just as we settled in and pushed our bags beneath our chairs, the train began to move. I probably breathed for the first time since leaving Niana's home. I'd never been on a train, or any moving vehicle besides a car, and the feeling wasn't one I loved. The floor vibrated beneath my feet and everything shook, including the walls. It made my stomach upset, and I gripped the handles of my seat, sitting all the way back.

As we sped down the train tracks through the dome of the plaza and then exited the protection of the Ward, I peered outside the window. I knew we were no longer in the city when the clean, lively streets turned dim and dreary. The tall apartment homes became bunkers and shattered windows, broken pavements. Every block or so, a leviathan ran fiercely toward the train, only to be crushed beneath the tracks.

To quell my anxiety, Jon asked more questions. He sensed I needed the distraction, so he asked me silly things, like what my favorite color was and if I was afraid of heights. I told him I'd never thought about colors in that respect, that it was weird to favor just one when there were so many. But if I had to choose, I would have chosen red. He chuckled and said that was unusual, but I was sure of my decision. Red was synonymous with fire, anger, and even confusion. It was the color that perfectly summarized how I felt, and it was powerful, vivid, and vast. Red was the color that flowed through my veins, the color ballads were written about. It was passion and heartbreak all in one hue. Red was me, and it was him too.

I knew I wasn't afraid of heights. I'd climbed the tallest structure in Silo without a second thought. If anything, heights excited me. I loved knowing I had little control at the edge of a precipice, and I admired the view at being so high up. I told Jon this and he seemed to understand, saying he didn't know all his fears but heights surely couldn't be one. He was a wanderer and heights were one of the few places he could feel big in a world working against him. And there, he could see the sky—blue, his favorite color.

Jon asked most of the questions as I tried to keep my eyes off the window, but I snuck glances when he wasn't paying attention. Even though we'd completely left A10's outlands behind, the red sands that stretched throughout Caeshua looked far more barren. Hills and plateaus were the only things for miles, and the skies were empty save for the birds. They were the same birds I swore I saw on the street with Jon, and I knew because they were huge and unlike any animal I could imagine. They followed the train, their long wings casting shadows across the landscape, but were gone the next time I blinked.

I zoned out an hour into our trip and relaxed my head on Jon's shoulder while he tinkered with my radiocom. People moved around the cabin, eating and using the restroom, talking in hushed murmurs. I didn't fall asleep, but I was lulled by the noises of the train. I remained moderately still until I sensed a shift in Jon's mood. I didn't know how, but I heard his alert thoughts like they were my own. One moment he was trying to program the radiocom and then the next he was glancing around the train with an elevated pulse.

24B... Toward the rear... Behind... If the conductor heads this way, we'll have to move cabins, came his thoughts.

I stared at him and focused until I felt his psyche brush mine, then I spoke into his head.

Jon, what's going on?

He spun to look at me, his eyebrows drawn in confusion.

You're hearing me?

I nodded, not quite understanding how I was doing it. Our psyches linked together, as if tethered by proximity, and I could hear his thoughts clearly like before. Only now I was able to telepathically send him messages.

Up front, he thought.

I peered around the speeding train to where a woman toward the front stood to grab her ticket from her bag. A conductor took it from her to verify it, which explained Jon's mood change.

They'll throw us off the train if we don't show them tickets, I thought to him.

Then we don't show them tickets.

He picked up his bags and handed me mine, not saying a word. Calmly, we walked down the aisle to the door leading to the next cabin. Some people watched us too long and I felt hysteria skittering down the grooves of my spine. Would they report us? Would the conductor turn the train around and have us arrested? I walked faster, only a breath apart from Jon. But when we glanced through the door window, we recognized another conductor headed our way. And they'd find out we'd snuck aboard the train.

Moving quickly, we split up and pushed into the public restrooms—Jon in one and me in the other on the opposite side of the aisle. I slid the flap closed and turned the lock until it read 'occupied,' then stalled my breathing as the footsteps passed. Through the door I could hear Jon's thoughts, how he hoped the conductor hadn't seen us. While I was doubtful they'd throw us out in the middle of Caeshua, I didn't really know what to expect. We were outlaws—killers and thieves by design. We probably deserved more than exile.

Someone wrapped against the door of the bathroom and my breath hitched. When I ignored it, it came again, and louder. Finally, I slid the flap open and readied my excuse for the conductor. But instead of the bearded man we'd seen in the other cabin, I glanced down into the face of a small child as he bounced up in down while holding his crotch.

"Peepee," he cried, pointing to the toilet behind me.

"It's all yours." I moved out of the way and allowed him to go in. Then before the conductor spotted us leaving, Jon and I crossed train cabins, stepping carefully between the railings. We barged through the next two aisles and kept going until we came to the last door at the rear of the train. I knew it was the end because when Jon slid the door open, there was only a small, open terrace. No seats or people.

"Cozy," I said, slipping through the door and closing it shut. Jon and I held unto the balustrade of the terrace as the train sped along the tracks, A10 a speckle on the horizon.

"It docks in ten minutes outside of A4. We'll just have to wait it out," he said. We resigned to sit on the floor and I could feel every bump in the track as the wheelless train glided over them. And we lingered there, our eyes on the door and our hands clutching for security on the cold, metal floor. Of all the things we had yet to endure, I knew the worst was still to come.

TWENTY-THREE

"BLACK DUST"
BIONIC: MATHAI-0329

Caeshua *was as dry as* it was empty. I nursed a bottle of water as we crossed the plains outside of A4, following the map in my codex. We'd only stopped in the city for a few minutes to look through the Most Wanted ads, and while I'd distracted the street vendors, Jon had flipped through their papers in search for familiar faces. He had no recollection of our legion, but he thought if he saw their faces the memory would swim back. And they had to be wanted if they weren't at Silo.

Jon didn't recognize anyone except us, though, and our faces were always at the top of every list. We'd left A4 then, passing the steps to the train and instead escaping the Ward on foot. We now regretted that decision with the sun bearing hot on our backs and a thirty-minute hike still ahead in our journey to the coast.

"Do you think they're looking for us?" Jon asked. He turned the map around to find our exact location since my radiocom only showed us on unmarked land.

"It would be easier for them to find us," I said. "All they need do is follow the sighting reports." And there were plenty. We just never remained in one place long enough to be caught.

We were trailing the path I'd drawn on my map, stopping intermittently for breaks. The sun began to set a while after we left A4 and I'd recorded it, noting how the days were getting shorter. Like we were running out of hours. Like we were losing time. When we eventually neared a crater, Jon handed me the codex and pointed. "It should be in there," he said, probably more perplexed than I was. A coast meant water, and I didn't think there were seas so far out in Caeshua.

I jogged, sweat sticking my clothes to my body, and stopped at the mouth of the crater. It was much deeper than the last one I'd been in. "In here? You're sure?"

"That's what your map says." Jon examined the chasm, then handed me my codex. "Stay here, I'll check." He dropped in with his feet first, skidding along the side to control the motion of his body. Then he waved me down once he reached the bottom, yards away.

"Do you see any water?"

"I see dirt," he said, walking away. Clutching my bag, I followed him into the crater and rolled ungracefully to the end, picking rocks out of my hair. Something was amiss, however, when I patted down my pants. The wall of the crater was rough and had ripped a whole in my back pocket. I poked a finger through, sighing. My bandages were no better. They were dirty like they'd never been cleaned.

"You should rewrap that," Jon said, walking around me. He glanced up as if looking for something, but the abyss we stood in was solely open to the sky.

I wiped the sweat from my forehead, ignoring the bandages. "Remind me when I get my memories back. Now where's the coast?"

Jon turned around in a complete circle and saw exactly what I saw: nothing. Unless the Ucilei coast was a dried up crater full off clay rocks, we'd come to the wrong place.

"This can't be right." I flipped through my codex and took a second look at the map. I'd drawn our path with a bold, black pen and we'd definitely followed it, step by step. There was no way we'd made a mistake.

"Wait here." Jon crossed the crater and knelt, his hands on the ground. He swished the sand from side to side, digging for something, and then growled, pounding an angry fist into the dirt. "They moved it," he called.

"Who moved what?"

"The stones. They *had* to be here."

I was going to ask how he knew, but then I saw the evidence. Jon's hands were black with it. "Presidium must have known we'd come looking for them. They could have moved them anywhere by now." The ditch Jon found had remnants of **black dust** scattered among the red sand. Upon a closer look, I realized it wasn't really black dust but black pieces of the stones. They'd been crushed to a fine powder, like they'd extracted the stones from the crater without care.

"No, but my map—"

"—Is from Silo. For all we know, Mathai, they marked this place in all their books, just to keep people away." He stood back, running his hands through his hair and pulling. "We have to find the real coast."

"Which is where?" I glanced back at the ditch, refusing to let it go but struggling to derive a positive from this loss. "It's not like we can go back to A4 and ask around. People will think we're crazy."

"And they'll know who we are."

"Niana." My heart dropped in my chest a little. I kept thinking about her face when she said we'd find the stone. She was so sure. "What are we supposed to tell her?"

Jon dropped his hand to his pocket and opened his mouth to say what we both knew—that we absolutely couldn't tell her—but he chose to leave it unsaid. So I closed my codex and readied my bag to go. To where, I wasn't sure. But I knew we couldn't spend the night in a crater. At the last second, I picked up a handful of the black dust and spilled it into a pocket of my bag. *For Niana*, I lied to myself. I knew it was merely for my curiosity.

I took one step forward then froze in place, feeling the ground shift around me. But it wasn't just the ground; the walls of the crater began to crumble in and Jon shot a look at me like I'd triggered something hidden in the sand.

"What is that?" I asked. Jon's eyes went to the sky and there was more to see this time. A hovercraft, torched in flames, exploded from the clouds and fell like a shooting star above our heads. The propellers blew off with the sound of a failing engine. If someone was flying it, I couldn't tell, because the shield was completely obscured by smoke. The craft dropped so fast I was afraid to blink and miss everything, so I stared as it spiraled into the ground.

"We need to move."

"We need to see who they are," I retorted, climbing back out of the crater and hefting myself up with my bag in tote.

"*Mathai*, it could be Reapers."

"I know, but why would they crash their only means of dragging us out of here?" When I stood and screened my eyes from the sun, the crashed hovercraft lie feet away, planted front first in the desert. Jon was right—it could have been Reapers, but that didn't explain how and why they'd gone down in flames.

"There's someone in there," Jon said, coming from the crater to stand beside me. He squinted against the heat and pointed at the fractured side of the silver craft.

Just then, one of the doors flew open with a burst of fire, and we quickly drew our guns, aiming them straight ahead. I steadied my finger on the trigger, preparing to shoot if I had to. "That thing fell from the sky like lightning. There's no way anyone's alive," I said.

Jon waved his pistol to the other side. "Just take left."

The craft still burned as we inched closer, circling slowly around it. I eyed the splintered screen and the ejected seats through the cracks of the metal. It would have taken a lot to bring down a craft this large, which made me wonder what did it. "See anything?" I called out.

"No, you?"

I walked around my half of the craft again and got as close to the flames as possible. When I peered in through the open door, I noticed a hand sticking out from the rubble. "Over here!" I holstered my gun and, carefully, navigated the flames enough to stretch into the craft. The person was lying down on the back seat, their hands tied behind their back. It was a girl—shoulder-length hair and fair skin. She was unconscious, but the rising of her chest let me know she was still alive. The person who'd been flying from the front had collided with the shield, however, bleeding from a gash on their forehead. They, too, looked unfamiliar, but their colorless skin and white clothes was reminiscent to that of a Jacket. My decision on who to reach for was simple.

"Give me a hand," I said to Jon. He stood at my back, and after a moment's hesitation, he dropped his gun to his side. With a wave of a hand, he cloaked the flames surrounding the craft. It was the wrong time for it, but I felt envious. Jon definitely knew how to control his abilities better than I did.

"Here, go in," he said, gripping the door and pulling it back. With both hands, I reached in and unbuckled the seatbelt around the girl. Her hands were bound with thick rope, her mouth taped shut, so I had no choice but to lift her up and carry her out. She weighed little to nothing in my arms, but I was concerned about the bruises on her skin. I knew some were because of the ropes, but others looked like she'd gotten them from a struggle.

She's their captive, I suspected, and I was sure Jon heard the thought.

When I brought her out completely and kneeled with her on the ground, he made quick work of removing the ties on her arms and the tape on her face. And I gently shook her shoulders, rousing her to wake. She couldn't be any older than sixteen. She was small, fragile. It took her some time, but she finally opened her eyes. They were a soft brown, and they were probing. She glanced from me to Jon, and then from Jon to me. She did this several times before noticing we'd freed her. I expected a smile, or even tears of joy, but instead the girl seemed angry. Her gaze stopped on Jon and she shot to her feet, diving for him with her hands out.

"You idiot!" she screamed, attacking him with her fists. They fell to the dirt with her on top of him, Jon trying desperately to restrain her. "I won't go back!"

"We're here to save you!" Jon told her, shielding his face from her blows. I stepped in, somewhat baffled that the little girl had so much strength, and pulled her off him. She still lashed out, mighty arms swinging a mile a minute.

"We're not going to hurt you. We saw the craft—"

In rapid motion, she grabbed my gun from my back and spun away, keeping her eyes on Jon. She eyed him like he was her worst enemy and not the stranger who'd just rescued her from a burning craft. "Yeah, I know what you saw. Just another criminal, right? Well, I'm not going back there," she said.

Jon and I shared a look. The girl had to be confused. Surely she'd hit her head on the way down, because we looked nothing like the man who'd been flying the craft. "We don't want to take you anywhere, but we can help you get back to the city. People can help you there."

"No," she said, waving the gun around. She held it firm like she knew what to do with it, but she was shaking. The girl was scared. "They don't want to help me. They want to *use* me."

"You're a legionary," Jon understood. He approached her slowly with his hands up. She was all of four feet tall, but she had jumped at him with speed I'd never seen before.

"What's your name?"

Looking at me, she said, "Elektra. No prissy nickname, either—just Elektra."

Jon offered her a smile and I watched her shoulders relax. She dropped the gun a fraction, but her guard was still up.

"We're legionaries too. We were here looking for the Ucilei coast when we saw the craft going down," I said. "Why were you on it?"

"They caught me sleeping under a bridge in A4. Didn't take much to guess I had gone rogue."

Rogue. "You're one of the wanted?"

"Are you?" She cocked her head, her hair slipping over her face. When she gave Jon and I another once over, something clicked in her head. I couldn't tell what it was, but it caused her to put the gun down, switching the safety on. "What are your names?"

"Jon and Mathai. Have you seen our faces too?"

"Yeah, years ago." Through her exhaustion, she smiled a smile of relief. She flung her arms out lazily, saying, "Where have you guys been?"

"Um …" I was utterly lost. Why was she suddenly talking like she knew us? "Looking for—"

"It doesn't matter; you're here now. Only took you several weeks, but,"—she shrugged—"we've been waiting for you."

"We?" Jon asked.

As he said the word, the air swirled around the desert, picking up my hair. When I glanced up, the two birds from the alley, and then from the train, descended with their large wings engulfing the sky. *Wings,* I thought. *And faces.*

They weren't birds at all.

TWENTY-FOUR

"MY LEGION"
BIONIC: MATHAI-0329

O*ne had eyes so white* they shone. Her hair was the same, colorless and flowing in waves around her shoulders. She was fair-skinned with a round face, and had wings sharp enough to rival daggers. She descended with one foot pointed forward, like a deity in the heavens.

The other, I noticed, was like her in various ways but different in so many others. His wings were bigger, shielding the entire sun, and his eyes were dark and calculating—a cool shade of gunmetal. Where her skin was light, his was dark, defining every muscle of his body. He dropped into the desert like an asteroid, fist to the ground. And the force rocked the ground we stood on.

"You took long enough," Elektra said to them, waving my gun

around. But the two winged people stared at Jon and me, much like we stared at them.

"You know each other?" I asked.

Elektra frowned. "What do you mean? Of course I do."

"They have no memory, Elektra," said the girl with the wings. She didn't have an accent, but she pronounced her words clearly, like a finely tuned machine. It was almost sing-songy in a way.

"How do you know us?" Jon asked.

"Because we're your legion," said the one with the gunmetal eyes.

I took a step back to unravel the thoughts flaying my mind. I picked them apart until all I had were questions, because none of this made sense to me. Why were they able to remember us and we weren't, if they really were the other members of **my legion**?

"I'm Lexyn," said the girl with slanted eyes and long white hair. She walked toward me with an innocent smile and waved to her counterpart behind her, who had yet to speak. "And this is Cameron, my brother."

Brother? "But you guys—"

"Look nothing alike, I know." She hunched her shoulders and her wings moved behind her. They weren't feathers, I knew. They appeared to be a synthetic metal, and they grew right out of her shoulder blades. "We are siblings by bond, not by DNA."

"But Lex is the prettier one," Elektra cut in. "Cam is a bit of an airhead." She jabbed Cameron's stomach and he swatted her away with his left wing like she was an incessant bug and she was thrown several feet back into the ground. She stood after a second, laughing and chasing after him again. Though I sensed Cameron liked her playful nature and, in some way, they were close like siblings too."

Jon brought me back to our conversation with Lexyn, saying, "But I don't understand how you found us? We've been discreet about where we stay."

"Not discreet enough," Lexyn said, grinning. "We've been following Mathai since she left Silo."

"What?"

"We've been following Ma—"

"No, no. I got that. But why didn't you talk to me sooner? I've spent days looking for you ... my legion."

Lexyn's face fell as she picked up on my frustration. "It wasn't the right time. I knew you wouldn't remember me; I thought you'd changed who you were again. And after the crusade, we honestly didn't know if you two were alive."

Well, joke's on me, because I did end up swapping personas.

"You remember the crusade then?" Jon asked. "You remember the Outliers?"

"The who?"

Cameron and Elektra walked up, looking just as confused. Elektra bit her nails as she said, "Who are the Outliers?"

"We hadn't planed to meet anyone during our crusade? Anyone ... *peculiar*?" I asked.

"Besides Jon? No," Cameron said, and his voice was surprisingly deep. He, too, watched me with innocent eyes.

"Wait, hold on. You're saying I wasn't on the crusade, but you planned to meet me?" Jon said.

"We always did," Lexyn answered, as if this were common knowledge. "You found us during one of our very first crusades outside of the Ward and those at Silo never knew."

So then Niana was wrong and we hadn't conspired with the Outliers? But then why did Manis think I was withholding information? Why was he so sure he'd break it out of me? *What did I know that I didn't know I knew?* And why would the Outliers free me from Silo?

I scrutinized the three new people we'd stumbled upon, digging their minds for some sign of a lie. But I got nothing. Lexyn was wondering why I was staring at her, Elektra was thinking about her next meal, and Cameron was … blank. I couldn't read him at all, but neither of them knew what really happened to us.

"This isn't right. We need to go back," I said, swiveling on my heels and trekking through the desert, headed for A4.

"Mathai, wait. Where are you going?" Jon followed me, stopping me with a hand to my shoulder.

"It doesn't make sense! If the Outliers had absolutely nothing to do with our crusade, then what could Silo have wanted from me?" I didn't stop to breathe; I was too angry. "Jon, what did I do?"

He put his hands on my face, counting. For what, I didn't know. But he counted to thirty before letting go, and that somehow calmed me. "You said you met with an Outlier—Petra. What did she tell you the last time you saw her?"

"She said to find my legion, and then to meet her in the Seeming."

"The Seeming?" Elektra stopped biting her nails and her face lit up with recognition. "I know where that is!"

Lexyn and Cameron turned to face her. "You do?" they said in unison.

"Yeah, sure. It's a valley between those two rocks that look like feet. Or at least that's what the drunkard told me when I was fishing through trash last week."

Lexyn sighed like she didn't believe her, but I did. I had to. It was something to go on, even if it sounded awfully ridiculous. "Would you be able to give us directions?" I asked.

"Sure. We just have to look for the feet rocks."

"Wait, we can't just go now," Lexyn said.

Jon glanced around the group. "Why not?"

"We were looking for you because Silo took you. We're meant to stay together, *always*, and we got separated." She swished her wings, her white irises trained on me. "We thought Alessia was with you."

"Who's Alessia?" Jon asked.

"Mathai's sister," Elektra answered. "Did you guys forget everyone?"

I had a sister? *I had a sister.* I'd told Jon as much, but the words were full of air at the time. I'd seen a girl in my dreams and she'd said a lot of things ... but I never fully believed she was real.

I had a *sister.*

"Where is she?" I crossed my arms over my chest, hoping they knew at least this.

"We don't know," Cameron stated. "Now it's been weeks; she could be anywhere. We were going to return to Silo, but then we saw our faces in a Most Wanted ad."

"We knew we couldn't go back until we found you," Elektra added.

"So the last thing you guys remember is waking up after the craft crashed during the crusade?" Jon was finding it hard to digest too.

Lexyn nodded. "And then we saw Mathai and Alessia being taken away. We've been out here waiting ever since."

I breathed in deep and held it, allowing the hot air to bring feelings back to my numb limbs. So many things were falling together, and so much was falling apart. I feared that if I couldn't find the perfect balance, I'd lose it all.

"Here's the thing," Jon said. "A friend of mine told us that Mathai was meeting with people called the Outliers when you left for the crusade a few weeks ago. This may have something to do with why Silo is now a threat to us, but we can't remember."

"And clearly neither do we," Elektra said.

"But there's a stone that can help. Before we pulled you from the burning craft, that's what we were looking for."

"A stone?" Lexyn's forehead furrowed, and she pinned her hair behind an ear, as if to hear better. "What could a stone do?"

"It's not a typical stone. It has healing properties, ones strong enough to restore our memories."

"Then where is it?" Cameron asked.

Jon sighed, saying, "Presidium moved its location—all of them."

"Then we need to find them. And Alessia. If she's a part of our legion," I took a moment to look at each of them, even Jon, "she needs to be here. We stay together." The prospect of having family was a wild one, even if Alessia wasn't my sister by DNA. But we needed the six of us together if this was going to work, if we were going to take our lives back.

Cameron moved his wings restlessly. "Where's the Seeming?"

"Like, on the other side of Caeshua," Elektra said, sounding exasperated. She pulled debris from her brown hair, and then looped my pistol in her waistband. I had a feeling I wasn't going to get it back. "It would take weeks by foot, days by train."

"No, that's too long," I said.

"Then we need something that moves faster," Jon concurred. He was sweaty and his shirt had been ripped at the hem. His hands were still black from the dust in the crater.

"We can fly," Lexyn said, shrugging like she missed the obvious.

Elektra rolled her eyes. "But *we* can't. We need something that can fit all of us."

As Elektra spoke, my gaze went to the hovercraft in the distance, sparking an idea I was almost ashamed to breathe life into. But it was the only shot we had.

Smirking, I said, "We're going to steal a hovercraft."

They were silent for a beat, and then everyone started talking at once, Jon telling me how crazy of an idea it was and Elektra jumping up and down with far too much excitement. Lexyn argued with Cameron on whether or not they could carry the three of us back to A4 themselves, even though it was impractical and a hard risk. And I tried to get Jon to understand that it was our only option. We'd pass out from hunger or dehydration before making it to the Seeming on foot. It would make us vulnerable, and so would an hours-long train ride. So it was hovercraft or bust.

Lexyn screamed to shut us up, but Jon kept talking, looking at me with confused, hazel-green eyes as he paced the desert. Elektra and Cameron were screaming, and in the back of my mind I knew this was chaos. We had no order, no memories. It would be a miracle if we survived *each other.*

"Hey!" Lexyn screamed. In a fit, she brought her wings up behind her back and flapped them down quickly. We had no warning before a spell of potent energy shot us through the air, parting us like a wave. Pain fissured through my body like a vice around my throat. Elektra was thrown to the right, Cameron to her left. Jon and I landed somewhere feet away, kissing the ground as we landed with a rough *oomph.* When I coughed and peered around, Lexyn's wings were still tall in the sky.

"Ow," Elektra groaned. She sat up and held her head, then started chuckling. "You could have used your words."

"I don't like when we fight," Lexyn said, her tone stern. "I want to go with Mathai's idea." She walked to me and held out her hand to help me up. Her entire body blocked the sun and I watched her eyes for deceit. Only moments ago I believed she had been another bird in the sky, *not* a winged legionary. Not a member of my legion. Though all I found in her mind was innocent intent. She truly wanted to help us. "We're going to steal a craft," she said.

I took her hand and she helped me stand. Right away, a wide smile touched her lips. She reeled me in for an unexpected hug and wrapped her arms around me tightly. Touching was still a new phenomenon for me, so I awkwardly put my hands out, patting her back in little circles.

Laughing, she said, "You're supposed to squeeze me back. Like this."

She clutched my body and I cringed. "Sorry, I don't know how this works."

Lexyn pulled away and held me at arm's length as the others regrouped at her back. She nodded, understanding. "You will when we get your memories back."

"So how are we doing this?" Cameron budded in. His stance was pensive; he was definitely the quieter one between him and Lexyn, like he had a complexity of worlds behind his mind. I tried to read him again and got nothing. He shot me a look from the corner of his eye like he knew what I was doing and I quickly looked away.

"Don't worry," Elektra said mischievously. "I know just the hovercraft." She began trudging toward the looming city ahead of us, her hair swaying as she moved. She walked like she danced to her own beat, a natural-born leader. The rest of us trailed alongside her with the sun in our faces, the crater of black dust to our backs. To get myself through the silence split between the five of us, I forced myself to believe that knowing the truth of my past would set us all free. That Silo would no longer see us as a threat and we'd clear our names for good.

Lies. It was all lies.

TWENTY-FIVE

"DRY LIGHTNING"
BIONIC: MATHAI-0329

"I *don't know how I feel* about this anymore." Lexyn peeked around the corner, then ducked behind the wall.

"Too little too late for that," I said. The sun had set by the time we reentered A4, passing through the neighborhoods Elektra swore by, insisting the job would be easy. But when we'd arrived at the corner, a block away from the armed citadel marked with Silo's green insignia, we began to doubt our plan.

"There are about six districts that way," Lexyn said, pointing down the narrow street. At this time of night, the only people outside were liars and beggars. "Why don't we look for a craft there?"

"No, we're doing this," Elektra said. She sat on the pavement with her legs crossed, my radiocom in her lap. "I can program this as a conduit. It picks up on emotion, strong energies, *power*. Zap this thing with enough of that and it'll blackout any city within a ten mile radius."

"It's practically a funnel," Cameron said.

"Exactly. We knock their lights out and they have no choice but to flee the building."

"So they rush out and we rush in?" I asked, squatting low to see what she did with the radiocom. If I had known it could do more than alert me of the time, I doubt I would have spent such useless effort in the outlands of A10.

"They won't all leave, so someone has to stay outside to be a distraction." She glanced up, giving us an uneasy grin. "Then someone else has to slow them down when they eventually find out rogue legionaries are trying to steal a hovercraft."

"Elektra!" Lexyn cried.

"What? It's what we have to work with. The crafts here can fit all five of us and carry enough gas to get us to the Seeming. Any other might have us diving out of the sky again."

"Get on with it then," Cameron said, keeping a sharp eye on the citadel.

"I'm going to program it for five minutes. That should be enough time before lights-out. From the roof, I can disarm the cameras."

"I'll distract from the outside," Lexyn said.

"No, that should be me," Jon countered.

"And me," Cameron agreed. "And I'll power the radiocom."

"You've got enough pent-up emotions for it," Elektra teased. She handed him the radiocom that flashed a set of numbers before counting backwards. When he fit it around his wrist, the band glowed, recognizing him as LEGION BLUE.

"The rest of us will head in the warehouse. The crafts are kept in a garage toward the back. You can't miss it."

"And if we get lost?" Lexyn asked, taking another look at the citadel.

"Yeah, don't do that."

Together, blanketed by the night, we crossed the road and made it to the fenced barricade surrounding the citadel. Round, white lights tanked the roof, rotating the circumference of the building. Through the barred windows I saw people working behind computers. Every door was guarded by a Generator from the inside.

"What is this place?" I whispered.

"Some sort of militia?" Jon guessed. Though that made no sense. Why would a facility like this not be in Silo?

While Lexyn and Cameron flew over the barrier, their wings like tails behind them, I mounted it, dodging the barbed edges to jump off on the other side. But Elektra stopped and stared at the fence in annoyance, immediately turning to Jon.

"Give me a lift," she said, nudging his side. He stooped and put his knee out for her to step up and she accepted the help, holding on with both hands. It took her a while to find her footing, but once she did, she was jumping over the barricade in seconds. Glancing over her shoulder, she said, "You know, you're kind of cute."

Jon wiggled a brow, making me smile. "Kind of?"

"Yeah, your haircut is stupid."

Cameron laughed a loud, belly laugh and Lexyn capped her hand over his mouth to muffle it. "No time for jokes. Let's *go*," she hissed. But behind her hand Cameron still cackled. Jon seemed to think it was amusing, too, and I detected a tonal shift between the five of us. It was as dramatic as it was sudden. It was like we'd spent no time apart at all and picked up where we left off, naturally.

Jon crossed over the barrier and followed Cameron to the front of the citadel, talking softly as they discussed what they had to do. We watched them stealthily dodge each camera and the blazing lights until they vanished around the side.

"How are you getting on the roof?" Lexyn asked Elektra. We walked swiftly to the other section of the citadel, where enormous trucks were parked in a numbered lot.

"There's a door around the side here. I'll go left, you guys go straight in."

"And you're sure this is going to work?"

"It has to."

We searched around until we found the grey metal door conveniently marked 'warehouse.' I moved aside for Elektra and she stopped before the door, hovering a hand above the knob. Using her telekinetic abilities, she gradually turned the gears within the lock. The clicks of the metal resonated in the dark, and then the door popped open.

"See," Elektra said. "Easy."

Lexyn grunted her response. "Your enthusiasm for breaking and entering concerns me."

"I've had too much time on my hands." Elektra felt around the wall for a light switch. She pulled a cord above the door and everything wired to life, surprising me. There was a table in the corner, an upturned chair, and too many file cabinets. They lined the walls, rising to the ceiling. Elektra kicked everything aside and grabbed a ring of keys from the table. Tossing it to me, she said, "Pick a craft, but be quick about it. Take it out to the lot, but don't fly it until we're all in."

"How do you—"

"Like I said: lots of time." Elektra was small, young. At first glance she seemed fragile and innocent, but she wasn't. And I was sure that misconstrued perception always worked in her favor. "I'm heading to the roof. Don't fly until we're in, got it?"

We nodded, dumbfounded. While she backed down a hall, Lexyn and I traveled straight through the warehouse. For a while all we saw were offices and storage rooms full of books. More paperwork, more data, and tons of computer screens. We even stopped to read a floor guide on one of the doors, but it was old and most of the print had been rubbed off. The only things still labeled were the exits. Finally, Lexyn called me back after we passed a white door and she pointed through the room's window. It wasn't the hovercrafts; it was another computer space, but the screens must have been linked to the cameras outside.

"There's Cam," Lexyn whispered. There were five screens displaying the perimeters of the facility and Cameron and Jon showed up on the third one. They stood in front of the building as the time on the radiocom ticked by. Slowly, Cameron raised his wings and clasped his hands in fists. The look on his face could only be described as *menacing*, because there was nothing about his stance and the power brewing around him that implied otherwise. He seemed to concentrate, and then when he opened his hands again, static orbs formed in his palms, growing in size as he continued to use his abilities. He then fixed his unwavering gaze on the facility. Jon moved behind him, his jaw clenched.

"Energy emission," I whispered. "He's funneling his energy into the radiocom."

Lexyn nodded. "We need to go. That stuff is strong enough to turn this place over, and we're running out of time."

"How much time do you think we have left?"

I spoke too soon, and not too long after we broke away from the window to continue looking for the crafts, the warehouse went pitch black and the screen blinked to nothing. "No time," Lexyn said. We took off through the steel-floored hallways and opened a two-way door into a corridor. The darkness provided no help, but we searched anyway. Lexyn did a blind sweep of each room and she returned with no luck.

"It's not here," I mumbled, trying to think. Our deep breaths were the only thing I heard for a minute, and then the walls of the facility shook, Cameron's energy rocking us from side to side. The blast of power kept coming, blinking the lights on and off like strobes. And somewhere in this section of the building, I heard the unquestionable drone of Generators.

"I don't think we've gone far enough," Lexyn said, her white eyes glowing in the dark. "Let's keep going."

We jogged further down the hall and I lost sight of the room we'd left Elektra. Darkness swallowed our backs and alarms went off in my head. But even though we were going in the exact direction I'd heard the Generators coming from, we had to find the door leading to the garage of hovercrafts. A little trepidation wasn't enough to turn me around.

When the lights blinked again, Lexyn and I spotted glass doors at the end of the hall. We sprinted for them, holding onto the walls as the confusion elevated outside. I didn't know much about her yet, but Lexyn's wings moved incessantly when she was frightened. She kept them tucked behind her, the ends nearly touching the floor, and they trembled more than she did. I wanted to tell her that things would be okay, but I couldn't tell her that. I couldn't even tell myself that lie.

"It's locked," she said, coming to the door and pulling on the handles. She tapped the panel on the wall and it flickered with a handprint error. "We need DNA."

"Well, we've got the wrong kind," I said breathily. My mouth was dry and the back of my throat felt itchy. I collected my thoughts and strategized ways to open the door, though none would provide us with sufficient time to get the hovercraft to the others. Lexyn beat against the door, but the glass was thicker than a glacier. And purposely so. Anything that had to do with Silo was different.

I tried my palm on the panel, only to receive the same error. After several tries, it asked for a code.

"A code? What kind of code?" Lexyn asked.

"A four-letter word." The keypad glowed as I shakily typed in *s-i-l-o*. I bit my bottom lip as it configured, then flashed the error code again. *Too obvious*, I thought.

"Try 'ward,'" Lexyn said, still trying to pry the door open.

I tapped in *w-a-r-d*.

Error.

Infuriated, I slapped the panel and turned to tell Lexyn we had to find another way in, even if that meant Jon and Cameron had to secure more time. But I never got to tell her. Three Generators crashed through a door to our right and collided with the wall. They didn't notice us until Lexyn moved, and they tracked our faces with their flashlights.

"Ari—0329, Lexyn—0097," they called. Their robotic forms shifted as they advanced on us, faster than we expected. With nowhere left run, we dove for them. Lexyn blazed ahead with her wings out, kicking and punching at every chance she had available. Her wings were both her shield and her weapon, thwarting the bullets that came for her chest and ripping into anyone that got too close.

I was only a step behind her, a blur in the dark. And deprived of my gun, I had to use my abilities. Concentrating on the vibrations in my body, I turned my form from corporeal to incorporeal, ebbing away in that same cloud of red smoke. I didn't skid like I had when escaping Silo. I flowed in and out of the fog without fault. When I appeared again, I had a hold of a Generator's neck from over my shoulder. I pulled down, mustering all my strength in my hands and legs to lift it over my head and threw onto the ground. Then before it could get back up, I shoved a fist through its suit and tore out its glowing, green life force.

"The door!" Lexyn screamed, her wings slicing through a Generator.

I swiveled back in time to see the third Generator headed for the garage door. To secure it or open it, I didn't know. But I would have bet the money I didn't have on the aforementioned.

I lunged for the Generator, zigzagging to evade its bullets that lit up the hallway, and gripped its hand, cranking it out until its suit bolts crunched beneath my fingers. Then, as soon as the idea dawned on me, I spun around with the Generator and placed my finger over its gun's trigger, showering the door with bullets. The kickback was ridiculous. Chippings of the door flew around us as it broke away, piece by piece. When the glass finally shattered, I knocked the Generator out with a fist to its head and kicked it aside.

"Come on." Lexyn grabbed one of their flashlights and took my arm, pulling me into motion. Without sparing a glance behind us, we exited through the broken glass doors and thundered down the staircase. We wound down two floors before reaching the bottom and breaking into an open space full of tall shadows.

Lexyn slowed her stride. "This has to be them," she said, her voice echoing in the recess. She shined the flashlight across the area and the obscurities were slowly unveiled from the dark. Hundreds of hovercrafts—every size, shape, and color—were lined in rows through the garage. I breathed a sigh of relief, calming the race of my heart, and started running through the lanes.

"Which one do we choose?" said Lexyn, speed walking behind me. She eyed every craft as I did, even though they were all the same.

"This one." I pointed to the one in the very front, the one that had to be the easiest to maneuver out of there. Pulling the ring of keys from my pocket, I sifted through the different numbers until I landed on key twenty-six, the same number on the craft.

"Do you know how to fly it?"

I winced, shaking my head. "Do you?"

"No time like the present to learn, I suppose."

The key was more of a button, and when I pressed it, the hovercraft's interior illuminated, showing the seats and control desks inside. I pressed the button again and the ramp dropped down at our feet.

"I really hope there's a manual in here," Lexyn muttered. We went inside and were taken aback by how much room there was. It looked two times smaller from the outside. Though we'd never flown, we immediately sat in the front seats behind the shield, poring over the million-and-one flickering buttons that created the control center. "That lever right there," Lexyn said. "Push it."

I pressed the yellow button that released the lever and the craft revved around us. Outside, the wide garage door slid open to the night. I forced the lever upwards next and we began to move forward, steadily shifting out of the warehouse and inching into the madness that awaited us.

Dry lightning cracked across the sky, igniting the stormy clouds. When I directed the hovercraft into the lot, we got a full view of Cameron blasting bolts of energy at the citadel. Jon fought off the armed men and Generators that tried to tackle him, and then every so often he moved toward a truck to cloak it with a wave of his hand. By cloaking them, he rendered each one invisible to the naked eye. And while it hadn't been a part of our initial plan, I knew he did it to slow them down.

Lexyn hit a button on her side of the hovercraft and the overhead window slid back and out of the way. She stood up on her seat and cupped her hands around her mouth as she started shouting. "Cam, Jon! We need to go!" They didn't hear her until she was prompted to scream louder, and then they finally saw us. Jon dropped the fight and immediately started running toward the craft. Cameron, amid the onslaught of flying bullets, released his last burst of energy into a group of Generators and began plowing through to us.

But there were about fifty men to their two-person team; they didn't glide through the chaos with ease. I watched Jon take a blow to the face, another to the stomach. They restrained his arms behind him while, not too far away, Cameron's wings were tugged back at an unnatural angle.

"No," I breathed. "They need help." Before I talked myself out of it, I ran out the back of the hovercraft and dashed for Cameron. The minute

I was close enough, I jumped at the Generator holding him back, my fist coming down in its face. It staggered back. With a growl, I yanked it away and pivoted, slamming my foot so hard into its side that it collided with an armed man approaching from my left.

"Go to the craft, now!" I shouted at Cameron. He limped to his feet, adjusted his wings, and shot into the sky with groundbreaking speed. After I watched him enter the craft in the lot, I swung back around to attack another Generator, smashing its suit to nothing. My fists heated. My body felt hotter than it had ever felt before and my mind was a muddled wreck. An eager mix of power and adrenaline pumped through my veins—the perfect drug.

I crushed another Generator below my feet, and then, with my hair sticking to the sweat on my face, hurried to Jon. He wrestled a Generator off of him only to be shook by another. Though he managed to break every one of their necks, he was struggling to keep it up. He moved around in a haze of fists, and after a moment I saw his fire. It lit up his hands as he fought, kindling sparks of blue. And he fought like he was in a trance, like he was blind to everything but the rage. In that moment I was both frightened and enthralled by him.

"Jon!" I ducked to evade a hissing bullet and got close enough to him that he could see me.

When he did, his eyes were almost unrecognizable. He was lost to the flames. Unthinkingly, I pummeled a Generator with its own gun and then reached for Jon. I only succeeded in touching his arm because he moved around so much, but the instant our skin met, blue flames consumed my body, encasing me in a heat so vile I felt it in my bones. I felt his energy, his emotion—I felt *him*.

"Mathai!" Jon yelled, shooting at two Generators. "Use it!"

He was referring to the flames. I glimpsed at the fires wrapped around my fingers, admiring the energy. With a single touch, Jon had shared his abilities with me. Or he'd triggered mine through a connection neither of us could explain. I didn't know how it was possible, but the fire scorched something from my past. It cleaved through my psyche, fracturing the walls Silo had built to keep my memories locked away.

I threw my entire body into the fight. Streaks of blue flames lit up the night, thunder above our heads. Back-to-back, Jon and I attacked the Generators that stomped toward us, fighting in a series of swift movements. They advanced with real bullets. The armed men that accompanied them wore black and red suits. I guessed that they worked with Presidium, because I'd never seen them before. They were trained. They knew our patterns, our tendencies. And though it was dark, their cruel, bottomless eyes, lit by the lightning in the sky, said it all. They were there to extinguish us, not take us back to Silo.

Mathai, someone spoke into my mind. *They found us in the craft!*

It was Lexyn. Though she had only spoken to me by way of thought, I sensed her fear and knew she was in trouble. My eyes scanned over the lot until I saw the craft under siege. Lexyn and Cameron stood at the edge of the ramp shooting colossal waves of energy into a team of five men who charged from a few feet away, carrying guns that looked more like canons. When they kept coming, Cameron flew out and barreled through the group. It would have been simple for Lexyn to get behind the wheel and divert their attention, but she couldn't. Not until everyone was inside.

The Generators came less and less and Jon and I didn't hesitate to run, booking it to the craft. But when I glanced up at the roof, I realized we were still missing someone. "Where's Elektra?" I asked Jon.

"She was up there a second ago," he said. Another scan of the roof got me nothing and I immediately began to worry. Lexyn and I saw the cameras go out with the lights, so if Elektra succeeded in erasing them, she would have been in the craft by now.

"We can't leave her," I said. Jon gave me a look, like he knew what I was about to do. But before he could open his mouth and try to persuade me, I said, "Tell Lexyn to fly it."

"Mathai—"

"Go! I'm right behind you."

Reluctantly, Jon ran for the craft, knocking out the men that stood in his way. When he neared the others, Lexyn helped him onboard. He told her what I said and I watched her face fall as I began retracing my steps to the citadel, though I knew she'd do it. If we stood any chance of getting out of here, the craft had to fly. Or else the Generators would damage it enough to render it useless.

"Elektra!" I screamed into the night, running at a slower pace. *Where the hell is she?* Generators tailed me as I struggled to take deep breaths. I was about a yard away from the craft when, finally, I saw Elektra's head of brown hair. She stood on the edge of the roof, tinkering with a set of wires. Her hands moved hastily, tying and snapping. When it seemed she had it figured out, she whipped it above her head, waving at me.

"Get to the craft!" I shouted, pointing ahead as I pumped my feet faster.

Her gaze followed my hand and she dropped the wires. Hopefully she'd erased the cameras, but in the end, it didn't matter as much as her getting on the craft. She took a step in the right direction, and then suddenly cried out, calling my name. A streak of lightning revealed a man in black appearing from behind her with a blade pressed to her throat.

"*Elektra, no!*"

She shouldn't have gone up there alone. The shock of seeing the man drag her back and out of sight hit me hard. I stopped running, a solitary breath *wooshing* from my lungs. Had he done it? Had he hurt her? I felt an ache seize my chest, like her fear was my own. I didn't know how to separate it from my own emotions. The corners of my eyesight blurred. My defenses powered off and I crumbled as pain blossomed at my hip. When I looked down, blood poured from a gash in my side.

Hurt.

I was hurt?

Jon yelled for me somewhere in the background, but he felt a million miles away.

Shot, my mind registered. I'd been shot.

I'd stopped running.

I'd lost focus.

I looked up and saw Elektra pounding away at the man's masked face. She was tiny compared to him; however, something dark shined within her eyes. She attacked him, grunting as she scratched at his face, kicked away his blade, and pulled his hair. A water tank sat behind them and she dragged him over, using all her might to throw his head in. I wanted to scream and tell her to just run for it, but like Jon, Elektra was lost in a daze I couldn't pull her out of alone. Her face turned red with sorrow as she held the man's head under water, mouthing a countdown from ten until the man stopped moving.

Dead.

"Mathai!" Jon called. Lexyn began flying the craft down the lot's runway and I spurred myself into action. As a Generator hurdled toward me, I swept my foot out to trip it. It dropped like a boulder and I crept over its form with a shaking hand covering the laceration at my hip. There, I saw my reflection in its suit. My blue and green eyes looked feral. They looked unnatural, because the last time I had seen them so bright I was holding a gun to Manis' head.

With a knuckled fist, I beat against the Generator's face, screaming louder than the thunder. The citadel was on fire and warfare wreaked havoc around me. But I didn't quit punching until the pain grew unbearable in my side and the Generator dropped its gun. Then I ran. I ran faster than my legs could carry me, and then tripled the effort. On the roof, Elektra raced to keep up with the craft. We ran at the same pace, and she peered down to signal to Cameron with a sequence of jerky hand movements. *We're going to jump*, she told him. *Get ready.*

I pinned my gaze on Jon as a flock of men chased me down. He stood on the ramp with a hand outstretched to me, the other gripped tight to the craft. His face was pained, as if it took everything in him not to rush over and pick me up himself. I looked at his hand and knew that it was both my lifeline and death sentence. Because his touch either fuelled or weakened me.

I could hurt him.

Or worse, we could hurt each other. Irrevocably and totally.

Elektra approached the edge of the roof and Lexyn ascended the craft to at least six feet in the air. I knew my time was running out when the wind picked up beneath its huge propellers.

I wasn't ready.

I was never ready, I'd learned, but I hadn't succeeded so far without a little trial and error.

Releasing the hand on my hip, I jumped into the air and grasped Jon's hand. Elektra took a step off the roof and her body fell from the sky. In my head, everything happened too fast. A Generator was an inch away from taking me back and the gunshots kept going. Elektra landed on top of the craft and into Cameron's arms, swaying as Lexyn flew it off the lot with accelerated speed. Jon held my arms the entire time and hurriedly pulled me in. But I might as well have been dead weight. My feet dangled miles into the sky, the cool air hitting my face. He didn't see what was happening as he called to the others for help, though I did. I saw the black veins slither up my arms and wrap around my elbows. I saw them creep up his neck and snatch that beautiful wonder from his eyes.

"Mathai, hold on!" Lexyn shouted from behind the wheel. Once Cameron and Elektra were safely inside the craft, they aided Jon in pulling me up. But the agony was too great. By the time they'd dragged me in and closed the ramp, darkness had swallowed all the light behind my eyes.

TWENTY-SIX

"ACTUALLY, I CAN"
BIONIC: MATHAI-0329

ruckus of whispered voices drew me to consciousness. My eyes fluttered open and the first thing I saw were their four concerned faces as they kneeled over my body, counting my intakes of breath like each one could be my last. Then I saw the walls of the craft and felt the rhythm of us moving through the air. When I binked and tried to sit up, Lexyn was the first to move. She pointed a flashlight at me and gently nudged my shoulder to lie back down.

"Go slow," she said.

"No," I groaned, holding my head as I moved to sit anyway. The image of me jumping for Jon's hand replayed in my mind, over and over again. The black veins, Elektra being attacked, and the shot to my side. It all came rushing back to a focal point. We almost didn't make it; we had come so close to losing everything. "We need to get to the Seeming," I said.

"But you're still dizzy," Lexyn argued.

"We've been tracking their movements on the ground using the sensors up front. They're not following us," Cameron said.

"But I suspect they've alerted Presidium," Elektra added, playing with the loose threads of her pants. Besides the small cuts on her throat, she appeared okay. At least, on the outside she did. I couldn't feel her emotions anymore, like she'd blocked me out. I didn't understand why this bothered me so much, but it did. "We have a day, at most, to find the Seeming. Even with the cameras erased, they'll know the exact craft we stole."

I nodded. "Then we won't spend too much time in the sky. How long have we been flying?"

Cameron glanced to the front as the monitor beeped with an AUTOPILOT notification. Beneath it was the time: ninth hour. "About forty minutes," he said. "You were asleep the whole time. We worried you ..." His words trailed off, his eyes going to my stomach.

I remembered the pain just then. I'd felt the bullet pierce my torso the second I stopped to look for Elektra on the roof. I roamed my hands over my body, searching for the bleeding wound, but when I lifted my shirt the skin there was completely smooth. "I removed the bullet," Jon said, his expression grave. "Your body did the rest."

Of course it did, I thought wryly. Irritated, I stood and wobbled to my feet. The front shield showed that the storm clouds had condensed into a thick, grey matter. It parted as the hovercraft navigated the aphotic zone. "How do we get to the Seeming?" I asked.

"I did a search and found the coordinates using natural landmarks," Elektra said. I followed her to the front of the craft and observed everything she'd programmed. Not only coordinates, but maps of Silo and Asylum 4. And even a map of Caeshua that was better, and more accurate, than the one in my codex. She tapped several buttons on the holographic screen and zooms of each city popped up. "The rocks that look like feet are south of where you guys thought the coast was. It's a straight flight this way." Using two fingers, she increased the size of the photo and made a trail from *Fake Ucilei* to *Feet Rocks*.

I grinned at her, surprised. "You're an evil genius, aren't you?"

"It's what they made me for." She shrugged, looking away. After she showed me how to reset the coordinates, she rejoined the others in the back and left me to tinker with the controls. I sat behind the wheel in one of the chairs, clicking away. I didn't notice that Jon had come to my side until I felt his energy shift behind me. His hands were in his pockets, but now I guessed he did that so often to refrain from accidentally touching me. He dropped into the next seat, his jaw working as he watched me. Regardless of our connection, I knew what he was going to say.

"You risked a lot out there."

"And I'd do it again," I said, turning away from my view of the sky. The others in the back lounged tiredly on the floor, but I knew they were listening. "You don't like taking risks, do you, Jon? That's why you try to stop me."

He didn't answer.

He just silently listened to me, taking in my words, and I couldn't begin to describe how that made me feel. To be *listened* to.

"You were reluctant to find the coast, to search the craft Elektra had been in. And it's not fear, either. I'd sense that from you." My gaze wandered his face. "I've spent what feels like eons of my life being told what to do and how to feel. If risks come with my freedom, I'm going to take them."

"And I've spent most of my life playing it safe," Jon finally said, his tone deep. The way he watched me sent a chill through my core. His eyes seemed darker as he spoke. "But when it comes to you, I want to be reckless. I want to *rage* with you, and that frightens me. It's the biggest risk I could ever take."

"I don't—"

"I want to hate you, but I can't. I'm *stuck*."

Stuck like he had been in A10. I bit back what I was going to say, jostled by his confession. Our connection was scary. Jon had literally crashed into my life and turned everything upside down. I couldn't blame him for wanting to hate me. I wanted to hate him, too, but I couldn't. He was in my head, under my skin. When I thought about those eyes and arms I'd felt in the darkness, I thought of him. Because although I'd been created with so much knowledge, I had no knowledge of him. Of how he worked. He was entirely new to me, an unknown category in my psyche. And like the calculations that filtered through my mind at every waking hour, I wanted to pick him apart.

And he wanted to consume me.

We were a conflict of interests, destined to tear each other apart.

As the hovercraft flew on autopilot, Jon and I settled into a long quiet. There was still a lot left unsaid, I could tell, but it wasn't the right time to say any of it. I pulled my knees to my chest on the chair and ignored the hungry growl of my stomach. The last time we'd eaten well was at Niana's and I regretted not packing the extra food she'd given us. Jon had burned through his ration by the time we left A4 for the crater. I only had a half-full water canteen, a can of fruit, and the yellow snack bag we stole from the food store. It was enough to last me a day or two, but split between the five of us, it was nothing.

A loud chiming broke me from my thoughts and a square panel on the wall began lighting up with a message. Lexyn jumped up and went to it, tapping until the chiming finally stopped. But she frowned, turning her head this way and that to read the words.

" It says ... we have a video call?" she said.

A video call? Jon and I strolled over and peeked over her shoulder, squinting to read the small, blue text. It was paired with an envelope icon and a timestamp. Dated four minutes ago.

"Yeah, it says video call. What's a video call?" Elektra asked, ducking beneath Lexyn's wings to get to the front of the group.

"I don't know," Lexyn answered.

"It's a phone call, but you can see the person's face," Jon explained.

"But who would be trying to call us?" Cameron asked.

"Only one way to find out." I tapped the envelope and everyone took a minor step back, like it was about to explode. But it blinked open with a live video that covered the whole screen. At first all we saw was a room that looked like a lab. The white walls were too familiar, as well as the machines and tables in the background. The audio took a while to come in, but when it did a faraway screeching boomed from the panel speakers.

"I don't understand what's going on," Lexyn said. "Maybe it was sent to the wrong craft? Or it was here before we got on?"

Jon denied it. "No, the call was made four minutes ago."

Elektra pointed to the corner of the screen where, toward the top, all five of our names were addressed in the envelope. "Look! Maybe it's someone who wants to help us."

Static raced across the panel with a loading bar at ninety-six percent. When it was nearly finished, a face came into view. Even though it was all holographs, the person might as well have stood right next to us. Every color of his face loaded onto the screen and I knew help was the last thing we'd be given.

"*Manis*," I said between tight lips.

His gruesome scar looked worse than the last time I'd seen it, but he had the audacity to smile. His bird-like features and pale skin were still haunting. He sat at a desk in the white lab as, what I now recognized to be Jackets, worked around him, righting chairs and installing equipment. Silo—he was in Silo. Which meant it hadn't been completely destroyed by the Outliers.

"It's so nice to see you again, Ari," he responded, his voice a faux sticky-sweet.

"I go by Mathai now," I said, speaking into the panel. "My *real* name."

Cameron moved around agitatedly. "You know him?"

"Unfortunately."

Manis observed the craft behind us, amusement in his eyes. How had he managed to contact us, miles away in the air? Most importantly, *why* was he contacting us? We were rogue, he knew that, and we weren't turning ourselves in anytime soon.

"What do you want?" Jon asked him.

Manis' huge eyes lifted to him and his smile broadened. "When your legion was created, we had no idea of the power we unleashed into Caeshua. It was a trial to see which legionaries would withstand the rigorous training. We had our doubts, but congratulations…"

I hated him so much. I wanted to reach in and gouge out his eyes for what he'd done to me, to us. We were their toys, their disposable playthings.

"We've been watching you, each of you," he continued. The screen changed and a video clip of me jamming the glass into the leviathan's eye in A10 began to play. Then came footage of Elektra sleeping under a bridge, Jon pickpocketing a stranger, and Cameron and Lexyn soaring through the sky. The clips rotated, switching to different times and locations. Every moment we thought we were alone, we had been watched. The finishing blow was the clip of us at the citadel, not even an hour ago. Every second of our time there had been recorded. We had been defending ourselves, but when our motions were slowed down and analyzed this way, we looked like cruel beasts. "Even though you fought against it, you turned out to be exactly what we wanted you to be. Smart, quick, and relentless. *Together.*"

"No!" Lexyn groused, slapping a hand to the screen.

The videos faded away and Manis' face returned. He looked at me like he I was scum on his shoe and I wished I'd pulled the trigger what I had the chance.

"Return to Silo and we'll help you."

I scoffed. "Help with what?"

"I know about your ... *memory* dilemma. And it must hurt for you two to touch ..." He glanced from me to Jon. "I can restore all of it."

"What's the catch?" Elektra asked, crossing her arms.

Manis flashed his teeth at her. "You surrender to Presidium and—"

"Absolutely not! Are you *kidding* me?" Angered, I started pressing buttons on the screen to end the video call, but none of it worked, like Manis controlled its power from his side.

"You're strong, Mathai, but you can't fight against what comes naturally," he said, talking so fast he spit everywhere. "You're monsters, killers. Programmed assassins—easily resettable. You can't live out your lives in the desert like scavengers, running like fools! You can't *win*."

My hand paused on the screen and the others behind me went silent. There it was—the truth. We'd known it all along, but Manis had always dressed it up for me, never actually saying what was on his mind. But now I'd heard it, and I was so furious my body shook. I wasn't going to let my DNA tell me what I could and couldn't do—not Jon, not Manis, not Presidium. I wasn't going to bargain with my freedom or my happiness like they were pebbles in an auction bid. They were invaluable. I fought too hard to give everything away.

Looking Manis straight in the face, I said, "**Actually, I can.**"

Elektra reached to the right and picked up a wrench from a toolkit beneath the control desk, then violently swung it down over her head, hammering it into the panel. Manis' surprised face flickered and sparked, and then he was gone, leaving nothing in his wake.

No one moved for a solid three minutes, and then Lexyn turned to me, tears in her eyes. "We're not giving up," she said slowly.

"It's not even a thought," Jon agreed. I nodded dazedly, afraid to speak in case my words sounded as confused as I felt.

Elektra dropped the wrench with a sigh, kicking it away. "We should land somewhere for the night," she said. As she moved to the wheel, a rustling at the back of the craft, toward the ramp, caught my attention. I stopped to make sure it wasn't me, but it happened again, along with unmistakable sound of soft footsteps.

"Do you guys hear that?" I asked.

"Hear what?" Jon scrutinized the dark corners, and when the rustling continued, he nodded. "Yeah, I hear it. Hit the light over there. White button."

I slid my hands along the wall of sleek knobs until I touched the switch. I pushed it, and the long aisle leading back into the craft lit up with luminescent floor lights. I shadowed them all the way to the closed ramp and small bathroom door. There was a sink and a cupboard, and then an empty crate. Ammunition lined the open racks, but none of it could have made the noise.

"I don't see anything!" I shouted to the others.

Cameron shrugged. "Maybe it's something outside. We can—"

"*Wait.*" My eyes raked lower and I saw a pair of feet poking out from beneath a control desk. When I dropped down on my knees, I stared directly into the bright, scared eyes of a girl. She trembled in the corner, holding the wrench Elektra had just dropped. Her hair was a frizzy, tangled mane around her head and the medical gown she wore was splattered with blood. She blinked, refusing to talk or to come out. But I recognized her. Not because my memories had instantly returned, but because she had been the prime focus of my dreams for days.

"Alessia?"

TWENTY-SEVEN

"COLD-BLOODED KILLER"
BIONIC: MATHAI-0329

lessia didn't remember who I was. I knew it when she flinched as I reached out for her, like she expected me to be violent. She held the wrench close to her body and didn't move at all. She was petite, maybe no older than twelve. I was afraid of scaring her away, though. I didn't understand how or why she was on the hovercraft, and I knew it couldn't be any typical coincidence, but my heart was racing frantically while I sat there with her.

I couldn't believe I'd found my sister, my only family.

"Guys!" I yelled. "It's Alessia!" I took in her tan, round face. She jumped a little when Cameron and Jon walked up to see her, but then calmed considerably, fascinated by Cameron's wings. Her grip on the wrench loosened and her lips moved to form words.

"It's okay, we won't hurt you," Jon assured. When I reached out my hand again, she released her weapon and slid it over, almost apologetically. Then with her eyes trained on me, she stood and slowly crawled out from beneath the control desk.

"What's going—" Elektra froze in the aisle and Alessia's legs quivered, her eyes as big as saucers. She itched at her skin and gawked at each of us, especially Lexyn. Alessia seemed enthralled by her wings the most.

"Do you know who we are?" Lexyn asked her.

Alessia nodded slowly and we held our breaths. Was it possible she still had her memories?

I stood to give her space. However, it took a lot for me to not put my arms around her and protect her in some way. I envisioned her face from my dream, her tears turning to blood as she was ripped into the sky, and I became cold. How long had she been hiding here?

"I was scared," Alessia finally said, her nails digging anxiously into her skin. Her tone was gentle, though I could tell she had a hard time mentally processing what was happening. "I heard the noises and the lights went out, so I ran."

"That's why you were on the craft?" I asked.

She nodded, whispering a soft *yes*.

"And why were they keeping you there? That's a paper facility, isn't? They store records, files, and documents. Not legionaries," Elektra said. "Were you running away from them?"

"No…" Alessia answered, looking confused now. "I've lived there all my life."

I took another step back and bumped into Jon's chest. She had to be wrong. She couldn't have spent her life there if, just weeks ago, we'd all been caught in an electrical storm. I glanced at her dirty feet, and then her face, feeling sad. What had they done to her?

"How do you remember us?" Cameron asked.

"You were in my training," she said. "They made me … learn you." She shivered again and I couldn't hold back any longer. I went to her on my knees, rubbing my hands in circles on her arms to warm her up. She accepted my touch without flinching this time, and I felt the trace of a new connection in my psyche. Whatever they did to her, we'd find a way to undo it. She was safe now; she was home.

"Let's get her some fresh clothes," Jon said, moving around me. He went to look for my bag he'd brought aboard and came back with the extra shirts and pants Niana had given me. He held them out for Alessia and she grinned at him.

"They said you were the sweet one," she said in a small voice, blushing. And Jon could only awkwardly stand there, scratching the back of his neck.

"Welcome back, Les," Elektra said, genuinely looking relieved. She walked back to the wheel at the front and pressed a few buttons, and then pushed the lever down. "I'm landing it, guys. If we're in the air for too long, we'll burn through the fuel," she said.

"Yeah, I'll help." Lexyn smiled at Alessia one more time and then turned around.

Alessia watched them leave and her timid, frightened features turned sad and curious. I questioned if she knew what she was, if she knew what we had once meant to her. And I hoped she didn't believe everything they told her at the citadel, for surely they were nothing but lies.

"Why did they look at me like that?" she asked.

"Like how?"

"Like I'm an apparition."

My gaze dropped to the floor as I tried to formulate the words. Even then, I didn't think there were words right enough for what I was about to say. "They're scared, like you. Like me. We don't know what's going on, but we're trying to pick up all the pieces to puzzle that we can. And you were one of them. We're just figuring out where you fit."

I felt that she understood, but she gave me no indication. So I kept talking, overwhelmed by her presence, her realness.

"You may not remember me, but I'm your sister. Though I suppose not by DNA," I said, now looking into her light eyes. "I think I've been searching for you for a while. At least, subliminally."

"How did you know where I was?"

"We didn't." Jon watched us from behind her. "I didn't know you were real until a few days ago, and I-I know that sounds bad. But a lot of things were out of my control and I'm trying to fix them now. I'll protect you, I swear." Alessia touched my hand on her arm and she began to play with my fingers, far more comfortable than she had been several moments ago. "I'm going to get you some help."

"Okay," she said gently. "I believe you." I leaned in and kissed her forehead, thoughts of us sitting in the crater and eating fruit coming to mind. I wanted to do that again, be that again, for her. A safe haven.

With her hand in mine, I led her to the bathroom and fought the urge to ask whose blood was on her gown. A quick inspection of her limbs showed no wounds, but the blood led sticky, dry paths all the way to her toes. *Maybe she ran into one of the men from the citadel*, I thought darkly, recalling how she'd held the wrench. Fear had the power to incite anyone to do anything.

While Alessia changed her clothes, Jon and Cameron strapped into the seats that folded out from the walls. Elektra and Lexyn set in the codes to land the craft safely in the desert and I felt the air vibrate beneath the floorboards. Everything tipped sideways. I held on to a handle above my head and counted silently to fifteen, feeling my stomach dip. And as we soared beneath the clouds, my thoughts turned to Manis' words. I snuck a peek at Jon's face, half-veiled by his hair. We'd never give in to Presidium, but I wondered...

What would it be like to touch him without restraint?

The moons shone beautifully here. They looked enormous, and there was enough of the sky to remind us of how small we really were. I saw the stars for the first time, too, and I imagined each one was a new, immense journey that I could pluck from the night and keep in my codex. Then I'd have it forever, and our voyages would be endless.

"Light takes so long to travel to Caeshua that these stars may have died thousands of years ago," Cameron said thoughtfully, shocking me. He sat with his legs crossed, his wings tucked behind him. Beneath the moon, his gunmetal eyes seemed to glow.

We sat by a crater in the middle of nowhere, our bed for the night. Alessia—who appreciated the nickname Les—snuggled deeply into the blanket Jon found in the craft and rested her head on my shoulder. We'd only been out here for an hour, but not much had been said. By anyone. I had a feeling no one wanted to air their insecurities, as our situation now weighed heavier than ever before. Manis could have been watching us from Silo right then and there wasn't a single thing we could do about it.

"I don't want to talk about the stars," Lexyn mumbled from the end of the group, her knees to her chest. "What if the Seeming isn't real? Where are we supposed to go? Silo was our home."

"Silo wasn't our home," I said, brushing back loose curls of my hair that moved with the wind. "Our home can't be somewhere we're not accepted."

Jon stirred beside Alessia with his elbows to his knees. He hadn't said much either. Actually, he hadn't spoken directly to me since he confessed to wanting to hate me. But he spoke then, looking at Cameron beside him. "We can't worry about going back. I think restoring our memories is the most important thing right now."

"And what if I don't want them?" Elektra asked, her eyes gazing into the crater. I peered around Alessia's head to see her face. It was blank, emotionless, which was completely uncharacteristic for her. She'd been nothing but a ball of energy since I'd met her. Although, I'd noticed a change in her attitude after she fought the man on the roof, and then during the call with Manis. She was quieter, as if it all hit her too quickly and she didn't know how to internalize it. She stopped joking with Cameron and I could no longer sense her emotions like I had at the citadel. Elektra was angry, I understood, but something darker was spinning in that head of hers. "We're murderers," she said sadly.

Cameron immediately tried to console her. "Don't say that."

"Why not, if it's true?" she shot back. "I held that man under water until his eyes had no color! I killed him ... and I liked it."

Her words pierced my heart, because she was only sixteen, living on the streets and stealing to make it by. And though she'd always been a legionary, fighting and killing was all new to her again. It was traumatic, and when I'd watched her on the roof, I'd wanted nothing more than to trade places with her. She wasn't a murderer—no **cold-blooded killer** cried while they did the deed.

"We're anything we want to be, and we're not murderers," Jon said. "We're not their weapons, and we're not disposable. Disregard everything you heard Manis say. They'll do anything to split us apart, because we're *stronger* together."

Les buried her face in my arm. She'd been the most quiet, but I knew it was because she didn't understand everything happening. While we hadn't gone to the citadel for her exactly, we were there because of her. To get the craft and search Caeshua until we found her. We'd risked a lot and nearly lost it, but I'd relive the moment a hundred times if it meant we got her back.

Elektra fussed with her hands in her lap and then said, "That doesn't make what I did any better."

"We've all had to do things we don't like."

"But I didn't—"

"No, you *saved* Les!" I shouted, vexed. "You killed someone who wanted to harm us. Who wanted to tear us apart and misuse us." Lexyn wrapped her wings around her body as my voice echoed in the sky. The stormy clouds rolled together and it began to rain, wetting through our clothes. But no one got up to leave. "That doesn't make you a murderer. That makes you family."

"And we're the only family we've got," Jon said, his eyes on me. Elektra's ire died out with the word 'family,' as she was probably hearing it for the first time. Or maybe she wasn't and we'd been a family before losing our memories, and maybe we'd have to tell her this every night under the moons until she believed us. And that was okay with me.

Lexyn had said it best: we were family by bond, not by DNA.

The rain continued to pour and we sat there soaking it in as it muddied the terrain. After a spell of silence, Lexyn shook out her wings and threw her legs over the edge of the crater. "I always find myself next to these. Just thinking ... about nothing, really."

"Craters?"

She nodded. "They're comforting, like the sky. They make you feel safe. Hidden away."

And free, I thought to myself. A crater had been my escape from Silo and one had been in my dream with Les. They were no more than holes in the earth, but they provided an unalienable security.

Cameron chuckled. "Crater Knights."

"Huh?" Elektra looked up from her hands.

"*Crater Knights*. We're the Crater Knights."

Alessia was the first to giggle, and the sound of her happiness was so infectious that was all began to laugh, there in the middle of a rainstorm. Lexyn slung her arm around her brother's neck and pulled him close, teasing his hair. "I like it. Fighting crime and slaying bad guys!"

"Pew, pew, pew," Elektra goofed, making fake guns with her hands and pointing them at the crater. She'd been crying, but the rain washed her tears away. The unease that had settled over my legion evaporated, leaving us hopeful, even though there was so little to feel hopeful about.

But I had an inkling we'd be all right.

TWENTY-EIGHT

"CEASELESS WONDER"
BIONIC: MATHAI-0329

opened up the crinkled paper I'd taken from the bunker in A10 and smoothed it out on the surface of the ramp. I had almost forgotten about it in my bag, but now that I had a moment alone with everyone sleeping in the craft, I admired the drawing of the iris in the moonlight.

Besides the torn edges of the paper, it looked exactly the same. I wished I'd taken the other ones to complete the whole drawing, though. I wished I'd taken more time to admire it all together. I held the paper out in front of me, shielding it from the blowing rain beneath the hood of the craft. Then I slid my fingers over the pen markings, memorizing each line that captivated me, wanting to climb into the picture. I couldn't quite comprehend why I loved it so much.

"Hiding something?"

I spun from my position on the ramp, my heart jumping in my chest. Jon stood behind me with his probing gaze on the drawing in my hand.

"It's nothing," I said, quickly folding it away and tucking it into my back pocket. "I thought you were asleep."

He walked up and sat beside me, his legs dangling off the ramp with mine. Then he sighed deeply. "I couldn't sleep. To be truthful, I haven't slept well in what's felt like years."

"Why's that?" I asked.

"I'm thinking too much, I guess."

I nodded, understanding. However, I spent my nights purposely avoiding sleep, afraid my dreams were darker than my reality. "I've been doing some thinking too."

"What about?" His hazel-green eyes wandered my face.

"About my past," I confessed. "About what my life would have been like if I was like other legionaries."

"But you're not like the others."

"I know that, and I don't want to be." I absentmindedly rubbed my knuckles together. "But I wish I knew what I did to make this all so bad."

Jon frowned thoughtfully, and the dimple appeared above his eyebrow. "You don't always have to be strong, you know?"

"What do you mean?"

"You don't have to worry about knowing everything all the time. You don't have to know all the answers and you don't have to be afraid. Being strong isn't your only option," he said. "Sometimes a state of **ceaseless wonder** is beautiful too."

"But what if I'm the only one? Who will be strong then, if not me?"

Jon's gaze moved from my eyes to my mouth. We were sitting so close on the ramp that I could feel his body heat warming me from the cold rain. "You could never be alone, Mathai. People will try to shame you for it, but there's nothing wrong with needing someone, or wanting to be needed."

"And what if I am afraid?" I whispered, my voice drowning out with the storm. "What if I'm afraid of not being strong enough?"

"The best of us always are, the irony in this all."

I grinned. "What do you have to be afraid about?"

But Jon didn't share my smile. The look on his face was intense as he gazed at me. "I'm frightened by *you*, your smile. Your laughter is my worst fear and your eyes haunt me even in the daylight. Your naivety is noxious." He stopped to angrily run his hands through his hair. "But I'm also afraid that I've grown obsessed with fearing you; afraid that I'm attracted to the darkness in you. That I'll *consume* all of you, and my fear of you will be beautiful instead of the terror I thought it would be."

I sat there motionless, a touch away from him. I didn't know whether to apologize or be insulted, but I loved knowing I affected him in that way. I loved hearing the raw truth from his lips. Because he did the same to me, and my mind, my mission, and my life hadn't been the same since he found me in A10. A week ago I had spent my days locked in a room with empty, white walls and now I was thinking of ways I could touch him and still remain sane.

Reading my mind, Jon held up his palm to me. "Let me show you," he said.

I slowed my breathing and put my hand out to his, hesitant to make contact. "Will it hurt?"

"Only for a second."

Biting my bottom lip, I placed my palm to his, intertwining our fingers. The pain began at a slow burn. I felt it in my fingertips first, and then the numbness spread to my wrist. I watched in part awe and part agony as black veins traveled down my hand like a lattice and slowly inched to my elbow. My lungs felt as though someone chained them up on an exhale, and no matter how hard I tried I couldn't inhale to relieve the pain. But when I looked into Jon's eyes—eyes now drained of color—I understood what he meant. The pain dulled to a tolerable level the longer we touched, even though I knew the black veins would kill us. Soon I didn't ache at all. In fact, the pain became something like an aphrodisiac, drugging my mind and creating an unhealthy addiction to him and this feeling.

And I *felt* what he meant about being obsessed with the fear of me. Because although it was scary and painful, to revel in it was bliss.

I snatched my hand away and we took in deep breaths of air. When my lungs no longer felt on fire, I scooted over on the ramp and rubbed my temples.

"I don't know what causes it," he said, his breathing still off.

"I told you that I can't control—"

"No, it's more than that."

I glanced up, preparing to argue with him, but my gaze got sidetracked, going to something outside in the rain. I couldn't see it clearly from where we sat, but it had a distinct shape, even in the rain.

"Jon, do you see that?" Raising a shaking finger, I pointed to the unusual ditch beside the crater, where water collected like it was a well.

He looked where I pointed and squinted. I wasn't sure if he saw, but curiosity made me stand and start walking anyway. And then I walked faster, hastened by the storm.

"Mathai!" Jon called.

Sprinting madly into the night, I searched for the ditch, the one that I was sure wasn't supposed to be there. It wasn't big enough to be a crater, and neither was it deep. It was like a small sink in the turf, a dip in the sand. As I got closer to it, I realized the ditch wasn't manmade, for it was too wide and too random. The sand grew soft beneath my boots and the land sloped to the center. When I got down on my hands and knees and felt around beneath the water, I knew they were there.

The stones.

"Jon!" I screamed, waving over.

He reluctantly followed me out from the craft, the rain soaking through his clothes. The look he gave me would have been hilarious if I hadn't just found our memories buried in Caeshua.

"What are you doing?" he shouted above the storm.

"Look!" I dug around blindly until I could wrap my hands around a bunch of them, and then I pulled them up. The stones were practically invisible against the dark sky, but the shiny surfaces were unmistakable. "*This* is the coast!"

Jon gaped openly at me. He didn't move for a second and we stood there, knee-deep in water. "How did you—"

"I don't know. I just saw the ditch and followed my first thought," I told him. I gave him a handful of the stones and then fished my hands beneath the water for a few more. When my arms were full, we ran back beneath the hood of the craft and dropped them all on the ramp.

"These are it, right?" I asked, shaking the water from my hair.

"These are definitely it." Jon ran a hand down the length of his face, his body shaking from the cold. But he ignored it, and instead picked up one of the black, smooth stones, turning it over in his hands. "I can't believe you found them."

"Do you know how they work?" I asked hopefully.

"Niana never told me, but I assume it can't be too hard." He held out the stone to me. "Can you feel anything?"

I took the square-shaped stone and pressed it in a palm, only to get nothing. I doubted some divine light was supposed to shoot out from the sky and bestow upon us our memories, but I expected *something*. "No, what's supposed to happen?"

"Niana didn't say," he said, looking lost. We moved through the different stones, picking up each one and shaking them like they contained juice. But none of them did anything, no matter how long we held them.

"What's going on?" Lexyn appeared from the craft, standing at the top of the ramp. Her wings bristled in the cold air as she rubbed the sleep from her eyes. When she finally saw that we were dripping wet and digging through stones like mad collectors, she rushed to our sides.

"Where did you guys find them?" she asked. Her hands went to the large, round one in the middle and she placed it between her two palms, marveling at it.

"Out there in the storm," I said. "But we don't know how they work."

"Maybe we're supposed to eat them?"

"That doesn't sound right," said Elektra, rousing from her sleeping corner on the hovercraft's floor. Alessia jumped up behind her and Cameron poked his head out from the front seat.

"What if we organize them then?" I said.

"Organize them how?" Jon questioned.

I took the stone he held, together with the one Lexyn was sniffing, and laid them out on the ramp. There were twenty in total, and as I moved them around, something in my mind began to connect the dots. I saw numbers and shapes, colors and symbols. I recalled the three letters I'd found in Silo as I aligned the stones. The others silently watched me work, my hands moving faster than I, myself, could keep up with. Then when I was done, when every black stone had a place, I stepped back, gawking at what I'd put together.

"It's a word," Cameron said. "Can you read it?"

There were seven letters and it didn't make sense how I knew their order. It was like I had subliminally evoked the word when I touched the stones, possessed by the need to get my memories back. It was almost chilling, and through our connection I knew Jon thought the exact same.

"Phoenix," I said. "It says phoenix. What does that—" I never got to finish the sentence. A bolt of lightning struck the craft and the ground parted beneath our feet, blowing wind and rain in our faces. A piercing ring split through the air and we dropped to our knees with our hands over our ears. And the stones ... they vibrated on the ramp like they were *alive*. The last thing I remembered before my eyes rolled back into my head was the cries of my legion.

*"**It appears the six of** them have found each other."*

"Was the girl freed?"

"Yes, and placed on the hovercraft as you asked. What should we do now?"

"Watch them. She'll know what to do when the time comes."

"That's it?"

"Well, what else is there to do?"

"Bring them in? They're going to discover what we're hiding."

"Let them. If we go to them now, she'll run. She needs to come to me."

"What if she doesn't?"

"She always does."

TWENTY-NINE

"DRUG OF FANTASY"
BIONIC: MATHAI-0329

The *first memory came to* me *like an old friend. It swathed me in unbearable heat, and then the flipping images began.*

I was young, not a day over five-years-old. I knew it was me because the incubator in the lab read 0329. I was small, with all the same features and the enquiring blue and green eyes. I sat with my back against the glass and my eyes trained on the lab entrance door, and I waited for something to happen. I didn't know what, but I felt it coming. And I didn't move until a light blinked above the door and the Jackets entered the room, wheeling in a second incubator.

He was young too. I stood and pressed as close to the glass as I could, my small mouth open in awe as I stared. They placed him next to me and I noticed he was still sleeping. But he was like me; that was my very first thought upon seeing his head of dark, wavy hair. They'd made me someone to play with, finally.

I watched him for hours. The Jackets left after they connected his incubator to mine and the room went dark, save for the neon blue lights above our station. To pass the time as I waited for him, I hummed. They had tried to break the bad habit for weeks, saying it was unusual, but I was stubborn. I hummed a random tune and busied with the toys in my incubator. I didn't like any of them, though. They were too hard, too cold, but I wanted to share them with him.

I piled my books and stuffed dolls by the small hole at the side of my incubator, where Jackets often pushed through with my meals. I stacked everything so high that when I stood on them, I could reach out my little, bandaged hand to my new friend. And I would help him, because he'd be just as scared as I was.

He finally woke after the neon lights dimmed, signaling my bedtime. His big, sleepy eyes scanned the lab with panic and his bottom lip jutted out over his top one as he began to cry loudly. His confusion struck me immediately; I felt him. I slapped my hand against the glass until he saw me, and then his cries instantly hushed. Like he knew who I was.

I smiled and grinned with a missing front tooth, waving at him. He probably thought I was the strangest thing he'd ever seen. I pushed back my wild hair from my face and pointed to the matching hole in his incubator. I went to mine, and after a moment, he went to his. I climbed up my stack of books since he was much taller than me and I pushed a hand through, all the way to my shoulder. I mumbled something he probably didn't hear, then indicated how to use his hand. It was okay if he didn't know, because I'd teach him.

Still pouting, he glanced at his hands and moved his fingers around, admiring at how they worked. He looked at mine next, outstretched for him in the space between our incubators. And maybe he saw the desperation and loneliness on my face—I'd never *know. He stumbled to stand, getting used to his own legs, and tiptoed to reach for me too. The Jackets were watching us, but I didn't want him to know. I didn't want him to be afraid. Our little fingers strained to touch, to hold on. Until I leaned more into my books and his hand finally grasped mine. His skin was so warm compared to that of a Jacket that I gasped. When he giggled, I giggled too, because I wanted him to be happy here. And with tears in my eyes, I promised to be his friend, to protect him from what they were inevitably going to do to him.*

By the time they came for us the next morning and began carting us away in different directions, all my toys sat in Jon's broken incubator.

The memory morphed immediately into a new one, and I was several years older, sneaking into Jon's room and tackling him as soon as he opened the door. We played chess and hide-and-seek in the dark, going until they found us the next day, sleeping under his bed with a flashlight and blankets. But then I'd always find a way to come right back, or he'd find a way to me. Always. The memory lapsed quickly—Jon and I eating, training, and laughing together in stolen moments at Silo. We were never allowed to be together. Not in the same room, not for long. And I always had to wear my bandages. These moments eclipsed until the day Niana took him away, and I cried with a hand outstretched my window, begging him to come back.

But he never did, and he disappeared outside the Ward as the memory changed.

I remembered Lexyn and Cameron next, and Elektra and Alessia. I remembered seeing them for the first time in the refectory and being introduced to them as a legion member. Our differences didn't matter since we had all been created at different ages. Cameron and Elektra were the only ones with permanent wings and Alessia had wild hair like me. They were quiet, but then they welcomed me to the table like they'd known me *forever. Elektra shared her porridge and Cameron made silly faces to cheer me up. Lexyn always smiled and Alessia taught me how to eat with a fork. And while they made me feel happy for some time, my nights were usually spent curled up on the floor of my room, missing Jon and haunted by the **drug of fantasy**.*

The crusades began when I turned sixteen. We trained more than we slept, more than we ate. I was a studious learner during camp. I picked up on forms quickly and practiced everyday before dawn when everyone else was still asleep. I was troubled by the images of my dead clones—the girls I used to be—and couldn't rest until I completely exhausted myself. Manis drilled the fear into me well and I never tried to run again after they pulled me from the room with Kyra in my hands; so well that when I left for my first assassination outside the Ward, I froze at the sight of a leviathan. It chased me through the outlands while Lexyn and Cameron tried to tag it down and kill it. And I ran so fast that I was unaware of the boy climbing out the window of a bunker. I didn't see him until he wrestled me to the ground and vanquished the leviathan with a yellow-amber bullet to the head.

My memories rushed to the forefront in a blaze of dizzying colors. One moment I was recognizing the boy as Jon and then the next I was traveling down a dark cavern, completely alone. I used my hands on the walls to guide me, and then stopped at a steel door. Before opening it, I glanced behind me to check if anyone followed.

I looked too guilty for this memory to be innocent. Inside the room, I dropped my bag on a table and shrugged off my jacket. I settled into a chair and Petra walked in just as I was pulling out a book.

"Did you get it?" she asked me.

I slid the book over and nodded. "Everything is there, like I said it would be. Now can you help me or not?"

Petra glanced over the book, flipping through the pages to make sure it was all there. It was my codex, I realized. She cast her eyes on me after pocketing it. "Are you sure about this?" she asked.

"I'm sure. They need to be stopped, Petra, and I want to help. I need to be there to watch them fall."

"No, are you sure this is the way?"

"It has to be," I said, wincing. "I'm sticking to this."

"And Jon?"

I looked away and the memory came back with a lot of pain—heartbreak.

"When will it happen?"

"Your next crusade," Petra said. "You won't remember anything, but you'll see me there. I'll help as much as I can."

"Thank you."

"Don't thank me for aiding in your suicide, Mathai." She frowned. "Now go before they know you're here."

The memory was banked with the others and I saw myself leaving Silo a few days later, my legion beside me as we exited the Ward and boarded our hovercraft. They acted normal, like they did every other day, but I was quiet. I kept to myself and my thoughts were all over the place. I was both nervous and terrified. We were on our way to meet Jon in Asylum 10, and then to complete our crusade in Asylum 26. Petra would meet up with us along the way, and we'd finally put an end to years of torture.

But we never made it.

A sudden electrical storm interrupted our communications with Silo and all of our signals were lost. Lexyn screamed for Elektra to quickly land the hovercraft away from the current, but the engines had shut down long before then. Alessia was frantic as she looked for the seat ejection button and Cameron urged me to let him fly us out, one by one. But we dropped too fast, the desert hills rushing into view. The dark sky opened with hail and thunder and we fell in. On the way down, clinging tightly to my seat, I remembered the storm not being a part of Petra's plan. I remembered thinking that Jon was somewhere out there, and that I wouldn't get to say what I needed to tell him.

The memory changed again as Petra and a team of Outliers carried our broken bodies from the desert and transported us to a covert facility. They disposed of our craft like we were never there. Days passed as they healed us, repairing us without leaving a single new scar. Jon was there too, but in far better condition than the rest of us. Petra supervised the surgeons, barking orders and giving directions. And hours after they pulled us from the storm, she had them sit us in the chairs.

They were the same chairs from Silo, with the restraints and glowing lights. Our unconscious bodies were strapped in and Petra watched from in the room as they injected us with the purple serum—Evermore—and promptly erased our memories. This was what I had agreed to, alone with Petra only days before the storm. The scenes played back-to-back, hammering in everything I had forgotten.

My plan with the Outliers had been to infiltrate Silo in order to shut down their labs, to stop them from creating any more legionaries with the Y-506 virus—like me. But to do this successfully, I had to forget everything the Outliers taught me. I couldn't retain any information, or else the Jackets would yank it from my mind. Which was why Manis suspected I knew things he didn't—because I did.

Using a series of numbers they called keys, the Outliers reset our minds and made us into the perfect assassins once more. They assigned Lexyn, Elektra, and Cameron to A4, Jon to the outlands, and Alessia and I were given to people they called handlers. We lived with these handlers for months, only knowing them as our parents. They fed us, took care of us, and kept up the charade so that we'd never know who we really were. But the Reapers found us anyway, tearing into the faux Ward they'd built in the Seeming. Alessia was captured and taken away and I jumped from a cliff to escape their beeping guns, only to find myself numbly walking back to Silo as my programming bided.

That relinked my memories to me waking in my pod weeks after we left for the crusade, submerged in water—right in the beginning where this all started. Jon had been captured and taken back to Silo as well, but he fled, leaving me behind to wander the dark halls until they found me. Until Petra found me, disguised as a legionary. And while I had no recollection of my time with the Outliers, my subliminal mind had dropped hints:

The P with wings beneath the table, the H whispered on the wind under Silo's Ward, and the O on the key that gave me access to my files. The letters led me to the word phoenix, which was the key the Outliers had given us before setting us free, saying it was our only way back.

The Outliers were our allies and Manis was the dirty liar I had always believed him to be. And even though he had worked hard to program my mind, and the Outliers had done their best to reset it, something in me always itched to crawl out.

I couldn't be controlled. And neither could my legion.

I played through the memories one last time. I found them hard to believe, but they were there in my head and I couldn't deny them. I kept going back to the storm, however, and all the emotions that came with that day. Through the fog of my panic, I'd seen something unusual. It was colossal and moved like a ship on water, gliding through the tempest effortlessly. Before we had hit the ground, it looked right at me, and a feeling much more harrowing than fear sent fresh pain through my body.

THIRTY

"STERLING CASTLE"
BIONIC: MATHAI-0329

Opening my eyes after my memories resurfaced was cruel. I floated somewhere between sleep and consciousness and I knew that once I sat up, I'd have to face them. I'd have to face the truth.

The sun grew too bright for my eyes, so I turned over, digging my hands into the desert ground. It was still wet from the rain and tracings of mud dried beneath my nails. To my left, Jon rolled over on his back and cast his gaze on me. He looked defeated. If the memories were still as fresh and raw for him as they were for me, I couldn't blame him. The trance-like state the stones had put us in was disconcerting. Unreal. In a span of what had to be hours, I went from knowing nothing about my past to knowing almost everything.

The others groaned, rocking around in the soil. When I glanced up, I noticed we lay in a complete circle, far from the craft. Lexyn shook her head, squinting. "Did you guys…"

"Yeah," Elektra groused. "The stones triggered *something*. I've got a wicked headache, too."

Cameron helped Les stand and brushed the dirt from her back. Les sneezed and rubbed her nose, then grinned wryly at me. "I remember everything now," she said.

"Me too," Cameron added. "The Outliers are the good guys."

Sighing, I rolled to my feet and Jon followed. We glared at each other, feeling whole and empty at the same time. While getting our memories back was what we wanted, it also aired many things we didn't know about each other. And even about ourselves.

"Maybe," I said, hating how vulnerable my words sounded. "I think Petra was leading us to each other from the beginning, but that doesn't mean her or her people are good. They're still withholding information from us."

"Do you think she knew about the stones?" Cameron asked.

Lexyn pulled mud from her white hair with a distressed grunt. "Definitely. It's the only way Mathai would have known to spell the word. She told her."

Elektra smiled. "So we're like … double agents?"

"Not so much," Jon said, chuckling. "But we were obviously on to something with the Outliers. Presidium is threatened by us."

I agreed. "We're among the few legionaries who can't be controlled. We know things they'd *kill* to know, which is why we were the perfect choice to take them out from the inside."

"But how do we do that now? We're not working from the inside anymore," Lexyn said.

"Then we'll work from the outside."

"And the Outliers?" Jon asked.

"We can't trust them, not completely," Elektra said. And she was right; we couldn't trust them. Even though Petra had helped me when I needed her most, her motives were questionable. Why risk so much for six kids?

"Then we're not going to the Seeming?" Cameron asked.

"We're going," Jon answered. "No where else is safe."

"And right now anywhere is safer than Silo," I said, digging the heel of my boot into the sand. "They're trying to make us into the monsters that we aren't. They're trying to create more like me—super legionaries. For what, I don't know."

"We can't let them do that," Les whispered. The clothing I'd given her was too big. The shirt's sleeves fell past her fingertips and she had to roll them up to keep them at a good length. She wore an old pair of Lexyn's shoes, too. They clunked around when she moved, but she liked it—said it sounded like she was making thunder with her feet.

"We *won't* let them do it," Cameron decided, and then he turned to me. "Right, Mathai?"

"Right." Five pairs of eyes pinned me to the desert and I felt compelled to say something that would make them feel better—something worthwhile—but the words were stuck in the back of my throat. I couldn't say them, because then I'd have to mean them. And if I ever let them down, after everything that happened...

Jon sensed my hesitation and jumped to my rescue. Walking around me, he said, "Look, guys, it's been a rough few days and none of us were prepared for what we've been through. But we *did* go through it, and we're still going through it. And we'll probably be going through it next week."

I admired the hopeful glint in his eyes. "What are you trying to say?"

"At least we're going through it *together*."

"As a legion," Cameron agreed.

"With super cool powers," Elektra said with a giggle.

"And *wings*," Lexyn yipped, hugging her brother. Les joined in and pushed herself to the middle, dragging Elektra along. They chattered like a bunch of birds, joking and teasing one another. They acted like we hadn't just plotted to take out an entire city and the virus destroying our world, the same virus used to create me. Though I wished I could have felt even an iota of that blindfolded bliss, I knew it was flighty. Any plan we'd strategize would begin and end with me, the Y-506 virus.

Holding out a hand, Lexyn said, "Come on! Get in our hemisphere."

I laughed. "Hemisphere?"

"Hemisphere." Cameron smiled and it was the first time I'd seen him do it. I couldn't read his thoughts, but his whole face lit up. I didn't need telekinesis to know he was happy.

Jon and I moved into the group hug and Lexyn began bouncing us around, rubbing our heads together. Alessia laughed so hard her little face turned red.

"Alright, enough, fob off!" Elektra yelled, breaking away from the hug. She hid a smile beneath all that false bravado. "Can we find the Seeming now?"

"Yeah, let's go," I said, sticking my tongue out at her. "I liked my own hemisphere anyway."

We headed back to the hovercraft and collected the phoenix stones from the ramp. Then when everyone was inside and strapped in, we followed Elektra's coordinates to the Seeming and disappeared into the clouds, searching for the **sterling castle** in the sky.

THIRTY-ONE

"ROOM 211"
BIONIC: MATHAI-0329

The wide, wispy fields of the Seeming were exactly how I remembered them. The valley stretched for miles between the two boulders, fading through the horizon. The sharp, twisted buildings, though not as tall as Silo's, appeared dark and moody against the bleeding sky. Like daggers through the clouds. The paved roads glimmered with flecks of silver, the air with arched, winding skybridges. Rock islands revolved around steel risers like planets. And the lights ... there were so many lights to look at that I gave up trying to choose and watched them all, drowning in the city's ambiance. Lanterns, humming street lamps, sky ships, and giant holographic screens—they were a solar flare all on their own.

"So, this is it?" Les whispered, who stood hand-in-hand with Jon as she ogled the red hills.

"This is definitely it," I said. I took a step down from the rock we'd climbed to see the city and picked up my bag. We'd parked the hovercraft in the desert and hiked the rest of the way to the valley. While I had a feeling the Outliers were expecting us, flying directly into new territory hadn't bode well with me. I didn't want them to have access to everything we had, and the craft was it.

"Do we ring a bell or something?" Elektra asked from Cameron's back. She snacked on my last bag of food, tipping her head back to get all the crumbs.

"I'm sure they're waiting," Lexyn said. "They probably have it down to a science, too, and knew the time and day we'd come back."

"Think they're watching right now?" Jon asked me, and my eyes were still on the lights.

"Wouldn't make much of a difference, right? They've always been watching."

We trudged down the red duns and grassy fields until we parted into the incoming flow through the metropolis. There were no Generators to monitor the crowds like there were in the Asylums. Instead, two enormous prongs created a force field of a gate. When we walked in, its scanners roamed over our skin, identifying us as LEGION BLUE.

They definitely know we're here, I thought.

We ebbed into the city and stood out like sore thumbs. Our clothes were dirty, torn, and our eyes probably appeared wild from sleep deprivation. The people here didn't wear usual clothing, either. They wore a lot of suits, cloaks, and used big umbrellas to shelter their faces from the sun. I couldn't tell the difference between a man and a woman, and crying children were swaddled in so much cloth I wondered how they breathed.

"Is it supposed to be cold?" Cameron whispered.

"I'm not feeling—"

"Mathai, up there," Les said, pointing. I looked and the central holographic screen that hung above the speedways displayed Petra's face. She spoke, reciting an automated, irrelevant message to the public. Whoever she was, though, she was important. The pin on her collar matched the star-shaped building in the background.

"Come on. I know where she is."

Steering through the traffic, we hustled across the city, dodging inquiring glances and beeping cars. I was awed by the beauty of the Seeming, but I didn't stop to marvel every little thing, because it felt familiar to me. A good familiar, a familiar that made me feel at home. A familiar that let me know my memories had served me right and we were going to the right place.

We arrived at the building and quickly climbed its grandiose, black staircase. I didn't know what to expect, but it surely wasn't for the doors to part and open as we ascended. I nearly hoped for a fight. Les paused on the last step and her hesitation spread throughout the group. Elektra climbed down from Cameron's back and we watched, wide-eyed, as a figure appeared from the darkness of the building and stepped into the light of day.

Her blond hair caught me first, and then I remembered her snarl as she'd handed me a napkin in the refectory to wipe the porridge from my hair. She looked exactly the same, only her casual jeans were a total toss-up from Silo's uniforms.

Petra smiled a knowing smile. "I knew you could do it."

"Yeah, well you didn't make it easy," I said. Cameron huffed beside me as if to say: *hell no, she didn't.*

"Come in and get settled," she directed, motioning us forward. She turned and began heading into the building and my head swam. When we followed her through the door, a flock of men dressed in suits took our bags and left the room with them. Elektra frowned as they snatched away her food.

"Your rooms are on the fifth floor, dinner is at seventh hour every night—"

"Whoa, whoa," I called, chasing Petra down the halls of the foreign building. The interior surely didn't match the exterior. Dark woods and cream colors adorned every inch of the place and my boots left scuff marks on the pristine floors. There were lit fireplaces and living room furniture where I expected office desks and lab vaults. Looking at Petra, I said, "Are you going to explain what's happening? We *literally* just woke from a memory-healing stupor and haven't eaten in days. Please, tell me what's going on."

Her eyes went from the group, to me, and then she nodded sympathetically. "Let's go."

I held on to my questions as we moved through the building and wound down a flight of stairs. I gawped openly at the old portraits on the walls, trying to read the names on the labels. The downstairs room we moved into looked more like what I expected to see when I first entered—steel floors, lab tables, and workrooms. At the back was a training room and a gun range, similar to the one at Silo. It was like they'd crammed two worlds into one building.

"I know you must have many questions," Petra began, walking backward. "But I'm assuming most of your memories are back now?"

"Most, but not all," Jon said, glancing around the room. We stopped in in a room with a long table and a screen. When Petra tapped a few numbers in on the radiocom around her wrist, the screen blinked on, displaying UNDERGROUND.

"Welcome to the Underground," she said, motioning to everything with her arms out. "You found us—or we found you, Mathai—months ago in A26. You knew about our mission and you wanted to be a part of it, without Silo knowing."

"Your mission?" asked Lexyn.

Petra answered, "Our mission to destroy the leviathans."

"So this isn't about Silo creating more legionaries with the Y-506 virus?" I asked.

"No, it's about that too," she said. She played with the loose strings of her top and waved us further into the room. It was peculiar seeing her here, sweater and jeans among what had to be a first-rate facility. We sat around the board table in the glass-enclosed room and she continued. "Silo needs to be stopped, but the leviathans have always been our top priority."

"Why?" Elektra said. "If you stop Silo, you stop the leviathans, right?"

"Wrong." Petra tapped her radiocom and a video of wild leviathans running rampant through the outlands began to play. "How much do you know about where they come from?"

"The virus," I said, because I'd read it a thousand times in my codex. "They fell from the sky years ago. No one knows their origin, but they gave Presidium access to the virus. That's when Manis used it to create me at Silo."

"Almost," she retorted, and I cocked my head in confusion. Lexyn leaned into the table, engrossed in the replaying video of the leviathans and Les slowly inched closer to me, her hand around my arm. "Presidium knows the origin of the leviathans. They've kept the truth locked away in order to have reason for legionaries."

"No leviathans, no legionaries," Cameron said, understanding.

"Correct. Leviathans were the only reason you were created. Presidium wants to hold on to their power for as long as they can. In other words, they want to keep the virus spreading."

"That's *madness*," I whispered, sitting back in my chair. It was mayhem and genocide. Had this been Manis' plan? Was this why he'd been so eager to pry information from me? I peered into the soulless eyes of the leviathans on screen, feeling determined. "How do we stop them?"

Petra stood at the front of the room, still distractedly playing with her shirt. She froze to process my question and my mind was transported to the night she came to my room after the Jackets had forced me to eat, when she took me to the vault to see clips from my past. Her face looked like it did back then: guilty. "This was where our plan began weeks ago. As Presidium's most valuable legionary, you'd go back in, covertly, and pinch the information from Silo. But you were supposed to find your legion sooner, and the phoenix stones. You were taking too long, and I sensed Manis was purposely keeping you guarded for this reason. Which is why I took you out that night and gave you the push you needed to get out of there."

"But where's the information I was going to leave with?"

"You didn't take it because you didn't remember," she said.

"I did?" I asked, internally kicking myself. How had I missed something that was right under my nose? "

"I tried to help by showing you little things, like your codex. The codes that were removed? That was your legion. I forced you to realize there was an error, to figure out why it wasn't the same."

"But then how'd she miss the information?" Jon asked. He leaned back in his hair with his arms crossed over his chest. He was soaking in everything Petra said, but his veiled expression told me he had a hard time believing her.

Petra moved around the room as the video of the leviathans replayed in the background. She tapped her radiocom again and the screen separated into four different angles of an asylum. I couldn't tell which one it was, though, and the angles changed before I could distinguish any buildings.

"It was stored in the building you climbed during your first attempt to escape Silo," Petra said. "It's a disc that's moved around Caeshua everyday to keep its location unknown. That day, it was in Silo's storage branch." She looked at me with probing eyes, and I thought back on the day I'd run from the White Room. The building had been the first thing I'd seen because it was the tallest in Silo. I didn't think much about the choice back then, but had I subliminally known the disc was there?

"So stop beating around the bush already," Elektra said, standing and pressing her hand to the table. "Where is it now and how do we get it?"

Petra offered her a demure smile, and then pointed to the screen. She enlarged portions by tapping and sliding things across the monitor. "Asylum 54," she said. "The disc will be relocated to their storage branch in three days."

Sun-up wasn't that far away and a trip to A54 would be more than worth it if we managed to get the disc. I shared a look with Jon before quickly looking away. While Lexyn asked more questions, I spoke into his mind so that Petra wouldn't hear.

We need to get that disc, I sent to him.

His jaw clenched. Even though we didn't look directly at each other, I knew he heard me. He arched a brow, like he was waiting for me to say the words.

Asylum 54 is the second most guarded asylum in Caeshua. It won't be like sneaking through A4, he thought.

Then we'll do better. I glanced around the department Petra called the Underground and scrutinized each room. *Do you think we can find blueprints?*

Of A54's storage branch? Definitely.

He glanced at me from the corner of his eye and I nodded once to keep our conversation discreet. Getting that disc was now more important than anything else. If Presidium had continual access to what was on it, their limits were practically nonexistent. They'd continue creating leviathans, legionaries, by the dozen. And when they'd finally amass a totalitarian army of super legionaries, the virus will have killed everyone.

"What's on the disc, exactly?" Lexyn asked, pointing to the picture of the small, silver disc Petra had pulled up on the screen.

"*Everything*," she said. "The total number of legionaries in Caeshua, the height of the tallest mountain in the eastern region, the names of your human counterparts...

"Human counterparts?" asked Cameron.

Petra moved closer to the table and with her standing so close, I realized she looked a lot younger than she probably was. Which was why she'd fooled so many people in Silo. She removed her radiocom and placed it on the empty seat in front of her. "All legionaries have a human counterpart their DNA was extracted from. Most are long gone now, except Mathai's."

Everyone looked at me. "Mine is still alive?"

"She's old, but still breathing," Petra said. "She's not like your clones, though; she doesn't have the same weaknesses as you do."

"Weaknesses?" Of course I had them—everyone had them—but why would I expect her to have the same ones me? "Is she here? Can I see her?"

After a pregnant pause, Petra nodded and we stood, following her out the room. It wasn't their human counterpart, but Lexyn and Cameron walked fast behind me like it was. We turned right through a set of doors and I the scenery shifted. When we passed a stretcher and a few rooms with empty medical beds, I realized this division was the infirmary.

"She's in here?" Elektra whispered, casting quick glances around the halls. "This is a bit ... creepy."

"You're telling me," I mumbled.

Petra took us to the very end of the hall—**room 211**. She knocked twice, and when someone said to come in, she turned the knob and opened the door for Jon and me.

In my head I imagined an old, sick woman lying in bed with tubes pumping oxygen into her lungs. But the bed was empty and I had to look twice before I found her. She was sitting on the floor pouring tea into a tiny teacup. She took a few sips, and then set it down, flattening a napkin to her lap so that she didn't make a mess on her gown. Then she heard us come in and glanced up, and I think my entire reality shattered when her eyes met mine.

Niana.

THIRTY-TWO

"UNBREAKABLE BOND"
BIONIC: MATHAI-0329

"*I need everyone to leave, except* for Jon and Mathai," Niana said. Petra ducked out first and Lexyn and Cameron followed, though I suspected they had no idea what was happening. Elektra tried to stick around, but Les dragged her out. When the door shut behind them, Niana patted the ground beside her. "I think we need to talk."

Yeah, we do, I thought, still in shock. I couldn't believe Niana was my human counterpart. We'd seen her just days ago and she hadn't said a word.

Jon and I sat around her table setup and she handed us her extra teacups. Humming a tune I recognized, she poured the hot tea into the cups, as if we were still in her home in A10. Then after she fixed the napkin on her lap several times, she looked at us. "I owe you an explanation."

"Why didn't you tell me?" I shot back. "You knew more than my name. You *were* me."

"If I had told you in A10, you wouldn't have believed me," she said.

"Then why lead me to believe you were a Jacket for years?" Jon asked, his eyes dark. "Why would you lie to me?"

"They were all good lies," Niana rushed to say. "And I wanted to protect you, Jon."

"From what?"

"From the *truth*." She clasped her hands in her lap and pressed her lips together. "I didn't tell you about Mathai because you had to learn on your own. You had to find each other yourselves."

"You're Jon's handler," I gathered, and Niana nodded her head. It finally made sense to me. Niana hadn't been a female Jacket. She hadn't been a Jacket at all. Jon had been living with her before the crusade, but she'd always been working with the Outliers.

"It was all a part of the plan."

"The plan to stop Presidium," Jon said. He was talking to Niana, but his gaze was all over me.

"No, a different plan," Niana said.

I blanched. "A *different* one?"

She picked up her teacup and took a sip. I may have missed it back in A10, but her hands trembled to the point she couldn't hold the tea to her lips for too long. She then set it down, wiping her mouth with her napkin. Without looking at us, she asked, "What happens when you two touch?"

My heartbeat thumped in my ears and I quickly looked away from Jon, feeling my cheeks heat.

"We stop breathing," Jon said slowly. "Her pulse skips, and then her face loses color. Her blood turns black in her veins. At most, we have two minutes before her heart stops altogether."

And she's beautiful through it all, I heard him say through our bond. My gaze shot up to his, surprised. He thought I was ... beautiful?

Niana took in a deep, shaky breath. "That's what I feared."

"Do you know why that happens?" I asked her.

"Jon is like you," Niana said, rolling her hands in her lap. "They told me to wait before taking him, but I couldn't. I saw Silo's testing procedures, and he was just a small boy ... he didn't ask for all that pain."

"What are you talking about?" Jon asked.

"When Presidium discovered Mathai was powerful enough to create new identities for herself, they needed something that would be able to fix and control her. And if it had to—kill her. So they created the one thing that would. *You,* Jon. They created you."

Jon's whole face fell. He rocked back visibly and all his pain gathered in his hazel-green eyes. "I was made with the virus too?"

"No," Niana said sadly, and she slaughtered something whole in me. "You were made with the cure."

My eyebrows nearly met my hairline. Inside my chest, I felt my heart flit like a caged bird. There was a *cure?* And Jon had been created with it? It didn't make sense if we were in the same legion, if our connection was so ... instinctive. Why would they do that?

But perhaps that was the *ceaseless wonder* in it all—being attracted to the thing bound to kill you.

I was the virus and Jon was the cure.

Jon was the antidote and I was the epidemic, undeniably.

"That's the real reason I took him away," Niana said. "I did it before anyone at Silo knew what he was, what he could do to you."

"Why would you do that?"

"I was you once, Mathai," Niana said, trying to smile through her sadness. Her old eyes appeared weary, tired. Sick. "I remember the way you two used to look at each other, even if you don't. I didn't want them to destroy what you had, and could have again. You don't get much good in a world like this."

But what did we have, as two people who couldn't touch without the chance of killing each other? As if Jon read my mind, he grunted and stood to his feet. He was storming out the door before I could call him back, and I sat there in front of my cold tea, feeling adrift.

"Time is running out, Mathai," Niana told me.

I shrugged helplessly, shaking my head. "What am I supposed to do?"

"Protect him, in the same way he'll protect you. Presidium will try to split you apart; forge an **unbreakable bond**."

"A-And if that kills us?"

She picked up her tea again and blinked sleepily. "Then you will have died knowing no one quite completes you like he does." She took a sip from her cup, and then set it back down. While I sat chewing my thoughts to pieces, Niana went to the bed and got in below the blankets, falling asleep almost immediately.

Knowing someone wasn't supposed to be difficult, and yet knowing Jon was easily the hardest thing I could do. I couldn't even walk away, because he'd crawled too deep between the cracks of my bones and I couldn't shake him from my system. I was *stuck*; we were stuck together.

Before leaving the room, I pulled the blankets up to Niana's neck and pushed her feet completely on the bed. Then I kissed her forehead, thinking that I would have looked like her someday ... if only we aged.

Petra told me our bags were placed in our bedrooms upstairs and I took my time climbing the marble stairs, moving extra slow. I couldn't avoid Jon for long, though. Not that I was trying to; not that it was possible. I walked down the clean, mahogany hall with my room key in hand, pushing my hands through my hair. I'd meant to check in on the others after leaving Niana's room, and I still had so many questions for Petra, but my mind was too fatigued to process anything other than my head on a pillow.

I got to my room and the door was already open. He was there, standing by the wooden desk in the corner as he pored over something in his hands. The room was big, but he made the space between us feel electric-charged and miniscule. A full-sized bed was in the center, dressers lined the walls. I silently moved in behind him and tried to see what he held, but his body hid it from view. He'd showered and changed, I noticed. The wavy ends of his hair dipped into his face as he looked at what he held, and his shirt clung to his defined muscles. The window in front of him cast warm, yellow tones across his tan skin. And how he looked at what was in his hands ... I realized he looked at me that way, with complete, unhindered intensity.

"How long have you been standing there?" he said without turning around.

"Only a few moments," I told him. When I shifted into the light of the window, I finally saw what he held. He'd flattened the wrinkled edges of the paper so that every line used to create the iris was prominent again. I hadn't been hiding the drawing from him, but it felt obscenely private to have him here staring at it. I didn't understand why until the long lost memory replayed the moment I first saw Jon in the outlands during a crusade, emerging from the same bunker I'd hidden in. Undoubtedly, the drawing was his. He was the unknown artist who'd created a mural of papers on his wall, and I hated that it took me so long to realize.

Jon was the eyes and arms in the darkness.

"It's your eye," he said, giving it another look before putting it down. He spun to face me and I crossed my arms to shield myself his sharp gaze.

"It's really great," I said. My feet moved on their accord, drawn to him. I stood on the other side of the desk and looked at the drawing again. "Elektra would definitely approve."

That made him smile. "It's that good, huh?"

"Oh, yeah. She can't laugh at a worthy piece like this." I grinned, and then when Jon grew closer, I sobered, feeling him reach out to trace my chin with his fingertips, then my lips. "You remembered my eyes," I whispered.

"Presidium could wipe my memories again and I'd still never forget them." Again—that *intensity*. His eyes were suns and I basked in all their burning heat. He didn't have to touch me for me to feel it. It streamed through our connection and overwhelmed me. "I don't know how to stop," he said dejectedly.

"I don't know if I want you to." I felt horrible saying it out loud, like an addict finally owning up to their transgressions. But I didn't want to stop knowing Jon. I didn't want to stop touching him or making him laugh. Because he was beautiful when he laughed with his whole face, and I never wanted to miss a moment of it. I wanted to be the reason behind all his smiles. And that's what frightened me the most—my want for him. It overrode all common sense and standing beside him made me feel ten-feet tall. The feeling was so wholesome that, suddenly, touching him until my heart slowed didn't seem such a bad way to go.

I began to cry. The tears came with the onrush of emotions and I vehemently rubbed them away, only to stare at the wetness on my bandages like I'd opened fresh wounds. I hadn't cried since I was at Silo. *Despair*, I understood.

"I was created to destroy you. It's innate, my need to fix you, but there isn't—"

"I want you to know that I don't need you," I said quickly while I still had control over my words. I settled my shaking hands at my sides and searched his face as I spoke. "I don't need you to fix me. I can exist outside of you. I saved myself before and I can do it again. My story didn't begin with you." He let me get it out on one breath; he didn't interrupt me or move to leave. Instead, he listened, and the inexplicable feelings I had for him deepened. "But then you tame the violence in my head and you make everything so okay. So okay that I worry my story will never conclude without you. That there will be no story at all, that I will lose myself in the rhythm of you. By fateless choice. So I *don't* need you, Jon,"—my breath hitched—"and then I *do*."

When I finished, biting my lips to hold in my pathetic sobs, Jon still watched me with drawn eyebrows, a war behind his mind. As he finally made a decision, I felt the difference in him first. His anger and confusion let way to compassion and empathy. He reached out and touched my face with no hesitation; he took what he *wanted* and he was so sure. His skin met mine and I breathed deep, readying my mind for the sweet ache that was sure to come.

"I was going to say that there's nothing to fix about you—"

Before he could get the words out, I tiptoed and crushed my lips to his. We gasped immediately, our mouths touching with an onslaught of pain. But he kissed me back, his hands at my back as he pressed me closer. His hands clawed at my shirt and I wrapped my hands around his neck. I'd never been kissed before, but the slide of Jon's lips over mine incited

feelings that made me want to tie myself to the end of his next breath and hang there forever. It was unhealthy, delusional, and a little perfect. I tasted my tears and I tasted him, a heady concoction that surpassed the ache and the black veins creeping up my neck.

"One," I counted against his lips, fighting through the pain.

"Two," he continued, slipping his hands beneath my shirt to touch my bare skin. I gasped into his mouth and he kept kissing me, his tongue slipping past my teeth. I felt like I was floating, like the ground had disappeared beneath my feet and I existed in an open space with him, where pain was pleasure and we didn't have to ration our time when we touched like this.

"Three." Without removing my hands from around his neck, I unwrapped my bandages and threw them to the ground. He was the reason I had to wear them, but I didn't want to hide behind them anymore. With free hands, I touched Jon's face, his hair, and his chest, right over his racing heart.

"Four." His kisses grew mad, a snarl on his lips. He knew he had to let me go soon. We counted quickly to one hundred twenty and Jon tore away before we got too close. But when he did, my vision blurred and I stumbled into him, losing feeling in my feet. The pleasure melted away and there was nothing, but slow, agonizing pain.

"Mathai? *Mathai*, talk to me." Jon's tone was concerned. He pushed back the hair from my face and surveyed my eyes. I could see him, and I could feel him, but my mind was shutting down, like I was falling asleep. The hand over his heart was devoid of color. "I need you too," he whispered fearfully, pressing his lips to my cheek one more time. He lifted me—one hand supporting my back and the other swept beneath my legs—and brought me to the bed.

I barely remembered him tucking me in, but I memorized the feeling of his lips on my forehead, his hand in my hair. He stole touches while my breathing grew shallow, and then he left the room.

Weaknesses—I had them. I had many. But Jonathus was unquestionably my greatest.

THIRTY-THREE

"ASYLUM 54"
BIONIC: MATHAI-0329

Three days passed swiftly.

We gathered every morning in the huge basement facility—the Underground. Petra greeted us with food and handed us daily schedules, then taught us how to read the blueprints of A54 so that we knew the storage branch inside and out. She told us the Underground was a training academy for Outliers and, because of us, rogue legionaries. I'd only seen a few Outliers around the building, and they were often in too much of a rush to stop and notice me. But they had school bags and uniforms, textbooks and notebooks. Which meant Petra's stories were matching up, and I gradually began trusting her again.

We were expected to enroll and begin classes immediately. Elektra had growled around a mouthful of her breakfast sandwich and Cameron had seemed genuinely excited. Lexyn and I were impartial to the idea of school, but if it meant the Outliers would help us take down Presidium and the leviathans, then we were in.

We trained in quartered, padded rooms with skilled specialists, throwing ourselves into hours of tactics and drills, testing our agility and improving our endurance. Petra pushed our limits as a group and forced us to redo drills even when we did them correctly. Though the work was exhausting and left me feeling sick at the end of the day, it worked. By the end of the second day the six of us were not only in synch mentally but physically too. We drew from each other's strengths and motivated each other to succeed—together.

When we weren't training with guns and knives, we sat around the table going through my codex, lab notes, and strategizing ways to get into A54. Through our research, we discovered that Elektra's human counterpart died only three years ago and that Elektra was originally from legion GREEN. But after a series of events during their crusades, she was moved to legion BLUE with the rest of us. While the lab notes Petra gave us hadn't been documented with a specific reason, we were grateful Elektra was there in the Seeming and not still at Silo with the other mindless drones they called soldiers.

We also unearthed the names behind Presidium—Vera and Falkor Myrmidon. Petra flashed their faces across the screens and we studied them, downloading all the information to or psyches. They were siblings who controlled all four asylums, including Silo, like deities. They'd inherited a lot of riches from past successors, including all the lands of Caeshua. The only territory they had no claim on was the Seeming, because the Outliers had established themselves as aliens long before the leviathans fell from the sky.

The Myrmidons were obsessed with making each asylum the best. They pushed technological advances and synthetic medicines without testing them and the public often suffered from it. And though they were hated by many, they were feared by many more. Which was why their clandestine plans to create more leviathans and super legionaries had made it so far already. They wanted to generate an audience. While the leviathans would run rampant through outlands and incite terror throughout the cities, they'd approach the people of Caeshua with the idea of super legionaries. They'd dress them up and show them off and people would believe their lies. The new super legionaries wouldn't be like me, or like Jon; they'd be one hundred percent unstoppable. And then like in every great tale ending, the world would burn.

We knew exactly what we were going to do by the third day. We woke early that morning before dawn and boarded our hovercraft outside the Seeming. Three days was hardly enough time to recharge, rewind, or process how much we'd learned, but we'd have time to figure it out in the end, after we leaked the information Presidium was trying to hide.

This time, I was ready.

The invasion of **Asylum 54** was now.

THIRTY-FOUR

"THE HIEST"
BIONIC: ELEKTRA-3522

The truck jerked to a stop, spitting out a cloud of black smoke, and I slapped the steering wheel before pressing the button to turn off the ignition. As I jumped out to grab the package from the back, I made a show being angry. The people walking around the plaza paid me no mind, but the idiots in black suits guarding the storage branch fed right into it.

"Stupid truck!" I yelled, slamming the door. The rusted hinges screeched and I hid a smirk behind the collar of my glittery shirt. The older the truck, the better.

"Can we help you?" one of them asked as I approached the revolving door.

ASYLUM 54.0

I turned my sneer into one of those pouty frowns Les taught me how to do and said, "I have to make a few more deliveries today, but my truck broke down. Is there anyone who can help me?" *Like the technician who works in room C9*, I thought wryly.

The man peered at me over the top of his tinted sunglasses. Then he took a look at the pink truck parked haphazardly on the other side of the street and rolled his eyes. "Wait here," he said. The second he turned around, I whistled a sharp, short tune and Mathai walked casually down the sidewalk. I nodded once, giving the signal, and she darted behind the storage branch building and broke into the stairwell. It happened so fast in a span of seconds that when the man came back, he was completely oblivious. He gave me the go to head inside and I waltzed in with a smirk.

Asylum 54 was celebrating a new holiday called Glad's Day. Petra had told us something about a party, but I must have fallen asleep with my eyes open. *Tragic.* All I saw was food when I walked into the storage branch. Tables lined every hall and servers bounced back and forth, balancing trays on their hands. I made a beeline for the security room, which was to the right of the welcome desk and a little ways down the corridor. I held the package in my hands and kept up the charade of Little Delivery Girl, smiling at everyone who passed. But when no one was looking, I swiped two cupcakes from a table and booked it for the security room.

They didn't keep the door locked since it made it easier for guards to check the camera tapes at any given time. I crashed through the door, setting my cupcakes down on the messy desk, and immediately began to search the drawers. "If I was a ten-digit code in a highly-guarded facility office, where would I be?" I said to myself. I knew right away that it wouldn't be in plain sight and ditched my hunt through the drawers. Then something clicked in my mind and I sat upside down in the chair, scooting myself under the desk. Sure enough, there was the code.

I wrote it down on the underside of the package with a marker and then wheeled back out. Before exiting the room and leaving things exactly as they were, I tapped a few encryptions into their screen monitor and shut off all cameras on floor five. *Only* floor five.

The hall was empty as I crept my way to the printing room. Everyone was on level two for the party and the only people who still roamed the halls were guards and servers. Or so I thought. I turned a corner to enter the printing room and came face-to-face with a man whose nametag read *Fred*.

What a name.

"You're not supposed to be here," he said, stating the obvious. He glanced skeptically at the package. "No one's allowed in these halls. They've been closed off to the public."

I stared at him dumbly for a good three seconds before going with the first thing that came to mind, "I got a little lost, sorry. I'm here to hand out ... *treats*." I remembered the two cupcakes in my hands and held one out. At first I thought he wouldn't accept it and I'd have to tie him up in a closet somewhere, but he did. He grabbed the cupcake and took a hearty bite out of the side, mumbling about how great the texture was.

"Superb," he said, and I nodded my head like I actually cared. "What's the name of your company?"

I smirked. "**The Heist.**"

"That's an odd name for a pastry business," he said.

Oh, you have no idea.

I told him I was on my way back to the party and watched him walk away. Then when he was completely out of sight, I made quick work in the printing room, dropping the package down the shoot and into the mailroom. And since I had the extra time, I peeled out of the glittery shirt, revealing my new bodysuit, and tossed that down the shoot too.

There, I thought. *Much better.*

BIONIC: JONATHUS-6254

He wouldn't stop talking. The man had a penchant for blood-red drinks and pretty women. He wasn't the most important person here at the party, but he sure made it seem that way. He laughed loudly, slapping his hand on the table like his joke was anything more than mediocre, and called for someone to bring more food.

I leaned on the bar about six feet to his left, watching his every move while still trying to blend in. I had borrowed a suit and tie from Petra. I was okay with sneaking in with a t-shirt and jeans, but Lexyn had insisted on the suit. So earlier that morning Mathai helped me get ready, making sure all my pockets were flipped in and my bowtie was pulled tight. Then she wet my hair enough that the waves were no longer frizzed, making sure our skin didn't meet when she slicked down the sides. We hadn't talked since we kissed in her room and I was afraid I'd ruined something between us. It had no name yet, but I felt it when her mouth met mine. And then again when I had to stand so close to her with her hands on me, and do nothing.

I'd never felt so intoxicated by someone's touch before.

We had to go before I had a chance to talk to her, but I vowed I would when this was all over.

The man made a move for the bathroom and I followed him through the streamers and balloons. When I was close enough, I purposely bumped into his side, throwing him off. He let loose a bizarre squeal as everything in his pockets tumbled to the floor. He turned around and his arrogance was present in every line of his face.

"Oh, I'm so sorry. Let me help you with that," I said, quickly kneeling to retrieve his things. It was his wallet, a set of keys, and a hair comb. I picked up the open wallet first and glimpsed through all of its contents in seconds. Then when I saw the flashy ID card tucked beneath a few scraps of paper, I furtively pulled it out, tucked it into my hand, and gave him everything else. "Here you go. So sorry for the trouble," I said, but my eyes weren't even on him anymore.

I glanced at the hologram above the performing stage as the clock struck twelfth hour. I only had a few moments to do this or we'd blow the whole thing and lose the disc. So I set my new radiocom with a ten-minute countdown and sent the notification to Lexyn, hoping she got it in time.

Without paying any mind to the partygoers, I left the auditorium through the glass doors and ran through the level two hallways in search for the mailroom. Elektra had given me direct instructions and I recited them to myself, turning left and right down the too-white halls marked with red circles above the door.

I found the mailroom a little after I heard the music blast from the auditorium, cueing the festivities were about to begin. The room was flooded with boxes and carts, but the package Elektra had sent down was at the very top of a mound of letters. I turned it over on all four sides until I found it—the code. She'd written it on the bottom in small handwriting, and then had drawn a smiley face at the end. I took a second to memorize it, and then swiftly left the mailroom like I was never there.

Glancing down at my radiocom, I cringed at the four-minute marker. Wherever Mathai was, I hoped she didn't run into any trouble. Because we had no overtime in this. It was now or never.

I made it to the elevator and hit the silver switch, my gaze perusing the halls for guards as I waited. When the doors finally pinged and slid open, I set the package down inside, the code facing up, and scanned the stolen ID along the elevator screen. The little light glowed green and I pressed the button for the fifth floor.

There wasn't much I was sure about in that moment as I watched the elevator take the package up, but I was sure about where this heist would lead us, about what we had to do if we made it through this day. And it wasn't anywhere or anything remotely good.

BIONIC: LEXYN-0097

"Do you have to chew so loudly?" Cameron munched on his food, mouth wide open, and then threw one of the chips at my head. "This is a heist! To be taken seriously, Cam." I set down my binoculars on the roof ledge and turned to him. He was sitting on the ground, smiling, while Les egged him on.

"What?" she said, giggling. "They're good. Want to try one?" Her little hand held out half a chip and I couldn't even muster the anger, because we were running out of so much time.

"They're going to be okay," Cameron said, serious now. "How much time is left?"

I glanced down at my radiocom and tapped the countdown Jon had sent me, shaking my head. "A minute. I don't think that's enough. Maybe we should have waited for the disc to circulate back to Silo."

"She'll make it," he said. Then he stood and put Les on his back between his wings, preparing to fly.

I turned back and watched Mathai through my binoculars as she jumped down the trap door and into the fifth floor. I hoped she remembered the plan well, because once the distraction bombs went off, she only had about three minutes to get back to the roof before the targeted buildings around the city exploded, one by one. While Cameron, Les, and I had made sure they were evacuated, burning buildings were going to do some damage to the city. Especially if Presidium discovered we were behind it. And we had to be gone long before then.

I watched the sky impatiently, counting down with my radiocom.

Where are you, Petra?

BIONIC: MATHAI-0329

I dropped from the trap door in the roof of the storage branch and squinted to see around the dark office. It was some sort of library, with wide shelves of books and papers, but it wasn't what I was looking for. I felt around until I found the doorknob, and then broke into a run down the hall. If everyone had followed through, no cameras detected my movements here on the fifth floor and I had exactly one minute to get in and get out before nearby buildings began to erupt—a mission that would prove to be easier said than done.

I pivoted right and ran all the way to the end of the hall, just in time to see the elevator doors slide open with the package. "Thank goodness," I whispered. Breathing deeply, I picked it up and read over the code Elektra had written on the bottom. It was ten digits long and easy to remember. It was the only code that accessed room C9, where they kept the disc locked in a vault. A vault I was now going to breach.

I retraced my steps and eyed the halls for the right room, and then came to a full stop. The keypad on the door was similar to the one from A4 and it took me no time at all to punch in the ten numbers. When the light dinged and the latch slid away on the other side, I transferred the package to my other hand and entered the room.

It was actually more of a closet, possibly smaller than my room in Silo. Humming monitors covered every inch of the walls and a stand to my right carried A54's extensive collection of video data. There were at least a hundred there, organized by color and date. And hopefully one of them was the one I was looking for.

I moved through the room, dropping the package on a steel table, and began digging through the records. I didn't look at my radiocom, but I knew I literally had seconds before the bombs went off. I had a cushion of three minutes to get out if I needed it, but that wasn't guaranteed. Not if the bombs took out the storage branch too.

I sifted through the first row of cases with no luck. All the discs were too big or they had the wrong markings on them. I was looking for something that related to the leviathans and most of everything here had to do with the history of Presidium. I quit my search halfway through the second row when something caught the corner of my eye. It was a small green safe beside the stands, but it wasn't locked. In fact, things stuck out of it like someone had recently been in here to quickly throw something in it.

I eyed the door, seeing no one, and then knelt to open the safe. There were files with highlighted text, and though none of it made sense to me, the words 'leviathan' and 'virus' instantly grabbed my attention. I dropped the papers, digging to the bottom. When my hand brushed against a case, I gasped and pulled it out. Right on the front, with bold, capitalized letters, it read: CAESHUA—Y-506 VIRUS.

That had to be it, undeniably. I went back to the steel table in the center of the room and tore open the package Jon had sent up in the elevator. It was a case with a disc similar to the one I'd just found, except the one we brought was blank. I swapped them, clipping the right disc into the case I was leaving here with. Though, as I was about to close it up, an unlikely idea hit me. I knew it was wrong the second it came to mind, but I had to know.

I had to know what was on it.

Petra intended to use it to expose Presidium, and while I was onboard with that idea, I needed the instant gratification of knowing where the leviathans came from, and why I'd consumed the virus instead of allowing it to kill me like the other legionaries it was tested on.

I popped the disc into one of the monitors on the wall and pressed play with a shaking finger. The stagnant blue screen fizzled with static, and then the video began to play. It was different from the others I'd seen, in that someone moved the camera around the sky. There were loud, frantic voices in the background and I couldn't make out what they were saying. But I knew they were afraid of something. Many people ran around, yelling at the person who held the camera to get away. A screaming child and a hushing mother sounded from right next to them.

They zoomed in on the sky as madness erupted beyond what looked like a Ward. I didn't see anything but clouds for the longest time, and I stood right in front of the monitor. But then they shifted their angle and I saw exactly what people were running from.

Black, wraith-like creatures dropped from the sky like asteroids, turning the sky grey and the moon blue. They buzzed through the air and flew right into bodies, infecting their hosts. People didn't need to be bitten to turn savage. As soon as one took over their mind, they dropped to the ground and writhed at unnatural angles, their bones shifting and snapping. And it didn't take the five hours Jon had told me about, either. One moment a woman was running away, terrified, and then she was crawling to her feet, her head twisted in the opposite direction and her eyes completely black.

It was a mass reaping, I realized. I heard the first bomb go off around me, but I was rooted to the spot, watching unblinkingly as more leviathans fell like rain. They came with a storm and there was something eerily familiar about how the tempest moved. It could have been anything with the video's poor quality, so I pressed pause to be sure.

And I was right.

A tall giant moved through the skies with red, piercing eyes. The night shifted around it, and where it moved its hand, the leviathans went.

It was the same thing I'd felt during the crusade, right before we crashed.

This thing was controlling them.

This thing was neither human nor legionary.

I stumbled back into the table, my hands clutching the sides. Petra had to see this, and *before* she gave it to the public. Their plan of extinguishing every leviathan just got a hell of a lot more difficult if this ... *thing* was hiding in the clouds, waiting to amass more hosts.

I fast-forwarded through the scene, grimacing as the person behind the camera finally dropped to the ground, infected. I didn't expect there to be any more footage on the disc, but there was. I stopped halfway through the next scene that took place in a different location and, probably, a different time too. I noticed the white walls of Silo straightaway. Masked Jackets moved around the room, setting things up. After a moment, a small child was rolled in on a stretcher. I began to think it was just another video of Manis torturing me when I looked closer and saw that it was a boy.

They hooked him up to machines, much like they'd done to me, and turned him to face a glass. He was screaming, crying, begging to be let go. They moved around him like he wasn't there, and then Manis slowly entered the room. He said and did nothing for a while as he watched the boy and I felt hatred creep into my heart. But in a way, it had never left. Not since I realized what a dangerous man like Manis could do.

The visual on the monitor shifted and I got a better look at what was on the other side of the glass. It was a bony leviathan limping around on one shoe, its jaw broken. It clawed at the glass with bleeding fingers, and the boy nearly ripped his arms off trying to free himself.

They took his blood, driving the needle into a vein. Then they transferred the vial to a gun and loaded it like a bullet. I knew what was happening, but I didn't want to believe it. And I didn't, not until Manis took the gun and shot the leviathan with the boy's blood. I shook my head and began beating against the monitor, whispering *no, no, no.* Because when the leviathan dropped to the ground and the black in its eyes slowly ebbed away, I knew it to be true.

The boy in the stretcher—the cure to the Y-506 virus—was Jon.

And they had it all on the disc.

"I see you've found my masterpiece."

I instinctually drew the gun from my black jumpsuit, turning it on the object of my hatred. Manis stood in the doorway, grinning like a fool.

"You're *vile*," I spat at him, my finger trembling on the trigger.

"And you've got your memories back." He came into the room with his hands clasped behind his back. He wore his lab jacket like it was the only damned thing he owned. "Then I suppose you also remember that you're quit vile yourself. If his blood could heal them, imagine what yours could do." I was disgusted with the prospect, but Manis, the devious bastard, looked excited.

"You'll never find out," I said. "How many people have seen this disc?"

"Just you and me, for now," he answered. He moved closer and I backed away, my gun still trained on him. "But it could be more if you like."

"*No.*"

"Then I have a proposition for you, Mathai."

He used my name for the first time and I didn't like the way it sounded coming from his lips. "The last proposition you had for me, I ended up facedown in the streets of Silo while you had your men drag me back to my room."

"That was a causality," he said, like I meant nothing. And I knew Manis was truly delusional, stepping into this room without a weapon. "But this one is quite different. I know your legion means a lot to you, which is why I'm offering them my protection."

"*Your* protection?"

"*My* protection. Don't you know they're wanted by Presidium? And if they get their hands around the five of their necks, imagine the pain they could cause, Mathai. They want to build an army of super solders, so guess who they'll start testing on?"

"*No*," I breathed, letting my shock slip through to the forefront of my mind.

"*Yes*," Manis said. "But if you come with me, I'll protect them. Together, we can safeguard—"

I promptly started laughing. I laughed so hard I started to cry, and I thought I was losing my mind. Or that I'd gone too many days without sleep. Manis watched me like I was insane, but he truly, *truly* had no idea.

"What makes you think you're any better than Presidium?" I said, wiping the tears from my eyes. "Why would you think I'd ever place the protection of my legion in your hands before I placed it in mine?" Manis' face was stone hard. He saw he was losing, and like the child he was, he threw a fit.

"You are *my* creation!" he yelled, picking up a chair and throwing it at the wall near me. I ducked as the steel chair crashed to the ground.

He clenched his teeth and they appeared black, like he was chewing on something inky. When he realized what he did, though, he settled down. He fixed his lab jacket and acted like he didn't just have a psychotic break.

"I'm not going with you," I stated simply.

"B-but don't you trust me, Ari?" he said, and he flinched when he made the mistake. "I mean ... *Mathai*."

"Ari doesn't answer to those keys anymore. Neither do Kyra and Desni. And Mathai never did."

"Mathai, listen—"

"I'm done listening now." Without even blinking, I aimed and shot Manis in the head, right between his eyes. His chin knocked back and his blood splattered the wall. I expected to feel some remorse as I watched his eyes roll back in his head, but I got cold indifference instead. Manis had tested on me like I was an animal. He'd tortured me, even made me torture myself, and then had attempted to reprogram me every time I didn't turn out to his liking.

In truth, he deserved more than death.

I went back to the monitor and stopped the video. I pulled the disc out and hovered it over the case, hearing the screams of people and the *booms* of the bombs outside. My time to go had long run out, but I took a moment to stare at the silver disc. The same disc that revealed who and what Jon really was. I could have easily taken it with me and begged Petra to keep it a secret. Maybe only publicize the beginning and leave Jon out completely, but it wasn't a sure thing. And I heard Niana's voice in my mind, begging me to protect him in the same way he would protect me.

And I knew what Jon would have done in that moment, which made making the decision ten times easier.

I threw the disc to the ground and crushed it beneath my boot, shattering it until it was unfixable. And then I ran out the door, leaving Manis' lifeless body behind.

No one was going to protect my legion but me. I fought for them, I bled for them, because they were *my* family. And I would do anything for them, even kill.

I sprinted back to the dark office I'd entered through and I heard their voices. They panicked, shouting my name down the trap door. When I opened the door to the room, Alessia's face brightened immensely. Lexyn reached her hands in to pull me out and Jon's eyes were dark with worry.

"You're covered in blood," Lexyn said as I crawled out onto the roof.

"What?"

"*Blood.*" She ran her hand over my cheek, smearing Manis' blood. I didn't even realize it was on me.

"I'm okay, I'm okay," I assured them. When I stood and looked up at the sky, a swarm of Reapers covered the rooftop from their hovercrafts, their guns trained on us. I looked at Jon, confused. "Why didn't you guys go? You had all that time to get—"

"We weren't leaving without you," Cameron said. "We're a legion of six, not five."

"And you brought us together, so we're staying together," Lexyn said.

"For good," Jon agreed. Our eyes met and there was so much I wanted to tell him right then. And I think he sensed that, giving me a small smile.

"Where's the disc?" Elektra asked, looking at my empty hands.

"It's a long story I'll explain later. But for right now..." My eyes went to the sky again. People screamed in the streets as the three buildings Lexyn had blown up crumbled to the ground. "Why aren't they shooting at us?"

"They're waiting for us to surrender," Les said.

"But where's Petra? She was supposed to meet us here with the hovercraft."

Les shrugged, appearing even smaller in her black jumpsuit from the Underground. "She never showed."

"I think something happened to her," Cameron said. And though I couldn't sense his emotions, I saw the concern on his face. The disc meant a lot to Petra and the Outliers too. She wouldn't have purposely deserted us.

"Fine, then we'll get out of here ourselves," I said.

"Mathai—"

"We can *do* this." I looked at them, my legion. "Make a run for the adjacent building and just keep running. *Don't stop.*"

"I think she's lost it," Elektra joked. But I was deadly serious.

I walked around them and stood out on the open roof. Jon nodded and joined me, and then slowly, so did the others. The lined up beside me, putting one foot forward as they prepared to run off the rooftop.

"Don't. Stop," I said, pinning my gaze on the tilting building in front of us. I didn't give them a countdown or a signal. We just started running, putting the last bit of our energy into outrunning the Reapers. Bullets poured from the sky, following us across the roof. And when we neared the edge, I had a flashback of me jumping from a crater. I had been alone then, feeling like fleeing my only choice to survive. But I was in the company of my legion now. My family. And I couldn't be controlled or tied down by anyone.

When I flew, I flew with them too.

Our bodies fell from the edge of the roof, soaring across the city below. At the last second, Lexyn rocketed into the sky and grabbed one of the hovercrafts with her bare hands. Her fists went at it with bright, burning energy. And with her wings stretched across the sky, she sent the craft spiraling into a blazing tower.

We crashed through the window of the tilting building and began to roll. I didn't get see where Lexyn went before pain shot up my right leg and blindsided me. My hands reached to grab onto something, but most of the furniture had slid out the windows. spiraling until our bodies hit a wall.

"Ugh," I groaned. I slowly opened my eyes and squinted into the sun through the broken window. The building was a wreck. Broken ramparts and splintered furniture lay strewn around the room. Wires dangled from the ceiling. Jon rubbed his neck with a wince and Cameron sat upside down on his head, his feet in the air.

"*Woo!*" Les screamed, standing and whipping a fist in the air.

"Les…" Elektra deadpanned her and blew her hair out of her face. "Don't."

"I think I lost my spine," Cameron mumbled.

When I coughed, dust motes fluttered through the air around me. The entire building was tilted, almost certainly hanging on by a thread. As we shifted on the floor, everything rocked beneath us. If most of the furniture in the room wasn't broken, it had fallen out the window, where the hovercrafts still guarded the sky.

A whipping sound vibrated from outside and Les dropped in with a skid, her eyes hard as she tucked in her wings. "We need to go, now. They're watching us," she said. "There should be an exit over here."

We stood and together searched around for the exit door, finding it to our right and through a set of steel doors.

"How are we getting out of here?" Elektra asked, out of breath. We moved quickly down the stairs, jumping over scattered trash.

Jon and I shared a look, and then said in unison: "Train."

When we reached the main floor of the building, we tore through the foyer and exited the front door. Breaking back out into the day was like seeing the light after years of darkness. Hovercrafts flew to and fro, looking for us. Effortlessly, we moved into the traffic of the city, disguised by the other bodies. There were too many people, too many faces. Even if they did find us, they'd never shoot at innocent people.

Ahead of us, not even ten feet away, was the sign leading us to the train. "It leaves in five minutes," I called, picking up my pace. I turned to make sure everyone was together and saw two men dressed in black, fissuring through the crowd, their gazes locked on us.

And they were gaining ground.

"The back of the train!" Elektra screamed. With my hand in Les', we zigzagged through the mobs of running people, pushing through to the front. We ran, determined to get make it back to the Seeming. Determined to free ourselves, determined to stay together. Regardless of our circumstances. When the doors to the train slid own, we pushed through, never stopping until we were in the last cabin and the door was sealed tight behind us. The guards who tailed us looked around confusedly before turning back around.

Only then did I allow myself to breathe. But even so, staring out the window and into the burning sky of Asylum 54, I knew my time of breathing easy had come to a full stop. Because we'd never rest until every leviathan was dead and Presidium's plot to create an army was dismantled and buried beneath the sands of Caeshua.

And if they thought we'd disappear and never return, they were wrong. They were always wrong.

We were watching.

THE CRATER KNIGHTS WILL RETURN IN...

SANCTUM 92

THE BIONICS SAGA

Made in the USA
Lexington, KY
10 July 2017